MEET ME
at the
LIGHTHOUSE

MARY JAYNE BAKER

A division of HarperCollins*Publishers*
www.harpercollins.co.uk

Harper*Impulse* an imprint of
HarperCollins*Publishers*
The News Building
1 London Bridge Street
London SE1 9GF

www.harpercollins.co.uk

This paperback edition 2017

First published in Great Britain in ebook format
by HarperCollins*Publishers* 2017

Set in Birka by Palimpsest Book Production Ltd,
Falkirk, Stirlingshire

Printed and bound in Great Britain

Robert Fletcher, this one's for you.
To Crazy Golf, Cheeky Vimtoes and the carefree
seaside days of our youth. Cheers.

Chapter 1

The day I turned 28, I bought a lighthouse and met the love of my life.

I mean, as you do. Get up, have boiled egg, meet love of life, buy lighthouse. We've all been there, right?

Of course I didn't know, when I was right in the fog of it, that I was meeting the love of my life. I didn't know I was less than an hour from buying my very own lighthouse either. Sometimes these things just jump out at you with a tummy-flopping, life-changing "boo!".

Cragport's Victorian lighthouse stuck up out of the chalk cliff that jutted into the North Sea's foam-crusted swill, rotting itself quietly into the ground just as it had for years. A red-and-white-swirled job like a fairground helter-skelter, half bleached by slashes of seagull guano. It was about 90ft high and indecently phallic, arched windows long denuded of glass at intervals all the way up and a round knob crowning the lantern room on top.

Once upon a time, this beacon-that-was had beamed Cragport's fishermen safely home. But its light had gone out for good decades ago, and these days all locals saw was an eyesore – if they noticed it at all. Cracked and graffiti-covered, the one-time colossus was just another broken thing in a town full of them.

I passed it every morning walking Monty. Barely noticed it, like everyone else. It was just furniture for a background, marked daily as Monty's property through the medium of a sly little wee up the side.

That day a man was there, nailing a notice to the half-rotten wooden door at a little distance from us. I put Monty on his lead before he decided both man and lighthouse belonged to him and it was damp trouser time.

"Morning." The man turned to flash us a bright smile that had no place on any self-respecting person's face at that time on a damp Saturday. It was like he wasn't even hungover. Surreal.

"Morning." I nodded to him as we passed, but something in his smile made me stop.

I hadn't seen him around Cragport before, though he had the town's own Yorkshire twang. Squinting at him in the sun's white glare, I could just about make him out: tall, broad, with longish hair and a rash of stubble, dressed in jeans and a padded jacket to keep out the chill nor'wester.

And he was gorgeous, really bloody gorgeous. I mean, if you went for that chiselled, rough-hewn look. He wasn't my type, but still, it was hard not to stare. You didn't see many bodies like that around town, not since Jess had dragged me off to see The Dreamboys last year.

"What's it say?" I asked him, pointing to the notice. I had to raise my voice a little so he could hear me over the yammerings of an increasingly toothsome clifftop wind. "They're not pulling the old thing down, are they?"

"They can't." He tapped in the last nail and turned to face me. "Listed building."

"Oh. Good." I wasn't quite sure why I said that. Something about the derelict lighthouse disappearing from my skyline rankled. "So what's the notice for? Is it for sale?"

"Yep." His face broke into a broad grin. "Why, you want to buy it?"

"A lighthouse?" I laughed and gestured down at my scruffy stonewash jeans and too-big hoodie-with-fashionable-bleach-stain combo, my hungover dog-walking costume of choice. "Don't let this well-heeled exterior fool you, mate. I don't start the day with a swim in a Scrooge McDuck money bin, you may be surprised to learn."

"You don't need to. Here." He beckoned me to his side and I skimmed the laminated notice fixed to the door.

Mary Jayne Baker

LIGHTHOUSE FOR SALE
£1
First offer gets it – NO TIMEWASTERS
Call 01947 482704 to enquire

"A quid?" I said to the man with a puzzled frown. "Oh, and it's Bobbie, by the way."

I was hoping he'd tell me his name in return so I could stop thinking of him as "the man".

"I know," he said, bending to stash his hammer in a small toolbox on the ground.

I cocked a quizzical eyebrow. "You know what?"

"I know you're Bobbie."

Er ... what? Unless the extra year I'd added to my age that morning had just shoved me arse-first into a full-on senior moment, I was pretty certain I'd never seen this bloke before in my life. Monty was tugging at his lead, keen to claim the rest of his walk, but I ignored him.

My stomach gave a sudden lurch. Could there have been some drunken hook-up I'd forgotten about? If so it'd have to have been a bloody long time ago: it was getting on for nine months since I'd last seen any action in that department. I mean, yes, it was only six months since the big break-up – but that was a whole other story.

The man straightened to face me. Now the blinding sun had disappeared behind a cloud, I could see him more clearly.

4

The deep green eyes were flecked silver, lightly sparkling as he squinted into the wind. And there was something in his face, a crinkle round the eyes ... as if he was enjoying a private joke at someone else's expense. He reached up to push away the rusty brown hair that was whipping round his forehead.

That face ... it did seem familiar. A half-remembered smile...

"Ross?" I said, blinking.

He grinned. "Knew you'd get there eventually."

"Oh my *God*!" Impulsively I threw my arms round him, a wave of pleasure sweeping through me. So it was Ross Mason: the boy in the band. What was he doing back here?

I couldn't believe I hadn't recognised him – but then he'd beefed up a lot since sixth form. I released him from the hug and drank in the well-built frame, trying to match it up with the beanpole of a lad who'd sat next to me in English. Not that Ross hadn't always been good-looking in a cheeky, boyish way, but I never thought he'd grow up to be ... well, buff was the only word for it.

And ... there had been a hook-up, hadn't there? My first kiss. School disco, Year 9, slow dancing to *Angels* by Robbie Williams. We'd managed a fair amount of experimental tongue action and some hormone-fuelled top-half groping by the time Mr Madison dived in to separate us, then spent the next two weeks avoiding each other in embarrassment.

He'd still had his braces in back then. Long time ago that it was, I could remember running a tentative tongue-tip over the ridge, tasting them; that same moist, metal flavour you get in your mouth before a rainstorm, made erotic through the thrill of inexperience.

I wondered if he remembered.

"Er – phew. Thanks," he said when I'd let him go, looking a double dose of windswept from the weather and the unexpected hug.

I turned my face to one side to let the biting wind cool my suddenly overheated cheeks. Had that been a bit much, after ten years? Maybe should've gone with a polite handshake...

"Sorry," I mumbled. "Didn't mean to launch myself at you. It's been a long time, that's all."

"Don't apologise. Not every day attractive women throw themselves into my arms, I wasn't about to start complaining." He nodded down at Monty. "Your friend doesn't look impressed though."

Monty had fixed him with a resentful doggy glare. He was still pulling at his lead, demanding to know why we couldn't ditch this joker and get off down the beach.

"Yeah, he's a possessive little bugger," I said with a smile.

"What do you call the lad?"

"Montgomery. But it's just Monty to his friends."

"Oh." He reached down to tickle Monty's ears. "Hi, Montgomery."

"So when did you get back?" I asked.

"Few months ago. I guess my mum told you about me and Claire splitting up a while back. Once we'd put our old flat in Sheffield on the market, it felt like a good time to make a clean break of it back in the old hometown."

I fumbled in my grey matter, trying to remember what Molly Mason had said about Ross's life post-school in our various bus-stop chats. Proud mums always sent me into nodding auto-pilot. Claire ... that was the girlfriend, wasn't it? They'd lived together for years.

"Yeah, she did mention something. I'm sorry, Ross."

I could sympathise: it didn't seem so very long ago I'd been marking CDs and crying into a pile of unpaired socks myself. A not-so-clean break with the emphasis very much on the broken.

Ross shrugged. "Well, it's been 18 months now. Onwards and upwards, eh? Can't force these things if they aren't meant to be."

"Won't dispute that." I summoned a grin and gestured across the bay with a broad sweep of my arm. "Anyway, allow me to officially welcome you home to Drizzle-on-Sea. Still the finest selection of mucky postcards and adult-themed novelty rock this side of Bridlington."

He laughed, showing perfect straight, white teeth to

prove the childhood braces had done their work. "Cheers love, good to be back in the land of the Kiss-Me-Quick-Shag-Me-Slow hat. So how about you, you get married?"

"No, still muddling along on my own." For some reason I found my cheeks heating again, despite the bracing air. Monty picked that moment to let rip with an accusing bark, which didn't help.

"Just the Westie with the Oedipus complex, is it?" Ross leaned down again to ruffle Monty between the ears. The little chap submitted to the caress with a resentful aloofness that clearly said he could take it or leave it.

"Yep, just us two and our Jess. We're living in Grandad's old cottage at the top of town."

"You still writing? Back in school we all thought we'd see your name in lights one day. Or at least in embossed gold print on an airport paperback."

I smiled at the image. Somehow Roberta Hannigan didn't sound like the right sort of name to be emblazoned across pulp fiction. It might just about work for the tweed-clad girls' school headmistress in an Enid Blyton book.

"Bits and pieces." With a wince of guilt I remembered the neglected first draft of a novel sitting in the drawer at home and hastily changed the subject. "You still play?"

He flushed. "When I get a chance. Surprised you remember."

"Well, you were pretty good." I turned to scan the notice

again. "So why the bargain bucket price, is the place haunted?"

"Dunno," he said, sounding relieved the conversation had moved on. "All I know is old Charlie wants rid, soon as he can. Says he can't be arsed fixing it up at his age and since he's not allowed to knock it down he just wants someone to take it off his hands. Put a stop to those letters from the council about it making the horizon look untidy and scaring off tourists."

"Oh." I subjected the notice to a puzzled stare. Ross's great uncle had always been eccentric, but a £1 lighthouse sale was a new level of bizarre. Even in its current state, the thing must be worth a fair bit.

"So? You going to go for it?" Ross asked.

"What would I do with a lighthouse?" I said with a laugh.

Monty's tugs were urgent now. I crouched down next to him to administer an apologetic stroke. "Ok, Monts, let's get you to the beach for your run." I stood and threw Ross a parting smile. "See you around, yeah?"

"Hope so." He bent down to give Monty a goodbye pat. "Bye, pup. Look after her."

"Oh, and Bobbie!" he called as I walked away.

"What?" I said, turning around.

He flashed me another smile, crinkling those merry eyes. "Happy birthday, love."

***

9

My stream of consciousness as I wandered aimlessly along the beach's blanched pebbles, Monty splashing happily in the baby waves, ran something like this:

He remembered my birthday!

The lighthouse … who the hell sells a lighthouse for a quid? Charlie Mason must've gone off his melon.

I mean, he remembered, after ten years. How cute is that?

God, a lighthouse for a quid … it'll get snapped up by the first pillock who sees it, won't it? Probably turn it into a crack den or something.

Wonder if he remembers when we snogged that time. Heh, bet he doesn't know I got grounded for a week when Mr Madison grassed me up to Mum.

I hope whoever buys it does something good with it. It'd be great as a restaurant. Bit short on floor space maybe, but … oooh, or how about a bookshop? A bookshop in a lighthouse, a gimmick like that could really pull in customers. Or … art gallery?

Hang on. Did he say I was attractive before?

I wonder how much it costs to do up a lighthouse. More than I could ever afford, probably. Still, with a bank loan…

It probably doesn't mean anything, that he remembered. Sweet though. Wish I could remember when his was. He's older than me, isn't he? Autumn baby, start of the school year some time…

I bet it'd be a piece of piss to get investors, if you wanted to renovate a lighthouse for a business venture. Guaranteed success, surely. It's a bloody lighthouse.

October, that's it. His birthday's in October.

Oh my God! I'm totally going to buy a lighthouse!

The next minute I was tearing up the uneven steps cut into the crag. I could see Ross there still, sitting cross-legged against the little outhouse that joined the main building and looking dreamily out to sea.

Monty was at my heels, adding some drama to proceedings by barking his lungs out like the Westie of the bloody Baskervilles. He obviously thought I was treating him to his favourite game of Runny-Chasey-Barky-Catch.

"Ross!" I panted as I reached him, clutching my stomach. The burst of exercise had given me a stitch.

He looked round in surprise, tearing his gaze from the fishing trawler he'd been following.

"Hi again. That was a short walk."

"Yeah, just wanted … God, I'm out of shape." I stopped for a minute while I caught my breath. "Just wanted to ask you to … tell … your uncle … I'll take it."

Chapter 2

It was early evening when I met up with Jess at the Fishgutter's Arms for a birthday drink. By the time we got there, the dark little pub was heaving.

"Sorry I can't stay out late, sis," Jess said as we made our way to a table with a glass of white wine (me) and an orange juice (her). A junior doctor, her Saturday nights were often swallowed up by erratic shifts at the local infirmary.

"That's ok, not really in the mood for a big one." I sat down, Jess plonking herself opposite. "I'll just have a couple then curl up in my PJs with a book and the dog, I think."

"God, sounds like heaven. Wish I could join you. The only birthday treat I've got to look forward to is a night babysitting drunks in A&E." She cocked her head like a budgie with Tinkerbell hair, listening to the soft indie-style music playing in the background. "Tell you what, this is a bit better than the usual live acts they have on."

"Yeah, not bad, is it? Improvement on the glam rock covers they normally inflict on us on a Saturday night."

"So you do anything nice for our birthday then?" she asked.

Bought a lighthouse.

"Not really, just took Monty Dog out..."

Bought a lighthouse.

"... popped round Mum's for a cuppa, picked up our presents from her..."

Bought a lighthouse bought a lighthouse bought a lighthouse.

I groaned. "Jessie, I need to tell you something."

"Oh God. What this time?"

I let my head sink on to my folded arms. "Mmmf mmf mmfmmf," I muffled through a mouthful of sleeve.

"Sorry?"

I lifted my head and fortified myself with another swallow of wine. "Bought a lighthouse."

"Oh. Right," she said, looking puzzled. "Bit of tat for Mum's mantelpiece?"

"No, love, not an ornament. An actual lighthouse. Charlie Mason's lighthouse. He was selling it for a quid."

Jess's eyes widened. "For a *quid*? Not finally cracked, has he?"

"Don't think so. Ross told me he'd just got sick of the council badgering him about doing it up."

"Ross Mason? Not seen him since school. Is he visiting?"

"No, he's moved back. I bumped into him this morning."

She shook her head, a bewildered look spreading across her features as what I'd told her sank in. "Yeah. So my sister bought a lighthouse. Welcome to another day in my world."

"It was a quid, Jess. What else was I going to do?"

"Well, not buy a lighthouse is the thought that springs immediately to mind." She shook her head again. "You daft cow. You know, you could get three Freddos for that and still have change."

"I'm on a diet." I tilted my head as another song started. It was a more upbeat number this time, a bit Kaiser Chiefs-influenced. "You're right, this is good stuff. Who's playing?"

I glanced over at the singer, seated on a stool providing his own guitar accompaniment, then jerked my face away before he saw me.

"Oh my God!" I hissed at Jess, reaching across the table to grip her arm. "It's only him!"

"Him? Who him? Him who?"

"Ross. That's him on guitar. Look."

She examined the singer whispering into his microphone, eyes tight closed as the music carried him away.

"Bloody hell, it is as well." She blinked. "Hey, he's changed a bit."

"Yeah, looks good, doesn't he?"

Jess narrowed her eyes. "Oi. Did you buy his uncle's

lighthouse just because he fluttered his pretty-boy eyelashes at you?"

"Oh right, because I'm that shallow. Yeah, the whole thing was an elaborate chat-up effort actually. I was like 'Is that a lighthouse on your coastline or are you just pleased to see me?' and he was like 'Yeah, you can polish my lamp up any time, darling'—"

"All right, no need to take the piss. So what're you planning on doing with this lighthouse then? Please say selling it on."

I shrugged. "Dunno yet. Thought I'd look into how much it'd cost to do up. I mean, yeah, if it's going to be more than I can afford I'll sell it on; can't go wrong on something that cost a quid, can you? But it'd be nice to do something with it, sort of a fun little project. It's a shame it's been left to get into that state."

"Well, be careful, that's all. Try not to bankrupt us with your 'fun little project'." Jess glanced over my shoulder and groaned. "Oh God. Did you put your pulling pants on tonight?"

"No, why?"

"Because we're about to get chatted up." She jerked her head behind me and I looked round to see two beefy, ruddy-faced blokes in rugby shirts making their way to our table.

"Ugh, not again. Really hoped we could just have a nice, quiet night."

"Bagsy your turn to wingman," Jess said quickly.

"Oh, right. Forcing me to wingman on my own birthday."

"It's my birthday too."

I sighed. "Go on then."

I plastered on a fixed smile as the two men reached our table.

"Evening, ladies. Looking good tonight," said the dark-haired talkie one. In any group of lads on the pull, there had to be a talkie one: the one designated charming enough by the others to open negotiations.

Jess threw me a sideways look to let me know this one was mine. Excellent. Just what I wanted to do on my birthday, be lumbered with the bloody talkie one.

"Hi," said the other lad, the quieter, better-looking one with the light curls. "Er, just thought we'd say hello."

"That was very friendly of you," Jess said with a flirty head-toss. She was good at all that stuff.

"You know, you two girls could be sisters," Talkie said, looking at me as he cracked out his smoothie routine. Obviously no one had pointed out to him that line only worked for mother/daughter chat-ups.

"We are sisters."

"Oh," he said, on the back foot for a moment. "Well, you know ... you look like you could be."

"We're twins actually," Jess said to Shy Boy.

"Are you?" He sent a puzzled frown from Jess's blonde

pixie cut to my long, highlighted brunette job. "Sure you're not winding us up? You don't look that alike to me."

"Yeah, we're the other kind," Jess said. "Although if they ever remade *The Shining* I reckon we could be a shoo-in. You two want to join us?"

"Thought you'd never ask," Shy Boy said with a grin, pulling up a seat next to her. I groaned internally as his chatty friend took the chair next to me and not very subtly shuffled it closer.

"What do they call you guys then?" I asked.

"Oliver," Talkie said. "This is Gareth. We were out on a rugby team social but the other lads abandoned us to go to the sports bar up the road."

Christ, not rugby players...

"What about you?" Gareth asked, not taking his eyes off Jess.

"Jess." She nodded to me. "And Bobbie. It's our birthday, you know."

"Well it is now we've turned up," Oliver said, grinning.

I made an effort to smile at him. "That line ever work for you?"

"I'll let you know later."

Ah, a joke, sort of. Maybe this talkie one wasn't so bad. Maybe my birthday wouldn't be a total write-off after all...

***

I was wrong. Long after Jess had dragged her pull to the dancefloor for a snog, I was leaning on the bar with another wine, forced to listen to Oliver's limitless supply of yawnar-ific stories about his job as a mobile phone salesman. I'd noticed the nickname "ET" on the back of his rugby shirt earlier and assumed it was because his eyes were a bit googly. Turned out that like his alien namesake, the man was literally obsessed with phones.

"... yeah, so if you come on down the shop I can sort you out an upgrade, mates' rates. Latest Samsung, all the extras—"

"You're all right, mate. Got a phone."

"What is it?"

"Dunno." I yanked it out of my pocket and pushed it over the bar to him. "Phone."

He tried not to curl his lip too obviously. "Oh. The 4680. This is well out of date."

"Well it works, which is as much as I ever expect of it."

"Nah, you need the 4880 with the Go Anywhere tariff..."

Oh God. Oh God oh God oh God. Was this it, the best Cragport could do for me? Was this my bloody life now: heading for 30 with no prospects for either shags or rela-tionships but this tedious neckless wonder of a phone salesman?

"Hiya, Bobbie. Didn't expect to see you again so soon."

Ross. Thank God.

He'd finished his set and was standing at my elbow waiting to get served, his guitar case propped against the bar. I shot him a smile of gratitude for giving me an excuse to turn away from Oliver and his interminable tariff talk for five minutes.

"Hi Ross. Loved your stuff tonight. You write some of those?"

"Yeah, plus threw a couple of covers in. They like a bit of cheese at the weekend."

"Do you do a lot of these pub gigs?"

"Couple a month. The extra cash comes in handy."

Oliver glared at him. "Rude. Can't you see you're interrupting? Bloody musicians, think they can just waltz up to any girl in the place."

I shot Ross a sideways look, a wide-eyed look of please-save-me, hoping he'd get it.

"Right you are, sorry mate. Didn't mean to be bad-mannered, just wanted to say hi to an old schoolfriend," Ross said to Oliver, smiling apologetically. He slapped me heartily on the back. "Anyway, nice to run into you, Bobbie. Oh, and really pleased to hear your chlamydia's clearing up, by the way."

"Er ... yeah, thanks, Ross. Doctor said the antibiotics should see it off in well under a month."

Oliver was looking from me to Ross nervously, trying to

work out if we were taking the piss. I kept my face firmly fixed, Ross doing his best deadpan at my side.

"Um ... suppose it's about time I went to find the rest of the team," Oliver said eventually, obviously deciding it wasn't worth sticking around to find out if it was a joke. "See you, Bobbie. Don't forget to come down the shop for that upgrade, yeah?" He pushed his stool back and hurried to the exit.

I turned to smile at Ross. "Thanks."

"Glad I could help. Sorry I didn't have a more dignified excuse for you, was on the spot a bit there."

"That's ok. What worries me is how you found out I had chlamydia." I grinned at the expression on his face. "Joke."

"Thank Christ for that. So can I get you a birthday drink?"

"Yeah, go on. White wine please." I patted the recently vacated barstool next to me. "And then you can come sit down, Ross Mason. I want to talk to you."

"Hey, Bobbie." Jess was tapping me on the shoulder. She was hand in hand with Oliver's mate Gareth, who was grinning all over his face. "I'm going to get off so I can change for my shift, Gareth's walking me home. You coming?" She nodded to Ross. "Hiya, Ross. Nice to see you again."

"Hi Jess, been a while," Ross said, leaning across to kiss her cheek. "Happy birthday."

I glanced at Ross. "Actually, sis, I'll stay for a bit. Me and Ross are overdue a catch-up."

I tried to ignore Jess's suggestive grin. "Oh yeah? Well, enjoy the rest of our birthday then. I'll see you later." She gave a very slight wink. "Probably," she added under her breath.

Chapter 3

"Another drink?" I asked, voice slurring under the influence of too many birthday Sauvignons.

"Not sure I haven't had enough really." Ross blinked
unfocused eyes into the dregs of his red wine. "But go on,
twist my arm. Is it my round?"

"Yeah. No. Dunno. Lost track a bit, to be honest."

"Ok, let's say it is, since you're the birthday girl." He
smiled at the barmaid and she came scurrying over with
that simper good-looking guitar players seem to be able to
summon at will. "Same again please, Gabbie."

"So. You always finish your set with Angels?" I asked
when our glasses had been refilled.

"Not always. If it's a weekend I usually do something
slow and cheesy though, bit of a crowd-pleaser."

"Brings back memories, yeah?"

He frowned. "Er, yeah. I mean, does it?"

I nudged him. "Ah, come on. You know what I'm on about."

"I don't, you know. You're not confusing me with Robbie Williams, are you?"

"Look, d'you remember kissing me that time or what?" I blurted out.

Ross snorted. "You what? When?"

"Really? You don't remember snogging to Angels at the Year 9 disco? And that was my first ever go at it as well." I stifled a giggle that was at least half drunken hiccup and punched him on the arm. "Have to say, pretty rude. You're s'posed to tell me I was unforgettably awesome and I triggered the sexual awakening that made you the smoking-hot studcrumpet you are today."

"Right. Might have to Google studcrumpet before I'll commit to that."

He was looking sideways at me across the rim of his glass. I noticed his face change suddenly, losing the droopy drunken grin and going all keen and intense. His eyes flickered over my features and down my body.

"Hey, Bobbie Hannigan from school," he said softly. "You're sexy, you know." He put his wine down and twisted his stool to face me. "Fancy giving me a memory jog on this snog? Sure it'll all come flooding back once we get going."

I let my gaze run over the square contour of his jaw, the dusting of stubble; full, sculpted lips a little stained by the wine. God, he was gorgeous. Who had I thought I was kidding when I'd told myself he wasn't my type?

Anyway, what the hell. Nothing we hadn't done before.

"Yeah, go on," I said. "It is my birthday."

I let my eyes fall closed and tilted my face to his, waiting for the kiss. What would it be like? Different than last time, obviously; he was 28, he must have learnt how Frenching worked by now. Soft? Passionate? Bit of both?

After a while I opened my eyes again. He was still scanning my face, his gaze lingering on my lips.

"Look, d'you want this snog or what?" I asked, folding my arms.

He grinned. "Yep. But I think you're going to have to give it me another time. You're pretty sloshed, aren't you?"

"So what? So are you."

"Not as much as you, you've been drinking longer." He leaned one elbow on the bar and propped his chin on his fist to look at me. "Sorry, love, nice boys don't do that sort of thing."

I scoffed. "Nice boy my arse."

He lifted an eyebrow. "How very dare you, madam."

"Come on. Can you deny you once got me hyped up on sugary pop and Space Raiders then took advantage by copping a feel?"

"Ha! Yeah, and I was having a grand old time till that bastard Madison grope-blocked me. That was always going to be the highlight of any 14-year-old lad's night, to be fair."

"I knew it!" I jabbed an accusing finger in his direction. "You do remember."

"Well. Course I do. Never forget your first kiss and go on a girl's boobs, do you?"

"Ooooh. I knew you were having me on. So it was your first too, was it?"

"Yeah." He reached out to give my hand a tipsy squeeze. "Glad I got to have it with you, Bobbie. Not sure I said so at the time, but ... you know, cheers and everything."

"You're welcome," I said, shooting him a slightly wonky smile. "Not that I really had any boobs to speak of back then. Still, long as you enjoyed yourself." I took another swallow of wine and blinked bleary eyes at him. "I'm glad you came home, Ross."

"Me too."

I smiled absently. What were we talking about? Oh yeah, he didn't want to kiss me. My smile morphed into a glare.

"Right. If you won't snog me you have to do a tequila slammer."

He grimaced. "You're kidding, right?"

"Nope. My birthday, my rules." I gestured to Gabbie and she came over to take the order. "Couple of tequilas with salt and lemon please, love."

"Coming right up," she said with an amused grin, taking the tenner I fished out of my purse. The best thing about the Cragport pubs was that the phrase "Don't you think you've had enough?" had never really taken off.

Ross shook his head when Gabbie placed a tequila each in front of us, a couple of lemon wedges and a salt cellar on a dish with my change. "And me such a clean-living lad, never afraid to show tender morning-after eyes to my mother. You know you're a bad influence, Hannigan?"

"Yep. S'why you like me."

He smiled. "One reason. So what do I do with this random assortment of booze, fruit and seasoning then? Make a sorbet?"

"Here. Watch me." I sprinkled salt on the side of my hand, chucked some over my shoulder to compensate the gods of superstition for a bit of spillage, licked it, knocked back the shot and squeezed a lemon wedge into my mouth.

"Ugh! Good stuff." I nodded to Ross. "Your turn."

"Er, right. Fetch us that lemon then."

"Salt first, lemon after. Here." I passed him the cellar and smiled as he sprinkled it on the heel of his hand with a puzzled, interested air, like David Attenborough watching a bunch of spider monkeys mating.

"Ok, so you lick it then down the shot," I told him.

"Why am I doing this again?"

"Because I say so. Anyway, it's rock and roll. You'll disappoint your fans if you don't knock back a bit of hard liquor after a gig."

"Sounds like gateway rock and rolling to me. Slippery slope, that sort of thing," he said, shaking his head. "Not going to make me go the full Keith Richards, are you? Chuck a telly out the window, snort lines of coke off your boobs?"

"Sounds like the flashbacks I get to mine and Jess's 18th. Go on, get it down your neck."

He sucked back the salt and downed the tequila, grimacing at the taste. "Oof! Bloody hell, lass. When you're out drinking you don't mess about, do you?"

"Lemon, quick!" I handed him the wedge and he crushed it between his teeth.

"So how was popping your slammer cherry?" I asked when he'd removed the lemon husk.

"Bleurghh." He stuck his tongue out and gagged comically. "Dunno, bit rough? You might want to ask me again in the morning."

"Is that a proposition?"

He clicked his tongue. "You want it to be?"

"Maybe."

"Well, you're only human." He winced as the slammer made a second assault on his brain cells. "But that had better wait till we're sober. Let's get out of here."

"Ok. Hey, let's go back the beach way. Love walking by the sea at nighttime."

"Me too."

After he'd arranged with Gabbie to stash his guitar behind the bar until morning, we jumped off our barstools and he pulled my arm through his.

"Thanks for tonight, Ross," I said as we weaved unsteadily through the empty tables. Most of the Saturday crowd had long since abandoned the place in favour of nightclubs or bed. "Best birthday I've had in ages."

"Best night I've had in ages. You're fun, Hannigan. Although doubt I'll be saying that tomorrow."

"Pfft." I waved a dismissive hand in front of my face. "Bugger tomorrow. Tomorrow can do one."

"God, you're sexy when you're being a mean drunk. Come on."

***

We stumbled along the shingle arm in arm. The creamy glow from the vintage-style lampposts above us, mingling with the multi-coloured neon of the amusement arcade, made the beach's chalky pebbles look faintly radioactive.

"Don't look now, but there's a murder of seagulls putting the evil eye on us over there," I muttered, jerking my head towards a gang of glass-eyed birds perched on one of the coloured beach huts.

"Nah, murder's crows. Seagulls're –" Ross squinted over at them "– er, a bastard."

I giggled. "Really, that's the collective noun: a bastard of seagulls?"

"Well it is if we're basing it on that little bruiser," he said, nodding towards the bastard of gulls. "Looks like he just got out of borstal."

I followed his gaze to a mean-looking thug of a bird, clearly the leader, yarking at us with a nasty look on his squat face.

"God, you're right," I said, shuddering. "Reminds me of that Hitchcock film. What's it called, with all the birds?"

"Um, *The Birds?*"

"Not that one." I paused. "*Psycho*, that's it. Lad looks like he'd beak you to death in the shower in a heartbeat."

Ross laughed as I mimicked his gory, beaky shower death with my nose on his arm, complete with blood-curdling sound effects.

"Stop pecking me, strange girl." He twisted my face to one side to free himself from my relentless nose attack.

"Scared the birds away though," I said with a grin. "Let's sit on Gracie's bench a minute, watch the waves."

The old bench had been a favourite place for kids to come for a smoke and a snog back when we were at school. In memory of Gracie Hasselbach, who seized every day, from her loving husband Harry – I must've read the plaque a thousand times.

We sank on to the slatted wood. Ross slung one arm around me and I let my head fall to his shoulder.

"So what's the thing with you, Ross Mason?" I asked softly, staring out over the gently swelling silver foam.

"Which particular thing are we talking about?"

"Any thing. The main thing."

I felt the broad muscles of his shoulder shift under me as he shrugged. "The music, I guess. Not that I've got any delusions of hitting the big time. I just … well, I had this idea. Or more of a dream really."

I looked up at him. "What?"

He laughed, looking sheepish. "Nah, I can't tell you. It's daft."

"Ah, go on. What's said between two people trashed on tequila slammers stays between them, that's the rule. It's like doctors and that hypocritical oath."

"Hypocritical oath, right," he said with a grin. "I wouldn't let your sister hear you call it that."

"Come on. Promise I won't laugh."

He sighed. "Well, it sort of goes back to when we were in sixth form. Me and the lads used to play the pub circuit round town."

"Yeah, I remember. Went to see you a few times."

He looked down to where my head was cradled by the arch of his neck and shoulder, gazing dreamily at the lapping tide. "Did you? Didn't notice you."

"No, you never noticed me in those days," I said with a smile. "You were the boy in the band. Enough lasses seemed to go for that to knock me right off the radar."

He planted a kiss on top of my hair. "Shows what you know. Just because I was working on my aloof and brooding act doesn't mean I didn't notice you."

"Didn't spot me at the gigs though, did you? Had my rock chick hair on for you and everything."

"Well, I was concentrating. I'm professional like that." He laughed. "Terrible, weren't we?"

"Yeah, you weren't great," I admitted. "I mean, *you* were good. That sausage-fingered keyboard player though ... ouch. What was it you called yourselves?"

"Oh God." He pinched the bridge of his nose. "It used to change pretty regularly, but for most of Year 13 it was ... oh God."

I smirked at him. "Come on, 'fess up."

"Ok. Nietzsche's Jockstrap."

I sputtered into laughter. "Where the hell did that come from?"

"Our bassist Chris was a philosophy student. Thought it'd impress lasses."

"And did it?"

"It did actually. Turns out teenage girls are just as stupid as teenage boys. I was doing alright for myself for a bit."

I nudged him. "So I recall, slutty. Hey, weren't we talking about something else?"

"What?" His brow knotted into a booze-muddled frown. "Oh yeah, you asked me about my thing."

"And what is your thing?" My hand flew to my mouth. "You're not reforming Hitler's Y-Fronts, are you?"

"Ha, Nietzsche's Jockstrap. No, luckily for the pub-goers of Cragport that ship's sailed."

"What then?"

"You really promise not to laugh? Because we artistic types are sensitive flowers. And you've already been pretty rotten about my band name."

"Well, that you had coming." I looked up at him. "Tell me, Ross."

He sighed. "I just ... I had this plan. Or more a castle in the air, something to keep me dreaming when things seemed bleak." In the glow of neon I could see his eyes glittering. "I want to set up a music charity for kids. Something to encourage young acts who want to fight the *X-Factor* clone wars, help them to everything they need to get a start – rehearsal space, workshops, open-mics, all that. Everything we wished we'd had." He looked down at his trainers with an embarrassed smile. "Like I said, it's daft. And probably never going to happen, unless I buy that winning lottery ticket."

I lifted my head off his shoulder to look at him. "Why is it daft? Sounds a brilliant idea."

"You know how much something like that would cost?"

"No. How much?"

He frowned. "Ok, I don't know exactly. I just assumed it'd be lots."

"What, you haven't even costed it up?"

"Well, no, not properly. Suppose I've avoided it. Putting a price on it'd just push the whole thing further away."

"So you don't really want to do it then."

"Yes, I want to, but ..." He laughed. "Hey, you're good at this. What is it you do when you're not writing?"

"Teacher. Adult education."

"Ha! Should've guessed, bossy."

"What's your day job when you're not playing pubs then? I thought your mum told me you were an artist or something."

"Nothing quite that glamorous, unfortunately. Freelance graphic designer." He sighed. "I dunno, Bobbie. There was a time I really thought the music thing might happen. Started putting money away, looking into venues. But I could sense Claire wasn't keen, so it got pushed to one side."

"And now that's not an issue."

"No."

"Then stop making excuses and do it. I'll help, I'm good at planning."

He flashed me a grateful smile. "Would you?"

"Course, whatever I could do. We need more creative stuff for kids round here."

"Thanks, love." He gave my ear an affectionate flick. "You know, you're pretty cool."

I didn't reply. I was staring out to sea, watching the distant lights of a pleasure cruiser making its final trip of the day.

"Bobbie, you ok?" he said, waving a hand in front of my eyes. "I can call us a cab if you need to get home."

"I bought a lighthouse today."

He laughed. "I know, crazy girl. What're you going to do with it?"

I fell silent again, letting my pupils lilt up and down with the shifting silken waves.

"Oh God, you're not going to do the eccentric writer thing and live in it, are you?" he asked.

"No ..." I turned to face him. "I've got a lighthouse, Ross."

His eyes flickered over my face and I saw his expression change. "Oh no, Bobbie. No. That's just ... it wouldn't work."

"Why not?"

"Give over, there's about two foot of floor space. You could barely fit a cymbal in."

"I bet it's bigger than you think. Anyway, there's plenty of room. You know, vertically."

"What good's that? I can't push it over."

"You could install platforms though. Then the music

34

would sort of … drift up." I stood. "Let's stumble along a bit. Feel like I need to walk off some booze."

He curled an arm around my shoulders as we continued our meandering way along the seafront.

"So?" I said. "What do you think?"

"I think it's the most ridiculous idea I ever heard." He bent to kiss the top of my head. "And you're a ridiculous girl."

"Ridiculous girl with a lighthouse." I stopped walking for a moment to face him. "I'm serious, Ross. A music venue in a lighthouse: with a unique selling point like that, we'd have investors falling over themselves. Bet there's loads of grants we could apply for, my mum'd know …" I fixed him in an earnest, drunken gaze, not quite believing what I was about to suggest but hell, diving in anyway. "Let's do it. You and me."

"God, you're not even kidding, are you?"

"Nope."

He let out a short, shocked laugh. "That's crazy, Bobbie. I mean, seriously off-the-chart crazy. Practicality aside, we haven't seen each other in ten years. We hardly know each other, in a lot of ways. What makes you think we could pull off something like that?"

"Nothing to lose by giving it a shot, is there?" My mouth spread into a grin. "Come on, mate. For once in your life, take a chance on something wilder than a tequila slammer."

His brow had tightened into a thoughtful frown. "Would you really take a risk like that? On me?"

"Course. You're a talented guy, Ross, I know you could do it. And it could be something really good for this town." I reached out to take his hands, seeking his eyes in the dim light. "Hey. I'll trust you if you'll trust me. Let's have an adventure."

He smiled. "Well, I do trust you. Still, I don't know ... there's the space, for one thing. And the money. Then the shape, the acoustics could be way off..."

"We can work round it."

"But it's your lighthouse. Your birthday lighthouse."

"Yep. And I'm offering you, Ross Mason, your very own half-share. I'm going round your Uncle Charlie's next week to get the deeds signed over. If you're up for it we can ask him to put the paperwork in both our names."

"God ... is it crazy you're actually starting to make sense?"

"Yeah, it's crazy. Still a great idea though. Come on." I held out my palm to him.

He looked down at it. "What's that for?"

"You have to give me 50p. For your half. Then we can say it's a deal."

"Oh." Ross fished in his pocket for some change, looking bewildered and excited all at once. He rummaged out a 50p piece and handed it to me, then burst out laughing.

"Are we really doing this? I mean, you hear these stories about people getting hammered and waking up with their best mate's name tattooed on their arse or handcuffed to a lamppost, but never with half a lighthouse."

"Well now people can tell that story about you. Shake on it."

He held out his hand and I gave it a firm press. "Look forward to working with you, partner. Get the key off Charlie and I'll meet you up there tomorrow at 11, ok?"

"Jesus. You really do mean it." He lifted a palm to his forehead. "Think I'm starting to feel that tequila. Did we just decide to do something completely insane or is it the DTs starting?"

"Yep. And we shook on it so it's legally binding according to the law of the playground. Plus –" I held up the shiny coin he'd given me "– got your 50p. No going back."

"Good. Probably the booze talking but I'm pretty sure this is the best idea ever. Me and you and the lighthouse ..." He squinted up at the old lighthouse on the cliff, blanketed from view by the darkness. "It is, right?"

"Has to be. In vino verity and all that."

"Er, don't think that's how that saying goes. Verity was in our year at school, wasn't she?"

"Oh yeah." I giggled and stumbled towards him, the heady combo of wine, tequila and sea air suddenly landing me a punch square between the eyes.

"Whoops. Careful, tiny drunk," Ross said, laughing as he caught me.

I gazed up at him through cloudy eyes, fluttering my lashes in a way I hoped looked flirtatious rather than sleepy. "So slammer's hit you at last?"

"Yep."

"And you're pretty smashed, all told?"

"I'd say so."

"How about that birthday snog then, if we're as drunk as each other?"

His mouth curved at one side. "Does sound nice, with the sea and everything. Still, feels like I'd be taking advantage."

"Ah, go on, Gentleman Jim, nothing we haven't done before. Call it a business snog. Can't seal a deal properly with just a rubbish floppy handshake."

"Oh right. I'll have you know that when sober, my handshake is as firm and manly as my lovemaking, darling."

"Wouldn't know, would I?"

"Not yet," he said, his voice suddenly gentle as he pressed me closer. "But there'll be time for that. Let's just enjoy right now, eh?" He reached up to stroke my hair away from my face, caressing my cheek while he pushed the escaping strands back. His fingertips on my skin felt rough, hardened by guitar strings, yet gentle too. I loved the way the tickle sent little vibrations through the nerves in my face. "Oh …

go on then, lass, if it's just a business snog. It is your birthday."

"Ha, I win. Knew I'd crack you in the end." I let out a dizzy giggle. "Crack you like a big handsome walnut."

"Yep. Caught in the nutcracker of your charms."

"Ok, let's stop with the walnut thing now."

"Yeah, think we've exhausted the nut-based flirting." He stroked a gentle palm down my hair. "Hey," he said softly. "I really like you, Bobbie."

"I like you too, Ross."

He brought his lips to mine and we held each other close as we kissed, listening to the leisurely waves plashing against the pebbles behind us.

Chapter 4

Next morning, I woke with the thundering of the mighty ocean in my ears, an army of goose-stepping jackboots kicking the backs of my eyeballs and a fuzzy sort of numbness around the mouth. A hangover, basically. And a bloody nasty one at that.

I winced as unwelcome memories of the night before assaulted me. God, I didn't really call Ross a big handsome walnut, did I? And tequila slammers, ouch – what had I been thinking? I was getting too old for this.

Oh shit ... there was another thing, wasn't there? The lighthouse ... we were going to...

I glanced over at the dressing table. Yep, it'd really happened. There was Ross's 50p, glinting wickedly as it reflected the chink of spring sunlight intruding through the blinds.

My eyes shot wide open and I grabbed my phone to check the time. 10am! I'd agreed to meet Ross at the lighthouse at 11. I jumped out of bed, grimacing with pain as my head adjusted to the change in gravity, and started rummaging around the cupboard for some jeans.

Would he even turn up? If our lighthouse plan had seemed unlikely under the influence of countless wines and a tequila slammer each, it looked nothing less than full-on surreal in the cold and sober light of day.

I stopped rummaging for a moment. Full-on surreal ... yeah, that about summed it up. In the space of one day I'd managed to buy a lighthouse, drunkenly get off with a man I hadn't seen since I was 18 and invite him to go into business with me. And the weirdest thing was, the idea didn't seem any less appealing now I'd sobered up. It seemed exciting. Exhilarating.

For so long now, life had been the same. Not that it wasn't rich enough, in its way. There was my job at Cragport Community College: that could be pretty rewarding. Some of the adults who enrolled for GCSE and A-Level English hardly had any formal education to start with, just a love of the subject and a determination to succeed. It was pretty incredible, taking them from the faltering, fawn-like things they often seemed when they started to bright, confident people ready to tackle the next step in their lives. And there was Jess, Mum, Monty ... but still, it was all so boring, every day like every day like every bloody Cragport day. No new faces, no new experiences. No new anything.

And now, suddenly, there was adventure, excitement, my very own Five on a Treasure Island moment. And there was Ross Mason, the boy in the band. Witty, warm, smiley Ross, his dancing eyes full of passion and fun, who'd somehow become part of it all. In spite of the hangover I felt my heart leap with that fluttering feeling: a path to travel, a step beyond the mundane.

The only thing was, I wasn't sure whether the leap went with Ross, the lighthouse, or both. The two things seemed to be knotted up somehow, and I couldn't see where one ended and the other began.

Ok, I knew it was insane. I knew the project would be difficult, maybe impossible. Expensive. Time-consuming. But it'd made my heart jump. God only knew how long it'd been since that last happened.

Bugger caution. I was doing this.

***

As I walked to the lighthouse, a sulky Monty in tow, I wondered whether I'd find Ross there. Assuming he even remembered our plan, there was no guarantee he wouldn't have changed his mind about the whole thing now all the booze was out of his system.

I needn't have worried. When I reached the clifftop he was waiting, looking a bit green around the gills but with a welcoming smile on his face. The sea breeze was whipping his hair around his face just as it had ... God, had it really only been yesterday we'd met again?

He looked bashful as I approached.

"Er, hi," he said, scuffing at the grass with one toe.

"Hi yourself."

"You feeling as rough as I look?"

"Worse." I shook my head. "Can't believe I let you talk me into that tequila slammer."

That seemed to break the ice. He laughed.

"Foul and hideous lies. But suppose I shouldn't expect any less from the girl who's inflicted the hangover from hell on me."

There was an awkward silence for a second.

"So, do you remember?" he said at last.

The lighthouse plan or the kiss? I leaned down to let Monty off his lead, a handy excuse to avoid eye contact. The little dog flung us both a dirty look before galloping off to chase his tail round the lighthouse.

"I'm here, aren't I?" I said eventually.

"And do you – you didn't just come to give me my 50p back?"

I shook my head. "I told you, Ross, I think it's a great idea. That wasn't the booze talking. I'm in if you are."

"I am if you are."

I laughed. "Then that makes four of us." I nodded to the

lighthouse. "If it's possible, that is. Let's check out the damage before we get too carried away, eh?"

Ross pulled a key out of his pocket and unlocked the old door. I noticed a brand new sliver of pink graffiti across it as I followed him in.

Oh God ... my stomach muscles went rigid as I cast my eyes over the inside. It was worse than I'd expected. Much, much worse.

Everything was the same shade of mottled pearly grey all over, like a three-week-old orange that had been left in the sun. And as for the smell ... Christ. A herd of cats could've spent a year pissing into every nook and it would've been more fragrant. The glassless windows meant hordes of seagull visitors had left a slimy layer of droppings over every surface.

The spiral staircase running up the middle was a slide of rubble, moss poking through every crack. Burst, festering sandbags were piled haphazardly at the base, along with a load of rancid wood and rope that might once have been lobster pots. The whole building looked like an unsalvageable mess of rock, guano and plant matter.

"Jesus, Ross!"

"Yeah, I know..."

"Is it even safe?" I asked, running one fingertip along a wall. My finger actually sank into the wet, powdery dust that seemed to cover everything. Pulling out a tissue, I wiped it off in disgust.

"Well there's no asbestos or anything, I asked Charlie. Just dirt and rot. Still, don't think we should spend longer inside than we have to."

"Oh my God ..." I felt suddenly lightheaded and my stomach flipped uncomfortably. Turning to the door, I stumbled blindly through, blinking dust out of my eyes.

Outside, I sank against the lighthouse's sloped wall and burst into tears.

So that was it. The adventure was over before it had even started. That ... that was it. Well, it had been a nice dream while it lasted.

Monty bounded up and put his little paws on my lap, blinking sympathetic brown eyes, but all I could do was stare at him through a fog of brine and disappointment.

Ross appeared at the door. "Hey, no need for that," he said gently, coming out and sitting down on the grass next to me. Seeing a rival comforter had arrived, Monty turned his tail to us and trotted off. "It's not so bad."

"Not so bad, are you blind? It'll cost a fortune to get that place sorted out. How could Charlie let it get like that?"

"He hasn't been up here since Aunty Annie died." He slipped an arm round my shoulders. "It was hers, you know. Think that's one reason he wants rid: sick of those letters

45

from the council, reminding him she's gone and it's still here."

"Poor Charlie," I said with a sigh. "But it doesn't matter. We can't do it, Ross. The place is beyond repair." I turned to bury my head in his shoulder and gave way to sobs.

"Come on, what happened to that girl from last night, the one who robbed me of 50p and told me we could do anything?"

"She ... sobered up, that's what," I gasped through the tears. "Sobered up and hit that bastard called reality head-on."

"Don't say that." He reached up to stroke my hair. "Honestly, I wasn't just trying to make you feel better, it really isn't so bad. We can do it."

"You ... really ... think so?" I sobbed into his coat.

"I really do. Come back inside a sec, let me show you."

I wiped my eyes on his collar, stood and followed him back in.

"See? Structure's fine, all the stone apart from the staircase," he said, blowing a layer of dust away and knocking against a solid-sounding wall. "And look." He took a few long strides across the floor. "You were right, it is bigger than I thought. Must be 30, 35 feet across."

I sniffed doubtfully. "You think it could work then?"

"Yep. We'll have to get someone to survey it, but I'm certain it's basically sound." His eyes sparkled as fervour for his pet project took hold. "Can't you just see it, Bobbie?

A stage down here, two or three viewing balconies, and then maybe a little bar at the top where the old lamp is, looking out to sea." He stopped to relish the image he'd conjured, a smile fluttering on his lips.

To be honest, I couldn't see it. All I could see when I looked around the lighthouse was dirt, decay and a hell of a lot of work. But I couldn't help smiling at the enthusiasm shining in his face.

"It'll be a new lease of life for the place," I said. "That's if we can pull it off."

"We can, I know it." He came over to squeeze my shoulder. "You and me, lighthouse girl."

"Yeah, but—" I broke off into a fit of coughing as some of the dust got into my throat.

"Come on, let's get out of here," Ross said, guiding me to the door.

"But how will we do it?" I asked when we were back in the fresh air. "I mean, even if it is salvageable, the state of it … where will we get the money?"

"You said yourself there are grants we can apply for. It is a listed building. And I've got some savings I can invest if things get desperate, sort of an emergency fund."

"You'd really do that?"

"Absolutely. I told you, Bobbie, I've been dreaming about this for years. This is my chance to make a difference and I'm going for it heart and soul."

I looked into his passion-kindled eyes. He was really prepared to fight for this, wasn't he?

I thought about the money I had sitting in my building society account. Jess and me had never known our dad, but he'd left us each £10,000 in his will when he passed away three years ago. I'd never been able to bring myself to touch it; it felt dirty, somehow. But the lighthouse project, something for the town...

"I've got cash I can invest too," I said. "My dad left me ten grand."

He stared at me in surprise. "Really, that bastard left you money?"

"Yeah. Deathbed guilt, I think."

"But Bobbie, this is my dream, not yours. Your dad left that for you."

"I don't want his money. Let it go to a good cause; I'll never spend it."

"But—"

I raised an imperious hand. "Don't try to talk me out of it, Mason. There's no point arguing when I get the bossy face on."

He smiled. "So I remember. Seriously though, you don't want to talk it through with Jess or your mum first? I won't hold it against you if you back out."

"Look, we shook on it, didn't we? If we do this, we do it together. Musketeers never say die."

"That's Goonies. But I take your point." He slapped me on the shoulder. "Well, lass, if you're really positive, I can match that. In for a penny, in for a pound, eh?"

"Are you sure you can afford it, Ross? I know freelancing can be unsteady."

"Oh, I'll cope. Anyway, there'll be the equity from my old flat once it finally sells, plus some joint savings of mine and Claire's. I won't have access to those until the divorce goes through, but at least it's on the horizon."

I stiffened under his arm.

"What?" I said quietly.

"There's nearly six months yet until we can get the ball rolling. Even when these things are amicable it has to be two years' minimum legal separation. Don't worry though, I'll have enough in the meantime with a bit of careful budgeting."

Divorce ... oh Jesus *Christ*, he was married! Oh God, I didn't snog a married man!

Ross frowned at my glazed expression. "Everything ok, Bobbie? You've gone all quiet."

"Yeah." I summoned a smile. "Yeah, course. Just thinking."

"Look, about last night. I mean, kissing you and everything – sorry. I shouldn't have done it when we were like we were." He grinned. "Obviously under the influence of tequila your charms just overwhelmed me."

"Last night was last night," I mumbled. "Nothing to beat yourself up over."

"So can we go out again, do things properly this time?"

God, I needed to bail out of this conversation. Married! How could I not have known he was married? That changed everything.

"I'm not sure it's such a good idea while we're working together," I said at last. "And while you're – your personal life. Let's just focus on the lighthouse for now."

"My personal life ... with Claire, you mean?"

"Yeah. Better to wait for your divorce till you plunge back into the dating scene, don't you think?"

He frowned. "Never really thought about it like that. We've been separated 18 months ... I suppose the actual paperwork just feels like, well, paperwork."

"Still, it doesn't feel right to me. I'm sorry, Ross, I can't; not now. Maybe ask me again in six months, eh? That is, if you still want to."

"We're friends though, aren't we?"

I shook my head. "More important than that. We're partners."

Chapter 5

Back at the cottage, Jess had finally dragged herself out of bed and was enjoying Chillout Sunday in front of the telly. I chucked myself down and dropped my head to her shoulder.

"What's up with you?" she asked, giving the wind-tangled strands tumbling over her PJs a vague pat.

"Hangover. God, Jessie, I've had the weirdest 24 hours."

"Tell me about it. Hey, want to play 'Guess where they stuck the vegetable' with last night's A&E loiterers?"

"Let's do news first. How'd it go with Gareth?"

She pinkened slightly. "Not bad. I mean, he didn't get lucky or anything, just a bit of a fumble. Seems a nice lad, for a rugby player."

"One night nice or second date nice?"

"Second date nice," she said with a soppy smile. "We're going for a drink tonight. Proper drink this time, I'm not working. Maybe I'll get to find out why he's got 'Tripod' on the back of his rugby shirt."

"Heh. Knowing your luck he'll just be a really keen photographer. All right, let's do the thing." I lifted a hand for her to high five. "Ow! Not so hard."

She looked down at my head on her shoulder. "So now your news. What did you and Ross Mason get up to last night, apart from what by the state of your eyes I'd say was a pretty heavy session?"

"You had to ask. Listen, Jess, this is going to sound bizarre, but ... I may have just slightly, I mean accidentally, while I was pissed ..." I groaned. "Me and Ross're going into business."

When I'd filled her in on the lighthouse plan, I was expecting a pretty vocal reaction. But Jess just stared.

"Well? Aren't you going to say anything?"

She didn't answer. I picked up an open box of Maltesers from the table and waved them under her nose like smelling salts.

"Helloooo? Is my sister in there?"

Eventually she picked her phone up from the arm of the sofa and started tapping at the screen.

"What're you doing?" I asked.

"Googling what I need to do to have you sectioned under the mental health act, since you've clearly gone totally off your chump."

I sighed. "It does sound a bit insane, doesn't it?"

"A *bit*?" Jess looked up from her phone to twitch an eyebrow at me.

"It's just ... well, it's some excitement, isn't it? I've been bored stiff for months. Bored of my job, bored of blokes, bored of this stupid small town..."

She snorted. "If you're bored get a hobby. Take up bloody ... I don't know, decoupage or bondage or something. Better still, finish your damn book."

I flinched at the reference to the long-neglected novel.

"Honestly, Jessie, I really want to do this."

She narrowed her eyes. "This is about him, isn't it?"

"Who?"

"Come on, don't play innocent. You're talking to someone who's known you since we shared a womb," she said. "Ross Mason. You fancy him. We both know you never lure a bloke on to the slammers unless you're trying to get into his knickers."

I winced. "That's the other thing I wanted to talk to you about. Did you know he's married?"

Her eyebrows shot up. "Christ, seriously?"

"Well, separated. They're filing for divorce as soon as they're allowed to. Ross just casually dropped it into conversation today as if he thought I knew."

She shook her head. "See, this is why everyone should be on Facebook. How else are you supposed to stay on top of 500 old schoolfriends' relationship statuses?"

"And last night ... God, I was this close to going to bed with him, Jess. I feel awful."

"You didn't know, did you?"

"I should've. Molly must've mentioned it a dozen times."

We both went silent for a minute, and I knew we were thinking the same thing.

"Are you remembering—"

"—when Corinne came?" I said. "Yeah."

We never met our dad, James, before he died; not even once. Mum's relationship with him had been all over by the time she found out she was pregnant, which according to family legend hadn't stopped Grandad having to be narrowly restrained from punching the guy, and he'd never shown any interest in us after that. When we got older and learned the whole story, the feeling became more than mutual. But the day Corinne had come to visit loomed large in my little kid memory.

She'd been pretty – beautiful really: a tall, willowy woman in middle age, with silvery skin and long, silken hair, prematurely white, like something out of a fairytale. We were only seven, but we could tell by the way Mum paled when she answered the door that it wasn't a welcome visit.

They'd been closeted in the kitchen together for nearly an hour when they eventually emerged. Mum's cheeks were wet, and Corinne's eyes looked red-rimmed too.

"Can I have five minutes with them?" Corinne asked Mum quietly. And there was a sort of hungry, longing expression in her eyes as she looked over to where me and Jess were watching cartoons obliviously on the rug.

Mum looked uncertain, but eventually she gave a slight nod, and Corinne came to kneel by us. I don't remember all she said, but I remember her hugging me, and a whisper, very faint: "You should've been my little girl, you know." She pressed a tenner each into our hands – more money than we'd ever had in one go, back then – and she was gone. Although she and Mum grew close in later years, the two of us never saw her again.

After she left, Mum called us to her on the sofa and cuddled us like she'd never let go. It scared me. I think I was half afraid Corinne was going to come back and take us away, for some reason I didn't understand.

"Who was that lady, Mummy?" Jess asked.

"A kind person I hurt once. Her name's Corinne."

"How did you hurt her?"

"Well, chickie, her husband lost his job because of something I did and it made her very sad."

"Why did you do it then?"

Mum smiled and stroked Jess's hair. "Oh, I was too silly to know better. It was a long time ago."

"What did she hug us for?" I demanded.

"Didn't you want her to, my love?"

I shrugged. "It was ok. She smelled nice. She doesn't know us though."

"She's lonely, that's all. The man she's married to goes away a lot, and she doesn't have any children."

"That's mean to leave her on her own." Jess looked thoughtful. "If I was her, I'd get married to somebody different."

Mum sighed. "So would I, Jessie."

"Did you know her a long time, Mummy?" I asked. She always encouraged us to ask any question we liked, and gave a frank answer whenever she could.

Mum shook her head. "This is the first time we ever met. I used to know her husband."

"Was he your friend?"

"Sort of. He's your dad."

"Oh." I pondered this new information for a second. "Hey, can I have a Jaffa Cake?"

And that was that.

"But this isn't like that, Bobs," present-day Jess reminded me. "Ross is getting divorced."

"So was James. That's what the lying git told Mum, anyway." I shook my head. "I know it's not the same, but ... well, I think the two of us know better than anyone that you don't mess about with married men. People get hurt."

"He's only married on paper though. If he's here and she's in Sheffield, it has to be over, doesn't it?"

"Still, it's not right. You wouldn't."

"No. I'd want to wait till it was all signed and sealed, I think." She examined me carefully. "You're just friends then, are you?"

"We're ... partners."

"And this lighthouse malarkey is nothing to do with you fancying him?"

"I do like his company," I confessed. "He's a good laugh, easy to be with. But that's all there can be, at least until he's actually divorced."

She sighed. "Yeah, you're right. Better to wait till it's simple."

I summoned a smile. "Well, let's cheer up. Go on, chuck us those Maltesers and I'll play your manky doctor game."

"All right. So. Parsnip."

"Bum?"

"Correct. Butternut squash ...?"

***

It was a spectre-grey Thursday afternoon when I met Ross outside his Uncle Charlie's bungalow on the outskirts of town, ready to sign the deeds that would make the light-house ours.

The ivy-covered house looked the same as always. It never did change much except for an occasional addition to Charlie's collection of lecherous-looking garden gnomes on the front lawn, the ones he'd been using for years to wind up his property-value-conscious neighbours.

I'd been a pretty frequent visitor once upon a time. When Jess and I were small our grandad, Charlie's long-time drinking buddy, used to bring us round to be plied with Madeira cake and pineapple squash by Charlie's wife Annie while the two men watched football. But Annie and Grandad were gone now, and Charlie was all on his own.

He and Annie had never had kids, so, at 83, he was left at the mercy of his brother's children – a niece and nephew. That was Ross's dad Keith, well-known tight bastard and all-round mardy arse. I wasn't quite sure how the same genes had managed to produce someone like Ross.

"Ivy only grows for the wicked," Ross muttered as we stood in front of the curling tendrils twining themselves around Charlie's front door.

"Sorry?"

He smiled. "Oh, nothing. Something my aunty used to say to wind the old boy up when he was working out in the garden, a silly superstition. Just came back to me."

I examined him with concern. He seemed vacant, purple rings bruising his eyes.

"You ok?"

"Just tired," he said, flushing slightly. "Up late on a design job."

"Hi, Uncle Charlie," Ross said when the door eventually opened, pumping the old man's hand heartily. "Good to see you, you old bugger."

"You too, lad. Come on in." Charlie ushered us into the dimly lit house that for some reason always made me think of soup – something in the musty smell – and closed the door behind us.

Charlie looked the same as ever – which was to say, a bit like one of his own gnomes. Short, stocky and weatherbeaten, with the large arms and broad chest that came from 40-plus years hauling things around on boats back when he was a trawlerman, decked out as always in jeans and silk smoking jacket like a smart-cas Hugh Hefner. His expression was the same combination of mischief, grumpiness and wry humour.

"How've you been, Roberta?" he asked in his pipe-roughened voice. "Your mam keeping well?"

"She's fine, Charlie." I gave him a hug. "Our Jess says hi too."

"Well, you're good girls. So." He jerked a thumb at Ross. "This young idiot tells me you got him blotto and talked him into opening a pub in my Annie's lighthouse."

"Er ... yeah, something like that. That ok by you?"

He shrugged. "No business of mine, not once you've signed on the dotted line. Come through, kids."

"Charlie, you sure you want to do this?" I asked when

Ross and I were seated on his uncle's beige sofa with him in an armchair opposite. The lighthouse paperwork was all laid out on the coffee table, waiting for the solicitor Charlie had booked to witness the sale. "I mean, you haven't got a few marbles missing or anything?"

"Only the same handful that've been rolling around upstairs for the last 20 years, flower," he said with a shrug.

"You could get a good price for it, you know."

"I could. And do what with the money?"

"I don't know, get yourself new carpet slippers or something; you're old. Or buy another pervy gnome, scare the kids on their way to school."

"You're a cheeky lass." He grinned, a wide smile showing off his few remaining teeth. "Knew I liked you for something other than being Bertie Hannigan's granddaughter."

"She's right though, Uncle Charlie," Ross said. "We don't want to take it off you unless you're absolutely sure you want rid at that price."

"Look, son, you and the rest of the family must've worked out by now I'm a miserable, cantankerous old bastard whose only joy in my old age is causing trouble for you all."

"It has been noted, yeah."

"Good, then you'll know it's easiest to shut up and let me have my way. I can't be arsed faffing with estate agents and the like, it might well finish me off. You kids just sign the deeds, take the bloody lighthouse and bugger off." He leaned over the coffee table for his pipe and started stuffing it with fresh tobacco from a tin on the arm of his chair.

I frowned. "There isn't any more to this, is there?"

"How d'you mean?"

"Well, you're not about to pop your clogs or something?"

The old man shrugged. "Not that I know of. Might last a few more years if I keep eating my greens."

"So you really want to do this then? You, Charles Mason, being of sound mind and body and all that jazz?"

"Yep." He sighed as he took a match to his old Dublin pipe, wreathing the room in brown-blue wisps that tickled our eyeballs. He inhaled a deep draw before he spoke again. "All right, if you really want to know, there is another thing. The bloody council."

"They written to you again, have they?" Ross said.

"It's worse than that. Bastards are threatening to sue me."

"*What?*" Ross shook his head in disbelief. "On what grounds?"

"Reckon they can make a case based on me letting the old place fall into disrepair, affecting the tourism industry. Some jumped-up little bureaucrat at the town hall sent me an ultimatum. Sort it out, sell it on or face the music."

"Bastards!" Ross's brow knit dangerously. "Who threatens to sue an old man? I'll bloody well go down there."

"Oi. Less of the O word." Charlie's papery face broke

into a smile. "But ta, lad. Nice to know someone in the family gives enough of a monkeys to watch my back."

Ross sent an affectionate smile back. "Well, you're not a bad old sod. You know I'll look after you. So is that why you're selling then?"

"That and I just want rid. Anyway, it's worked out well, this young lady convincing you to take an interest." He bobbed his silver head in my direction. "Lighthouse would've gone to you in the end anyway. Was going to leave it you in my will."

"Me? What for?"

"Piss your dad off, mainly. And to see your face from the great beyond when you realised I'd saddled you with a lighthouse."

"Ha. Yeah, I bet."

"I still don't know, Charlie," I said. "Not sure we should take it if the council have bullied you into it like that."

"Trust me, you're doing me a favour." His expression softened. "Look, she'd want you to have it. My Annie. Seems right it should go to our Ross, keep it in the family."

"What was the lighthouse like when Aunty Annie was young?" Ross asked. "Don't remember her ever talking about it."

"Well she did, all the time. Still, you were only a nipper when she passed, doubt you'd remember." Charlie took another long draw on his pipe, his crinkled eyes unfocused.

"It were an impressive sight in its heyday. There was still a keeper back in the thirties, Annie's grandad Wilf. Lived there with his wife. Proper old-fashioned battleaxe her Granny Peggy was, scary as the Old bloody Gentleman. And by, but she were houseproud. Every day she'd be out there topping up the paint, scrubbing the front step with sand. The floor were bare stone – they'd no brass for carpet – but she'd have you take your shoes off and walk round in your socks like she had ruddy shag-pile down." He smiled wistfully. "Pride of the town, our lighthouse, in them days."

"So how did it end up like it is now?" I asked.

"Oh, the war came. Light had to go off, Peggy and Wilf moved out. When peace broke out they decided they didn't want to go back and leased it to other keepers, offcumdens who didn't take the same pride in it. By the time Annie inherited it, the day of the lighthouse was over. Ours were a husk of what it had been by then."

"So it's just been left to rot?"

"No, when Annie were here she did what she could with it. The paint always shone when she were alive. She wanted everyone to see it, pride of the town, same as when Peggy had it." He blinked, and I thought I saw the hint of a tear in the already watery eyes. "And then my Annie were gone, and no amount of paintwork could bring her back. It's been years since I could bear to look at the thing." He summoned a gap-toothed smile. "Ah well, no good getting weepy now, I'll see her soon enough. You kids take the lighthouse. Make your aunty proud, eh, our Ross?"

I glanced at Ross, and was surprised to see tears in his eyes too.

"I'll do my best for her, Uncle Charlie."

"Ross, can I have a word?" I said. "I mean, in private."

Charlie grinned. "I can take a hint. I'll brew us up a pot."

"He's grieving," I whispered when Charlie had tottered off to the kitchen.

"I know. He misses her."

"Then we can't take it, can we? We'd be taking advantage of a lonely old man."

"We wouldn't though. She's been dead 18 years, he's not exactly rushing into it." He shuffled on his cushion to face me. "Look, the lighthouse makes him miserable. Every time he hears about it, it reminds him the love of his life is gone and that bastard's still standing."

"Yeah, but … well, it isn't right."

"You heard him, Bobbie. My Aunty Annie loved the thing." His brow gathered into a determined frown. "Well, you make your choice, you're entitled to back out. Me … I never thought about it till he told me all that. But I'm doing this. For Annie."

"Hey. If you're doing it I'm doing it, partner." I leaned

round to look into his eyes. "Don't be angry, Ross. I care about the lighthouse too."

His face softened. "Sorry, got a bit carried away. Anyway, it's your lighthouse."

"No, it's your lighthouse, I think that's clear now. But if you want me ... well, maybe it's our lighthouse."

He shot me a smile. "I do want you, Bobbie. I want it to be our lighthouse."

He was looking at me with that keen expression in his eyes, the one that was so often the prelude to a kiss, and I stiffened. But before things could go any further, there was a loud rap at the door.

"That'll be the lawyer lady," Charlie called from the kitchen. "Can you get it, lad?"

I sent a silent prayer of thanks to the invisible solicitor for getting me off the hook. Kiss awkwardness averted.

Ross jumped up, coming back in a few seconds later closely followed by an official-looking solicitor in a black pencil suit. And in what felt like no time at all, Charlie had an extra pound in his pocket – and Ross and I were the proud owners of a pair of cheesy grins and our very own lighthouse.

Chapter 6

"Don't be nervous." The kind-faced receptionist who manned the front desk at Cragport Town Hall smiled encouragingly.

Ross was clutching a folder of notes against his chest, moving his lips silently, while I tried to distract myself with an old *Elle* I'd found. We'd been there half an hour, waiting to make a pitch to the town council for funding to get the lighthouse cleaned up.

"That obvious, is it?" I said to the receptionist.

She nodded at the magazine on my lap. "Well you've been staring at that feature on what to wear to hide a lopsided bosom for 15 minutes." She lowered her voice. "Honestly, there's nothing to worry about. Those pompous old duffers are desperate to see something done about the lighthouse. You've got the winning hand here."

Ross looked doubtful. "You really think? We're asking for a hell of a lot."

"Absolutely. Stand your ground, that's all. The chairman can be a bit of a bully."

"Thanks for the heads-up," I said. "Let's just hope we catch him in a good mood."

"I don't think he has good moods. Sorry."

Ten minutes later, I was still staring at on-trend summer looks for the wonky-titted fashionista when some sort of pager on the receptionist's desk buzzed. She looked up from her book to examine it.

"You're up," she said, jerking her head towards the ornate wooden doors leading to the council chambers. "They want you in the meeting."

The councillors – ten of them, all in suits, all men and with an average age of at least 60 – were seated in a horse-shoe around a large table. The only one I recognised was Alex Partington, the youngest councillor. He tried to catch my eye but I ignored him.

No chairs had been provided for me and Ross, who huddled together on the carpet as if we were being tried for murder. The bony, leather-skinned man with the watery eyes who was chairing the meeting – Councillor Langford, he'd introduced himself as – had us fixed in a stern gaze.

"So. Mr Mason and Miss Hannigan: welcome," he said without smiling. His flat-toned voice echoed off the chamber's oak panels, and I could tell that good moods were out. "Let's make a start, shall we?"

Councillor Langford put on a pair of reading glasses and looked down at the document in front of him. "I see you're asking for £60,000 to have the town lighthouse cleaned and repaired." He glanced up at us from over the rim of his glasses, not lifting his head. "Now. That's a lot of money, isn't it?"

"Yes," I said, squirming under his unsympathetic gaze. "The place is in quite a state, as you can see from the photographs. But we're not asking for money towards maintenance; the project we have in mind will be self-funding. And we've already been approved by the Coastal Heritage Fund for a £70,000 grant that'll partially cover repairs."

"It's a lot of money," the man repeated, as if he hadn't heard me. "Public money. We see a lot of projects here, Miss Hannigan. Just this month we've considered bids from the Cragport Clean Beaches Association to have the beach huts weatherproofed and another from the Women's Institute to repair the Edwardian bandstand in the park. What makes you think we should choose your lighthouse over competing bids?"

"Well..."

I faltered. This was harder than I'd expected. Despite the nerves that had hit me before coming in, I'd been quietly confident the council were so desperate to see the place done up that they'd cough up a grant with ne'r a grumble. And now this demon-headmastery old bastard seemed determined to give us a hard time before he rolled over.

"The lighthouse is over 100 years old." Ross jumped to my rescue with something from the notes we were both supposed to have memorised. "It's a historic icon of the town, one of the first things visitors notice. We want the emblem of Cragport to be something we're proud of, don't we, gents? Not a broken-down wreck."

That hit a nerve. The chairman kept his face fixed, but I noticed a few nods around the table.

"So can you tell us why you decided to launch this project?" Langford asked, once again ignoring the point raised. He shot Ross a pointed look. "I believe the lighthouse has been in your family some years, Mr Mason, with no attempt made before to tackle the state of decay it had fallen into – in spite of our frequent requests."

I could see Ross was trying to keep up a polite, detached expression, but his hand clenched at the reference to the council's persecution of poor Charlie.

"I've just moved back to the area," he said with forced calm. "The lighthouse was my uncle's property, as you all know, and he's too elderly now to keep up with repairs. The deeds were only signed over to us in April."

"A month ago. Have you done any work since then?"

"No. We only got approval for our Coastal Heritage grant last week. Plus, of course, we wanted to wait until we'd seen all of you."

"And this young lady is your ... business partner, is it?" Langford said, examining me with lip curled.

"Yes, and an old friend."

"So you have some expertise in this area, do you, dear?" Langford asked me with that patronising air we ladies just bask in.

"What, renovating lighthouses?" I gave a nervous laugh. "Not exactly. Well, who does? But I've got experience setting up projects like this one. My mum – Janine Hannigan, some of you know her – started the Cragport youth club a few years back."

"And you were instrumental in that, were you?"

"Not exactly instrumental. I helped a bit." I noticed Langford eyeing me with a barely concealed sneer. "A lot," I corrected, meeting his gaze. "I was involved with all the planning, start to finish. I can show you the paperwork if you need me to prove it."

"That won't be necessary." Langford shuffled his documents, taking his time; an obvious power-play that I had to admit was bloody effective. Out of the corner of my eye I could see beads of sweat standing out on Ross's face, and felt sympathy prickles on my own forehead.

"I notice you haven't answered my question," Langford said at last. "Why did you decide to commence this, frankly, bizarre-sounding project – this music thing?"

God, he had to ask. We could hardly confess it had been

a drunken plan fuelled by tequila slammers and snogging.

Ross recovered before I did. "It's been a long-held dream of mine, to open a performance space for young people," he said, his voice carefully formal. "I'm a musician myself, and I know from experience how hard it is for kids in this community to find the support they need. But I'd never considered the lighthouse. It was Roberta who convinced me it could work." He flashed me a little smile. "She's got a talent for spotting potential in things others don't see."

"This could put us on the map," I said to Langford, sensing the tourism angle might be the way to win them round. "How many seaside towns have got their own music venue inside a lighthouse? Cragport could have something nowhere else in the country – the world, maybe – has got."

I thought that was a pretty strong argument, but if Langford was impressed he didn't show it. He was sneering again, not bothering to hide it now. "Right. And this madcap plan you concocted over, what, a couple of beers in the pub is something you think the two of you, with next to no experience, can pull off?"

In the pub … shit, he only bloody knew, didn't he? We should have realised the ever-restless town tongue-waggers would've been at work. Well, that was it then. He'd clearly made up his mind against us. Unless we could win round the other grave, silent men at the table, it looked like it was game, set and fucked to Councillor Langford.

Alex had been trying to catch my eye all the time we'd been talking, and so far I'd done pretty well ignoring him. I'd spent a week mentally preparing myself for seeing him, knowing full well I needed to stay calm and professional if we were to have any shot at the funding. But he finally managed to arrest my gaze, flashing me a warm smile before he turned to face his chairman.

"Sorry, Arthur, I have to take issue with you. I think you're being rather harsh." Alex patted the paperwork in front of him. "No matter where the idea came from, Bobbie and Ross have come to us with a solid, well-researched plan. That alone should deserve applause from us rather than censure, whatever our ultimate decision." He caught my eye again, but I kept my gaze fixed straight ahead. If he thought that little intervention was enough to earn him a place in my good books, he could think again.

"I agree," another man joined in. "I think this music venue idea is capital, something the whole community can benefit from. Vital as it is to our economy, I've long argued this council needs to think less about tourism and more about the people resident here all year round."

"They already have a sizeable grant from the Coastal Heritage Fund," Alex said. "If that body were willing to put their faith in this project, I see no reason we shouldn't be."

There was a rhubarb-rhubarb murmur around the table,

but whether it represented assent or disagreement I couldn't tell.

"Questions from the council at the end, gentlemen," Langford said, not taking his eyes off me and Ross.

"My granddaughter's in a band, they're very good," the second councillor went on, ignoring his chairman and speaking directly to us. "This sounds like it could be just the thing for her. She's always saying how hard it is to find anywhere to practise."

Alex nodded. "Very true, Bill. I'm sure lots of young people would benefit from somewhere to rehearse without disturbing people. It's about time the council started encouraging creativity instead of punishing it."

"Questions at the end," Langford repeated firmly, turning to frown at Alex. "Due process, please, Councillor. Keep to your agenda."

"Yes. Sorry, Arthur." Alex looked down at his papers, but I saw him flash me a smile as the chairman gave his attention back to us.

"I repeat," Langford said. "What makes the two of you believe you can pull off this little scheme?"

Ross glared at him. "We're perfectly capable, thank you, Arthur – er, Councillor. We've got drive, energy and incentive: the rest of it we'll learn as we go. Anyway, it seems to me you don't have much of an alternative, do you?"

"There is one alternative, one your uncle always stubbornly

refused to countenance," Langford said, his mouth twisting into an unpleasant half-smile. "You could sell the lighthouse to us. The two of you would get a tidy payout each and the lighthouse would get the future it deserves."

"Future? What future?"

"A visitor centre, like lighthouses the country over. Pay a pound to see the view from the top, get a sandwich and a cuppa in a little tearoom at the bottom. It's a relic and it ought to be preserved, not filled with feral adolescents doing God knows what damage."

Ross looked angry now. "It bloody well isn't a relic. It deserves better than that. It's ..." He paused.

"It should be alive," I chimed in. "Not just a pretty thing to be kept in bubblewrap. It was someone's home, once. It's saved lives—"

Langford scoffed. "You're too sentimental, my dear. It's a building, not a pet. A historic building, which should be admired as just that. Not used as a –" he paused, fumbling for the word "– a damn ... speakeasy."

"Performance space." I crossed my arms. "And you can't just buy us off. We won't sell and that's that." I turned to Ross. "Will we?"

Ross crossed his arms too. "Abso-bloody-lutely we won't. If Uncle Charlie wouldn't sell to these people, there's no way I'm going to."

Langford smiled, a nasty ear-to-ear Grinch smirk, as he

prepared to play his trump card. "We thought you might say that." He paused. "£70,000."

"You must be ..." I trailed off. "Wait, what?"

"£70,000. That's the figure this council has agreed upon as a fair offer. Not the full value, of course, but a neat little sum each, and far more straightforward than trying to sell on the private market with the lighthouse in its current state. Plus you'd have the pleasure of knowing you've done your civic duty by returning it to the town – finally." He shot a loaded look Ross's way. "One nod and the pair of you walk away with £35,000 each to do as you like with. No one in this room will think any less of you, I assure you."

I turned to Ross. "It's a lot of money," I muttered in a low voice.

"It is, isn't it?" he muttered back. "You thinking what I'm thinking?"

"Yep."

"Can I do it?"

"Be my guest."

"If the two of you would like to take a moment to discuss it—" the chairman began.

"No thanks, we've said all we need." Ross glared at Langford. "So. If you're willing to put up that kind of public money, that tells us you can easily afford the 60 grand we're asking for, can't you?"

"That's not really how the funding works—" Langford said, but Ross cut him off.

"We're not stupid, Councillor. We thought you might have some sort of offer for us, and we can see it for what it is: desperation. Well, listen carefully." Ross leaned forward, enunciating his next five words with great deliberation. "We're not going to sell. Not to you, not to anyone, not under any circumstances. And you know you can't force us to, not legally. I'm not an old man you can harass with dodgy threats to sue."

"And if we up our offer?"

"Sorry, Arthur." Ross shot him a wry smile. "No deal."

Langford narrowed his watery eyes, mask cracking to reveal some real anger simmering below the sternly calm surface. He was evidently a man used to getting his way.

"Fine. I had hoped you might be persuaded to put the town first, but clearly not. And please be aware, Mr Mason, that this council does not respond well to being held to ransom." He turned to face his colleagues. "Now then, gentlemen. Any questions for these two –" he hesitated a fraction of a beat "– people before we vote?"

The other councillors' questions were far more reasonable than any Langford had asked us. Alex asked about our Coastal Heritage grant and our other ally, Bill, made some helpful suggestions on potential funding sources for the rest of the renovation work. Another man wanted to know how child protection would be managed when the band performing contained minors, and an elderly councillor in a monogrammed blazer, who was very sweet and looked like he must've been elected some time during the reign of Queen Victoria, asked if we'd be having any brass bands on.

Luckily we'd done our homework and I didn't think we did a bad job answering. Once Ross had been through our plans – the balconies and speakers we wanted to install, the workshops and open-mic nights for under-21s he was planning, all with his trademark energy and enthusiasm – I could see some of the stern expressions beginning to thaw.

"Right, are we done?" Langford asked the others when we'd answered all the questions. There was a hum of assent.

"In that case, would the two of you leave the room please?" he said to us.

"What?" Ross looked suspicious. "Why?"

"The council will need to discuss your case privately and take a vote on the allocation of funds." He managed a joyless, tight-lipped smile. "All above board, I assure you, Mr Mason; it's how these things are always done. We'll call you back in when we've reached a decision."

"Er, right. Ok." Ross moved hesitantly to the door, me following. Before going out, he turned to face the council again. "Look ... just quickly, before we go. You've got your bits of paper there with the details of what we want to do, and I'm sure you know your jobs. But I can promise you, there's no one in this room the lighthouse means more to than me and Bobbie. And we won't sell, not at any price – but we will work, hard, to make this thing happen. So if you want to get your precious lighthouse back to its glory days then it seems to me you've got no choice. You can allocate the funds or you can watch it rot. Your call, gentlemen."

And with that parting shot, he left the room.

"Oooh. That was bloody good," I breathed when we got back to reception, looking up at Ross admiringly. "Langford was all like, 'It's our lighthouse, mwahahaha! Sell it or you won't get a penny, mwahahahahaha!' and you were all like, 'It's my way or the highway so you can all go swivel, you bunch of knobs. BAM!'" I punched the air enthusiastically.

"That is literally exactly what I said."

"Well, how'd it go?" the friendly receptionist asked when we'd wandered over to throw ourselves into a couple of the high-backed green Chesterfields in the waiting area.

"Awful," I groaned.

"Arthur Langford?"

"Yeah. God, what a nightmare." I shook my head. "You poor woman."

"He doesn't scare me. I've worked here long enough to

know he's all bluster and no trousers." She flung me a reassuring smile. "Don't worry. The others'll let him talk just to test your mettle, but he won't influence them if they think he's being unfair. As long as you made a strong case they'll be on your side."

I turned to Ross, who was leaning on his palms looking worried. "Did we make a strong case?"

"Dunno. I can't remember a word except me telling them all to fuck off at the end there." He groaned faintly, pushing his fingers into his hair.

"You didn't tell them to fuck off. You said something super manly and dignified, like 'so go suck on them apples, gentlemen', then flounced out. It was proper sexy."

"Oh. Great. As long as me buggering everything up for us turns you on."

The receptionist jumped as the pager on her desk buzzed. "That was quick. They've got a decision for you already."

"Is that a good sign?" I asked.

She hesitated. "Well ... it can be. In you go, guys."

***

"Thank you both for waiting," Councillor Langford said, his tone suggesting we could've been out in reception weeks for his money. "The council has reached a decision."

He paused, and at first I thought it was another ploy,

the carefully timed hesitation to intimidate us. Then I examined his face and I knew: it wasn't a power-play, not this time. Behind the stern frown, he actually looked glum. And I could see Alex, smiling slightly under his blonde mop as he tried to catch my eye...

Langford sighed and looked down at his notepad. "The vote came in at 18 in favour, two against. You've got the lot."

Chapter 7

My body vibrated with excitement. Sixty grand, we'd really got it! It was actually happening. The lighthouse project was actually, properly happening.

"Arghh! That was brilliant!" I said to Ross outside the town hall, giving his arm an enthusiastic squeeze. "God ... I suppose it didn't feel real until today. Hey, we can go ahead and book that clean-up company now."

"Yeah, guess so."

I frowned at his dismal expression. "Aren't you excited? This is your dream, Ross."

"I know." He summoned a smile. "It went really well, didn't it? Can't believe we turned it round. I thought Langford had us shafted for a minute."

But he sounded like his heart wasn't really in his gloating.

"You sure you're ok?" I asked. "Thought I'd have a job to stop you streaking through town playing a vuvuzela after that."

"Just tired, that's all. I am excited, promise. Didn't mean to kill the mood."

I shot a concerned glance at his baggy eyes. He did look drained. And I'd felt him flinch when I squeezed his arm, as if he was on edge.

"You're burning yourself out," I said gently. "You need to take a break, Ross. How about you come for a drink with me? We can swear off lighthouse talk for the afternoon and relax."

"Hmm. Dunno, socialising with you's always a dangerous business," Ross said, his mouth twitching. "God knows what public building I'd wake up with."

I laughed. "Well, I promise not to buy the Scout hut or anything. So you want to?"

He sighed. "Sounds fun, but I can't. Work to do. Sorry."

"Still on that big design contract?"

"Yeah, putting in a lot of hours. I can't really afford to turn jobs down at the moment, to be honest. Money's been a bit tight the last few months, paying my rent here and the mortgage on mine and Claire's old flat. I thought it'd get snapped up once we put it on the market but the place seems to be taking forever to sell."

And he'd just turned down a no-strings offer of £35,000, plus his half of the 20 grand sitting in our emergency fund. The project really must mean a lot to him.

"Then let me do more on the lighthouse," I said.

"Would you have time?"

"I'll make time. It's the long summer break coming up anyway, then I'll have two months off work to give to it."

Ross smiled. "Always look out for me, don't you?"

"That's what partners are for." I patted his shoulder. "Go on, get yourself home so you can finish your work and grab an early night. I'll see you at the pub next week."

"Ok. Cheers, Bobbie, you're a good mate." He chucked me under the chin by way of a goodbye and headed back to his car.

It was a glorious May day and the air was heavy with the seaside smells that always meant home to me: cigarettes and shellfish, saltwater and sweet things. And vinegar, always vinegar. In spite of the spirit-dampening conversation I'd just had with Ross, my heart lifted. It was a Punch-and-Judy world, but it was mine.

I inhaled appreciatively, hugging myself. It was too nice to sit indoors after nearly two hours closeted in a stuffy town hall. Turning in the direction of town, I took the scenic route down to the seafront for a walk.

The sea, when it eventually hoved into view, was deep blue and glittering, the beach's chalky pebbles radiant. Cragport always looked its best clad in sunshine. The old pier stretched invitingly into the water, and I bent my steps that way.

It was the town's third or fourth pier, which back in the less safety-conscious times of good Queen Vic had had a nasty habit of catching alight. The current incarnation was long, broad and meticulously fireproof, laden with the sort of seaside entertainment that kept tourists happy and towns-people solvent: a greasy spoon caf, penny arcade, kiddies' Teacup ride belting out a tinny circus tune, and a naff old cabaret club, Tuxedo's, that doubled as a bingo hall during the day. Right at the end was a glass pavilion, The Orangery Tearoom, which boasted the best sea view in Cragport. I shot it a smug look as I dawdled along. Once the lighthouse was open for business, they'd have to drop that tagline.

I was sauntering past the industrial 1970s-style cafe, smiling as I thought about the lighthouse, when I pulled up short and stared through the window. I gasped, blinking to reassure myself I was really seeing what I thought I was seeing.

It was Ross! Ross Mason, who not half an hour ago had assured me he was heading for home. Ross Mason, squirting ketchup lavishly over a plate of chips.

And he wasn't eating alone. A petite woman with long strawberry-blonde hair was sitting with her back to me, tucking into some chips of her own. Ross was laughing at something she'd said, crinkling his handsome eyes. As I watched, the woman leaned over and rested her long, mani-cured fingernails on his forearm.

I swallowed hard, then darted into the amusements next door before they spotted me.

Inside, the flashing coloured lights and assorted *buh-*

buh-bips of the one-armed bandit aisle greeted me. Schools hadn't broken up yet and it wasn't quite peak tourism season, so the place was nearly empty.

The proprietor eyed me suspiciously as I shuffled to one of the Coin Cascades. Rummaging in my jeans pocket, I located a few twopenny pieces and started feeding them mechanically into the slot.

With my free hand I pulled out my phone.

"Hm?" Jess said when she answered my call. It had been another late shift, or a late date with Gareth, I forgot which, and I'd clearly woken her up.

"Guess who I've just seen," I hissed.

"Well it'd better be someone pretty A-list if you're interrupting my beauty sleep."

"It was Ross. Having chips at the caf on the pier."

"Wow, living the dream. Very happy for him. Ring me back in two hours."

"Wait, don't hang up," I said urgently. "There's more. He wasn't alone."

"Sorry, can you speak up?" she said as one of my 2p pieces got lucky and the machine started paying out in a series of noisy chinks. "Where the hell are you?"

"Hiding out in the slotties." I raised my voice. "I said, he wasn't alone!"

"What?"

"WASN'T ALONE! ROSS!"

The stiff-necked proprietor was subjecting me to a properly filthy look now, the kind he reserved for customers who carried out loud phone conversations while winning all his tuppences, and I flashed him an apologetic smile.

"Look, I can't talk here," I muttered to Jess while I scooped up my winnings. "Come meet me in the playground, ok?"

"Oh, what, get dressed?" She groaned. "Can't you come home?"

"Please, Jessie. The natural light'll do you good. And you can bring Monts for his walk."

***

The old playground perched halfway up the hill, overlooking the sea. A fat, muddy cloud had swallowed the sun and the water wasn't sparkling any more. Instead it looked clotted and greasy, like my mood. I pushed my swing back and forth with my feet, eyes fixed glumly on Monty foraging for treasures in a nearby patch of shrubs.

"So it was probably just a mate," Jess said for about the third time as she swung past me. "Or a client maybe. Graphic designers meet with clients, don't they?"

"And buy them chips?"

"Yeah, when they're hungry. If someone's your bread and butter you have to keep them sweet."

"Do clients touch your arm and giggle and stick their boobs out at you?"

She shrugged. "If they're paying for the platinum service."

"Don't joke. It was a date, Jess. What else could it be?"

"Any number of things. Lass from school, maybe."

I slowed my swing down and twisted to look at her. "No. This was a stranger."

Jess stopped swinging too. "You only saw her from the back, didn't you?"

"Yeah, but I could tell it was no one we knew."

She sighed. "Look, I want to be supportive sister and all that, Bobs, but ... well, what's it to you? He's not your boyfriend."

"It's just he's – I mean, since we started this, it's felt like we've been—" I broke off. What the hell did I mean, exactly? "I can't believe he's still dating, that's all," I finished lamely.

"Why can't you believe it?"

"Because he's married, Jess! He told me he couldn't even think about seeing people until his divorce came through."

"Did he?"

I hesitated. Actually, thinking back, had he said that? Or had I told him that's what he ought to do and then just assumed his agreement?

"I'm not sure. I thought he did. I thought..."

"What did you think?"

I flushed. "That he liked me, I guess. The flirting, the

way we just seem to click. In the back of my mind I think I had an idea that eventually his divorce would come through and me and him and the lighthouse would live happily ever after. And now he's off guzzling chips with another woman, on top of the wife he keeps back in Sheffield for emergencies."

Jess stretched her arm around my shoulders and gave them a squeeze. "You don't know it means anything."

"It bloody well looked like it did."

I stared absently at Monty, still scrabbling in the shrubs like his little doggy life depended on it. It made me smile in spite of myself, watching him cover himself in dirt with his tail wagging excitedly.

The playground Grandad had taken us to so often as kids was steeped in a sepia layer of nostalgia and neglect now, just like the lighthouse. A fancier modern affair with a zipwire on the other side of town was more of a draw for local children, but Jess and me still liked to come sometimes to swing and reminisce. Whenever one of us felt down, it was safe money that's where we'd be.

I heaved a deep sigh. "The worst thing is, Ross lied to me about it. Why would he do that?"

"What did he actually say?"

"Said he was going home to work on a big project." I scoffed. "Actually had me feeling sorry for him, offering to take on more of the lighthouse stuff so he could get some rest. Turns out he's knackered from nights on a different sort of job."

"I could be right though, couldn't I?" Jess was like a dog with a bone when she got a fixed idea in her head. "If she's a client it could've been a working date."

"Pretty touchy-feely for a graphic design client."

Jess shrugged. "He's a good-looking lad. Not his fault if his lady clients want to feel him up."

"Trust me, he wasn't exactly fighting her off."

She laughed, pushing with her feet to get the swing swaying again. "Stick the bottom lip in, before you trip on it. You need to grow up."

"Shush your face. You do."

"Look, all it boils down to is you've seen a bloke you like eating chips with someone. It's not as if you've caught him inflagrante in a pair of frilly knickers bending over the kitchen worktop, is it? Ross Mason's a nice lad, I'd bet my medical degree on it."

"The one you bought online?"

"Ooh. Right, come here and take your punishment, you." She jumped off her swing and came over to get me in a headlock, rubbing my hair with her fist.

"Arghh, geroff!" I spluttered. "I've got mousse in, bitch."

"Make me."

Giggling, I pushed her away.

"So am I being a daft cow as usual then, our Jessie?"

"Yeah. But I can't help being fond of you. You're like a manky old cat living in a bin you just have to feel sorry for." She gave my hair another affectionate nuggy. "Come on, manky, let's go to the pub. I'll let you drown your sorrows if you'll let me have a go on the quizzer."

Chapter 8

I tried to follow Jess's advice and put the redheaded woman, whoever she was, out of my mind, and although I couldn't help being a little cool to Ross at our next meeting, it soon melted as we threw ourselves into our pet project with gusto.

Once the clean-up operation was under way, we decided the next step was to rally the troops: do the rounds of everyone we knew who might be able to help. Which was why I found myself one Saturday morning knocking on the door of a rundown bed and breakfast by the seafront, swilled over in peeling, pastel-pink paint.

It was answered by a short, slim woman in beads and tie-dye skirts, her green hair clashing eye-wateringly with the building's strawberry-milkshake façade.

"Well, if it isn't the prodigal daughter," she said. "Which one are you again? The doctor or the mad lighthouse owner?"

I tutted. "We're not identical, Mum."

"No, thank God. One of each is plenty."

I followed her along a yellowing hallway, pungent with the smell of greasy bacon and black pud, to the dining room. We navigated the tables of guests enjoying their full English then headed upstairs to her snug living room.

"So, what do you want?" she asked when she'd made us both a cuppa and we were seated together on the sofa.

"Can't a daughter visit her aged parent without needing a reason?"

"No. And I'm 46, missy. What is it then?"

"Want to pick your brains." I pulled out the notepad and pen that these days seemed to live in my handbag. "Lighthouse stuff."

She shook her head. "You must get this from your dad, you know. There was never any history of insanity on my side of the family."

"And was there on his?"

"I don't know, do I? If your art teacher knocks you up with twins when you're 17 and promptly buggers off back to the missus, popping round for a detailed medical history isn't the first thing that springs to mind. 'Bollocks' is the first thing that springs to mind. Followed closely by 'ow'."

I patted her arm. "Ah, who needed him? You and Grandad managed us all right."

"Some might say you and your lighthouses are evidence to the contrary."

"Well if Jess is a doctor then it's my job to be the idiot child no one in the family wants to talk about, isn't it?" I said. "Anyway, you know you think the lighthouse thing's a good idea."

"It's not the idea that worries me," she said, tossing back a mouthful of tea. "So what do you need advice about?"

"All of it, basically. Have you got the paperwork from when you started the youth club?"

"Yes, in the filing cabinet. I'll fetch it."

"Did you know Ross came to see me?" Mum asked when she'd brought a stack of ringbinders from her little office next door and dumped them on the table.

"Did he?"

"Yep. Popped round for a cuppa." She flicked her green braids with an offended air. "You should take a leaf out of his book yourself."

"Come on, I ring you all the time."

"Well you could come over a bit more, the pair of you. I haven't seen our Jess for ages."

I tried not to let her notice the flicker rippling across my face. I knew why Jess hadn't been round, she was putting off having the new boyfriend conversation about Gareth. It was weeks now since they'd made the jump from "just dating" to "officially a couple". Mum always worked these things out.

"All right, all right. The three of us'll take an evening class together or something," I said, waving a hand impatiently. "So why was Ross here?"

"Said he felt like he should visit now he's back, with his Uncle Charlie being my godfather and you two working on this thing together." She put her tea down on the table. "There, er, isn't any other reason he might be trying to butter me up, is there?" she asked in a carefully casual tone.

I reached over to pick up a ringbinder, give myself something to occupy my hands.

"Like what?"

"I wondered if you two might be ... well, you know." She nudged me. "Don't think I've forgotten grounding you for what your head of year called 'inappropriate behaviour' at the school disco when you were 14."

"Oh God. Please stop with the innuendo, it's more than my ribs can take."

"So are you?"

"You know I wouldn't do that. He's married, Mum."

She shrugged. "Only technically."

I stared at her. "Have you had a brain transplant or something? Since I was old enough to wear a bra, you've been hammering it into me that married men are off limits. You've grilled every boyfriend I've ever had on his intentions before we've made it to the second date. You're not seriously telling me you're giving me your blessing to start bonking Ross Mason just like that?"

"Well, maybe I'm softening in my old age," she said, draining the last of her tea. "Not that I don't think you're right to hold off until his divorce comes through. But Ross is a good boy, I've known him all his life. He'd be better for you than the motley selection you've introduced me to so far."

I sighed. "Well, it's academic now anyway. He's off the market."

"Only until his divorce."

"Not what I meant." I blinked back a rogue tear. "He's seeing someone, Mum. I saw them in town, shovelling chips in their gobs and tittering like love's young dream."

She snorted. "You think he's seeing someone because you caught him eating chips? I eat chips with the bloke who comes to deadhead the roses, I've never thought of it as foreplay."

"Not just that. They were flirting and ... and stuff. What made you think there might be something between me and him anyway?"

"Oh, maternal instinct. The way he was talking about you when he came over, maybe."

I brightened a little. "Was he talking about me?"

"Yep, he's a big fan," she said with a smile. "Singing your praises about this project. He said I must be very proud."

"And what did you say?"

"After I'd stopped laughing, you mean?"

I leaned over to prod her arm. "You're rotten, you are."

She grinned. "All right, so I'm proud of you. Now come on, tell me what you need to know for your crazy lighthouse business."

"Funding sources mainly," I said, rifling through the ringbinder I'd picked up.

"How much do you need?"

"Well, the council grant plus the money we got from Coastal Heritage'll get the rot out, which is the most expensive part of it, but there's still a lot to do. We want to get a loo installed in that little pokey-outy bit, insulate the walls with this acoustic stuff Ross says makes the music sound better." I started counting on my fingers. "Bottle bar in the lantern room, crescent viewing balconies, staircases. Oh, and speakers to help the sound carry, LCD screens so people can get a better view of the acts—"

"Ok, stop, stop!" She held a hand in front of her face. "Bloody hell, our Bobbie. That sounds like it'll cost a fortune."

"Yeah. Ross did a rough costing." I fished it out of my bag and handed it to her.

"£200,000! Jesus!"

"I know it looks a lot," I said, flushing. "But that does include the two grants we got, which come to 140. So that's really only 60 grand we need to find."

"I'll check down the back of the sofa, shall I?" She shook her head. "Only, she says."

"You think we won't get it?"

"Not necessarily, if you write good bids. But you could do it cheaper using the community for some stuff. Anyway, it helps get people invested in a project if they feel they were part of it from the off."

"Suppose it does," I said. "What sort of stuff?"

"The painting – does that have to be done by professionals?"

"Shouldn't think so, not once the inside's been certified safe."

"You remember when we got the old Guide hut for the youth club? We got everyone involved in helping out."

"Oh yeah, the painting party. Hey, that's a great idea. Cheers, Mum." I scribbled it down on my notepad, itching to ring Ross so I could share.

Mum was still scanning the list. "Here, give me the pen." I handed her the biro and she started working her magic, writing out the names of funding bodies next to some items. "So you could try the lottery for more expensive stuff: screens, platforms. See if you can get businesses to donate materials like paints. The Eric Godfrey Trust's a local thing, funds art projects, they might cover speakers." She looked up at me again. "And then there's fundraising. The usual, jumble sales and that. You could ask the schools and uniformed groups to organise events on your behalf, since their kids will benefit. We'll do something at the youth club, obviously."

"Thanks, Mum." I twisted round to give her a hug. "You know, sometimes you're a pretty handy person to be related to."

"Oh right, just sometimes? Ta muchly. Oh!" She ducked out of my hug and started scribbling again. "And you can ask local businesses about match funding. Try your college, for a start: sure they'll be impressed one of their staff is getting involved in something like this. Don't forget to stick a donations bucket out at your painting party as well, will you? Give everyone a few beers, that'll loosen their wallets."

I laughed. "You look like Ross. That same mad glint in your eye."

"So will you soon, I bet. This stuff's addictive."

To be honest, I was well past that point. The last couple of months working on the lighthouse with Ross had been the most alive I'd felt in years.

"See?" I said with a smug grin. "Told you you thought it was a good idea."

"All right, so I do," Mum admitted. "Have to say, when you first told me you wanted to open a music venue in a lighthouse with a lad you hadn't seen since school I thought you'd gone completely potty—"

"Er, ta."

"– but you're doing it all the right way, if you will insist on doing it."

"I think so too." I smiled at her. "I know you think I'm a reckless, impulsive moron, Mum, but I wouldn't have come this far unless it was something I believed in. It's the right thing for the lighthouse, I know it – and for me."

"I know," she said, rubbing my arm approvingly. "Now give us a proper hug."

"And I don't think you're a moron," she said gently when I was absorbed in a comforting Mum hug. "Impulsive maybe, like your mother, but there's nothing wrong with that if you're smart with it. I really am proud of you – of both my little girlies. Your grandad would be too."

"Well we're proud of you," I said, patting her frizzy hair. "Works both ways, doesn't it?"

"Suppose it does." She pulled out of the hug to look into my face. "Well done, Bobbie. I mean it."

"Thanks, old lady. Doing my best."

"All I ever expected of you," she said with a warm smile.

Chapter 9

When Jess and I arrived at the lighthouse for the painting party, Ross was already there setting up.

The building had been pretty much reset to Lighthouse Zero during the clean-up, filleted from bottom to top. The old staircase, the broken lamp, all the rot was gone. The walls had been rerendered, windows glazed, and a local business keen to support the project had donated rolls of acoustic insulation. Now, after nearly a month's work, the inside was a big, tapering grey tube; an empty canvas for what was to come.

Currently there were a load of old bedsheets covering the stone floor and some enormous extending ladders propped against the wall.

"All right, Hannigans?" Ross said when we walked in. He was slicing bread rolls behind a pop-up table laid out with polystyrene cups and a Thermos urn. The fact he was wearing his scruffiest jeans and a paint-stained old t-shirt didn't make him the least bit less gorgeous. If anything, it was worse. Made him look sort of ... rugged. And then there were those bare, rippling arms...

I tried to let my eyes wander anywhere but over his body.

"Hi Ross," Jess said brightly. I cast her an envious look. Apparently Ross's arms didn't have any effect on her, lucky cow. "You know there's graffiti on your door?"

"Yeah, little buggers," he said, scowling. "They better hope I never get my hands on them."

He came out from behind his table to give Jess a kiss on the cheek. With me he just exchanged a self-conscious nod. That was all the greeting I tended to get these days.

There'd been a change in him over the last six weeks, since we'd met with the council. I'd thought at first I was imagining it, but no, it was definitely there. He still seemed fond of me, still did the jokey banter thing, but he was ... different.

In the early days he'd been so warm and frank, often slinging an arm around my shoulders or pressing my hand like it was the most natural thing in the world. Now his touchy-feelies were more big-brotherly: a nose-tweak here, a hair-ruffle there. He'd stopped sitting next to me during our planning sessions at the pub as well, taking a seat opposite as if he wanted it to be clear they were meetings and not dates. And when I occasionally offered more intimate gestures like a squeeze of the arm, I noticed him flinch. His new girlfriend must be the jealous type, I thought bitterly.

It was easy to put it out of my mind, when we were enthusiastically making plans for the lighthouse over drinks in the pub. But sometimes, alone at night, I felt a lump forming in my throat. My feelings for Ross were becoming more complicated every second I spent with him, and the more he put me at a distance, the more I couldn't stop thinking about him.

I'd almost started to resent the Bobbie of three months ago for her stupid principles. God, if I'd just said yes when he asked me out then ... I mean, even Mum, the patron saint of wronged spouses since the day she was old enough to feel guilty, didn't seem to think Ross's marriage-on-paper was too much of a problem. And in just a few months his legal separation period would be done with; he could finally put in a petition for divorce. He'd be free, and I'd be ... too late.

I shook my head to banish unwelcome thoughts.

"So what's in the Thermos?" I asked him with forced brightness.

"Soup. Carrot and coriander."

"What, you made it? Didn't know you did soup."

"When necessary," he said with a smile. "Did you two bring the beer?"

"Yeah, couple of crates in the car," Jess said. "That should keep people going. Let's get the stuff in."

By the time we'd emptied my old Fiesta of paints, trays, rollers and booze, people were starting to arrive. Ross and Jess took soup duty, and when Mum turned up she joined me by the door to meet and greet. After everyone had assembled, there were an encouraging 30 or so packed in kipper-style.

Other than friends and family, I recognised a couple of ladies from the Women's Institute, my old Brown Owl, some kids and parents from Mum's youth club, a few students from the college I worked at and a load of others I didn't know. Some of the councillors from the meeting we'd gone to were there as well, including –

"Oh God, not him," I muttered to Mum.

She followed my gaze and frowned. "Alex. What's he doing here?"

"Representing the council, probably. But that's not who I meant." I nodded towards Councillor Langford. He was leaning against the wall, looking around the lighthouse like he owned the place. "That's the wanker who gave us such a hard time over the funding."

"Oh. Arthur Langford," Mum said. "Yeah, I've had a few brushes with him over the youth club. Man seems to think kids should be locked in a box till they're 21." She patted my arm. "Well, you got what you wanted. Don't let him ruin your moment."

"Er, right. My moment." I shot a panicked look over the

sea of faces waiting to be given instructions. "What do I do now then?"

"What, you haven't written a welcome speech?"

"Was I supposed to?"

She shook her head. "Useless, lass. All right, just thank them for coming, explain the project and tell them what they have to do. And don't forget to mention the donations bucket."

"God, can't you do it? I know half these people from when I was a kid. Look." I nodded towards a bespectacled older lady. "There's Mrs Abberley, our old lollipop lady."

"No," Mum whispered back. "You and Ross are the faces of Project Mad Lighthouse, it has to be one of you."

"Ugh. Fine." I summoned a weak smile and raised my voice so I could be heard across the room. "Um, hi everyone, thanks for coming. Er ..." I cast an anxious glance over my shoulder at Ross and Jess and they sent me a supportive thumbs-up each. "So, yeah. Welcome to the lighthouse project. Ross and me, er, we're hoping to give a new lease of life to the old place so that, with the help of all of you, we can take it back to its glory days. We've got soup and rolls for those who've offered their time, and a beer when we're done." I felt Mum nudge me. "Oh! And there's a donations bucket by the door, so please give generously."

The crowd were still looking at me expectantly. God,

what did these people want from me? Off-the-cuff public speaking wasn't exactly my forte. I cast around for a get-out.

"Well, that's all from me. Here's Ross with more." I turned to him with panicked eyes, silently begging him to come to my rescue.

"Thanks very much, cowardy custard," he muttered when he'd come over to flank me on the other side.

"Come on, you're a singer, aren't you?" I whispered back. "You should be used to this."

"Yeah, and you're a teacher."

"That's different. I don't have to teach Mr Madison." I nodded to an overweight, grizzle-headed man who'd once been head of our Year 9.

"Shit, it is him as well, isn't it? Oh God ... right. I can do this." Ross cleared his throat. "Er, hello, Cragportians." He gave the crowd a shy nod. "I wanted to say, um ... thanks for turning up this afternoon to support a project we hope will not only put the lighthouse back in her rightful place as queen of the coastline, but also provide a much-needed creative outlet for our young people. A project very close to our hearts."

Mum shot me a significant glance. She was right, he was good at this. I'd noticed it at the council meeting too, that eloquence the lighthouse brought out in him.

The crowd were all attentive ears as he went on.

"You all know my uncle, Charlie Mason. Many of you will

also remember his late wife Annie." He seemed to be warming to his subject now, the old fire in his eyes – lighthouse fever, I'd started to think of it. "This project marks the culmination of two dreams: Annie's of seeing our lighthouse restored to the pride of the town, and mine of providing young musicians with a place of their own to rehearse and perform." He gestured to me. "And I couldn't have taken it this far without the inspiration, hard work and sheer bloody-mindedness of my partner in this project, Roberta Hannigan, who convinced me those dreams combined could be the future of the lighthouse." He beamed across the crowd. "So I guess all that's left to say is thanks for coming and thanks for believing in us. There's some literature in the outhouse if you want to find out more about our plans. Now let's get our sleeves rolled up and do some work so we can all have a drink."

There was a ripple of applause and a few cheers as Ross came to the end of his speech, presumably from those who'd appreciated the offer of a drink.

"Bloody hell, where did that come from?" I whispered.

"I have literally no idea," Ross ventriloquised back from behind his teeth. "Sound ok?"

"Brilliant. Nice one, Mason."

He turned back to the crowd, noting the muttered conversations. "Oh, sorry," he said. "Any questions before we get going?"

"I've got a question," a silver-haired man who I recognised as chairman of the Cragport Clean Beaches Association called out. "How much is this going to cost?"

I flushed, thinking of Mum's reaction when I'd shown her the figure. "Well, it won't be cheap," I admitted. "But we're confident that with fundraising and grant applications we can—"

"Two hundred grand," a voice called out. "At a conservative estimate."

All eyes turned to look at the speaker. It was Langford, of course, still leaning against the wall with a smug expression on his face.

"Bloody hell!" a man in the crowd said. "And where's that coming from?"

"Your wallet, so far." Langford flicked at his cuff as if he'd spotted a speck of dirt sullying it. "They've had a large grant from the council already to cover the clean-up. We'll see them again when it runs out, no doubt."

I glared at him. "That's not true. Most of the clean-up money came from Coastal Heritage."

"Sixty grand of it was public money though. Wasn't it, Miss Hannigan?"

"I thought that costing was confidential," Ross said, scowling. "We've revised it since then anyway, it's closer to 180 than 200. And Bobbie and I have set aside a fighting fund of £20,000 we're personally prepared to invest should we need it."

There was a buzz through the crowd, but I couldn't tell if it was on Langford's side or ours.

"I think you'll find your costing is a matter of public record, Mr Mason. All there in our minutes," Langford said with an acid smile. "Not that it matters. One hundred, two hundred. It's still Cragport's pockets you're picking."

There was a definite hostile hum now. We were losing them.

"Shit, what do we say?" I muttered to Ross in panic, but he looked just as adrift as I felt.

"And how much public money were you planning to spend on the lighthouse, Arthur?"

Alex. I shot him a look of relief for coming to our rescue, then quickly pulled my gaze away before he noticed.

Langford seemed confused for a second, but quickly recovered. "The figure I proposed would have put the light-house in the hands of officials with its best interests at heart. It would have been an investment in the future."

"How much, Councillor?" Ross said. "Answer the man."

"How much is neither here nor there."

Alex turned to address the assembled crowd. "It was 70 grand. 70 grand of taxpayers' money. And that was just for the purchase, never mind the clean-up." He gave his colleague a falsely apologetic shrug. "Sorry, Arthur. As you say, all there in the records."

Langford glared at him. "You're out of order."

Alex snorted. "Please. We're not in a meeting now, you can't whip me into submission with agenda and due process. I'll speak my mind and damned if you'll stop me." He nodded to me and Ross. "Bobbie and her partner have shown passion and commitment you couldn't begin to understand. They're the future of the lighthouse, and as long as they're at the helm I'm behind them. So are we all."

"You can't speak for me, young man. I may have a few years on the clock but I can still just about form an opinion of my own," said an elderly gentleman, flashing Alex a resentful look. He turned to Langford. "You there. Cocky. What would you do with the lighthouse then, if you got your hands on it?"

Langford preened at the sudden, unexpected support. "Make it an asset to the town, of course. The council want to turn it into a visitor centre and tearoom."

"Typical," I heard a woman near me mutter to her husband. "All about bloody tourists as usual. The kids round here never get a look-in."

Alex scoffed. "The council. There is no council, Arthur. There's only you," he said. "Well, as you're a public servant with the town's interests solely at heart, perhaps you'd like to tell us what your daughter does for a living?"

"What?" Langford frowned. "What's that got to do with anything?"

"Every time we have a council meeting we're obliged to

declare vested interests in agenda items at the start, aren't we? And yet strangely, the fact Cheryl runs a catering company never comes up."

The crowd were vibrating now, and I heard cries of "Shame!" rippling through. Alex and Langford were still bickering, but the background volume was so loud I couldn't hear a word.

Mum peeled away from me, a determined look on her face, and moved next to a bemused-looking Jess behind the soup table. Taking off one strappy sandal, she bashed it loudly against the tabletop.

"Oi! Shut it, you lot," she yelled.

Instantly the volume dropped. No one messed with my mum when she was at her shouty, scary best.

"So. I get it now," Mum said to Langford when the noise had died down. "Cheryl Sharp of Sharp Sarnies. That's your daughter, is it?"

"Not a bad little earner, her dad pushing cafes into major tourist attractions so she can do the food," the Clean Beaches man called out. "We're not as stupid as you might think round here, Councillor, for all that we managed to elect you."

Langford looked nervous now, his back flat against the wall like a cornered animal.

"This is slanderous. My integrity as council chair is beyond question," he said, trying to sound indignant. "It's common knowledge my daughter owns a catering company, and I assure you we follow the correct procedures in every respect. All contracts for public venues and events must be passed by the whole council."

"And yet it always seems to be Sharp Sarnies that gets every catering contract in the end, doesn't it?" Alex said.

"That's right, Sharp's did the school funday on the council's recommendation," Mrs Abberley called out.

"And the Cragport Carnival," shouted someone else. "Sandwiches were crap as well."

Langford looked hunted, but he pulled himself up straight, ready for his last hurrah.

"And what about your vested interest, Alex? Have you declared that? Surely these people deserve to know."

"I'm sorry?" Alex said.

Langford nodded towards me. "This young lady. You lived together for a period, I think?"

Ross turned shocked eyes on me. "That's not true, is it?" he whispered.

I flushed. "Yes. We broke up last year."

"Jesus, Bobbie! Why didn't you tell me?"

I frowned. So Ross could go on dates and not say a word but I was obliged to share every detail of my relationship history with him, was that it?

"It's … complicated," I muttered back. "Messy break-up. Look, we'll talk about it another time, ok?"

"That's right, we were a couple," Alex said to Langford.

"This is a small town, there are plenty of people with a shared history. What of it? I don't stand to gain financially."

"Don't think we can't see through you, Alex," Langford sneered. "This transparent attempt to curry favour with your ex-girlfriend won't wash, I'm afraid."

But it was desperation speaking. The crowd were Team Alex now, and Langford's battle for Cragport's hearts and minds was lost. The cries of "Shame!" aimed at him were becoming louder, and I even heard a "Resign!" from one particularly terrifying WI lady.

"I don't know, it seems to be washing white enough from here," Alex said with a smug smile.

The crowd were closing rank, openly jeering now as Langford edged towards the door.

"Time to go, Arthur," Alex said. "Don't feel too bad. Happen you'll win the next battle." The crowd laughed as Langford turned and stalked angrily out of the lighthouse.

Chapter 10

Once Langford was gone, things calmed down a bit. Ross and I divided the crowd into two, half to tackle the inside of the lighthouse and half the outside, and people set to work with a bad-guy-defeated camaraderie that made for a very matey atmosphere.

An hour in, I was rollering a patch of wall with magnolia emulsion, Mum next to me in her faded denim dungarees tackling a patch of her own. There was a hum of happy chatter round the room, and some enterprising soul had gone home to rustle up a portable radio so we could enjoy a bit of music. Seemed appropriate, given what we were working towards.

"Not looking bad, is it?" I said to Mum, scanning the tube of lighthouse. The walls were about half covered with glistening snow-fresh paint. It made the place look brand new, and bigger somehow. So different from the grey, mossy mess Ross and I had stumbled into, nursing our hangovers and wondering if this was the biggest mistake we'd ever make, nearly three months ago.

Mum cast her eyes around the other volunteers approvingly. "Yeah. Lovely to see everyone come together."

"I know, never thought we'd—"

I broke off when I heard a "hem" at my shoulder. Turning, I found Alex, the hero of the hour, lurking behind me.

"Hi, girls." He smiled at Mum. "How are you keeping, Janine? Been a long time."

"Not long enough. Bye, Alex." Mum turned away and went back to rollering her wall.

He looked a little crestfallen at the rebuff, but he didn't leave.

"Bobbie, any chance of a word?"

"If you must," I said. "What is it?"

"In private, I meant."

I shook my head. "Don't think so, do you?"

"Just five minutes. I won't say anything to upset you, I promise. It's important."

"Lighthouse important or us important?"

"Both. Look, I'm not going to ask if you want to get back together or anything," he said when he saw me still hesitating. "There's something I want to tell you, that's all. Please. I earned it, didn't I?"

I could see Mum shaking her head at me, but I ignored her.

"Well … ok. Five minutes then."

Weaving through the crowd of painters, I followed him out of the lighthouse. I noticed Ross watching us from behind the soup table as we exited.

Outside, we made our way past the team of volunteers on ladders topping up the lighthouse's barbershop stripes to my battered Fiesta, parked a little way away at the top of the cliff. Alex smiled when he saw it.

"Are you still driving that old thing?"

"Let's cut the small talk, eh?" I said, folding my arms. "Just say what you've got to say."

"Oh, Bobs, please don't be like that." Alex reached out to take my hand, then thought better of it and dropped his arm to his side.

"How else do you expect me to be?" I swallowed. "Look, I know we're bound to see each other sometimes. You're right, it is a small town, and we're both involved with the community stuff now. But let's keep it strictly professional, shall we?"

He looked down. "Ok. I mean, we're adults, I'm sure we can manage to work together without our history getting in the way. But I want to say something to you first. Not as a councillor, as me – someone you loved once."

I blinked back a tear. Memories, feelings I'd spent the last year trying to suppress were coming back, and I didn't have the energy to deal with them: not right now.

"All right, off you go then," I said. "Make it quick."

"I had to say I'm sorry. I know I've said it before but I don't think I understood what it meant, not until just recently. I've been doing a lot of thinking lately and I'm really, really sorry for everything I did to you. And I know an apology doesn't even begin to make up for it, but I need to offer one all the same." His eyes were full as he sought mine. "You can't forgive me, I know. But maybe one day you can stop hating me?"

I sighed. "I don't hate you. But you're right, I can't forgive you either. We're not going to be friends, Alex. Let's just try to be ... I don't know, people who can manage to be civil to each other. More than that is asking too much."

"Look, that girl, the one I – it didn't mean anything. I was lonely, that's all. You wouldn't talk to me, kept shutting me out..."

"So it was my fault, was it?"

"No, it was my fault. And it was an awful thing to do, and I hate myself every day, even if you don't." He dipped his head to look at me, and I saw a tear starting to escape behind the geek-chic Wayfarers he always wore. "But I've changed, Bobs, honestly. I get it now. I've been doing a lot of reading, talking to people who experienced the same thing." He swallowed a sob. "God, what you must've gone through. I was such a bastard to you."

"No arguments here." I turned away to look at the lighthouse, my face twitching with emotion as I thought back to that whole horrible period of my life. "And you know what, Alex? I believe you. I know it didn't mean anything. And that makes it so much fucking worse, because it means you'd casually chuck everything we had away on some seedy, empty sex."

He put a hand on my shoulder and turned me back to face him. "It wasn't like that. I told you, I was lonely. You wouldn't even let me touch you when all I wanted to do was hold you, make the pain go away. Can you imagine how that felt?"

I scoffed. "Yeah, I'm sure you were having a terrible time."

"Look, I said sorry. I really have changed, Bobs. And I'd like to make amends in any small ways I can." He gave a bleak laugh. "The funny thing is, Arthur was right. I actually was just trying to curry favour. I thought it'd be a start, at least."

"What, you don't care about the lighthouse?"

"Not as much as I care about you," he said softly. "I know I can't win you back. God knows, I don't deserve to. But you'll let me help, won't you?"

I sighed. "I suppose. But don't think it means anything. We need all the help we can get, that's all."

"We." He shot a resentful look towards the lighthouse. "You and that chap Ross, right? Are you seeing each other?"

"How is that any of your business?"

"No, no, I know. Sorry." He took my hand and gave it a squeeze, and I didn't pull it away. "Thanks for hearing me out, Bobbie. Come on, let's go back in."

When I got back to my patch of wall, Mum was straight to business.

"What did he want?" she demanded.

"Just to talk. Apologise."

She examined me suspiciously. "And did you accept this so-called apology?"

"We made a sort of wobbly peace," I said. "He wants to help with the lighthouse. It's not like I thought I'd never see him again, is it? Especially since he got elected to the council."

"Hm." She jerked her head towards Ross. "And what does your partner have to say about it?"

"Nothing he can say. We're not going out, he doesn't get to play jealous."

"Right." She grabbed my roller off me and pushed me towards the soup table. "Go talk to Ross. You can swap with your sister for a bit. Unless my Mumdar is significantly off, our Jess has got something she's not telling me, and knowing you two I'm guessing boy."

I laughed. "Unless she's drunkenly bought a lighthouse as well."

"Oh God, don't even joke. Go on, off you bugger."

I headed over to Ross and Jess, who was slicing rolls, blissfully unaware of what awaited her.

"Sorry, Jess," I said when I arrived at the table. "You're being summoned for a Mum interrogation."

"Oh Christ," she said, her eyes widening. "Does she know?"

"Yeah. She always does."

"Knows what?" Ross asked.

I jerked a thumb at Jess. "About our Jessie's secret boyfriend. Anyway, sis, it's time you came clean. Gareth's a nice lad."

"That's what worries me," she said, pulling a face. "Don't want Mum going into full protective mode and scaring him off."

"Give over, she's not that bad."

"She bloody is." Jess sighed. "Ok, I'll leave you to the rolls. Try not to slice off any fingers, I'm off duty so you'll have to sew them back on yourself." She handed me her breadknife and went to join Mum for painting and the third degree.

"Still sulking about Alex?" I asked Ross when we were alone.

"I'm not sulking. Just wondered why you never said anything."

I sighed. "I don't really like talking about it. Too many bad memories go with that guy."

He flung a bitter look at Alex, painting a patch of wall next to our old teacher Mr Madison. "You seemed pretty matey from where I was standing."

"We have to be mature about it, that's all. Can't avoid each other forever in a place like this." I changed the subject swiftly. "So how's it going in the soup kitchen?"

"Great, the stuff's going down a storm. Tell you what, maybe I should jack all this in and try my luck on Junior Masterchef."

I picked up a cup and took an appreciative gulp of the hot-and-herby orange liquid inside. "Mmm. Maybe you should, this is good stuff. Where'd you get the recipe?"

"Er, Baxter's. There were instructions on the back of the tin. It was easier than I thought actually, it just had to go in the microwave for a bit and bam. Soup."

"You cheating little sod."

He grinned. "Only kidding. It's just veg and spices I chucked in a pot, think I got lucky."

I nudged him. "Funny boy."

"S'me. So what did Alex want then? I saw you going outside."

Wasn't going to let it drop, was he?

I busied myself with a roll, watching Ross from the corner of my eye for his reaction. "He wants to help with the project. I think he feels guilty about – well, what happened with me and him."

He frowned. "If he hurt you I'm not sure we need his help."

"I'd say we need whatever help's on offer. Alex is a

councillor, he's got contacts." I looked up at him. "Why should it bother you?"

"I just don't want to work with someone who can upset you this much." He scanned my face, and I reached up to brush the last shimmer of a tear from my cheek.

"Because we're friends, right?" I said.

"Yeah. Because we're friends."

He caught my gaze, and there was a look in his eyes, a feeling, anguished look I couldn't interpret.

For a moment I was on the brink of spilling everything: what I'd seen that day on the pier, my worries about his mood shifts, his tiredness, the distance he'd been putting between us. I wanted to ask him outright if he was seeing other people, and exactly what it was we were to each other.

"Ross, I—"

"Excuse me, Roberta dear." Mrs Abberley, my old lollipop lady, had approached the table and was eyeing the rolls critically through her spectacles. "Do you have any butter for these? They look a little dry."

The moment was gone, and the words died on my tongue.

"Oh. Yes." I managed a smile for her. "There's another tub in the car. I'll fetch it for you, love."

***

"Looks good, doesn't it?" I said after all the painters had drunk up and gone.

"Better than good." Ross was smiling up at the lighthouse with a faraway look in his eyes.

We were with Jess and Mum outside, draining a hard-earned beer each as we surveyed the old place. The candy-cane swirls looked fresh and new, the way they must've done in Wilf and Peggy's day, and the dying copper sunlight dripped off the fresh glass in the windows.

"It's lovely to see it gleaming again," Mum said. "Looks just like it did when I was a kid, when your aunty was alive, Ross."

"I'm going to bring Charlie up tomorrow," Ross said. "I think he'll want to see it now."

"Give me a ring when you do, I'll come with you." Mum jerked her head towards me and Jess. "Charlie and Annie gave these horrible children their first cot, you know."

"Really?" Jess said. "I never knew that."

"Yes, they did a lot for us when your mum was just a silly girl with no cash, no partner and two screaming babies. The whole community rallied round to help us get sorted. Just like they did today."

"It's not a bad old town, is it?" Ross said, his eyes still fixed on his lighthouse.

"No." Mum turned to smile at me. "It might have started

out as a mad drunken idea, but I'm proud one of my girls is putting something back in."

Jess glared at her. "Oi. Who's been working her fingers to the bone slicing bloody bread rolls all afternoon, Mother Dearest?"

"All right, both of you then. Or all three of you," Mum said, including Ross with a sweep of her hand. "Well done, kids."

"Come a long way, haven't we?" I said quietly to Ross. I felt his hand slip around mine and squeeze my fingers briefly.

"We have. Thanks, Bobbie."

"For what?"

"Being you. Don't think there's anyone else I could've made this work with."

I flushed. I could see Mum watching us, her eyes narrow as she downed the dregs of her beer.

"Ross, can I have a quick word?" she said.

"Course, Janine. What about?"

"I'll tell you when these two have gone." She turned to meet my glare. "Nothing to concern you, our Bobbie. Just family stuff. I need to talk about Charlie."

"That better not be a massive whopper," I said, frowning. "Don't you two dare be talking about me."

Mum laughed. "What, you think we can't find anything better to talk about?"

"I know you, Mother. Just don't—" I broke off, shooting a quick look at a bemused-looking Ross. "Stick to the small talk, ok?"

"I promise."

"You've got your fingers crossed behind your back, haven't you?"

"I have not!" Mum protested, holding flat palms up in front of her. "Now go on, girls, piss off home." She looked up at Ross. "And you. Stay there and listen to me."

I flung a last worried look over my shoulder as Jess and I headed down the hill. Mum was talking at Ross, who blinked dazedly in the flow.

"If she's interfering in my love life again there'll be hell to pay," I muttered to Jess.

Chapter 11

"So, what news on the Rialto?" I asked Ross. "Any word on that bid we put in to the Eric Godfrey Trust for speakers?"

We were having a planning meeting behind a dwindling wine each at the Mermaid pub. Ross was looking more upbeat than I'd seen him for ages, not tired or moody as he had been too often lately, smiling warmly across the table. But he was still across the table. Long gone were the days when his default position was in the seat next to me.

"No, not yet." He puckered his brow. "Sorry, what's the Rialto got to do with it? Is the trust based in Venice?"

"Shakespeare reference. Let my inner pretentious bitch out for a minute there."

"Oh. Right. Didn't even know you had one."

"Writer's prerogative," I said with a smile.

He was flicking the document pile in front of him unconsciously, and my eyes dwelt on his fingers. They were long and broad, nails ink-stained in the corners, the skin on the tips hard and a little calloused from his guitar. Idly, I wondered what they'd feel like brushing the bare flesh at the back of my neck. Sliding down my back, up inside my top to unhook my bra...

"Bobbie?"

"Hmm? Oh." I snapped out of it. "So, anything else to report?"

"Just this." Ross twitched a sheet of paper out of his pile and pushed it to me. "I mocked it up to go with the blue-prints, thought it might help with bids. It's not to scale or anything, but..."

My breath caught as I looked at what he'd handed me.

The print-out showed a cross-section of our lighthouse done in some 3D graphics program. Except it wasn't our lighthouse, because this one was gleaming and brand new. A tiny band was on stage at the base, with a tiny audience watching from the balconies above, and upstairs a tiny barman served tiny drinks from a tiny semi-circular bar where the old lamp had been. As I ran my eyes over it, the dream made sort of flesh, I found myself blinking back tears.

"Bobbie, you ok?"

"God, it's just like I imagined. Your aunty'd be proud." I threw him a smile. "Clever boy, aren't you?"

"I'm far too modest to say. But yes. So, any news from you?"

"Well, I finished writing that funding bid for the lottery money to cover balconies and staircases. I'll email it over so you can give it a read."

"Sounds good. Oh, by the way. Brought something for you."

He reached into the satchel he used to lug documents around and pulled out a little object wrapped in brown paper, handing it to me along with one of his pretty eye-crinkling smiles.

A present? I stripped the parcel of its papery skin, full of curiosity.

Inside was a little wooden fishing boat. The blue and white paint was faded and cracked in places and a tiny fisherman in a yellow sou'wester, his face long since rotted away, was standing on the prow looking into the waves.

"The workmen found it in the lantern room, I had to rescue it from a skip," Ross said. "Sent it off to be cleaned for you. I thought you might like to keep it, for luck or whatever."

I blinked at him, touched. This was exactly what I didn't get about Ross. One minute he'd be making with the back-off body language, flinching when he touched me, rushing off after meetings as if he didn't want to spend any more time with me than he had to. The next he was joking and flirting and being sweet as hell with toy boats. What was going on with that boy?

I set my lighthouse boat down on the table, where it rocked gently back and forth as if buoyed by invisible waves.

"Wonder who it belonged to," I said, running my eyes dreamily over the white stripe down its side. "Before, I mean."

Ross shrugged. "Annie maybe. Anyway, it's yours now. Hope you like it."

"I love it. Thanks, Ross." I reached down to stash the little boat safely in my handbag where there was no risk of a wine spillage in its direction. The poor thing had weathered years of neglect, I didn't want it perishing in a sea of alcohol right at the end. Although perhaps that's how the little fisherman would want to go.

There was an awkward silence for a moment. I was thinking about the boat, the gesture, what it meant. God only knew what Ross was thinking.

"Hi, Bobs. Mind if I join you for five minutes?"

I looked up to see Alex, who'd appeared from somewhere and was lurking next to our table.

"Oh. Hi. Er, yes, don't see why not," I said, indicating the chair next to mine. Ross opened his mouth as if he was about to protest, then closed it again.

Alex gave him a friendly nod. "Hello, Ross. Good work at the painting party the other week, the place is looking great. The council were singing your praises in our last meeting."

Ross didn't smile. "Good for them. So what're you doing here?"

I threw him a warning look, but he ignored me.

"I'm meeting a friend," Alex said, casting a glance over his shoulder to see if they'd arrived yet. "Spotted the two of you and thought I'd come get a lighthouse update while I waited. Anything I can do?"

"We're fine, thanks," Ross said. "All under control."

"Actually, Alex, there is something," I said. "Do you have any contacts at that self-storage place?"

"I've met the manager a few times. Why?"

"We're trying to arrange some secure off-site storage for sound equipment, but we're struggling to negotiate a charity rate. The manager's asking way more than we can afford."

"I wouldn't say struggling exactly," Ross said. "I'm wearing him down. Just need a bit more time to work on him, that's all."

"He might take it better coming from you," I said to Alex. "I mean, if you were serious about wanting to help."

"I don't think it'll make any difference, Bobbie," Ross said. "That manager's a tough old bugger. I was on the phone to him for half an hour yesterday and at the end of it I'd only managed to negotiate a fiver off his original price."

"Well, we'll see," Alex said. "I happen to be aware he's

just applied for planning permission to extend his premises. He might feel it's not a good time to upset the council."

Ross frowned. "You're going to blackmail him?"

"No. I'm going to have a quiet word about the lighthouse and never mention planning permission. The blackmail will come from his subconscious."

"Crafty." Ross downed the last of his wine and stood up. "Right, I'll leave you two to catch up. See you next week, Bobbie." He gave Alex a curt nod. "Alex."

"You don't have to go yet, do you?" I said. "I thought you could stay for another."

"I think we're all planned out for today. I've got work to do at home." His sullen expression lifted slightly. "Unless you want to walk back with me?"

Alex looked over his shoulder again and waved to a man in a business suit standing at the bar. "Looks like my friend's arrived. You're welcome to join us if you want, Bobs?"

The blue eyes peeping out from behind his specs were appealing, and for a second I hesitated.

"No, I should probably get off," I said at last. "See you, Alex. Thanks for your help with the storage."

"No problem. I'll let you know how it goes." His gaze followed the two of us as we left the pub.

Chapter 12

Ten minutes later, Ross and I were crunching along the seafront in silence, foaming waves slapping against the pebbles by our side.

"Did you have to be so abrupt?" I demanded when I was sure we were out of earshot of other people.

"Any reason I should be polite to that guy?"

"Well there's one massive one," I said. "We need him. Alex is on the council; he could be a big help. Especially with Langford gunning for us."

Ross just snorted.

We lapsed back into silence, listening to the waves and the strangled yarking of the seagulls. He was walking a little apart from me, and I couldn't help letting out a sigh as we passed Gracie's bench. I'd felt so close to him that night. To talk, to touch, to kiss, had just seemed the most natural thing. And now ... everything was different. Surely it couldn't be that when we weren't talking lighthouse we had nothing to talk about?

"What did Alex do to you, Bobbie?" Ross asked at last.

Ok, nothing except that.

"Do you mind if we don't talk about it?"

He frowned. "If that's what you want."

I glanced at him and sighed.

"He cheated on me," I said eventually. "It was complicated, but that's what it comes down to."

Ross stopped walking and turned to me, shock written across his face. "He did that?"

"Yeah. Girl from his squash club."

His brow knit dangerously. "Bastard! He's lucky I didn't know before, I'd have told him to shove his help."

I suppressed a smile. It was sweet seeing him go all protective, even if it was only as a friend.

"Well, it's in the past now," I said. "Nothing to do but move on."

"You're not even angry?"

"I was. I went through all the stages they tell you about in the women's mags: anger, grief, despair, etc. And time went by, and then I saw him at the council meeting, same as ever, and now I'm just ... resigned, I suppose. We both have to live here and things are the way they are."

He scowled. "You might be resigned."

"Look, what's it to you, Ross?" I demanded. "It's between me and Alex, isn't it?"

"I don't like the thought of him hurting you, that's all.

I don't like *him*." Ross dipped his head to look into my eyes. "Bobbie, can I ask you something?"

"Course."

"Are we ... what are we? I mean, who are we?"

I blinked in puzzlement. "Sorry, what?"

"What I mean is, we're partners, aren't we?"

"Well, yeah. Why?"

"Anything else?"

Where was he going with this? Was he asking me if I wanted to be something else? Was he telling me he didn't want to be? It had seemed easier to talk to him months ago, when we were still virtual strangers.

"Only I got an ear-bashing from your mum after the paint party that basically amounted to a demand to know what my intentions are," he said.

"She didn't!" I exploded. "I knew she was up to something. I'll kill her!"

"Oh, don't be too hard on her. She's only looking out for you." He twiddled his fingers awkwardly. "So ... did you want me to have some intentions?"

"Depends what they are." Suddenly I started laughing. "God, we're riddling like drunk bloody leprechauns. Come on, let's stop playing silly beggars and say what we mean. We're too old for games."

"And getting older by the minute." He sought my gaze. "Is something wrong? Things seem weird between us lately."

"No. Not really."

He hesitated. "Look – that night. Last time we were here."

"I told you, forget about it. It was the booze."

"Not for me it wasn't. I really liked you, Bobbie. And then next day you just seemed to cool off. I've thought about it over and over, wondering what I might've said …" He paused. "You didn't know I was married, did you?"

"No," I said, flushing. "Not until you told me."

He groaned. "Oh God, I knew it! So that's what it was all about. You wouldn't have kissed me if you'd known?"

"No." I wrestled my eyes away to glare at my sandalled toes. "It's just – well, my dad and everything. You know Mum's story. It's made me wary, that's all."

"Why didn't you talk to me about it? I thought we were mates."

I frowned at him. "Well it's not like you've been so bloody approachable lately, is it? Never coming near me, being all moody. And with the—" I bit my tongue. I really didn't want to go into what I'd seen on the pier, not until I knew for sure who the woman was. "With you working all the time."

He turned away to look out over the ocean. "I wasn't being moody."

"Come on, you know you were. I never know how you're going to react to me these days. I patted your knee the other week and you jumped about a foot."

I grasped his arm, turning him back to face me, and felt him shudder under my fingers.

"See?" I said as he jerked his arm away. "What's wrong with you lately? You're jumpy as hell, all the time."

"You really don't know why? You haven't worked it out?"

"No. Why?"

He swallowed hard. "God, you must know how it works," he said, his voice choking slightly. "When you get near me, when I touch you ... I mean, I can smell you, Bobbie. I can feel you against me. It's kind of torture."

I took a shocked step backwards. "What?"

"I had to back off, didn't I? It just felt like the more time I spent with you doing lighthouse stuff, the harder it was not to – to want more, you know? And then you've seemed so different lately, I didn't know if you wanted—" He flushed. "Well, the same thing I wanted."

"Oh. Right." I could feel my cheeks getting hot. "Er, sorry. For smelling and everything."

He smiled. "Don't apologise, I love how you smell. Not your fault you turn me on, is it?"

"No, um, I guess ... not ..." I mumbled, head reeling at the sexy turn the conversation seemed to have taken.

"So did you?"

"Did I what?"

"Want it?"

I hesitated, for what seemed like an age. But I was done with riddles.

"Yes."

He inhaled sharply. "Oh God. Why didn't you tell me, Bobbie?"

"You were being so weird with me. I thought maybe you'd … met someone. Or something."

"Met someone?" He laughed. "When would I have time?"

I managed a smile, and he took my hand to draw me closer.

"Why didn't you talk to me, if that's all it was?" I asked.

"And say what? 'Sorry I can't be close to you, it makes me fantasise about ripping your clothes off and ravishing you over the bar'? I didn't even know if you liked me like that. You've been so cold since the council meeting, and this thing between you and Alex—"

"There is no thing between me and Alex."

"But you hid it from me that you'd been a couple, didn't you? It was only when your mum told me off for dicking you about that I thought I might still have a shot."

The council meeting. The day I'd seen him down on the pier. Maybe I had been cooler, without meaning to be. Maybe my behaviour had seemed just as inscrutable to him as his had to me.

"I'm sorry, Bobbie," he said softly. "I didn't even think how the thing with your dad might've affected you. Seriously, I thought you knew I was separated."

"I know. It was just such a shock, when you said you were married. That poor woman ... my dad's wife, Corinne. God, he hurt her so much. My mum's never really forgiven herself."

"She needs to," Ross said earnestly. "Middle-aged teacher and seventeen-year-old pupil, seems pretty obvious where the blame lies. Your mum and his wife were both victims."

"I know. But Mum really drummed it home, you know? If someone's married you stay the hell away, or it's a sure-fire recipe for pain for everyone concerned. It became almost a gut reaction."

"Be logical though. It's been over between me and Claire for ages. Honestly, what is it but a piece of paper in the end, if the love's not there?"

"I just ... want to do the right thing. I don't want to hurt anyone. I don't want to get hurt, not again." I sucked my breath in sharply. The whole time we'd been talking he'd been touching me. Taking my hand, running his fingertips over the ridges of my knuckles and across my palm, gently tracing the bones of my wrist. Now, finally, he pulled me into his arms.

"This is the right thing," he whispered, and his voice was trembling. "Oh God, you feel it too?"

"Yes," I muttered as the sensation hit me. "Yes, I feel it."

Now I understood what he meant, about getting too close. I felt a spasm of arousal as I absorbed the feeling of being there in his arms, his scent, faintly caramel, and my body pressed against his. I struggled against the sudden ramp in my hormone levels, tried to slow the pulse that had started thrumming up through my body from between my thighs. But it was too late.

The next thing I knew he'd dropped his satchel full of lighthouse paperwork and we were kissing, kissing like we were fused, like we were never going to stop.

I lifted my hands to his neck, caressing the firm sinews with my fingertips. Ross's hot tongue teased my lips apart to explore my mouth with a hungry intensity that seemed to filter three months' worth of kisses that never were into this single one. And I savoured every second: the feel of him, his taste, his warmth. In a minute there'd have to be a conversation. But right now there was just Ross Mason, his arms holding me and his wine-laced tongue embracing mine.

When he finally drew back for a gulp of air, he was almost breathless. I felt my chest rising and falling rapidly against his and realised I was too.

"That was ... unexpected," I gasped.

"Yeah," he said, his breath coming through in sharp pants. "Did you like it?"

I attempted a casual shrug. "It was all right."

Ross grinned. "Go on, you can do better than that."

"Very nice."

"Nope, I can hear you panting. One more."

I sighed. "Ok, ok. Best kiss ever."

"That's more like it."

Suddenly I was conscious of the fact I was in his arms, his hands caressing my back, his obviously aroused body pressed into mine, and with a huge effort I dragged myself into the real world and wriggled out of the embrace.

"What's up, Bobbie?"

"We shouldn't."

"Why shouldn't we, if we both want to? Keep telling you, it's just paper. You do believe that, right?"

"I do. But it's not just that. There's the lighthouse too."

"Um, ok." He frowned. "What about the lighthouse?"

"People round here know you're married, don't they? And you know what Cragport's like for gossip."

"Everyone knows I'm separated though. Anyway, what's that got to do with the lighthouse?"

"Don't you think it might bother the powers that be if they hear we're suddenly sleeping together? By the time it got Chinese Whispered back to that knobhead Langford at the town hall, we'd be notorious local swingers with secret plans to turn the lighthouse into a leather-uphol-stered sex dungeon."

He cocked his head. "Hey, is it too late to ditch the music venue idea?"

"I'm serious," I said, smiling. "He'd be bound to hear

about it. People always do, round here. It might affect our funding chances if donors know we're not strictly business partners."

"Well, you could be right." He scrunched his eyes closed and I heard him stifle a groan. "Jesus, Bobbie, I want you so much right now, you know that?"

"Bloody hell, Ross ..." I swallowed hard, trying to still the banging in my chest. "It won't help if you say stuff like that. And stop making sexy noises."

"You were the one who brought up leather sex dungeons. Hey ..." He came forward to slip his arms round me, and I could feel the heat from his body flowing into me through the cotton of his shirt. I gasped as he tilted my head to one side and started kissing down my neck, his fingers burrowing up into my hair. "You know, here's a radical suggestion," he muttered against my skin. "We could just be really sneaky and not tell anyone. You could take me home right now and I'll make some more sexy noises for you."

"God, that sounds good..."

"Does, doesn't it? Here's a taster." Sliding his palms to my buttocks, he pushed himself firmly against me so I could feel his erection hard on my leg and let out a long, low, open-mouthed groan that just oozed sex. The vibrations from it tingled into the flesh he was caressing with his lips and sent the muscles below my abdomen fluttering alarmingly.

"Do you have to be so bloody erotic at me?" I choked back an answering moan, summoned the last shred of resistance I had and pushed him back so his body wasn't touching mine. "No, love, we can't."

"This is for me and you, it doesn't concern anyone else. Why shouldn't we enjoy each other if that's what we want?" He lowered his voice to a whisper. "Go on, Bobbie. Enjoy me."

I fought against another wave of lust that was threatening to surrender me. "Oh God ... look. Ross. Believe me, I'd love to take you back to mine and rip your clothes off right now." I paused to trail my gaze over the inviting contours of his body, then squeezed my eyes closed to shut it out. "But it's not just the donors. It's ... well, it's me. I'm sorry."

His voice softened. "Is this about your dad?"

"Partly. And what happened with Alex. I just think I'd feel better about myself if you were a man actually getting divorced rather than just a man not living with his wife, you know? I know it's just a piece of paper, but it's a bloody important one." I opened my eyes to seek his. "Would you wait for me? Just until the lighthouse is done. You'll have your petition in then, and all that time and energy we've been focusing on the project can be for me and you."

"Is that really what you want, Bobbie?"

"No, I want you. But it's what I think we should do."

"God. You had to go and say that, didn't you? Like this isn't hard enough." He swallowed another sexy noise and pinched the bridge of his nose. "Ok. We'll wait."

"You really don't mind?"

"Well, yes, I bloody do mind because I'm seriously horny right now." He gave a deep, throaty sigh. "But if it's what you need."

"Thanks, Ross, you're a good boy. Sorry I made you horny."

"Never mind. I've got a *Razzle* at home." He clapped his hands together. "Right, so what's the next thing, lighthouse partner?"

"Bloody hell, you're keen all of a sudden."

"Yeah. I could do with something to distract me before we get back out in public, if you know what I mean."

I laughed. "Ok, well, I'm going to put in that bid for the lottery money, and then we need to start planning some fundraising."

"What're you thinking, like a bikini car wash or something?"

"You really are horny, aren't you?"

"Yep."

"You can soap up cars in your trunks if you want, handsome. Then we might make some real money." I paused for a moment to savour the image. "Heh. Wish I had a *Razzle* at home."

"I'll lend you one. So, what're we really going to do?"

I shrugged. "Not sure yet, needs brainstorming. Let's get out of here before this goes all *From Here to Eternity* on us, eh? Apparently we're not safe alone together in beach settings."

"No." He shot me a warm smile. "Bobbie?"

"What?"

"Glad we understand each other again. Next time let's just talk, all right? No more secrets."

I smiled back. "No more secrets, Ross."

Chapter 13

Now Ross and I had cleared the air, everything seemed to slot naturally into place and I felt happier than I had since the day I'd seen him on the pier.

I still hadn't asked him about that. Jess was probably right, the woman was a design client: some local entrepreneur needing business cards or whatever. I didn't want to sound all stalkery by quizzing him. He wasn't seeing anyone else; he never had been. That's all that mattered.

He was occasionally tired still from late nights working, but the mood swings disappeared, the awkward silences were no more. We were as comfortable in each other's company as we had been in those early days, and when Ross put space between us, I just felt grateful to him for being willing to wait.

To be honest, since that night on the beach the keep-your-distance rule was as much for my benefit as his. The sexual tension hadn't gone anywhere, and our biggest problem now seemed to be keeping our hands off each other long enough to actually get the lighthouse finished.

"You sure we should do this here instead of the pub?" I asked when I met Ross outside the lighthouse for our fundraiser planning session.

"Just wanted to check out the speakers they're installing with that Eric Godfrey money. I'm sure we can stop it getting too sexy if we keep our distance." He nodded down at Monty, on his lead by my feet. "Anyway, that's why I asked you to bring this little chap. There's something about him giving me evils that puts me right off."

"Heh. Yeah, he's a bitch like that."

I let Monty off his lead. As soon as he was free, he bounded over to Ross and jumped up to rest his two front paws on the man's calves.

Ross frowned. "What's he doing that for?"

"He wants a stroke," I said, smiling. "Looks like you made a friend of him at last, Ross."

"Aww. Good lad." He bent to tickle the little Westie between the ears. "Finally decided your Uncle Ross isn't so bad, eh?"

Monty let out a short bark and galloped off to scamper around the lighthouse.

"Was that a yes?" Ross asked, turning to me.

I laughed. "No, he's asking you to chase him. But we'd

better get the lighthouse stuff done before we play with the dog."

Inside, the lighthouse was a mass of wires and cable reels. Workmen were part-way through installing large speakers up the side of the tapered walls, to give our audiences the best experience of the acts performing beneath them.

"Looks like they've still got a lot to do," I said.

"Well, they reckon they'll be done by next week." Ross sounded doubtful.

I glared at him. "You better not've hired a bunch of cowboys to fit our speakers, Mason. Where'd you find them?"

"My dad recommended them."

"Oh Jesus Christ. This is going to turn into a Fawlty Towers episode, isn't it?"

He looked amused, like he always did when he thought I was being stroppy. "It's fine, Bobbie. I checked out their reviews online, they're a five-star company. I'll give them a call later and check they're still on schedule."

I skimmed the room. It seemed like a lot of detritus for workmen who were supposedly nearly finished.

"Let me do it. You'll go too easy on them."

"All right, bossy knickers, I'll give you the number," he said with a grin. "So what about fundraising ideas? You got any?"

"One. It'll take a bit of planning, but ... well, you're a musician, aren't you?"

"Ah, I get you." He gave me a knowing nod. "Geldof this bastard. Charity single."

"Not exactly. Was thinking more of a benefit gig."

He frowned. "What, here? But there's no space, we won't get the balconies in for ages."

"I didn't mean inside."

"Oh. Oh! Right. Yeah, that might work." His eyes kindled into lighthouse fever as the idea took hold. "Big thing to organise, but I can definitely see it. Marquee, stage, barrier fencing to keep people away from the cliff edge. And then the bar inside the lighthouse, yeah? Let people get a look at what they're backing."

"Exactly, like your thinking. And maybe a barbecue, we can borrow that big one of the Crown's." I pondered for a second. "A charity single's not a bad idea, you know. We could sell it at the gig."

"We could, couldn't we? I could write something." Ross's fingers were twitching as if he couldn't wait to get back to his guitar and thrash out some ideas. "Right. Come on." He grabbed my arm and dragged me through the door.

He didn't waste any time, striding around outside to gauge the size of the area.

"Ok, so there's room for a stage here in front of the cliffs.

Probably best, keep people as far from the fencing as possible," he said, sweeping his arm across the balding, chalky area that bled off the edge of the crag.

I walked over to the grassy wasteland in front of the lighthouse and spread my arms. "And we could get a marquee here for a bit of shelter."

Ross frowned. "How much is all this going to cost though? Marquee hire doesn't come cheap, Bobbie. Nor does sound equipment. We've already put bids in to all the major funders for the renovation work, we don't want to push our luck."

"Well, we can go on the scrounge." I grinned. "Sorry, good-looking. I'm going to have to pimp you out."

"Oh God. I don't have to lap dance for the chairwoman of the WI, do I?" He turned his eyes up to the sky. "Again," he muttered.

I giggled. "No, fluttering your eyelashes should do the trick. First I want you to go see the vicar, see if she'd loan us the church's big marquee. Then when you've shown her a good time you can try your luck with the manager at Cragport Playhouse, they've got a collapsible stage. I'll find out what paperwork we need from Alex."

Ross scowled. "Do we have to involve him?"

"If we want the council on side. You know what Langford's like about noise, he might try to block the whole thing."

"Hmm."

I laughed. "Come on, don't be grumpy. You were in a good mood a minute ago."

"Can't help it. That guy winds me right up, with his Mr Nice act. I don't know how you stand to be around him after what he did to you."

"At least he's trying to make amends. That free storage he sorted out saved us a packet." I sighed. "I'm not saying it's easy, Ross, but in a small town where you can't avoid each other you just have to deal. It's all right for you, with the missus all the way over in Sheffield."

"It wasn't the same with me and Claire though. The split was pretty amicable, as these things go." He gave a resigned shrug. "Fine, it's your decision. If you think Alex can help, go ahead and ask."

I smiled. "Thanks, love."

"Well, let's not talk about him. Come on, back to planning," he said, tapping the lighthouse wall. "How much will we charge per ticket?"

"Depends what acts we can get, I suppose," I said. "Don't know Led Zep, do you?"

"'Fraid not. I once stood next to Peter Frampton at a urinal in Leeds, any good?"

"Not unless he gave you his number, in which case I'd have something entirely different to worry about."

"Sadly not, just a dirty look for breaking the male code

and giving him side-eyes. Still, I'd say that served him right for being Peter Frampton."

"So who else have you got?" I asked. "Don't suppose you ever met Alice Cooper while you were out cottaging?"

"No, just a few MPs." He shrugged. "I know some good acts based locally. What sort of thing were you thinking?"

"Oh, crowd pleasers. Rocky stuff, folky stuff, indie. Span the generations." I smiled. "Hey, why don't you headline? Your stuff's got broad appeal."

"Ha! You must be joking."

"I mean it, Ross. You're the talent round here, you should play a set."

"What, a crappy pub singer? We couldn't give tickets away, love."

"Give over, you're not a crappy pub singer." I sank down against the lighthouse wall and patted the grass next to me. "Here."

"All right, but not too close, eh?" he said, sitting down beside me.

"You don't really think that, do you?" I said gently. "You must know your stuff's good."

"Some days I think so. I'll write a snatch of something, a lyric, a few chords, and think it sounds pretty awesome. But then I'll listen to someone with proper talent and know I'll never produce anything that good."

"But you are that good. Honest."

He smiled. "As good as what, Bobbie?"

"As good as anything." On a sudden impulse I reached for him, drawing my fingers slowly down his rough, chiselled cheek. My thumbtip came to rest at the corner of his lips. "You're a very gifted man, Ross Mason."

He stopped my fingers with his, pressing my hand against his face. "Oh God, Bobbie, don't …" he whispered.

I could feel myself leaning towards him, the urge to kiss him overruling everything else; and Ross, as if magnetised, was moving towards me. For a moment there was nothing but Ross, absorbing me into his caramel musk, and the wind and the lighthouse and the hypnotic whispers of the sea…

But before our lips could meet, a jealous Monty jumped on my lap with a loud yap and the spell was broken.

Ross sighed, dropping my hand. "Thanks a lot, mate," he said to the little dog. "Just when I was starting to like you as well."

"You were right, he is useful for killing the mood," I said, swallowing a frustrated groan. "Let's get out of here. We'll be safe in the pub." I glared at Monty. "Come on, you little … dog. You can go home to annoy Aunty Jess and Uncle Gareth."

"Oh, something I wanted to ask," Ross said when we'd locked up. "You free a week Friday?"

"For planning?"

"No, I'm playing. Wondered if you wanted to come. It's not a long set, we can have a drink after."

"What?" I frowned. "Sounds a bit datey, Ross."

"It's not, it's research. I'm on at The Cellar in South Bay – performance space, a bit like our thing. A mate of mine bought it when it was a run-down beer cellar and did it up as a music venue. I thought we could scope the place out, see what we can learn."

"Oh." I hesitated. "Go on then. If there's other people we can't get too naughty."

"So I'll pick you up at 7?"

"Ok. See you then."

Chapter 14

"Hey," Ross said as we clambered out of his Mini in the neighbouring town of South Bay, just a little bit further down the coast towards Whitby. "You know what today is?"

"International Pie Day?"

"No. Well, probably, it's always international something day. But it's our anniversary as well."

"Bloody hell, is it?"

"Yep. Four months since I let a pretty girl buy me a tequila slammer and woke up with my own lighthouse." He smiled at me as we retrieved his guitar case from the boot. "Glad you're a bad influence, Bobbie."

I smiled back. "Me too."

"You look nice tonight," he said, scanning my outfit.

"Oh. Thanks." I'd dressed up for a change in a white satin top of Jess's with a lotus flower pattern, a pair of bootcut jeans and high heels with a floral motif to match the top. "Hope I've got it right, didn't know the kind of place it was."

Ross shrugged. "Anything goes in The Cellar. Anyway, you look great. I mean, you always look great. But tonight you look extra great."

"Back at you." He was looking pretty sizzling in a black blazer and matching shirt open at the neck, sleeves rolled to the elbow, with his usually tousled hair smartly gelled.

"Ta. I was going for young Johnny Cash, think I pulled it off?"

"Nah. Young Ross Mason's much hotter."

He tweaked my earlobe. "Sweet talker. Come on then, time to break up the mutual admiration society."

"So what're you playing tonight?" I asked, following him to the entrance.

"It's only a short set, there's another five acts on. Probably just do three or four favourites, maybe chuck in something new."

He looked flushed. I gave his arm a swift squeeze while we navigated the uneven stone steps down to The Cellar.

"Not nervous?"

"A bit. Funny, no matter how long you do this the stage fright never leaves you." We reached the bottom step and he barged open the heavy door.

It wasn't at all what I'd expected. I mean, if you go to a place called The Cellar that's in a cellar, you expect something that looks like – well, a cellar. Apart from the whitewashed beer barrel tables giving the place a slight smugglers' cave vibe, it was about as unlike a cellar as you could get. To borrow a favourite phrase of Mum's, it looked like a tart's boudoir. Red-glowing art deco lamps on every table, bevel-mirrored walls, pink ostrich plumes all over the place...

"I hope we didn't come for decorating tips," I whispered to Ross as we weaved our way through the crowded tables. "Bit flapper chic, isn't it?"

"You'll get it when you meet the owner, he's on bar tonight. Oh, er ... better brace yourself, he fancies himself as a ladies' man."

When we got to the large mahogany bar, Ross propped up his guitar case and reached across to slap his friend on the arm.

"Hiya, Travis. How're you keeping, matey?"

The young man serving drinks was just as offbeat as The Cellar itself. If someone had heard of steampunk but never seen a picture, they'd probably look like Ross's mate Travis.

His yellow hair was long and foppish, combed over the back of his head then curled up at the ends: very Brideshead Revisited. He was wearing a stripy pink and white blazer that looked like it might once have upholstered a deckchair, with a – yes, it was as well – not a tie but a cravat, a pink bloody cravat. His bobbly eyes were coloured in with dark eyeliner, and for some reason he had a pair of those steampunky goggles round his neck. The whole aura was of someone trying too hard to prove he had Personality with a capital P. Still, he was grinning happily enough so he obviously felt the look was working for him.

"Hiya, Mason, long time no see," he said to Ross. "How's the graphic design business?"

"Just about keeping me in baked beans and shoe leather. When am I on then?"

"I put you fourth on the bill." Travis nodded at me. "You going to introduce your girlfriend?"

"Oh, she's not – er, this is my partner Bobbie. I mean my business partner." Ross looked flustered, and I jumped in to rescue him.

"Hi," I said to Travis. "I'm an old friend of Ross's. We're working on the lighthouse project together, sure he's filled you in."

I stretched my hand over the bar for him to shake. Instead, Travis lifted it to his mouth and pressed his lips against the backs of my fingers.

Eurghh, hand kisser: hated those. When this guy decided to go the full Edwardian he didn't muck about.

"Charmed. Bobbie, was it?" he said in an affected drawl. Sounded pretty odd with the Yorkshire accent coming through underneath.

"All right, smoothie, don't push it," Ross said with a smile. "Get us a Coke and a glass of white wine then and we'll have a chat. We want to pick your brains."

"Whatever the gentleman wants." Travis turned to sort out our drinks.

"So what can I assist the pair of you with?" he asked when he'd dumped two glasses in front of us, leaning up on his elbows.

"We were hoping you'd tell us how you got this place off the ground," I said. "See if we can learn anything useful."

"Free business advice? Well, anything for a beautiful lady." He flashed me a smirk he obviously thought exuded sex appeal, and just the hint of a wink from one gooseberry-like eye.

Oh God. Ross was right, this was going to be hard work.

"Hey, she seeing anyone?" Travis whispered audibly to Ross.

"Yeah, Trav. Six-foot-seven cage fighter with tattoos up to his eyeballs. They call him Cuddles."

"Funny." Travis turned back to me. "Well, are you? Because if not there's no charge for the wine."

I rummaged in my handbag and slapped a note on the bar. "There's your answer. Come on, mate, stop flirting. No offence but you're not very good at it."

"Yeah, but I am keen." He shrugged. "Well, if you change your mind let me know. What do you need then?"

"Whatever you've got," Ross said.

"How far along are you?"

"Had the place insulated for acoustics, repainted, got some speakers in with grant money we got. Just getting the electrics and plumbing done and organising a fund-raiser we hope'll pay for the bottle bar to be installed. Oh, and we've got a bid in for lottery money to cover balconies. That'll be the most expensive thing."

Travis looked impressed. "Not bad for four months' work."

"Ta, mate, been going at it pretty hard. So how did you do it?"

"Bit different for me. All the renovations had to come out of my own pocket."

"Yeah?" I said. "How'd you pay for that, you a baronet or something?"

He tossed me another suggestive grin from his obviously abundant store. "Mainly through selling my body to women who wanted a good time, if you must know. Back then they called me The Orgasm Machine. Minimum three per session guaranteed if you fancy a go on me, love. And for you, no charge."

I turned to Ross. "How did he really do it?"

"His dad left him a house."

Travis glared at him. "Thanks for the cockblock, mate. Back in the day, me and you used to have a rule about playing along with chat-ups when we were on the pull."

"Well we're big boys now, Trav. And to be fair, you as a gigolo was never going to fly no matter how much I backed you up. So what did all this cost you then?"

He shrugged. "Hundred grand, thereabouts."

"Christ!" I looked around the room. "Still, you could probably've saved ten grand on plucked ostriches if things were tight."

Travis gave Ross a conspiratorial nod. "That's the way I like them, Mason. Funny and stroppy."

Ross shot me a mischievous wink. "Double trouble with this one as well, Trav. Bobbie's a twin, you know."

"Bloody hell." Travis stood up straight, looking interested. "What kind?"

"Why, how many kinds are there?" I asked.

"Well, there's the creepy kind and the sexy kind."

"Oh. Well not the creepy kind, I hope."

"Yeah? In that case, the two of you ever considered film work? I know this guy, really classy stuff, black and white and everything..."

"Seriously, you're cracking out 'I can get you into pictures'?" I rolled my eyes at him. "Didn't realise your vintage obsession extended to antique chat-up lines."

"You don't mess with the classics," he said with a shrug.

"Well before you ask, I don't want to come upstairs and look at your etchings, I haven't read any good books lately and I don't want to see your bloody elephant impression. Anyway, we're not identical, which I'm guessing is what you were angling for."

"Oh." He looked disappointed. "Can't have everything, I suppose. Offer's there anyway."

"So can we get back on the topic if you've got the sexy twin talk out of your system?" Ross asked. "Where did the hundred grand go, Trav? Apart from dyeing all those poor ostriches pink."

"There was all sorts needed doing," Travis said, waving an arm vaguely around the room. "Bar licence, stage, furniture, toilets. Soundproofing so we don't disturb the neighbours. Don't suppose that's something you have to worry about."

"Any tips?"

Travis pondered for a moment. "Well ... don't DIY it unless you know what you're doing, it'll end up costing you more down the line. Make the most of charity shops for decorating, you can save a fortune. Get four quotes minimum for any work – oh, and come to me when you're ready to install your balconies, I know a guy."

"Not the same guy who makes the tasteful twin porno, is it?" I asked.

He flung me another loaded smirk. "No, this is the guy who built my stage, but I can get you that guy's details if you're interested. And it's not porn, it's erotica."

"What's the difference?"

"He uses classical music for the soundtrack."

"Heh, just what your frustrated housewife needs when she's got a well-hung man round to fix the plumbing, sodding Vivaldi," I said with a snort. "You're all right, mate. Ta for the advice."

"No worries. Let me know if you want to drink for free, yeah? Offer'll be open all night."

I furnished him with a last eyeroll as we grabbed our drinks and made our way to a table.

Chapter 15

"Sorry about him," Ross said when we were seated. "Thought I was going to have to spread more rumours about you having chlamydia there."

"Persistent, isn't he? That routine ever work for him?"

"Nope. But he keeps trying all the same."

I looked at Travis, Edwardianly polishing a shot glass behind the bar and whistling to himself. "Odd bloke. How'd he end up like that?"

Ross shrugged. "He used to be pretty normal. Played the same circuit as us with his band and we'd go out drinking together. Then one day he just decided he wanted to be a Character, impress girls."

"And the fact it isn't working hasn't put him off?"

"I think he likes the attention. He's a nice enough lad, if you're prepared to work through the layers of laboured quirkiness."

"I'll take your word for it," I said, wrinkling my nose. "So how many acts before you're on?"

"Another three. Will you be all right on your own?"

"I'll be fine," I said, smiling. "Looking forward to hearing you again."

He twisted to face me. "How is it you never come see me, Bobbie? You haven't heard me play since that first night."

Well it certainly wasn't that I was afraid his deep, sexy voice – that voice that could always melt hearts and drop knickers like nobody else's, singing those beautiful tunes he'd written himself – might awaken something I wouldn't be able to fight back. Heh. Nope.

"Suppose I just never got round to it," I said with a casual shrug.

There wasn't much conversation after that, as a noisy heavy metal band, all leather and piercings, started up with their catalogue of Metallica covers and original songs that sounded like Metallica covers. After them came a Dylanesque folk duo, ageing hippy types who were actually pretty good, followed by a Britpop-inspired five-piece. You could say a lot of things about The Cellar, but you could never say it wasn't eclectic.

And then it was Ross's turn. I could tell he was experiencing the familiar stage fright from his pinkened cheeks. I gave his knee a swift squeeze before he grabbed his guitar and made his way to the stool Travis had dragged in front of the on-stage mic for him.

Once the music took hold he was fine though: calm and self-assured, as if there was no one else in the room. He started with a song I recognised, the one he'd been playing that night I'd first noticed him in the pub, then a couple of others I didn't know.

"Thanks, guys," he said with a sheepish smile when the audience applauded his third number. "Er, last one before I give up the mic to someone more talented. Hot off the strings, and like all the best songs it was written for a girl."

Oh God, he hadn't ... had he? Was that what all the blushing had been about?

"So this is Ivy Only Grows for the Wicked. Enjoy."

His face changed as he started thrumming his guitar, the look he always had when he was singing his own stuff: earnest, eyes closed, carried far away with the emotions he'd channelled into his music. Lips whispering against the microphone like a lover, like they had against my neck that night on the beach; lucky little microphone.

The music was sweet and mournful. Something lost then found again, second chances ... God, he'd only gone and written me a song. Felt like I was in a bloody Richard Curtis film.

I let my eyes fall closed, swept away with the weeping guitar, the lilt of his voice, lifting and rolling, surging and swelling, just like the ocean. Rippling through me, making my body surge and swell too. Echoes of Ross Mason singing me a song. My song.

That boy...

When he'd handed over the mic to some sort of jazz outfit, he came back to join me, looking bashful.

"You soppy, embarrassing bugger," I said when he'd sat down beside me, leaning across to kiss his cheek. "What did you go and do that for?"

"Dunno. For you. Did you like it?"

"It was beautiful," I said softly. "Can't believe you did that for me."

"Um ... cheers," he said, avoiding eye contact and flicking the zip on his guitar case. "I wanted to write you something. You're kind of musey."

"Why the ivy?"

He shrugged. "Suppose it reminded me of when we started all this. Charlie and Annie, how he misses her. The lighthouse and its history." He flashed me a fond smile. "Somehow all that stuff's tangled up with you, just like the ivy. Bobbie Hannigan from school, and the lighthouse, and the fun, wicked things I only dare do when I'm with you."

I found myself blinking back tears. God, that was ... why did he have to say these things? It made it so difficult.

"When did you get so sweet?" I summoned a smile. "At school you were just another swaggering boy. Prettier than the others, maybe, but I don't remember you going in for the sentimental stuff."

"Heh, that's all you know. Back then the 'wrote you a song' routine used to get me plenty of action, I can tell you."

"Oh right. I'm not the first then."

"Well, technically you are. In the Nietzsche's Jockstrap days it was always the same song. Me and the boys just used to tweak the lyrics to fit the girl."

"Ok, I take it back. You're not sweet. You're a devious little groupie-shagging sexaholic."

"That's me, addicted to sexahol." He grinned. "Come on, what lad wouldn't? It's called being 17, love."

"All right, fair point." I nudged him. "And between us, I still thought you were pretty adorable back then. Not that you noticed me by that time, when you had so many other girls throwing themselves at you."

"I did though." He looked serious now. "Did you really not know I liked you, Bobbie?"

"What, in sixth form?"

"Yeah. Didn't you ever wonder what happened to that lad Sean you sat next to in English before me?"

"Sean?" I fumbled for the memory. "With the ponytail? He got moved to the back, didn't he?"

"No, he got bribed to the back. I paid him a tenner to fuck off so I could sit next to you instead."

I squinted at him. "You never did."

"Yep. Still never had the balls to ask you out though."

"Come on, Ross, really? You barely spoke two words to me the whole time we sat next to each other. Every time I tried to start a conversation you went all monosyllabic."

"Heh, yeah, I was scared stiff of you. Weird, isn't it?"

"Bloody hell. That is weird." I thought back to Ross at school: lanky, cocky, good-looking Ross, joking and preening with pretty girls in the common room, strutting around like God's gift. He'd been a lot of things, but shy with girls was never one of them.

I shook my head. "So how come you never asked me out then? You asked just about every other lass in our year."

"Give over, I wasn't that slutty."

"You bloody were, mate."

"Well, maybe a bit," he admitted. "I dunno, you felt different. Like I'd only get one shot at it and I had to get it right. And I spent so long worrying about it, I never got round to doing it."

"Really, Ross?"

"Yeah." He smiled, one of his broad, devastating specials – sweet and warm and ever so slightly wicked in a way I wasn't sure I had much power left to resist. "Glad I got my shot in the end. Took me a while but I made it."

"God, you adorable bastard," I whispered with feeling. "Do you know how bloody much I want to kiss you right now?"

He stretched an arm around me and cuddled me against him. "Got a window in my schedule, darling. Go for it."

I shook my head, trying to shift the jumble of nostalgia and songs and Ross. "No, I ... better not, eh?"

"Why not though? Is there any good reason, except a bit of paperwork that'll be done and dusted by this time next year? I know you want to, you know I want to. Sod the waiting." He turned another sexy Ross smile on me, green eyes crinkling at the corners, obviously intent on finishing me off. "Come on, I wrote you a song. Can't resist that, can you?"

I laughed. "You are pretty charming. I mean, pretty nause-atingly charming."

"Aren't I just?" he said with a grin. "So, what about it?"

"I don't know, Ross. I do want to, but you know I've got previous in the being too impulsive department. Hence, you know, lighthouse. Something as important as this ... I want to do it the right way, that's all."

"You are doing it the right way," he said gently. He ran a hand along my hair, flowing over his shoulder while I rested my head on him. "It's nearly two years since me and Claire separated; even longer since we knew it was over. How long since you split with Alex?"

I did a quick calculation. Last summer ... God, was it really that long?

"Nearly a year, I guess."

"Exactly. We've been alone long enough, Bobbie. It's time now. Our time."

I tried to fight back the fog of schooldays enveloping common sense. The divorce. The lighthouse. Shagging, divorce, lighthouse, dating ... seemed a bit ... too much. Bad idea. Bad idea? Probably a bad idea.

"Not tipsy, are you?" Ross asked, clocking my vacant expression. "We can talk about this another time if you want to get out of here."

"Yeah," I said, smiling gratefully at him for letting me off the hook. "I mean, I'm not really tipsy, only had a couple. But I would like to get out of here. Let's go home."

Chapter 16

"Hey, can you come up to the lighthouse?" Ross asked as he turned the car back towards Cragport. "Thought since I've got the guitar I might as well test the acoustics, see how it sounds now the insulation's in. Could use a second opinion."

"You're going to sing?"

Oh God, not again. I'd managed to survive the last round. Any more and I'd need a cold shower.

"Just a few chords, hear how it resonates. I can't really judge it myself while I'm playing."

"Well ..." I hesitated. "For a bit then. Park down in town and we can stroll up. Something about Travis's interior decorating that leaves you feeling a bit smothered, isn't there?"

We abandoned Ross's Mini outside his flat and started walking up along the seafront road. It was a muggy summer night, stinking hot, and the breeze coming across the North

Sea breathed blessed relief against my overheated cheeks.

"Bollocks!" I said when we were about halfway, holding my hand out to catch a few plump drops that came thudding out of the cloud-bruised twilight. "We'll get drenched without coats."

"Who thinks to bring a coat in the glorious British summertime?" Ross said, laughing. "Come on."

He grabbed my hand and we started running towards the lighthouse, just visible in silhouette against the horizon.

"Quick, save the guitar!" I said with a giggle as I stumbled in my high heels up the shingled path, thumping raindrops churning up the clifftop around us.

Ross unlocked the lighthouse and darted in ahead of me. Dumping his guitar case, he flicked a switch to light up the room.

"Ta-da!" he said, turning to do the jazz hands thing. "Let there be light, eh? Anniversary present for you."

"Bloody hell!" I blinked rainwater out of my eyes, glad I'd worn the waterproof mascara. "It's like Cragport illuminations in here."

"Illuminations?"

"Yeah, we got another one while you were away. So when did the electrics get finished?"

"Yesterday. Electrician rang me last night."

"Sly bugger, you never said."

I crouched to take off my rain-filled shoes. Ross did the

same, stripping out of his wet brogues and socks. I smiled to myself when I remembered Annie Mason's Granny Peggy, so houseproud she'd make visitors take their shoes off before walking on her scrubbed stone floor.

"Was saving it as a surprise," Ross said as he busied himself with his laces.

"And when did you set this up?" I nodded to a grey woollen blanket on the floor, a bottle of something fizzy in the middle with a couple of champagne flutes.

"This afternoon. Thought once I'd lured you here we could christen the place, mark how far we've come."

"Ross…"

"What?"

"This was a date, wasn't it?"

"Er, yeah," he said with a guilty smile, standing up again. "You mad at me?"

I sighed. "No. Still, you're a tricksy bugger."

He cocked his head to one side. "Would you say tricksy? Or would you maybe say … adorable?"

"A bit of both," I said, smiling.

I pushed away the damp shoes and stood to face him, flinching when I took in his appearance.

Oh for God's sake, give a girl a break…

Ross's rust-dark hair was wet through, curled by the rain, and he was raking it out of his eyes with his fingers. His chest was still heaving from our run, rainwater dripping off his gorgeous body and puddling on the floor. By the time I'd run my eyes over him, I could easily have joined it.

Were the heavens mocking me, was that it? Surely there was only so much singing, sweetness and hot, wet man one flesh-and-blood woman could be expected to stand.

Part of me knew we ought to wait, just until Ross's divorce petition was filed, the lighthouse work was done and we were free to focus on us. That was the sensible thing. But unfortunately for sensible Bobbie, the other part of me – the impulsive, lighthouse-buying, currently very turned-on part of me who wanted to tear off Ross's wet clothes and take him right there on the floor – just shrugged and thought, what the hell?

"What?" Ross said, noticing me staring. "Is there something on my face?"

"There will be in a minute," I said hoarsely. "Come here."

I grabbed the wet lapels of his blazer and pulled his face down, covering his mouth with mine. I saw his eyes, blinking with surprise for a moment, fall closed as my tongue teased his lips apart. Powerful arms snapped round me, pressing me close.

"Oh God, really, Bobbie?" he asked breathlessly when I finally released him.

"Really. There's no one to get hurt here, is there? You were right, Ross, it's our time now."

He screwed his eyes closed, summoning one last effort

to do the right thing that was so Ross Mason. Which just made the potent need for him that had sprung up all of a sudden even harder to resist.

"I don't want you to do anything you're not completely comfortable with," he said after a moment, wringing the words out with an effort. "Are you sure about this? You weren't before."

"True." I gazed up at him through lowered lashes. "But don't you think we should get out of these wet things? We could catch our deaths." I brought my voice down to a seductive murmur. "We should probably, you know ... get naked. Wrap round each other a bit, warm up. Medically approved."

His eyes darted down my body, wet and dripping as his was, my satin top clinging to the breasts pressed against his chest, and sucked his breath in sharply.

"Bloody hell, lass ..." His voice was husky now. "That's it, I'm done. Come to me."

I gasped as he slid his hands to my buttocks and pushed my soaked body hard against his. He started planting scalding kisses down my neck, the tip of his tongue brushing the water droplets speckling my skin. I could hear him panting against me; hot, harsh, rasping breaths.

"What happened to your gentlemanly principles?" I breathed as I felt him fumble for the zip of my top. I raised my arms so he could peel the damp satin over my shoulders.

"There's a lot to be said for being a cad," he murmured,

flinging the top to one side. "You get to see girls with their clothes off, for a start."

Ross released me from his arms and led me to the blanket, moving the wine and glasses to make room for us. Sinking into a kneeling position, he guided me down so I was straddling him.

"Wrap your legs round my back," he whispered.

I did as he said, twining my legs around him. He hugged me to him and buried his face in my hair, gulping in deep, appreciative mouthfuls of my scent: coconut and passion-fruit or whatever shampoo I'd used that morning, seasoned with summer rain.

After a second he held me back and I heard him make an odd little noise in his throat.

"You are so bloody gorgeous when you're soaking wet. Get that bra off and let me look at you."

It was oddly sexy, him being the bossy one for a change. I unhooked my bra and chucked it to one side.

Ross reached out to run his thumbtip around an erect pink nipple. His skin was rough against the sensitive flesh, and I shivered with pleasure. Then he leaned forward to plant a cool, soft kiss, just brushing my nipple with the tip of his tongue and sucking ever so lightly. The gentlest of touches but it burned right through me.

I dug my fingers into his hair, encouraging him to try more, explore me, but he pushed back against my hand.

"Not yet, love. Saving you up."

"Cruel." I nuzzled into his neck, relishing the flavour of his skin on my tongue. "You now," I whispered. "Shirt off."

"You do it."

"Yes sir." I helped him out of his sodden blazer and shirt.

Bloody hell, when had he got that fit? Without his top he looked like a male model or something, the lanky lad from school all buffed up. And his skin was still glistening with rain. Made him look kind of delicious, like a cold drink on a hot day. Kind of … lickable.

Oh God … maybe it was the year's worth of celibacy or maybe it was the gorgeous, topless, teasing, dripping, panting boy gripped between my thighs, but I couldn't wait any more. I wanted him so much it was pain; needed him, that second.

Pushing him onto his back, I started peppering frenzied kisses over his chest. I slid my hands down to caress the tempting furrows and contours of his body, over the swell in the front of his jeans, and let out a low moan of longing.

"Hey," he gasped, stroking my hair as I scattered kisses over the well-defined muscles of his stomach. "Slow down, Bobbie. We've waited a long time for this. Let's savour it."

"Ah … yes …" I tried to stall the feverish beating in my chest. "Sorry. I just want to … feel you, that's all."

"Then feel me." Suddenly he rolled me over so he was on top and slid down to unbutton my jeans. He yanked them off over my hips then sent my knickers to join them, and I was completely naked, my tummy skin to skin with his chest.

I made a needy little noise in my throat when he ran the backs of his fingernails lightly along my inner thigh, tracing teasing patterns against the soft flesh.

"Ross ..." I whispered.

He flashed me a wicked grin. Then, without warning, he slid down to plunge his face between my legs.

I gasped and arched my hips as I felt him taste me with that hot, talented mouth, lips soft against me, so soft, so ... God, was he good at everything? His soaked curls dripping against my tummy, his fingers kneading my skin ... and his face, his gorgeous face, nestling into the wet, trembling fever at the top of my thighs, rough stubble firing every nerve, his relentless, eager tongue driving into me.

Ross bloody Mason, the first boy I ever kissed, making my body scream for him.

I cried out as the throb of orgasm took me, and I heard him laugh in triumph while that searing heat ripped up my body, shivering, painful, irresistible, until the moment was over and I sank against the blanket I'd writhed into bunches with a moan of satisfaction.

Ross slid back up and leaned on his elbows, his flushed face gazing down into mine.

"You look beautiful after that, you know," he panted,

shifting his weight so he could draw a finger along my heated cheek. "Makes you glow."

I let out a long sigh. "That was amazing. Thank you."

"My genuine pleasure." He claimed my lips, his delicious musk-laced tongue seeking mine.

When he drew away he rolled on to his back and guided me so I was astride him.

"You fancy getting the rest of my kit off then?"

"Since you ask." I helped him out of his jeans, but left his underwear on.

"Not going to take my boxers off?"

"Not yet."

I moved down to kneel between his legs and nuzzled softly against the firm sinews of his inner thigh, planting kisses hot and unhurried. I ran the tip of my tongue just under the leg of his boxers, then slid my hand up his hip, under the black cotton, to very gently trace the bone of his pelvis with my fingertips. Shifting up his body, I pulled the elastic down slightly to plant a row of light kisses under the waistband, where textured dimples guided me across his stomach like a map.

He was panting now, gasping with each meeting of my mouth and his flesh, his hips rising and falling gently beneath me.

Finally I guided his boxer shorts off, and swallowed a gasp of my own as his erection sprang free.

God, he was beautiful naked. I felt another throb of lust, but fought it back. He'd said he wanted to take things slow. I could take things slow.

I leaned forward again, but I didn't kiss him. I just blew softly, hot breaths against skin still clammy with sweat and rainwater. My body whispered over his, teasing him with the gentlest brushes of my breasts, and I could feel the tip of his erection grazing my tummy. He groaned, a needy, animal sound, and bucked towards me, but I moved back.

"Bobbie, please." His voice was pleading. "Don't tease. I have to make love to you, I'm going insane here."

"Well ... go on then. Since you asked nicely."

I slid up his body to bring my face level with his. His eyelashes were flickering rapidly, lips parted with quick, rasping pants. It was an irresistible sight. My mouth claimed his and he thrust his hands into my hair, pushing down greedily.

I broke away with a stab of worry.

"Did you bring something?"

"Yes. Wallet, back pocket."

"Thank God." I reached for his discarded jeans and located the foil packet tucked inside his wallet.

Ross pushed himself up into a sitting position. With trembling fingers I rolled on the condom, feeling him shudder when I touched him.

"Wait," he said before I could guide him inside me. He

drew one shaking finger along my cheek, brushing a strand of wet hair behind my ear. "I need to say this first. You're very special to me, Bobbie. You hear me?"

"Yes, Ross. I feel the same."

"Do I get to keep you after tonight?"

"If you want me."

"Oh God …" His eyes blinked closed for a moment, then in one swift movement he pulled me over him and thrust hard into me. "Then I'd better make this good, hadn't I?"

"Ah! Had you?" I gasped, letting my body rise and fall against his.

"You'll find I take my boyfriending duties very seriously." I heard him suck in a breath as I ran my tongue around his earlobe. "Bloody hell, lass, you can keep doing that as long as you like."

I let out a short, breathless laugh. "Never met anyone like you, Ross. You're … surprising."

He laughed too – God, there was something about the way he did that when he was aroused, half laugh, half pant, his mouth wet and open, that was so unbelievably hot. The buck of his hips under me was getting faster, sending delicious, torturous pulses of pre-climax thumping through me. I drove my fingers into his thick hair and grabbed a fistful, feeling my senses start to slide out of my grip in the sweet unforgiving agony of his body pressing into mine.

"Ah … sorry, I'm … hurting you," I panted when I heard

him take his breath in sharply. I tried to relax the white knuckles weaved into his hair, but I didn't seem able to let go.

"No, you're not, it's ... oh God, just keep moving like that ... Jesus *Christ*, Bobbie!"

I threw my head back, screaming out his name as he drove himself into me one last time and climax took us both together; those excruciating vibrations, greedy for every sense, until there was nothing but me, and him, and us – a single being in the long moment it took for our bodies to gorge themselves on each other and fall away.

***

"When you said we should christen the place, I thought you meant with the wine," I panted as we lay together on the blanket, sweat-gilded and cuddling breathlessly. "That was incredible, Ross."

"Pretty earth-moving yourself." He reached out to grab my hand, in lieu of the kiss we were still too exhausted to manage. "You know, I bet Freud'd have a few theories about people who bonk in lighthouses."

"I'm just glad to discover the fact you're from a long line of lighthouse keepers doesn't mean you need to overcompensate for anything." I leaned up on my elbow. "Did a good job testing the acoustics, didn't we?"

He grinned. "Well you certainly did. Surprised the place is still standing."

I pinched him on the arm. "And whose fault is that, shameless? Weren't exactly keeping the noise down yourself."

"That's the good thing about lighthouses, you never need to worry about waking the neighbours," he said, stretching out comfortably on the blanket. "Mind you, there're probably a couple of seagulls who'll need counselling."

"Yeah. Hugging their knees and shaking." I giggled at the image.

"Ok, enough seagull pillow talk. Now we've got our breath back how about a kiss, bonny lass?"

He pulled me to him and we locked lips, our hot breaths mingling.

"You know, after all that time at school worrying about how to ask you out I've done this totally wrong, haven't I?" he said when we came up for air.

"Oh, I don't know. Your methods were pretty effective."

He knit his brow. "Ok, I'm going in. Brace yourself to be asked out good and proper. I've waited 12 years to do this and I'm bloody well doing it right."

"All right, how would you like me?"

"Um ..." He rolled on top of me. "Here's good. Right, off we go. You ready for this?"

"As I'll ever be."

"Good." He cleared his throat. "Miss Hannigan, as your most ardent gentleman admirer, would you kindly permit me the honour of squiring you about the town?"

"I beg your pardon?"

"I really fancy you, will you go out with me?"

"Daft sod," I said with a giggle. "Go on then. Always enjoy a good squiring."

"Yeah, I'd heard that about you." He nuzzled into the arch of my shoulder.

"So you're really my girlfriend now?" he mumbled against the skin he was kissing.

"Yep."

"Brilliant. In that case, fancy sealing the deal by taking another crack at me?"

I lifted my eyebrows. "What, already?"

"Well, it's been a while." He jerked his head towards his wallet. "Got another if you fancy it."

"You certainly came prepared." I narrowed a suspicious eye at him. "Oi. Did you think you'd get lucky tonight because you wrote me a song?"

"Just thought I'd better be ready for the day you finally succumbed to my boyish yet manly charm."

"Maybe I'm not that easy," I said, tossing my head.

"Resist me then." He moved his lips to my earlobe and nibbled gently.

"Could if I wanted."

"Really?"

"Yep."

"Really though?"

I sighed. "No, not really."

"Good lass. Let's scare a few more seagulls."

Chapter 17

Back at the cottage, I dashed upstairs to change out of my damp, crumpled clothes. Once I'd got my pyjamas on and pushed my steaming hair through a bobble, I went down to the living room. Jess was snuggled against Gareth, watching TV with Monty asleep at their feet.

"Hiya, Bobs," Gareth said with a bright smile. "Missed you for film night."

"Liar," I said, returning his smile. "Bet the pair of you have had a great night without me, snogging your faces off."

"Heh, busted. So how was the gig?"

"Not bad," I said, throwing myself down on the sofa opposite them with a contented sigh.

"Thought you'd have been back ages ago," Jess said.

"Got chatting. Lighthouse stuff." The corner of my mouth kept twitching into a treacherous smile. I willed it back into submission.

Jess stared. "Not pissed, are you? Your face looks weird."

"No, I didn't have much." Just the two glasses of wine at the gig and a post-coital prosecco to celebrate the third orgasm ... "In a good mood, that's all."

She examined me suspiciously for a moment, then her eyes went wide.

"Oh. My. God."

"What?" I said, trying to sound casual.

"Oh my God oh my God oh my God!"

"Bloody hell, sis, have you found Jesus or something?"

She turned to her boyfriend. "Gareth, bugger off a sec, can you? Need to talk to our Bobbie. Twin stuff."

He frowned. "Er, right. What, like, cute little matching outfits, that sort of thing?"

"Something like that. Go stick the kettle on."

"Sexy cute little matching outfits?"

"Yeah, if you like. Crotchless PVC catsuits. Look, ten minutes."

Once Gareth had gone, I shook my head at her. "Can't believe you played the sexy twin card. How's the lad supposed to brew up with that image in his head?"

She shrugged. "He'll cope."

"Hey, you should meet Ross's mate Travis. He's got some tasteful erotica in production that'd benefit from your costume advice."

"Never you mind tasteful erotica. You had sex tonight, didn't you?"

I rolled my eyes. "Ugh. How do you and Mum always know stuff?"

"Ha, I knew it! Tell. Where've you been, his place?"

"No. Not his place."

"You didn't do it in the Mini?" Her eyes widened as she caught the look on my face. "Oh my *God*. You never."

My mouth spread into a smirk. "Yeah. Twice."

"Dirty mare!" She threw a cushion at me. "Not sure I fancy going to gigs in a lighthouse people've been having it off in. Any good?"

I sighed. "Bloody incredible. He sang me a song as well."

She frowned. "He sings while he's shagging? I mean, I've had my share of bizarre bedroom stuff, that lad who had to turn the photo of his parents to face the wall first and the one with the giant creepy teddy, but—"

"Not during sex, foolish child. Before, at the gig. He wrote it for me."

"Ha, is that still working? He used to do that at school to get girls into bed. Connie Hainsworth told me he wrote her one in Year 13."

"Yeah, he said. This was different though." I smiled when I remembered his lyrics, soft and haunting. "It was all about the lighthouse. Something about ivy."

"Ivy?"

187

"Ivy only grows for the wicked, this thing Annie Mason used to say. There was a whole metaphor. Think I might be the ivy, and then ... well, the lighthouse. That's symbolic too, isn't it?"

"Well it's got a pretty filthy silhouette if you go up at sunset."

I tutted. "Not what I mean, smut-for-brains. I mean it's ... the song, it was sort of saying the lighthouse is like me and him. As kids, and who we are now – those feelings. They were there, kind of dormant and half-forgotten, all the time. They just needed some attention, like our lighthouse."

"Or your novel."

"Shut up."

"Are you guys a proper couple now then?"

"Yeah." I hugged myself. "Yeah, we are."

Jess nodded approvingly. "Good."

"You think I was right then, letting him talk me into it?"

"Not for me to say really. Do you think you were?"

I hesitated. "I guess. He's nearly at the end of his separation period, seemed daft waiting just for form's sake. And he was right: there's no one to get hurt this time."

"Well, good for you, sis. Happy for you."

"Thanks. We decided we want to keep it quiet for a bit though, just until his divorce petition's filed." I glared at her. "So don't get pissed and tell everyone, gobby."

Jess assumed a look of innocence. "Would I?"

"Er, yes and yes and yes some more."

"Heh, is that what you were saying earlier?"

"Shut it, you." I sighed. "I'm serious, Jessie. It might worry people. The community's invested a lot in the light-house thing and they've put their confidence in us to pull it off. Maybe save going public until it's all settled."

"Right. So you don't want Mum finding out then."

"See right through me, don't you?" I said with a grin. "No, can't face the third degree straight off. You taken Gareth to meet the old lady yet?"

"I'm working up to it."

"Go on, you can't put it off forever. You know she'll love him."

"It's not her I'm worried about. A Mum interrogation isn't something you just inflict on boyfriends without careful psyching up. He could be running for the hills."

"Nah, he loves you."

She actually blushed – Jess never blushed. And she was picking at a loose thread on the sofa in a distracted sort of way...

"Oh my God!" I burst out. "He only bloody does! Did he say it tonight?"

She grinned. "He did, yeah."

"And did you say it back?"

She coloured a deeper shade of red. "Yes. Meant it too."

"Aww, you soppy cow. Give us a hug then."

"If I must." She came over to my sofa, chucked herself down and threw her arms around my neck.

"Pleased for you," I said, patting the back of her hair. "He's a great bloke. You know, for a rugby player."

She laughed and nodded to Monty, asleep on the carpet. "He must be, even the dog likes him."

"Oi. Can I come back in or what?" Gareth shouted from the kitchen.

"Yeah, come on," Jess called back. "We're done talking about you."

Gareth came through with a tray of drinks. He put on a look of mock disappointment as he handed mugs round.

"Oh. Thought you'd be modelling these catsuits for me by now."

I looked at Jess. "Are all men perverts about the twin thing or just the ones we meet?"

"All of them, I think." She went back to the other sofa to snuggle up with Gareth. "Hands off this pervert though, our Bobbie, he's mine."

"You say the sweetest things, Doc." Gareth twisted her face round for a kiss.

"Not the snogging again," I said, lifting my eyes to the ceiling. "Shame the dog likes you, Gareth, or you'd get a nip on the ankle for that. I think Mum had him specially trained."

"Worth it though," he said when he'd unplugged himself from Jess's face. "Speaking of, Jessie, you going to introduce me to your mum any time soon? You've met the drunken reprobates who pass for my family."

"Trust me, if you'd met my mother you wouldn't be asking that."

He looked puzzled. "Well no. Because I'd already have met her, wouldn't I?"

"You know what I mean."

"Go on, what's the worst that could happen? I'll turn on the charm, be Mr Perfect Boyfriend. And if she still hates me, I've got some cracking mother-in-law jokes I can whip out after rugby practice to entertain the lads. Win-win."

"Yeah, come on, Jess," I said, sipping my tea. "You can't leave it for the bloody wedding day, you know."

"Oi." Jess shot me a warning look. "No wedding talk. Let the boy handle one scary thing at a time."

"Still. You'll have to do it one day."

Jess sighed. "All right, I guess it is time." She turned to Gareth. "Have you got any strong booze at home? Whisky, brandy?"

"Er ... got some peach Schnapps from my sister's cocktail party, any good?"

She shrugged. "If that's the best you can do. Have a couple of stiff ones before our Bobbie's music festival next month, we'll do it then. You'll be safer in a crowd."

Gareth frowned. "Be a bit loud, won't it? I won't be able to hear a word she says."

"Fingers crossed, eh?"

Chapter 18

"Ross Mason playing his guitar for me naked. Think I had this dream once when I was 17."

We were in bed at Ross's flat, having what we'd rather creatively decided to call a planning session for our festival fundraiser. Ross was cradling his guitar against his bare chest, getting ready to play me the charity single he'd written.

He cocked an eyebrow. "Once?"

I smiled. "Ok, a few times. What's the song called?"

"Dark Sentinel."

"Oh." I rolled the title around in my head. "Yeah, I like it. Sort of sad though."

"The lyrics are a bit wistful. Optimistic too though, I hope."

I saw his normal, smiling Ross face change into his full-of-feeling singing face as he started the song. He was caressing the guitar softly with the same fingers that half an hour ago had played over my body just as skilfully, coaxing sweet, soft notes out of the strings just like he always could out of me.

… Watchman for the lost
In ruthless waters, weary-crossed
Sons and daughters, tempest-tossed
Were starred to shelter, hugged to home again…

The song seemed to channel all our feelings about the lighthouse, everything it had been, was, would be; all it had meant to the boatmen, the keepers, the town. As I watched Ross's face flicker with emotion and felt those deep, smooth tones quiver through me, I realised I was blinking back tears.

… Guardian of the light
Through grizzled dusk and deadly dark
The shattered husk once more will spark:
A spire of hope against the setting sun…

"That was beautiful," I said softly when he'd finished. "See? You made me cry."

He brushed a tear from the corner of my eye. "Wasn't that bad, was it?"

"It was perfect." I managed to push the tears back and smile. "You're a sentimental git under your jokes and your *Razzle* collection, aren't you?"

He tossed his head affectedly. "I was merely born with the deep, tortured soul of a poet, darling."

"All right, Lord bloody Byron. Is one's artistic temperament above a kiss for one's girlfriend?"

"Never." He leaned over to kiss me. "So you really like it?"

"I really do. How do we get it up on iTunes, do you know?"

"Travis knows a guy with a recording studio, he's offered to help me sort it," he said, putting his guitar down at the side of the bed.

I shook my head. "Only Edwardian Trav could have a carpentry guy, a recording studio guy and a porno guy side by side in his contacts book. So will you sing that at the festival?"

"Dunno, Bobbie, you honestly think I should play?" he asked, looking doubtful. "We've got some really good acts lined up."

"Yep, including you. And I'm not taking no for an answer." I pursed my lips. "See this? Bossy face. I'm boycotting any music festival that doesn't have a Ross Mason on the bill."

He tweaked my ear. "Cheers, love."

"What for?"

"Believing in me. Kicking me out of my comfort zone."

"Well, you're a talented boy," I said, blushing. "And I promise I'm not just saying that because of all the orgasms recently."

"Bet you are. But thanks."

"So what's next on the agenda?" I asked.

"Actually, you just gave me an idea about that." He leaned over to nibble my ear.

I giggled and pushed him away. "None of that. Planning first, sex for pudding."

"Meanie." He reached for his document wallet. "Fine, let's tally volunteers then."

"All right, who'd you get?"

He fished out a list of names. "My mum and dad, Judy from the post office—"

"Ha. Only coz she fancies you."

"Yeah, had to wiggle my arse like a right tart to get that one. It was like an x-rated Postman Pat in there. Pension day as well."

I looked up from the notepad I'd started taking notes on. "You trying to turn me on?"

"Always. Although I'm a bit disturbed that the image of me gyrating in a room full of OAPs gets you going."

"The pensioners are optional, if it makes you feel better. Who else then?"

"Chris from my old band says he'll be a steward if he can have a slot to perform his new single—"

"Oh God, no."

"What? You've heard him, he's not bad these days."

"If you like feeling depressed," I said. "I don't want herds of goths clambering up the barriers trying to chuck themselves into the sea, thanks."

"I can ask him to keep it light. Up the tempo or something."

"Right. And what's it called?"

"Er ... Death is the New Black."

"Yeah. Stick a drum beat on it, they'll be dancing in the aisles." I shook my head. "Sorry, Ross, no go. Tell him he can play a cover if he wants. Anyone else?"

"The usual conscripts. My brothers, Andy from the Crown, couple of his mates who said they'd man the bar. Oh, and Travis said he'd help if we let him distribute flyers for The Cellar."

I curled my lip. "Won't be on the letch again, will he?"

"Probably, but he'll be handy to have on board. He's got a van, for one thing. Anyway, you know you think he's funny."

"Ugh. All right. Is that it for you?"

"Yeah. Who've you got?"

"Well, Jess, obviously. Her boyfriend Gareth, my mum, some of the youth club kids to help set up; oh, and a bouncer I know said he'd lend us some lads for security."

"Reckon that's enough then?"

"Yep, that makes 14." I looked up from the notepad. "Hey. Aren't we forgetting something important?"

"You haven't kissed me in ten minutes?"

"That too." I leant forward to rectify the situation with a snog. "Mm. Watch the hands, gropey, we're not done. The other thing is, what're we going to call this? We need to make a start on publicity. It'll have to be something good, really hook 'em."

"Well, we're both writers. Sure we can think of something." He squinted one eye thoughtfully.

"So, you got anything?" I asked when he'd sat in silence for a while.

"Yeah, the horn. Shouldn't have kissed me first, should you?"

I shook my head, smiling. "You're terrible. Come on, we can't call it The Randy Git Benefit Concert."

He shrugged. "Worked for The Monkees."

I ignored him and started idly sketching the lighthouse's shape on my notepad. "Ok, how about … Festival of Light?"

"Bit obvious. Erm … Lighthousapalooza?"

"You still got the horn?"

"Yeah."

"You can tell, it's sapping your writing skills." Suddenly a lightbulb dinged in the back of my brain. "Ooh! Got it."

"What, the horn? Awesome."

I batted away the hands that had reached to embrace me. "Look, stop feeling me up for five minutes so we can name this bastard, can you? I've got the perfect thing."

"Go on then, blow me away."

"Ok, drum roll please."

Ross beat an obedient patter on the duvet until I held up my hand for silence. "Ladies and gents, I give you ... Little Stick of Rock and Roll."

He squinted one eye. "Meaning the lighthouse, yeah?"

"Yep."

"Ok, that is pretty good," he admitted.

"Ta. Since you're kind enough to say so, you can have another kiss."

"Your fundraiser planning skills are second to none. Also your hair is nice."

"Um, thanks," I said. "What was that in aid of?"

"Thought it might get me a feel of your boobs as well."

"Oh. Well you thought right, love. Help yourself."

Giggling, I let Ross pull me to him and planning was forgotten in the tangled joy of our two naked bodies.

Chapter 19

"Those bastards have been up with their spray paint again," I said to Ross as we walked up to the light-house a few days later, nodding to a fresh sliver of graffiti standing out against the old wooden door in the distance.

"They've ripped the thermometer too." Ross pointed to the laminated diagram we'd stuck up showing our fund-raising total. It was torn down the middle and flapping forlornly in the wind. "Little buggers need a slap."

I squinted at the door. There was something else, something not right...

Ross looked too, and I saw his eyes suddenly widen in horror. The next minute we were running as fast as we could towards the lighthouse.

"Jesus, Bobbie," Ross whispered. He pushed at the door, not needing the key. The lock had been forced, and the wood was creaking in the breeze.

I followed him in to examine the damage.

God, it was devastating. The floor was strewn with empty beer bottles, broken glass and cigarette ends. A puddle of vomit was giving off a rancid smell and the two windows nearest the ground had been shattered. But worst of all, the freshly painted walls were covered in graffiti, as far up as they'd been able to reach.

"Thank Christ we didn't leave the ladder for the lantern room, they'd have trashed the speakers as well," Ross muttered darkly.

I turned tear-filled eyes to him. "This is a disaster! What the fuck do we do, Ross?"

He slumped against the door frame. "I don't know," he whispered. "I don't know. After everything we did, the community ..." He shook his head, suddenly angry. "God, we should've seen this coming, that door's needed replacing for ages. Bloody idiots, the pair of us."

I felt the tears start to seep out and swallowed hard.

"Ross, the festival ... we'll have to postpone."

"What?" He turned to me, and I saw his eyes had water in them too. "No, Bobbie. All the acts have been booked, deposits paid, everything! We can't go back on it now."

I gave a bleak laugh. My head felt weightless, balloon-like, as if this wasn't quite real.

"We've only got a few weeks. There's no way we can get this sorted in time. No choice: we have to cancel." I gave in to heaving sobs and drooped against the arm he'd slipped round me. "Oh God, why would anyone do this?" I gasped. "They've ruined everything."

Ross planted a gentle kiss on top of my head. "Don't give up yet. We can fix it. Team Lighthouse, eh?"

"No, it's no good. It's ... too much." I could feel panic rising, threatening to black me out, and the smell of vomit was churning my stomach. "Oh God, oh my God ... I have to get out of here, have to ... sorry, Ross, I need to go."

I pulled myself away from him and ran out of the door, all the way to the cottage, sobbing as if my heart might splinter.

***

"Thought I might find you here."

Jess took a seat on the swing next to mine and started swaying gently.

I ignored her. I was staring at the little boat Ross had given me, which I'd set on the ground in front of the swing so I'd have something to gaze miserably at while I wallowed. There was a steady drizzle and my top was soaked through. I barely felt it.

"Still moping?" Jess asked.

"Yep."

"Hungover again?"

"Yep."

She stretched an arm around my shoulders, stilling my swing. "Come on, sis, it's been two days. This isn't like you. When there's a problem you look for a solution, then boss everyone about until it's sorted. You don't just give up."

"That's the thing, Jessie." I turned to sob into her arm. "I don't think there is an easy solution this time. You should've seen the state of the place. God, it feels like we're almost right back where we started."

She patted my head. "Then you just have to roll up your sleeves and sort it, don't you? You've come too far to leave it now."

"It'll take forever. And the festival ... it's ruined everything."

I stared blankly at the boat, the little faceless fisherman heading back to shore with his catch. There'd have been a real fisherman back in the day, in his sou'wester and hat, looking to the lighthouse for guidance through choppy waters just like in Ross's song.

It made me think about the place's history, what it had been when it was still a baby lighthouse. I could picture it back in the thirties, Ross's Great-Great-Great Uncle Wilf – was that enough greats? – sending out a huge spotlight to warn boats away from the deadly crags. How many lives had it saved that would've been dashed to pieces on the cliff? Poor old lighthouse.

"And what does Ross say?" Jess said.

"I don't know, I haven't spoken to him since it happened."

"What? Why?"

"He's been ringing me, but ... I can't face it, not yet. It'll make it too real."

"You're doing it again, aren't you? Hiding from something that scares you, just like you've been doing with that bloody novel of yours for the past year." Jess nodded to my jeans pocket, where my mobile was stashed. "Call him," she said. "You're partners. When there's a problem with the lighthouse you fix it together."

"Maybe that's what's so upsetting, Jessie." I choked back a sob. "The lighthouse goes with me and him, somehow. Seeing it like that ... I don't know, it's silly. All of a sudden I had this sickening feeling, like it's an omen or something. Like I might lose him."

"Don't be daft." She got up off her swing. "Right, you've moped enough. Come walk Monty Dog with me, clear your head. Then you can ring Ross."

"Don't want to," I said, sticking out my bottom lip. "Leave me, I'm staring at my boat. Got a lot of important boat-staring to do."

"It wasn't a suggestion, I'm telling you that's what's going to happen. Up."

"Nope. Fine here, thanks."

"Don't make me set Mum on you."

I rolled my eyes. "Ugh. All right, I'm coming. Hate you."

She smiled. "You don't though. Grab your little toy and let's go."

On the ground the little boat rocked lightly, as if buoyed by invisible waves.

***

An hour later Jess and I were following a yipping, frisking Monty along the pebbled beach. I was trying to avoid looking at the lighthouse; pretending it didn't exist so I could let the sea air clear my head unmolested by bitter thoughts.

Jess nudged me. "What's going on up on the cliff? Looks like a gang of people there."

I forced my eyes up. There was a crowd gathered around the lighthouse. Touching it. Touching my lighthouse.

"Oh my God!" I exploded. "They're back to do more damage, aren't they? Why can't they leave the poor thing alone?"

"Bobbie, wait!"

But I was already running for the cliff steps, Monty at my heels, determined to give whoever was up there the bollocking of their lives.

When I reached the lighthouse I froze in my tracks.

"Told you ... I'd get her ... here," Jess panted as she came up behind me.

Ross was painting over a patch of graffiti with a crowd of others, some I recognised from our painting party and some I'd never seen before. There must have been 50 or 60 people, painting and scrubbing like their lives depended on it.

I stared at them. "What's going on, Ross?"

He smiled, a warm smile that filled his face. "I made a few calls. Got a party together to blitz the damage. Nothing's impossible if we all pitch in, right?"

"You were able to get all these people here at such short notice?"

"Yep. Contacted the heads of the big local groups and asked them to email their members. People were queueing up to help when they heard what'd happened." He nodded to a man touching up one of the lighthouse's red swirls a little distance away. "Even him."

I blinked. "Langford?"

"Yep. Think he's finally realised opposing something as popular as the lighthouse project isn't a wise career move."

I just stared, feeling dazed.

"Come with me," Ross said. "There's a friend of yours here."

He took my elbow and led me to a man in his thirties painting out a streak of blue graffiti.

"Zaheer?"

He smiled at me. "Hi, Miss Hannigan. Strange seeing you outside college."

"I told you, it's just Bobbie. What're you doing here?"

He nodded at Ross. "Better ask him."

I turned to Ross, wordlessly demanding an explanation.

"I phoned Zaheer yesterday to ask if his company wanted to support the lighthouse project," Ross said. "He's going to be our official festival sponsor."

Zaheer had been in my A-Level English class for nearly a year now. Most of my students were adults who for one reason or another had missed out on the traditional qual-ifications and come back to them later in life: some with ambitions of going on to uni or improving their employ-ment prospects; others just for fun, to broaden their minds. I knew Zaheer was in the "just for fun" camp and that he owned his own company, but I'd never asked him what it actually did.

"What's the business, Zaheer?" I asked.

"Hussain Security," he said. "Heard of it?"

"No. What is it, bouncers?"

He laughed. "Not that sort of security. I've offered to donate materials to protect your property from future break-ins. My men will be up later today to fit a steel multi-lock door and repair the broken windows, and I'll arrange for an alarm to be put in as well. Anything for my favourite teacher."

"I said we'd include the firm's logo on all the festival publicity in exchange," Ross told me.

"Wow." I beamed at them both. "That's ... wow. Thanks, Zaheer."

"So do I get straight As from now on?" he said with a grin.

I grinned back. "Don't push it."

"Any idea who did it yet?" he asked Ross.

"No, but I took photos of all the damage. They're with the police now. Hopefully there'll be a few clues in there."

"Hope they get them." Zaheer shook his head. "Makes you sick, doesn't it? I'll never understand why some people want to spoil things for everyone."

"Yeah. Just to watch the world burn." Ross turned to me. "Here, Bobbie, come inside. Someone else you need to talk to."

I followed him into the lighthouse, and blinked in surprise when I saw who was there.

"Mum?"

"Hi, love," she said brightly. Her voice was muffled by the dust mask she was wearing as she supervised a group of youth club kids covering the walls in spray paint. "What do you think?"

"If we can't keep graffiti off the walls, better embrace it, right?" Ross said.

All around the room, covering the ugly graffiti, the kids were creating a sort of mural. It showed the lighthouse at sunset as it must've been in its heyday, light bursting forth from the lantern room, a fleet of boats just like my model heading to shore. The words Project Phoenix were coming out of the lamp beam a bit like the Bat Signal. It reminded me of Ross's song. A spire of hope against the setting sun...

"It's ... incredible, Mum," I murmured. "How'd you do it?"

"Young Josh is our Banksy. Made his day when Ross told him he could have all this space to play with, he's submitting this for his A-Level coursework." Mum nodded towards a lad of about 16 detailing the lighthouse's red and white twirls, frowning with concentration under his scruffy shoulder-length hair. "We can't take credit for the name though, that was Ross's. Now go on, get out, before the fumes knock you down."

"I can't believe you organised all this," I said to Ross when we were back in the fresh air.

"Just asked myself what my lighthouse girl would do." He threw an arm round me and gave my shoulders a squeeze.

"What she did was freak out and hide in a bottle of wine. God, I should've been here." I turned to face him. "Ross ... kiss me."

"What?" He frowned. "But there's people. Thought you wanted to keep it quiet till we were done?"

"Don't care any more. I want to kiss you and I want everyone to see."

"Bobbie, you sure that's – mmm ..." I stood on tiptoes to stop his mouth with mine and saw his eyes close as the kiss took him.

"So? What's everyone doing?" I whispered when we separated, still in the arms that had locked around me.

"Ignoring us, mostly," he whispered back. "Just got a thumbs-up off Mr Madison though."

"Heh. He's changed since school."

He held me back to look into my face. "So how does it feel to be my official girlfriend, Miss Hannigan?"

I sighed and nestled against him. "Never been happier."

Chapter 20

I dragged myself away from some festival publicity I was working on one Saturday morning to answer the door, expecting to find Jess, who'd gone to work without her key again. But the silhouette behind the frosted glass wasn't Mum or Jess or the postman. It was a stranger. I cursed the fact I was still in my dressing gown, flicking away a stray cornflake that had stuck to one lapel as I opened the door.

"Hello," a smooth feminine voice said. "Is this where the Hannigan twins live?"

The woman fluttering her falsies on the doorstep was an attractive, top-heavy redhead of about my age, with manicured emerald nails and eyebrows tweezed to within an inch of their life. She didn't look very Cragport, somehow.

"Yes, which of us are you after? My sister's not in, I'm afraid."

"Neither, I'm looking for Ross. His mum said I might find him here."

I felt my stomach jump suddenly. Redhead ... could it be her, the woman from the cafe? The hair was shorter but the colour was spot on. I tried to sound nonchalant as I answered.

"He's just upstairs. Who can I say it is?"

"Tell him it's Claire."

So that was it. The missus was in town.

***

I found Ross stark naked in bed, propped on one arm scribbling song lyrics into the notepad he always kept handy.

"Morning, sexy," he said when I'd plonked myself down, sitting up so he could give me a kiss. "Was hoping you'd come for a cuddle. Missed you when I woke up."

"Sorry, no time for cuddles now," I said, returning the kiss. "Someone at the door."

"Thought I heard it. Is it your mum? Should probably get some pants on if it is."

"No, it's for you. Claire."

I scanned Ross's face for his reaction, but he just looked blank.

"Oh. Right. What does she want?"

"She didn't say. Did she tell you she was coming?"

"No. My mum might've invited her, they're pretty close.

Or it could be about the flat. We agreed to lower the asking price when she was in town a few months ago so maybe we've finally got a bite."

I felt a surge of relief to hear him refer to it so frankly. So it had been Claire, the woman in the caf; not a date at all. And he hadn't lied to me, not on purpose. I should have known it was just my daft insecurities getting the better of me.

But there was something else mixed in with the relief. Jealousy? Guilt? As happy as we'd been since we'd become a couple, as confident as Ross was that we weren't doing anything wrong, a little nagging part of me still worried we should have waited for his divorce before getting involved.

"Well, better go find out what she wants." He threw off the duvet and started locating the clothes I'd ripped off him the night before.

"S'pose."

He turned to me, my tone alerting him to something not right.

"You ok?"

"Yeah ... guess so."

He pulled on his boxers and came to sit next to me on the bed. "Sorry, Bobbie, that was thoughtless. This must be weird for you."

"It is a bit," I admitted. "I mean, these last few weeks,

with you ..." I pinched my eyes closed a moment. "Sounds soppy, but I've never been so happy."

"Aww, love ..." He reached out to embrace me but I pushed his hands away.

"Let me finish, Ross. I want to get this out."

"Ok, go on."

"I've never had something like this before, even before it all went wrong with Alex. It's a bit strange knowing you have – that you cared enough about somebody to want to spend your life with them. It was easy to put it out of my mind when it was just me and you, but now ... now she's here, and I have to face up to it."

He took my hand and pressed the backs of my fingers to his lips. "That's the past. No need to be jealous."

"You loved her though."

"Of course, very much. But it wasn't the same as it is with you. I don't mean it was better or worse." He brought his hand up to caress my face, fixing me with that keen expression he so often had when he looked at me. "I don't know what I mean exactly, but I know you're unique. When I'm with you, it's not like being with anyone else."

I managed a weak smile. "That's how I feel."

He drew me into his arms. "I think me and Claire both realised it wasn't going to work about a year before it actually ended, to be honest. But we'd invested so much by then, made that massive commitment to each other, we felt we should try and salvage it if we could." He tipped my face up to leave a feather-soft kiss on my lips. "But I know it could work with you, Bobbie Hannigan from school."

"You're sweet." I lifted my hand to stroke his jawline. "Come on then. Let's go deal with the ex, then maybe we can have that cuddle."

He nibbled my ear. "Normal cuddles or sexy cuddles?"

I giggled. "We'll see what comes up."

***

When Ross and I were dressed and we came hand in hand down the stairs, Claire was where I'd left her in the passage. I hung back to let them talk.

"Er, hi," Ross said, smiling shyly. "You look well."

"You too," Claire said, looking just as bashful as him.

"You changed your hair."

She reached up to pat the seemingly immovable bob. "Oh. Yes. Do you like it?"

"Yeah, suits you."

"Yours is getting a bit long," she said with a smile, reaching over to ruffle it. Running her expensive manicured fingers through it ... the third finger sparkling through his hair, my boyfriend's hair ... Jesus, she was still wearing her wedding ring! After nearly two years separated. Ok, that was just plain weird.

Ross looked blank while the fingers combed through his hair. Claire blushed and jerked her hand away, as if she'd just realised what she was doing.

Suddenly, she started laughing. "Oh, this is daft," she said, flinging her arms around him. "Missed you, sweety."

Ross stood motionless for a second, then he laughed too and wrapped her in his arms, lifting her off the ground as he hugged her.

And all I could do was stand and watch. Because obviously I didn't mind, I mean, who would? If attractive, sophisticated women wanted to crush their double Ds against my boyfriend's chest while rubbing their fancy fingernails up and down my boyfriend's back, why on earth should I have a problem with that? Because I was unique, right? Brilliant.

"Oh," Ross said, disentangling himself from the embrace and blushing as he turned to face me. "Claire, this is my girlfriend, Bobbie. Bobbie, this is my – er, this is Claire."

"Hi," I said, doing my best to smile brightly while I shook her hand.

"Hi. Nice to meet you." I could see her doing the subtle eye-skimming thing down my body, curling her lip as she passed judgement on the faded jeans and t-shirt I'd hurriedly thrown on.

"So, shall we go through to the living room?" Ross asked. "If that's ok with you, Bobbie."

"Yeah. Great." My teeth were getting dry from maintaining the rictus grin I'd screwed on.

When Claire and I were seated, Ross went into the kitchen to make tea and I was left with the small talk baton.

"So what is it you do?" I asked.

"Graphic designer, same as Ross," Claire said. "You?"

"Teacher, adult education, when it isn't the holidays. Well, full-time teacher, part-time lighthouse keeper." I tried to summon a smile, but it seemed to come out one-sided, like a sneer.

She frowned. "Sorry?"

"Oh. Thought he would've told you." I jerked my head to the kitchen door. "Me and Ross have got a lighthouse. We're doing it up, sort of a project."

"Not Uncle Charlie's lighthouse?"

Seriously, she called his Uncle Charlie her Uncle Charlie? Oh, get me, I'm one of the family.

"That's right. Ross wants to turn it into a performance space for kids."

"Still on with that, is he?" she said with a dismissive laugh.

I tried not to glare. "Yes. He's very committed to it."

Luckily Ross came in before the icy tone-off could go to the next level. He handed out teas then looked from me to Claire, as if he couldn't quite remember which one of us he was supposed to sit next to, before throwing himself down on my sofa and curling an arm around me.

"So what's up, love?" Ross asked Claire when the awkward dust had settled. "Didn't expect you. Everything ok with the flat?"

Ugh, love, he was calling her love. He called me love. I mean, ok, this was Yorkshire: everyone called everyone love. But there was something in the soft way he said it that'd always made me feel it was mine.

"Sort of," Claire said. "We've got a potential buyer."

"Bloody hell, really?" Ross sat up a little straighter. "God, I thought we'd never shift it. Who?"

"Sweet young couple, just married," Claire said. "One viewing and they fell in love with the place. Bit of a problem though, they're stuck in a chain. It could still be a while before we see the back of it."

"Oh well, at least the wheels are turning. Sure I can leave it in your capable hands."

"Always, sweety," she said with a grin, fluttering her spider-leg false eyelashes at him.

Hang on. Was that flirting? Was she flirting over that capable hands line?

I could feel Ross's fingertips brushing my shoulder. At least that was reassuring.

"Oh. Brought this thing," Claire said as if she'd suddenly remembered. She reached into her handbag – designer, of course – and pulled out a little pearl-pink guitar pick. "Found it when I was clearing out the flat. I remember you used to say it was your lucky one."

He took it from her, their fingers brushing ever so lightly, not that I noticed. "Thanks, love. Good of you to remember."

He looked at her, and his face was different somehow. Frowning, but not angry. More like concentrating. Intense.

"Um, Ross," I said quietly. "The two of you have got things to discuss. Maybe I'd better leave you to it."

"No." He shook his head, as if to free himself of something. "No, Bobbie, there's nothing I don't want you here for. Don't go, sweetheart."

Claire looked at me with barely concealed dislike when she heard him use the endearment. "Yeah, stay if you want, it's nothing secret. I just wanted to drop these off."

She yanked a stack of paperwork out of her bag and dumped it on the table.

"Flat stuff," she said. "Needs signing."

"Oh. Right." Ross looked down at the pile of A4. "What, now?"

Claire shrugged. "No rush. I've booked a room at the Royal for three weeks, just drop it off before then."

"Bloody hell, three weeks! That's as much Cragport as most people can stomach in a lifetime. What for?"

"Just fancied a holiday. I thought it'd be nice to come and see the family."

The family, right. Ross's family. God, you'd think they were the sodding mafia the way she was going on.

"Anyway, you've got my number," Claire said, finishing the last of her tea and standing up. "Let me know if you're free for a drink while I'm in town – er, both of you, of course. See you, sweety." She nodded curtly at me. "Bonnie."

I knew it, I knew she'd do the fake name-forget! Classic. That must be page one, paragraph one of *How to be a Megabitch*.

It was weird. From the beginning, with Ross, it felt like there'd been a connection. Perhaps it had been a bit arrogant to think that was exclusively for me and him. But ... I had, all the same. And now, seeing him with Claire, it was like a carving knife to the ribs. Like he wasn't just mine any more.

Ridiculous. I knew he'd been married. That meant promising to spend his life with someone, and he wasn't the sort of man to take that on lightly. And yet to me he'd always just felt like Ross Mason, my boy from school. Suddenly he was someone else. Claire's Ross. Grown-up, married, 28-year-old Ross, with ten years of life under his belt I knew almost nothing about.

And it hurt. Irrational as I knew it was, it hurt like hell.

"So, what do you think?" Ross asked once Claire had

wiggled her tiny Versace-upholstered arse out the door.

"Nice rack on her. Shame she hates me."

"She doesn't hate you."

"Yes she bloody does. Most awkward cuppa I've ever had." I sighed. "Ross, are you sure this is all ok? I know it's a long time since you two were a couple, but … well, she's still your wife."

I badly needed him to reassure me. Guilt and jealousy were currently fighting each other for chunks of my insides.

"I keep telling you. She's my wife on paper, that's all." He pulled me closer to him. "I'm with you now, Bobbie. And there's nothing at all wrong with that."

"So is she seeing anyone new?"

"Not at the moment. She goes on dates though."

"What, she told you that?"

"Well, not in so many words," he admitted. "Not really something you talk about with your ex, is it? I'm assuming she does, she's got a pretty active social life."

"Hmm. So what was with the bitch queen from hell act then? She didn't seem particularly chuffed to find you'd moved on."

"Oh, don't worry about that, she doesn't mean it," he said. "It's always weird seeing your ex with someone new, isn't it? No matter how much you both know it's over. I bet you'd be just the same if Alex found someone else."

Someone else … I shuddered, remembering that whole horrible period of my life when I'd found out Alex had cheated on me and the painful break-up that followed. That awful feeling, knowing the person you loved had been touching someone else, betraying your trust in the most intimate way possible. It made me feel nauseous just thinking about it.

Ross looked at me with concern when he felt me shiver. "Sorry," he said softly. "I shouldn't have said that. Wasn't thinking."

"It's ok." I summoned a smile. "You're right, it would feel strange. I don't think I'd quite manage the full Joan Collins though. Claire seems to have a real knack for it."

"She'll come round. Honestly, you'll like her when you get to know her. She's a lovely girl."

"Maybe," I said, more to make him happy than anything. I was far from convinced the girlfriend and the wife were going to be braiding each other's hair and swapping friendship bracelets any time soon. "So come on, tell me the story. How did it end between you two?"

He sighed. "Not much to tell really. We met working for the same design agency in Sheffield, a couple of young people just out of uni. Went out, fell in love, moved in, got married. But it didn't work out. No one to blame, we just … fell out of love again. Grew up, changed. And in the end that's all the story there is."

"Ok, so what was all that about then?"

"All what?"

"All that. 'Ooooh, sweety, your hair's so pretty, I want to touch your face, have a sexy guitar pick', etc. Bit touchy-feely, aren't you?"

"I guess that was a bit weird," he admitted. "We were just together so long ... old habits."

"Well don't fall back into the old habit of sleeping together, will you?"

I was expecting a laugh, but he looked down at me, concerned.

"Don't trust me, my Bobbie?"

"No, I ... sorry, Ross. Just a bad joke."

"I wouldn't do anything to hurt you. You know that, don't you?"

"Yes ... yes, I know. I do trust you, promise." I leant across to kiss a stubbled cheek. "When did you know it was over?"

"Around three years ago, probably. We tried to make it work, but eventually we had to admit it was a lost cause. In the end we realised we were just too different to be anything more than mates."

"Different how?"

"In lots of ways. Hobbies, friends. And she never could get into the music. The more important it became to me, the more we drifted apart."

"She wasn't supportive of it?"

"It'd be easy to say that," he said, gazing wistfully into his past. "But no, that's not fair. It wasn't that she didn't support it, she just never got it. And Claire had dreams of her own just as baffling to me."

"So you were the one who broke it off?"

"No, it was mutual. We both knew we were fighting a losing battle." He sighed. "It's a funny thing, isn't it? When I made that commitment, I really believed it'd be for life. I don't know what's sadder in the end: saying goodbye to something you once believed in so strongly, or admitting that on some level you've failed."

I ran a finger down his cheek. "You didn't fail. Things change, that's all. None of us know the people we're going to end up being."

"Yeah, you're right. We were too young really. At 23, you're still finding out who you are." He smiled. "So are you going to stop being jealous and kiss me?"

"Yes. Sorry, Ross, I know it's bound to be a bit strange for you. Here." I pressed a tender kiss to his lips.

"Hey," he said gently, guiding me on to his lap so I was sat sideways across his knees. "Never mind Claire. Tell me about your dreams, Bobbie Hannigan."

I shrugged. "Not sure I've got any really. I mean, the lighthouse…"

"That's my dream, you just got pulled in. Come on, there

must be something you want out of life apart from tequila and lighthouses."

"Well ..." I started rubbing at a dusty mark on my jeans. "There's the writing, I guess. I've had the first draft of a novel sitting in a drawer for six months now. Always dreamed I'd finish it, maybe even see if there'd be any interest in publishing it."

"So why don't you?"

"I suppose it's like you with your performance space. I mean, how you felt before we started. Scared if I look at the manuscript again it'll show me it's worthless, and that'll be the end of the dream."

"Give over, you're a great writer. The publicity stuff you've done for the lighthouse has been brilliant."

I laughed. "It's only press releases, they're hardly going to win me the Booker."

"What about all those creative writing prizes at school?"

I heaved a sigh. "Long time ago."

"Look, why don't you let me read it?" Ross said. "I'm a writer too – well, sort of. I can give you some constructive criticism."

"God, you must be kidding. I can hardly bear to read it myself, let alone show it to anyone."

"You think I don't feel that way about my stuff?" he said. "All us creative types are insecure like that."

"That's different though. You're good."

"So are you. And once a few people have told you so, you'll be amazed what it does for your confidence."

"Well ... I'll think about it."

"That's my girl." He pressed another kiss to my forehead. "Now how about that sexy cuddle I was promised?"

"Thought you'd never ask. Let's go back to bed."

Chapter 21

The day of the music festival dawned grey but dry, which was as much as you could expect of Cragport. The weatherman said we might even get a glimmer of sun in the afternoon. I was a bit worried about Travis bursting into flames with that cellar-dwelling, undead vibe he had going on.

Tickets had been selling like hot cakes at a hot cake fan convention. It helped that Ross had got some really good acts on the bill – I mean, some of these guys had played Morecambe, they were that big. We'd sold around 150 tickets in advance and there were another 50 we'd kept back to sell on the door, which meant that at £15 a pop, fundraising was well under way. Ross had also managed to pull a few strings to get our one and only local celeb – an ageing thesp and one-time sitcom actor who'd been a pretty big name in his day – to open the event, a real coup for us.

Our little team of volunteers gathered early by the lighthouse to start setting up.

I'd just tipped out the bag of marquee poles and was puzzling over them, wondering which slotted into which, when someone tapped my shoulder. A nervous, smart Gareth was lurking behind me, his fair curls gelled and his cheeks even ruddier than usual.

"Hiya. Your mum here yet?"

"Oh yeah, it's your big meet-the-mother day, isn't it?" I said. "Where's our Jess?"

"She's abandoned me. Says I have to face it on my own. Your sister's kind of a terrible person, no offence."

"You don't need to tell me, love. She once fed my Barbie to the cat."

"Never mind that, is your—" He broke off as the words sank in. "Wait, how do you feed a Barbie to a cat?"

"Head first, apparently. Luckily Binky wasn't having it or that could've been a pretty solid vet's bill. Still, never felt right playing with that doll afterwards. The teethmarks round the eyes made it look like she'd had a dodgy facelift."

Gareth smiled. "You being funny to help me feel less nervous?"

"Yeah, is it working?"

"A bit. Thanks." He scanned the volunteers. "So is she here?"

I pointed out Mum, chatting animatedly to Ross as they slotted bits of stage together. "That's her."

Gareth's eyebrows shot into his curls. "What, with the green hair?"

"Yeah, why?"

He squinted at Mum. "She just looks so ... nice. Sort of young and fun. The way you two go on, I'd expected some rolling pin-wielding gorgon."

"Don't be fooled. I swear her fashion sense is just to lull our boyfriends into a false sense of security. Once she's decided she doesn't like someone, she goes the full dragon lady."

"Oh God." He sucked his lip nervously. "Er, hey, how about we jack this in and go for a drink? You fetch Ross, I'll text Jessie and tell her we're in the pub."

I laughed. "I have to run a music festival, you big wuss. Plus it's 9.30 in the morning. Look, she'll love you. You're easily the nicest lad our Jess has been out with."

He smiled. "Thanks, Bobs. Glad one of the family approves of me."

"So will Mum. Once you get the first ten minutes out of the way she'll be your biggest fan, I promise." I pointed to Mum giving Ross an approving slap on the arm. "See how she is with him?"

"Pretty chummy, aren't they?" Gareth said, shooting Ross an envious look.

"Yep. All she really wants is to see me and Jess with lads who treat us right. Once she's worked out you come under that umbrella, she'll be fine."

"Oh God, she's spotted me," he said, his eyes widening.

He was right, Mum was striding in our direction. When she reached us, she didn't muck about with idle chit-chat.

"I take it you're the young man who's here to see me?"

"Er, yeah. Nice to finally meet you, Ms Hannigan." He held his hand out, but she just eyeballed it suspiciously.

"What's that for?"

"Um, to shake?"

She scanned Gareth up and down. It was funny, watching the strapping rugby player quaking in his suit while this tiny woman examined him.

"Hmm. Let's see how it goes before we make with the handshakes, shall we?"

I laughed. "Come on, Mum, you're scaring him. This is a good one, I promise."

"I'll be the judge of that," Mum said, not taking her eyes off him. "Come over to the cliff for a private talk, young Gareth. I've got some questions for you."

Gareth's eyes saucered as she pulled a notepad out of her pocket. "Jesus Christ, you've got them written down? I've had less intense job interviews. Er, I mean, er ... Jiminy Christ, er, Cricket ... shit."

Mum grinned. "Don't worry, just a preliminary check. If

230

you pass we'll be best friends by the time our Jess gets here."

Gareth shot me a helpless look as he followed Mum to the cliff edge.

I could see them talking, Gareth's eyes glazed, Mum flipping through her notebook. After ten minutes she beckoned him to her and he planted a bewildered kiss on her cheek before wandering back to me.

"You passed then," I said.

"Er, yeah ..." He wiped his brow. "Wow. That was the most terrifying experience of my entire life."

"Well done. There aren't many lads who'd face a Mum interrogation for our Jess."

"Well. Love her, don't I?"

I gave his arm a pat. "You're a good lad. So what did she ask you?"

"God, it was like the Spanish Inquisition, minus the comfy chair. Everything from whether I'm a smoker to religious beliefs. No word of a lie, she actually asked me about my daily Vitamin D intake. Is she worried Jessie'll be left a widow when I die of rickets?"

"Heh, no. It's just to see if you crack under questioning. If she scares you off, it shows you're not committed enough."

"What, you couldn't have told me that before?"

I grinned. "That'd defeat the object, wouldn't it?"

He shook his head. "You Hannigans are all evil. Torturing innocent boys."

"Well, it's over now."

"For the time being." He grimaced. "Apparently me and Jessie have to go over for Sunday dinner next week. Or Round 2, as your mum calls it."

"Don't worry, me and Ross're going too; we'll protect you. And terrifying as Mum is, she's a great cook."

Ross was heading over now, leaving Mum to work on the stage with the other volunteers.

"Did you have to go through this as well?" Gareth asked when he joined us.

"Me? No," Ross said. "Janine's known me all my life, her dad was best mates with my Uncle Charlie."

Gareth glared at him resentfully. "You jammy bastard."

Ross grinned. "Yep. I learned early in life that schmoozing the mums of pretty girls would see me right one day. So have you come to help then, Rugby? Need another big, strong lad to help me sort the pop-up bar."

"Sexist," I said, nudging him.

He looked down at me with an amused smile. "Why, you want to do it, tiny?"

"I would if I was as big as you two. Don't see what being a lad's got to do with it."

He kissed the top of my head. "All right, She-Hulk. Next time I'll get you some protein shakes and steroids, then you can do the lot and me and him'll go down the pub."

I giggled. "And will you still fancy me when I look like an East German shotputter?"

"If I didn't I wouldn't dare say, you might beat me up." He turned back to Gareth. "So, can you give us a hand?"

Gareth glanced down at his Mum-meeting suit. "Not really dressed for heavy lifting. Might pop home and get into some jeans, have that stiff drink Jessie warned me I'd need. Won't be long, you guys."

***

Four hours later, we were nearly ready for the off. There were already a few people hovering by the gates, peering curiously past the two lads on security as we finished getting everything set up.

And I had to admit, it was all pretty bloody impressive. I mean, it was no Woodstock or anything, but for a small-town music festival it looked damn professional.

We'd done things on the cheap where we could and most of the stuff was a loan. There was the stage we'd borrowed from the playhouse, covered with an open-fronted gazebo Ross had scrounged from somewhere. Travis had lent a load of sound equipment from The Cellar, there was disco lighting from Mum's youth club and a couple of power generators Alex had borrowed from the council. Above the stage was an awesome banner Ross had designed for us. It showed a cartoon lighthouse made to look like a stick of rock, sliced in half with *Little Stick of Rock and Roll* written in a seaside rock font round the middle.

We'd left a clear area in front of the stage for people to picnic on the grass, with a huge marquee of the church's behind for shelter if it rained. Under it was a table with leaflets about the project, plus an industrial-sized barbecue of the Crown pub's. We even had merchandise for sale – t-shirts with Ross's stick of rock design on the front and a list of acts on the back, CD singles of Dark Sentinel and albums by some of the performers. Glasto could go suck it.

"How we doing then?" Ross asked, joining me under the marquee.

"Awesome. I think we're pretty much ready to go. Does everyone know their jobs?"

"Yep. Jess is taking first shift in the first-aid tent, Gareth's on merch and everyone else is on steward duty. Oh, and Trav's going to help us look after the bands. He wants to keep an eye on all his equipment."

"What about my mum?"

He grinned. "Oh God, it's hilarious. Haven't you seen?"

I frowned. "No. Seen what?"

"She's babysitting our star, they're at the bar. Honestly, you should see her face."

"Why, what's the matter?"

"You'll understand when you meet him. Come on. He's expecting to be introduced."

Ross took my elbow and guided me towards the lighthouse, where we'd set up the bar.

Anthony St John was Cragport's only "name". As a theatre actor, he'd been in rep at the Old Vic, worked with some of the greats – even Gielgud once, Ross had told me. But these days the old man was mainly remembered for a naff sitcom he'd starred in back in the '70s called *'Im Indoors*, one of those two-a-penny domestic affairs where the social-climbing wife's always throwing dinner parties and the hen-pecked husband's feuding with the neighbours.

Nobody saw much of him these days: in his early 80s now, he'd become a bit of a recluse. Occasionally locals would notice a reporter camped outside Anthony's gated house on the hill, trying to get a pic of him for a "whatever happened to ..." piece. But largely he was left to himself, which seemed to be the way he liked it.

The catch-up pieces the press sometimes ran on Anthony usually included phrases like "flamboyant", "tired and emotional" and "confirmed bachelor", those unsubtle codes the redtops use to let readers know when they think some-one's a camp old lush. In his glory days Anthony had always played up to his reputation. As Ross pushed open the lighthouse door, I could see not much had changed there.

"Did you tell him it was black tie?" I muttered to Ross.

"Nope. He just turned up like that."

The old actor was leaning up against the bar with a tumbler of something amber and alcoholic. He was in full evening dress: waistcoat, tails, spats, even a top hat. At a bloody music festival, Jesus.

Mum was next to him in her best tie-dye dress, green braids hanging over her shoulders and a glazed look in her eyes. It was all very odd couple. Jess and Gareth were milling around too, attaching decorative bunting to the walls to give the place a more festive atmosphere. Even with the bar to fill the floorspace, it looked very bare.

"Bloody hell, pretentious old bugger or what?" I said under my breath to Ross. "How did you get him here?"

"He's a friend of the family. Uncle Charlie was a mate of his when he was still just little Tony Johnson, they grew up on the same street."

"Really?"

"Yeah, the Johnsons ran a chippy down on the seafront. I reckon he only came so's I'd keep it quiet." He cleared his throat as we joined Anthony and Mum at the bar. "Um, Anthony, can I introduce my partner, Roberta Hannigan?"

"Enchanted," the old man drawled, holding out his hand to me.

"Er, yeah, nice to meet you —" That didn't sound like enough, with the level of formality he had going on "– er, sir," I added lamely, shaking his hand. "You didn't need to dress up just for us."

Anthony raised one bushy eyebrow. "Please, my dear! It's after luncheon." He drained the last of whatever it was he was drinking and turned to Mum. "So shall we abscond to the outdoors, Janine, my love? I feel I could benefit from a chestful of sea air."

"You sure you want to?" Ross asked. "There's a few reporters out there." We'd spotted a local news team parking up earlier, here to cover the festival.

"So they've caught up with me again, have they?" Anthony scowled. "Those appalling scavengers of the press. You know, all they ever wish to speak to me about is that damnable sitcom."

"Well it was pretty popular," I said in a flattering tone.

"'Pretty popular'?" he said huffily. "Sixteen million viewers is more than 'pretty popular', young lady. Not that it's much comfort to me now, when there were those who believed mine was a Dick the Third to rank alongside Olivier's."

I bit my tongue, willing back the giggle I could feel rising. Mum, noticing me struggling, came to my rescue and grabbed the conversation.

"Really, Anthony?" she said with forced brightness.

"Absolutely, my dear. I'm certain that if it hadn't been for that blasted sitcom I'd have had a knighthood in '76." He sighed melodramatically. "And instead I was pipped to the post by that bastard Attenborough. Yet there he is, with his bloody dinosaurs..."

Mum had a persecuted aura, like a woman who'd heard enough knighthood stories for one afternoon. I could see her eyes darting about, looking for someone to palm the old man off on to. They narrowed meanly as they lighted on Travis, who was just entering the lighthouse with more stock for the bar.

"Anthony, have you been introduced to this young man yet, Travis?" she said. "He's, er, very interesting."

Interesting was certainly one word for it. The gothic Gatsby had really outdone himself: tartan plus-fours and a straw boater, like a Wodehouse character whose valet was off his tits on magic mushrooms. Hearing his name, he glanced over, smirking suggestively when he spotted my mum. Over the course of the day, he seemed to have taken a bit of a shine to her.

"Talking about me, Ms Hannigan?"

She grinned back. Poor Travis, too innocent to know that was never a good sign.

"Certainly am. There's someone I want you to meet." He put down his crate of Heineken and swaggered over, looking pleased with himself.

"Travis, this is Anthony St John, the actor," Mum said. "Anthony, this is an oddly dressed pervert called Travis."

"Delighted to meet you," Anthony said, holding long, white fingers out for Travis to shake. "You're an interesting sort of young person, aren't you?" He examined Travis's Edwardian getup as if the younger man were a frantically flapping butterfly he was about to staple through the middle. "I assume you take both male and female lovers?"

Travis goggled at the casually personal question. I think it might've been the first time he'd met someone more genuinely Bohemian than he pretended to be himself.

"Er, neither, usually," he managed.

"But not through want of trying, eh Trav?" I said with a wink.

"You really should, darling." Anthony leaned confidentially towards him. "Let me give you a few words of advice from my 80 years treading the boards. Try everything once, be beautiful if you possibly can, always give of your best in life as in art, and get yourself up someone at least twice a week. That's the secret of a long life."

Behind Travis, Jess spluttered alarmingly. Gareth slapped her on the back, eyes watering as he bravely held back a snort of his own.

"Well, aren't you two getting along?" Mum said from behind her fixed smile. "Tell you what, Travis, why don't you take Anthony for a stroll around the clifftop? He's just told me he's gagging for some fresh air."

Travis's face was a picture. "What, on my own?"

"Mayn't that young man accompany us?" Anthony asked, nodding over Travis's shoulder.

Gareth's smile vanished. "Who, me? Why?"

"You look like a person of sentimental disposition." The old luvvie gave an artificial-sounding sigh. "You remind me of someone I knew well in my misspent youth. I should like to share with you some of my latest works."

"Your ... sorry, what works?"

Anthony tossed his white-maned head flirtatiously in Gareth's direction. "Why, my poems, you charming young rogue. Of course you know I write?"

I saw Jess nudge Gareth surreptitiously in the ribs with a look that said "humour him". I sent a look of my own to telegraph the same. Anthony was the only celeb we'd got, and I wasn't above pimping out friends and family to keep the old man sweet. If he wanted to read Gareth poetry and tell him he had beautiful eyes that was fine by me.

"Oh. Right. Er, yeah, course ... big fan, mate," Gareth said, smiling weakly.

"Really?" Anthony brightened. "Which do you favour?"

Gareth's eyes darted from side to side in panic, but there was no help forthcoming from any of us. We were all watching him with amused expressions – apart from Travis, who was sneakily trying to edge out of Anthony's eyeline.

"Oh, er ... what was that really good one you did?" Gareth fumbled.

"I take it you mean my epic narrative in iambic tetrameter, The Summer of Healing Hydrangeas?"

"Um, yeah, the epic wossit with the healing thingummies. Love it. Perfect beach read."

Anthony smiled indulgently at poor Gareth, but I'd noticed a twinkle in his eye. "Well I would be perfectly charmed to lend my moniker to your copy, if you happen to have it about you."

"Who's Monica?" Gareth whispered to Jess out of the corner of his mouth.

"He means he'll sign it for you," she muttered back, trying to suppress a giggle.

"Oh." He looked across at Anthony. "Er, you know what, it's – at home. Another time, yeah?"

Anthony's face spread into a mischievous grin. "You really are the most magnificent liar, darling." He nodded approvingly at Jess. "You have what we all secretly crave, dear lady. A beautiful young man who'll lie to you every day of your life."

Gareth's big, open face was a sight now, bright red and gaping like a tuna. Anthony was smirking all over, relishing the discomfort he'd created. Different as they were, I could see why him and Charlie Mason might get along.

"I won't, Jessie, promise," Gareth managed to gasp.

Jess grinned. "Ignore him, love. He's just winding you up." She turned to Anthony. "Come on, you old bugger, I'll mind you for a bit. You're kind of a laugh under your Oscar Wilde act, aren't you?"

"Pfft. Wilde." Anthony waved a dismissive hand. "A poor man's wit. If you wish to insult me, by all means compare me to Wilde."

She laughed and came round to link his arm. "All right, Noel Coward then. Let's get you some air before you drink the bar dry."

"Chip shop? Seriously?" I muttered to Ross as the two of them disappeared outside.

"Yep. It was his job to fillet the pollock."

"Well that was a lucky escape," Travis said to Gareth. "Thought he was going to drag the pair of us off for a poetry-recital-cum-threesome for a minute. Even I'm not hard up enough to be hitting the OAP crowd."

Gareth was still blinking. "Er, yeah – sorry, what just happened? Are my Jessie and the old actor bloke who fancies me best friends now?"

Ross grinned. "Sorry, Rugby, looks like it. She'll probably invite him round for Sunday dinner with us at Janine's next week. You two can play footsie under the table."

***

By the time the two security lads flanking the gap in the mesh fencing started ticket-checking, there was a huge queue buzzing excitedly.

I nudged Ross, standing next to me in an alcove by the stage.

"This is all right, isn't it?"

"Yeah. I reckon we're looking at a full house." He blanched suddenly and gripped my hand. "Oh God. Can't believe you're making me play a set."

"You'll be fine. You've got two hours yet to psych yourself up."

I noticed his face suddenly change, eyes narrowing as he watched people filter in. I followed his gaze to Alex, who was buying a ticket on the door.

"Oi. Be nice," I said, nudging him. "Alex did us a big favour getting all that paperwork fast-tracked, and the generators too. No glaring."

"Yeah," Ross muttered darkly. "Very committed to this project, isn't he?"

"What's that supposed to mean?"

"Nothing. Just nice to see so much public spirit, that's all."

I frowned at him. "Ross..."

He sighed. "Come on, Bobbie, I'm not blind. He still has feelings for you, it's obvious."

"What? Don't be daft."

"Then why's he doing all this?"

I watched Alex as he made his way through the thickening crowd to the lighthouse bar.

"He feels guilty about what happened, I think. Wants to make it up to me."

Ross snorted. "How can he make up for that?"

"Maybe he can't. Still, at least he feels badly enough to try. That's something."

"Does he know about me and you?"

"S'pose he must do by now. We've not exactly made a secret of it."

"Right. But you haven't told him."

"Well, no," I said. "Last time I called him it was about generators, it didn't seem the time for a chat about relationship statuses. Look, behave, Ross, please. I can't run a music festival while you're sulking."

"Why're you always defending him?" he demanded. "If someone had treated me the way he'd treated you, damned if I'd be having cosy little chats about bloody generators with them."

"I'm not defending him. I want a quiet life, that's all. Let's just try to be polite and stay out of his way, eh?"

But Ross wasn't listening. He'd been distracted by something happening over at the entrance.

I glanced over to see Claire, arriving arm in arm with Molly Mason, Ross's mum. She was all dressed up like a poodle's dinner again, festival glam in a pair of skinny jeans, low-cut top and some of those pink wellies with jewelled things on that morons wear to Glastonbury.

I turned an accusing gaze on him. "Oh no, Ross. You didn't invite her."

He looked down at the ground, kicking his feet against the stubby grass. "My mum did, all right? She won't be any trouble. I told you, she's a nice lass."

"Nice lass who hates me."

"Come on, don't be jealous. You're not allowed, not when you just told me off."

"I'm not jealous. I'm pissed off, it's different." I sighed. "Ok, ok, you're right. I guess I can be an adult about it if you can."

"Thanks, Bobbie," Ross said with a grateful smile. "I should probably go say hello to them. Can you babysit the first act for ten minutes?"

I forced an answering smile, pushing back the swell of jealousy rising in my gut. "Course. Take as long as you want, I've got it covered."

Still. I couldn't help feeling as I watched his shapely backside head in Claire's direction that trying to be the perfect girlfriend was a royal pain in the arse.

Chapter 22

Twenty minutes later, Anthony had managed to open the festival – albeit with the slightly slurred speech of a man who'd had a few too many whiskies for that time in the afternoon – and the first band had started up. Crooked Sixpence were a local four-piece who did a good line in Yorkshire folk-punk. I wasn't quite sure I believed in Yorkshire folk-punk, despite Ross's assurances it was a real thing, but it still sounded pretty good.

Ross was still with Claire. I was still in my alcove, minding the band and doing a bit of shifty side-eyes spying on my boyfriend and his wife. Which was one fucked-up sentence, when you thought about it.

Molly had left them to seek out her husband and older sons, all among the volunteer stewards wandering in high-vis vests through the crowd. Ross had just been to the bar to get Claire a drink and she was swigging red wine while she rested her emerald-green nails on his arm, just like I remembered her doing in the caf months ago.

She started laughing at something he'd said, jutting her sizeable cleavage in his direction like there were Ross-seeking magnets in her nipples. I couldn't hear what she was saying but I imagined it was something like "Oh sweety, you're soooo funny, do you like my enormous knockers? How about you leave Bonnie or Bessie or whatever and come back to mine for a Disaronno and a shag?"

"Ow," I said when I felt a dig in the ribs. I turned to find high-vis Mum, fixing me with one of her knowing looks.

"You know, if the wind changes that frown'll stick," she said, pushing my grumpy expression into a stretched-mouth smile.

"Mmmf. Geroff." I batted her hands away from my face. "Thought you were babysitting. Where's Anthony?"

"He's fine. Well, pissed, but he's used to that. Your sister's calling his car for him." She nodded at Ross and Claire. "I take it she's the one."

"Yep. The other woman."

"Technically that's you. You know, legally speaking."

I grimaced. "Thanks for the reminder, Mother. I've always been fond of the word 'adultery', the way it rolls off the tongue."

"I don't know what you're being all jealous for anyway. You know Ross isn't like that."

"She is though. Look, she's got her posh city-girl finger-nails all over him."

Mum shrugged. "So? He's with you now, love. Doesn't matter where she sticks her fingernails."

"Mm hmm." My gaze was still fixed on Claire feeling up my boyfriend's arm.

"You. Look at me," Mum said, tugging at my sleeve.

I sighed and turned to face her. It was easiest if you didn't try to resist, I'd learned while Jess and me were little.

"What? I'm not doing anything, am I? Just watching."

"I know you," she said, narrowing her eyes. "Don't you dare bugger this up with your trust issues, our Bobbie. Ross wouldn't cheat on you, no matter how many pretty girls poke their tits out at him."

"That's not just any pretty girl though, is it? It's his bloody wife. How am I supposed to feel watching her touching him up? Thrilled to pieces and up for a threesome?"

"Oi." She reached up to cuff my ear. "None of your smut, stroppy. Listen, I've known that lad since I held him in my arms as the tiny puking thing Molly Pennyman shoved in my direction to help me get some practice in for you two foetuses. I know what he's capable of and it isn't that."

"You don't know. He's been away ten years."

"Doesn't matter. You can't change someone's heart."

I pulled a face. "Eurgh, did you really just say that? You're like daytime soap opera Mum today."

"Yeah, all right, that did sound daft," she admitted. "I'm right though, take it from someone notoriously hard to please when it comes to daughters' boyfriends. Married or not, he wouldn't hurt you; not on purpose."

"I know. I mean, I think I know. It's just tough, seeing the two of them still so close." I nodded to Ross's mum, talking to her middle son Will near the lighthouse. "Claire and Molly seem pretty thick too. They were arm-in-arm when they got here."

"Molly's known her a long time, I suppose."

"Yeah, and she's known me all my life. She could make a bit more effort to bond with the current girlfriend. Claire swans around like one of the family when I've not had so much as a drinks invitation."

"I can have a word if you want? She probably hasn't realised it's upsetting you."

"No, don't make a fuss. Spose I've just been feeling it more since Claire turned up." I sighed. "So have you heard from Corinne lately? Been thinking about her."

Mum shook her head. "She can't write now her eyesight's going, poor lamb. I went to see her at the new place the other day though."

"Care home, is it?"

"Sheltered housing. She's got a lady who comes to help her out. There was a pile of washing up in the sink when I went round though, and no one had hoovered for at least a week. I sorted it, but think I'm going to have to have a word with the people who run the place."

"It's surreal, isn't it?" I said dreamily, my gaze still fixed on Ross and Claire. "You two getting so close. No offence, but if my husband had done that to me, you'd be the last person I'd want to see." My brow lowered as I thought about James. "Well, second to last."

"Your dad hurt us both. I think in the end it brought us together." She squeezed my arm. "But I can never bring myself to hate him completely. Not when I got my baby girls out of it."

"No, but I can," I said darkly. "Poor Corinne. You want me to come with you next time? I can get the place tidy while you two do the tea and chat thing."

"Best not, chick. I know she'd love to see you, but it'll only make her upset."

"S'pose so." I thought back to the one time we'd met, and her whisper when she hugged me: *you should've been my little girl.* "Can you imagine staying with someone after they'd done what he did to her? I can't."

"She doesn't see it the way you do though," Mum said. "You're young. It's hard to imagine how it affects you mentally, decades of being wholly dependent on one person. And trust me, your dad was a very magnetic man."

I forced a laugh. "So that's where I get it from."

Mum scowled. "What you've got is all your own. You

didn't get anything from him except life, and that only by accident."

"Good. I don't want anything off him."

"That's my good girl." She gave me another squeeze. "Wherever there are bastards there are cheating bastards, Bobbie. Married, single, men, women: there's Jameses and Alexes waiting for all of us who aren't savvy enough to spot them." She nodded to Ross. "But trust me, that lad isn't one."

"I know. I do know." I sighed. "Mum?"

"Yes, my love?"

"Do you think it was right, not waiting? I thought I was being silly, letting the James thing run away with me, but now she's here it seems ... Ross says it's all just paperwork, but I can't help feeling I'm doing something wrong."

She hesitated. "I don't know," she said at last. "You're not doing anything wrong, don't let that worry you. They're not a couple in any real sense. But waiting would certainly have made it all simpler."

"You think she still has feelings for him?" I asked, nodding to Claire. She was gazing at Ross while he talked, apparently rapt with adoration. Either that or her eyes were glazed with too much wine, but my money was on adoration.

"Maybe," Mum said. "But he doesn't for her."

"How do you know?"

She shrugged. "Dunno, feminine intuition? Trust me: whatever she's feeling, he's moved on."

I watched him laughing at something Claire had said, putting his arm round her shoulders briefly to give them a fond squeeze just like he did with me.

"Hmm." I dragged my gaze away with an effort. "Look, you better go relieve Jess in the first aid tent. The next band'll be starting in a minute, I'll have to show them where everything is." I sent another dirty look in the direction of Ross and Claire. "In the absence of anyone to help."

"All right, I'll leave you to it." She patted my arm. "And try to knock the jealousy on the head, eh? You can't let what happened with Alex or your dad ruin this for you. Just remember, she'll be gone soon. Then his divorce'll go through and everyone can live happily ever after."

"I know, I know, you're right. I'm just being daft as usual." I gave her a swift one-armed hug. "Thanks for looking out for me, Mum. I do appreciate it, you know, even when you're a right pain in the bum."

"Aww." She returned the hug. "It's worth being a pain in the bum to see you happy in the end. Just make sure you don't bugger it up, that's all."

***

"You took your time," I shouted over the music when Ross came back nearly half an hour later – not that I was counting. "Could've done with your help showing these guys how the equipment works." There was a blues and soul outfit on now, belting out an Aretha Franklin cover. I'd been doubtful when we'd booked them but they were actually really good. The singer had lungs on her that could bring down a zeppelin.

"Sorry," he said, looking guilty. "Got chatting about the old days, lost track of time a bit." He scanned the arena. "Where's Travis anyway? He was supposed to be helping look after the bands."

I snorted. "Over there, doing what he does best. Well, worst."

Travis, nicely recovered after his encounter with Anthony earlier, was sitting on a picnic blanket by a girl, leaning towards her with an oily smile on his face.

Ross blinked. "Is that Connie Hainsworth from school?"

"Yeah." I nudged him. "How does it feel to watch your former conquests getting Travised?"

"Heh. I did sleep with her, didn't I? Should probably do the chivalrous thing and rescue her." He shrugged. "On the other hand, let Trav have his shot. He's bound to strike lucky one day."

I tutted. "You're a bad boy, Mason. She'll be all right, as it happens. Her husband'll be back in a minute, I saw him go to the bar just before Travis turned up."

"Poor Trav. Oh well, he'll just try his lines on the next lass." He patted my shoulder. "Try not to be too upset, eh? I know you thought he only had eyes for you."

I sighed theatrically. "If I can, Ross. If I can."

***

Two hours later, the hippy duo on stage – the same one we'd seen at The Cellar – had just announced their final number. Ross's hand slipped into mine and I gave it a firm squeeze. His set was next, and I could see from the flushed cheeks that his stage fright had reached fever pitch.

"Don't be scared," I said. "You'll be brilliant. You're always brilliant."

"How the hell do I let you talk me into these things, Hannigan?" he hissed, his glazed eyes fixed on the 200-strong crowd. He put on a high-pitched voice and waved his hands about dramatically. "'Oh, hey Ross, remember me from school? Let's have a tequila slammer and buy a lighthouse, then maybe later you can make a tit of yourself in front of a fuckload of people ahahaha!' Think I've worked out who the evil twin is."

I elbowed him in the ribs. "Stop taking the piss. I did not say ahahaha. It's not really that much scarier than the pubs, is it?"

"Are you kidding? There's three times as many people

here as the biggest gig I ever played. And in the pubs they aren't even paying attention, it's just background music for a booze-up. This crowd –" he gulped "– these bastards are actually *listening*."

"Good. Then they'll realise how talented you are, won't they?"

"I hate you, Bobbie. You know that, right?"

"Look, you know once you're up there you'll be fine. The music in your head'll start playing and carry you away, same as always."

He turned to face me, looking surprised. "How do you know that's how it feels?"

"Shines right through your face," I said, smiling. "How come you still get scared, if that's how it always happens?"

"Recurring nightmare. Got this bone-crushing fear that one day the music won't play and I'll be left gaping like a turbot in front of a crowd of disgusted punters."

"And has that ever happened?"

"No. But it's only a matter of time."

"Well, here's something to bring you luck." I rummaged in my jeans pocket and handed over the present I'd got for him.

It was a 50p piece with a hole drilled into it, threaded onto a keyring. He dangled it in front of his face, looking puzzled.

"I don't get it, Bobbie."

"It's your 50p," I said softly. "The one you gave me the

night we got drunk. Thought it'd remind you ... you know, why we started all this. Like my boat does for me."

"Seriously, you kept it? That's really ... God. You're very sweet."

"When I'm not being bossy," I said with a bashful smile.

"Isn't it illegal to deface the queen's image though?" he asked as he tucked the keyring away. "Think it's technically an act of treason. Possibly a hanging offence. I mean, I'll miss you, but the law's the law."

"Yeah, and after that I burned a book of stamps and nibbled a swan. What you going to do about it, Mason?"

Ross laughed. "Think I'm supposed to make a citizen's arrest and drag you to the Tower. But it'll have to wait." He pressed a kiss to my forehead. "Thanks for making me laugh, love. Makes it harder to be nervous."

"That's my thing today apparently," I said. "So how about a proper kiss before you go up?"

"Mmm. Now that's the kind of luck I can work with." He pulled me into an embrace and brought his lips to mine.

After a minute I broke away. The hippy people had finished their final number. Crunch time.

"Your turn, Fonzie." I brushed a clinging Monty hair off his leather jacket and stood on tiptoes to peck his nose. "Ok, your collar's straight, your fly's up and you look handsome as sin. Get up there and give 'em what for, Ross Mason. Make me proud."

"Er, right. I'll try." He grabbed his guitar case, looking nervous again. "Break a leg, yeah?"

"Think I'm supposed to say that to you, aren't I?"

"Oh. Well, never mind, I don't really want to break my leg. If I can get off without being pelted with rotten veg it'll be as much as I can hope for." He shot me a weak smile. "See you on the other side, lass."

He turned to mount the stage, throwing me a final panicked rabbit look as he climbed the steps.

I was right, of course. As soon as Ross touched his guitar, he was away. Confident and calm, whispering against his mic like the crowd wasn't even there.

He was down to play a 45-minute set, all his most popular numbers. I was relieved he'd decided not to do Ivy Only Grows for the Wicked. Claire was lurking somewhere in the crowd, and for some reason it didn't feel right, having her hear my song.

Speak of the devil ... it was when Ross introduced Dark Sentinel at the end of his set that I realised the missus had threaded her way out of the throng and was standing at my elbow. She was slightly unsteady, her top even lower than it ought to be and her breasts heading chinwards with the aid of a push-up bra.

"Bonnie. All right?" Her voice was slurred, and I wondered what number the large red wine she was holding was.

"Come on, you know it's Bobbie."

"Ok, just a joke. You should get yourself a sense of humour, darling." I saw her scanning my outfit, not bothering to hide her sneer this time. "Like what you've done there. Heard retro was coming back in, very daring of you."

Ugh. Did this stuff come out of a book? Any minute now she'd tell me it was almost flattering.

"Makes you look quite slim. From a certain angle."

Yep, there it was. I glared at her, but remembering my promise to Ross, I forced a smile.

"Come on, you've had a few drinks. Let's drop the mega-bitch routine, eh? It'll only upset Ross. Don't want that, do you?"

"No." She blinked groggily. "No, I want to make him happy, like I promised. I ... I messed up before, didn't I? He went away." She glared at me. "D'you make him happy?"

"I hope so, yeah."

"I could do that. I used to do that."

"Well, people change. You weren't right for each other, that's all."

"People change. Right. What's his favourite colour then?" she demanded. "Bet you don't even know."

"Well, no, I..."

"It's aquamarine. Blue-green, like the sea. And his favourite film's *This is Spinal Tap*, and he likes raspberry sauce on vanilla ice cream but chocolate sauce on mint, and penguins make him laugh because of how they walk, and *Toy Story 2* makes him cry but he'll never admit it. And when he smiles his eyes sort of glitter and light his whole face up. Did you know all that?"

"The last one, I guess ... look, what're you trying to prove, Claire? It's not a competition."

"You're sure about that, are you?"

I pressed down another wave of irritation. "You're drunk or you wouldn't say these things. Let me call you a cab."

"Why're you being nice to me?" she said. "You're sposed to hate me. Go on, hate me, you know you want to."

I shrugged. "Maybe I don't know everything about Ross, not yet, but I do want to make him happy. And I know he cares about you."

Her eyes had clouded, and I could see her attention had wandered away to somewhere else in her drunken, sprawling mindmap.

"And what if we were right for each other?" she said absently. Suddenly, she burst into tears. "What if we were and I ruined it? Oh God, Bobbie..."

"Er, hey ... don't do that." I patted her shoulder, feeling helpless.

So this was weird, right? Me, comforting my boyfriend's wife while she sobbed. Yep, sounded like my life.

"Don't cry, love," I said gently. "It'll look different tomorrow. That's the booze talking."

Suddenly the head that had sunk down to her chest shot up. "What's this song? Did he write it?"

"Um, yeah," I said, bewildered in the path of her roller-coaster mood swings. "He wrote it for the lighthouse. We're selling it to raise funds."

She glared at me. "He didn't. He wrote it for you. Didn't he?"

I blushed. "He did write me one, but this isn't it."

"It is," she snapped. "The lighthouse ... he means you, I can tell. I've heard all his songs, the man's a wossit addict – metaphor, that's the badger. Listen."

Ross was singing the chorus, in tones hymnal and laced with longing.

… My dark sentinel
My friend and my support
Hold to me, my sentinel
Embrace me ever safely into port.
At the dying of the day, at the ending of the light
Keep my fear at bay against the lapping night…

Was she right, was it about me? Was the lighthouse always about me somehow ... about us? I wondered if Ross even realised, or if the idea was just there, lurking under his subconscious. Me and him and the lighthouse...

Claire was tottering ever more unsteadily at my elbow.

She'd just downed the last of her wine and was glaring at me with unconcealed resentment.

"Come on," I said firmly. "That's enough for today. I'll call you that taxi."

"I don't want a taxi. I'm fine here." She jabbed a finger at me. "You just want to get me away from him, don't you? I saw you staring at us before."

"Look, I'm not his keeper, Claire." I pushed back a half-smile when I realised what I'd said. Ugh, keeper ... it really was always lighthouses with us, wasn't it? "If he wants to see you, he will."

She looked at me suspiciously. "You're not even jealous?"

I laughed. "Well, I never said that. I'm not Supergirlfriend. But it's his decision who he sees, not mine."

To my surprise, her face broke into a grateful smile. "Really? You're jealous of me?"

"Er, yeah, I guess. I mean, you're his wife."

"Wife ... that's right, he loved me once. Enough to promise ..." She scowled. "It was supposed to be us against the world. How the hell did it all end up here?"

"It'll look different in the morning." I took her elbow and guided her towards the exit. "Time to go home now."

She blinked unfocused eyes at me. "Will you come?"

My eyebrows skyrocketed. So, what, we were friends now? God, this woman could make drunken mood swinging an Olympic sport.

"You remember who you're talking to, right?"

"Don't want to be on my own. We can go for a drink and talk about my Ross some more." She blinked in confusion. "I mean your Ross. Something like that."

I felt a stab of pity. She looked so vulnerable, her glazed eyes wide and her boobs about to pop out.

"Here, you're going to have a wardrobe malfunction," I said gently, helping her adjust her top. "I'll see if my sister can ride back to the B&B with you. You'll feel better after a lie-down, promise."

Chapter 23

When I'd finished putting Claire in a taxi, instructing Jess to stay with her until she was safely back in her room, I was hoping that was it for drama. All I wanted was for the rest of the festival to pass off uneventfully so me and Ross could get tidied up and go home for a cuddle.

No such luck, of course. I felt someone pluck my elbow as I strode down the side of the marquee and turned to find Alex, smiling vacantly.

"Oh. Hi," I said. "Glad I ran into you. I wanted to say thanks for sorting those generators. You've saved us a fortune on hire fees."

"Anything for you, Bobs."

I frowned at the flirty comment, and the slightly slurred way it was delivered. Alex seemed to be sagging, the blue eyes peeping through his Wayfarers just a little too bright.

"Have you been drinking?"

"Not much."

I knew instantly it was a lie. Alex had always been good at carrying his drink, but I'd lived with that man for nearly nine months of my life and I could tell we were in bottle-of-wine-and-best-part-of-another territory.

"Well, at least we must've made a killing on the bar this afternoon," I muttered to myself.

"What?"

"Nothing. Look, do you want me to get you a taxi? You look like you're all festivaled out."

"Not yet. I want to talk to you." He put one hand on my shoulder. It felt uncomfortable, like he was pinning me in position.

"Alex, please," I said in a low voice.

"Just give me a minute." His eyes flickered earnestly over my face. "I meant it, Bobbie, what I said at the painting party. I really have changed. You believe me now, don't you?"

I tried to shrug off his hand, but he shifted his weight to hold me there.

"Can you let go?"

"I told you, in a minute. Let me say what I've got to say first." He took a deep breath. "Is it true then?"

"Is what true?"

"What I heard earlier this afternoon. You and Ross."

I coloured. "What of it?"

His lip curled in disgust. "Oh God, you're sleeping with him?"

"He's my boyfriend, if that's what you mean. Look, could you let me get on?"

Alex's brow knotted into a worried frown. "You don't love him, do you?"

"I ... yeah." I flushed. It was the first time I'd said it out loud, although I'd known for a while in my own head. Funny the first person to hear it should be this one. "Yeah, I love him."

His face tightened in pain. "More than you loved me?"

I felt an instinctive stab of pity when I saw the hurt in his fast-filling eyes. But then I remembered who it was. What he'd done.

"I don't owe you an answer to that. Just go home, Alex. I can't talk to you when you're like this." With an effort I pushed the heavy hand off my shoulder and turned to leave, but he grabbed my arm to hold me back. When I tried to pull away he gripped hard with his fingers and spun me round to face him.

"Please, Bobs, just let me say my piece then I'll leave you alone. I love you, you hear me? No one could ever love you as much. Not Ross, not anyone."

I recoiled like I'd been shot. "You don't mean that."

"More than I've ever meant anything. I never stopped."

"Seriously? That's what all this has been about? Jesus Christ, Alex!" I shook my head in disbelief. "And you tell me like this, today. What the hell is *wrong* with you?"

265

"I wanted to tell you before, but it … it felt too hard. Talking to you so often these last few months about the lighthouse – it just brought it all rushing back, how we used to be together. When I heard about Ross I knew I had to—"

"Alex, please, my arm. You're hurting me." I made another attempt to writhe free, but he just held on tighter.

"Ok, so it was a lie, what I said that night at the painting," he said. "I mean, it wasn't a lie about wanting to make things up to you, but it was a lie about not wanting to win you back. Because I do want that, Bobs, even though I know I don't deserve it. It was never about the lighthouse, that was just an excuse to see you: it was always about you. I need you." He flinched in pain. "It's not really too late for us, is it?"

"What? *God*, yes!" I struggled again to pull my arm free of his grasp, but his fingertips dug painfully deeper into my flesh. "Let me go, Alex! I mean it, don't touch me. You're scary when you get this way."

"Just one more chance to earn your trust again. I swear you won't regret it." His features twitched feverishly. "I keep finding things in the flat … they've still got your smell on them, it's driving me insane. Just give me another chance to make you happy, please. It'll be all about you this time."

"About me. Right. Then tell me this: why'd you do it, Alex?" I was trying to keep my voice to an angry murmur so we wouldn't be heard over the soft-spoken female vocalist who'd taken over from Ross on stage, but it was a struggle. "If you're so sure we're perfect for each other, why'd you cheat on me in the first place?"

"I told you, I was lonely. All I wanted was to take you in my arms, help you, and you shut me out like I was nothing. God, do you know how much I needed to touch you?"

"So you went and found yourself someone who'd let you, did you?"

He cast ashamed eyes to the ground, but he didn't loosen his grip on my arm.

"Yes. Someone I could hold and comfort and pretend she was you."

I shook my head. "Do you even know how fucked up that sounds?"

"I'm not proud of it. I was selfish and immature. But I swear I'm not that man any more, Bobs. Everything I've done this last year, fighting the good fight on the council ... it's changed me. I can show you if you'll let me."

"Show me, are you insane?" I gasped, trying to fight the rising panic as I twisted to get free from his grasp. "Right now I can hardly bear to look at you. Get the fuck off me, it hurts. I'm not kidding, Alex."

"God, don't say that..."

Suddenly a man's hand reached around Alex and jerked the bruising fingers away.

"Not sure how it worked in whatever cave you crawled out of, mate, but round here when a woman tells you to get the fuck off her there's no debate: you get the fuck off her."

It was Ross. Of course it was Ross. Alex spun angrily to face him.

"Who asked you to stick your nose in? This is a private conversation."

Ross pulled himself up to his full height, towering over Alex like a ... lighthouse, for want of a better simile. "Care to come and have a, er, 'private conversation' with me, Alex? I'm not doing anything important right at the minute."

Alex sneered. "Really, you're asking if I want to take this outside? Aren't you supposed to throw a glove down first?"

"We're already outside. I'm asking you to leave my Bobbie alone before I thump you."

Alex fixed him with a resentful scowl. "She's not *yours*. She'll never be yours."

"No, she'll always be her own. Now are you going to fuck off or will I make you?"

At his side, Ross's hand balled into a fist.

"You wouldn't, I'd have you on an assault charge. This is real life, not that '60s *Batman* show."

"Maybe I wouldn't, maybe I would," Ross growled. "Touch her again when she's asked you not to and you'll find out."

"Just go, Alex." I shook my head. "You know, I'd really started to believe you'd changed. Everything you've done for the lighthouse, I thought you might be feeling some actual fucking remorse." I pulled up my sleeve and thrust my arm towards him. He recoiled in shock when he saw the angry red welts made by his fingers. "You see that? You know what that reminds me of?"

"Oh God," he mumbled, casting his eyes down. "Yes."

"You haven't changed. You didn't understand then and you don't understand now, and I never, never want to see you again."

Ross stepped forward to put his arm round me and we faced Alex together. "You heard the lady. Get out."

Alex hesitated, looked down at my sore arm again, then gulped down a sob. "Sorry, Bobs. I'm so sorry. I never ... just an accident, that's all. Accident," he muttered, before turning and sloping towards the exit.

Chapter 24

"Come on, love," Ross said gently once he'd evil-eyed Alex past the barrier. "Let's go up to the lantern room, eh? Trav can mind the bands while we take a break."

We threaded through the cheering festival crowd to the lighthouse. Inside, we navigated round the throng at the bar to the ladder we used to access the lantern room.

A few of those queueing chucked us a quizzical look, but most were too focused on getting the barmen's attention to notice us clambering over their heads. At the top Ross unlocked the loft-style door, heaved himself through and lifted me easily up after him.

We were letting acts use the room for storage and there were currently assorted guitars, a saxophone and – randomly – a banjolele propped against the circular window. Ross guided me to the bench in the centre and we sat, each with an arm around the other, looking out to sea.

"You ok, my Bobbie? Need anything?"

"Just you."

"You can always have that." He twisted round to kiss the tip of my nose. "How's your arm?"

"It'll heal," I said, rubbing at the sore part. "So you're very alpha male-y today."

"Aren't I always?"

"Only when it's sexy." I shuffled over a bit to snuggle against him. "Thanks, Ross."

"No need to thank me, gorgeous. Happy to be your knight in shining armour."

"I wasn't thanking you for me, I was thanking you for Alex. You just saved him from a pretty hefty kick in the balls."

"Ha! That's my girl."

"Did you hear much of that then?"

"Enough." He put one finger under my chin and tilted my face up so he could look into my eyes. "You want to talk about it?"

I made a choked noise as a sob stuck in my gullet. God, if we did this I'd have to go through it all again, the most painful – but it was him, wasn't it? Somehow it felt ok with him. Even if I didn't know his favourite colour.

Except I did, didn't I? Aquamarine, like the ocean. Our ocean.

"I'll try. It's tough, that's all."

"I know, sweetheart. Don't if you'd rather not."

"No ... no, I need to. No secrets."

"If you're sure," he said gently. "Just take your time."

I gulped, summoning courage from somewhere in my toes.

"It was all great, in the early days," I said. "We were happy. Not exactly love songs and rose petals but everyday sort of happy, you know? He seemed such a nice guy: thoughtful, principled. It was a bit of a whirlwind, and after three months when he asked me to move in with him, I just thought, yeah, why not? Then ..." I paused to swallow another sob. "Then this thing happened."

"What thing?" Ross's brow knit into a scowl. "Did that grabby bastard hurt you, Bobbie?"

"Not him. Someone else."

"Who?" I noticed his hand clench unconsciously at my shoulder and let out a tearful laugh.

"You don't have to go all punchy this time, this guy already got what he deserved. He's serving ten to twelve somewhere at her majesty's pleasure."

"Jesus Christ! What the fuck did he do to you?"

"Nothing. It's what he tried to do."

"What did he try to do?"

I lowered my head, fighting back the flood of tears threatening to overwhelm me.

"Hey," Ross said softly. "Don't go on if you don't want to."

"No ... I'm ok." I shot him a wobbly smile. "He ... this

bloke, he ... attacked me, down on the pier. Tried to drag me off down one of the ginnels."

"Oh my God!" Ross wrapped his other arm around me and hugged me tight, as if by holding me he could keep me safe in the past as well as the present. "Poor little Bobbie. You must've been terrified."

"Yeah, it was the scariest thing," I said, snuggling into the security of his arms. "If one of the doormen at Tuxedo's hadn't run over to help, God knows what would've happened." I pinched my eyes closed. "Well, no, I know exactly what would've happened. Same as happened to the other five girls who weren't so lucky."

"Shit! How did they catch him?"

"Gary, this bouncer, punched the bloke's lights out and sat on him till the police came. Then he stayed with me till I got home. Really nice guy."

"Did you have to testify?"

"Yes. God, it was horrible."

"That was brave," he said, rubbing a comforting hand down my back. "Proud of you, lass."

"It was worth it to stop him hurting anyone else. Came out in the trial he was a seasoned sex attacker round the coastal resorts, where he thought he could corner drunk women on their own." I scowled out at an unfortunate fishing coble that had bobbed into my eyeline. "Hope the bastard rots."

"Me too," Ross said darkly. "So Alex couldn't deal with it?"

"No, I couldn't. Just, the idea of sex, after that – made me feel ill, for the longest time. Started having panic attacks, nightmares, sleeping in a separate room. Didn't even want Alex touching me. When I remembered that guy's fingers digging into my skin, what nearly happened ... it haunted me. His smell, his face ... eurghh." I shuddered at the memory. "Every shadow was him."

"Only natural," Ross said, stroking my hair. "It takes time to heal after something like that."

"Alex didn't think so," I said with a bleak laugh. "He thought the guy would get put away and that'd be it, tra la la, back to normal, especially since – to quote him – 'nothing actually happened'. He couldn't understand why our sex life didn't just go back to how it had been before. So off he merrily fucked to find himself someone more accommodating." I shook my head. "Can't believe I was stupid enough to think he might've changed. Guys like him don't change. My dad taught me that lesson."

Ross directed an angry scowl of his own at the inoffensive fishing boat as it crested a wave out on the horizon. "God, if I'd known all that I'd have kicked him in the balls myself. What a first-class prick."

I lifted my head from his shoulder to plant a tear-dampened kiss on his cheek. "Thanks for caring enough to hate him, Ross. And for being everything he isn't."

"Well. I knew it was all an act: no one's that nice."

I smiled. "Come on. Did you think it was an act or were you just jealous?"

"Ok, so I was jealous. You were being all friendly with him, letting him help on the lighthouse ..." He kissed the top of my head. "Forgive me?"

"You know I do," I said. "Oh, speaking of mad exes, had to put yours in a taxi while you were playing earlier. She was well hammered."

"Really? Was she ok?"

"Yeah, she just needs to sleep it off. She was being pretty weird: she basically spent ten minutes slagging me off then asked if I wanted to go for a drink."

"Heh, sounds like drunk Claire," he said with a fond smile. "You two'd get on great once you got to know each other, she's good fun."

I fought back the jealousy I could feel prodding me in the belly. So Ross thought Claire was fun; so what? He thought I was fun. *Stop it, Bobs, you're ridiculous.*

"I did feel kind of sorry for her," I admitted. "She's lonely, I think. Hard to get to know her when she's gunning for me though."

"I know. But be nice to her, Bobbie, for my sake."

I sighed. "All right, if it's important to you."

"Thanks, sweetheart. I know it's a bit strange, but she won't be around long." He planted a lingering kiss on my

275

lips. "You know, you're something pretty special, lighthouse buddy."

"Not so bad yourself. Lighthouse buddy."

"Still a team?"

"Yep. Still a team."

But I couldn't quite squash the unsettled feeling in my gut as we made our way back down the ladder.

Chapter 25

It was with a sigh of relief that I heard the last act play the last note of their last song – Ross's goth friend Chris with his cover of Don't Fear the Reaper – and the crowd started filtering out, buzzing happily. Quite a few people stopped to tell us what a good time they'd had and wish us luck with the project, and some even offered to help tidy up.

When everyone had gone, we were left with about 20 volunteers armed with bin bags and marigolds.

"Did all right, didn't we?" Ross said as we spiked litter side by side. "Well done."

"Well done yourself. Forgot to say after all the drama: good job with your set. Proud of you."

"Thanks." He looked sheepishly down at an empty Coke can on the grass. "Did you hear them call for an encore? Must be my new lucky keyring."

"Yeah, I heard." I leaned over to kiss his cheek. "People know quality when they hear it."

I pinkened when I remembered what Claire had said. Dark Sentinel ... was it really all subtexty in a way I hadn't spotted first time round?

"Ross..."

"What?"

I shook my head. "Oh, nothing. Let's get some of the stuff packed up, shall we? Then I'm thinking we owe these guys a drink. Pub and a cuddle feels like the way forward."

"You read my mind." He glanced at the assorted family members, friends and people from the community who made up our team of volunteers, some litter-picking, others taking down the church's big marquee. "Although not sure about inviting these guys for a cuddle: maybe stick to buying them a pint. Let's get the sound equipment into the van while they're doing that, then we can all tackle the stage."

"Oh, hey," I said as we started dismantling the equipment. "You fancy coming round Saturday for film night with me, Jess and Gareth? Be nice to do the double date thing rather than watching them snog on my own."

"Hm?" He was taking apart a microphone stand, looking distracted.

"Film night, Saturday, my place. How about it?"

"Oh." He looked up at me. "Sorry, something on that night. Another time, eh?"

"Ok. S'pose I'll see you Thursday at the pub then, watch that new band."

He shot me a guilty look. "Did we arrange that for Thursday? So sorry, Bobbie, totally forgot."

I tried not to seem disappointed. "You can't make it?"

"No. Got plans I can't cancel now."

"You playing? I can come along."

"No, something else."

I frowned. Ok, that sounded pretty evasive. What something else, couldn't he tell me?

Since we'd become a couple, it had seemed like we'd naturally gravitated towards one another, spending most of our free time in each other's company. Was he ... Had I been monopolising him, not allowing for the fact he'd need his own space? Working together on the lighthouse and dating on top: maybe it was all getting too much.

"Ok, love," I said, trying to sound bright. "If you need some you time I get it. Let me know when you're free."

"Thanks, Bobbie," he said absently, his gaze flickering back to the mic stand.

I tried to squash a feeling of something not right lurking in the hollow of my belly – the same one I'd had when the lighthouse got trashed. I mean, it was nothing. Everyone needed time to themselves sometimes, right? There were certainly nights I'd rather veg out with a book than be with anyone else.

Still ... I hoped everything was ok.

***

Later that evening, our unofficial lighthouse committee was sitting round a table at the Fishgutter's with a drink of their choice each. Ross and I had splitsied a round for everyone, our treat. It felt like the least we could do after what for many had been a 12-hour day.

Somehow I'd ended up with Ross on my right and bloody Travis on my left. He was the only person at the table not having either wine or a pint, instead opting for a cocktail, some sickly concoction called a Flirtini he'd spent ten minutes describing to poor Gabbie behind the bar. I mean, with an umbrella and everything, he'd insisted.

Deep in conversation with Ross, I gradually became aware of Trav talking to my mum on his other side.

"Yeah, really tasteful, all the nudity's completely artistically justified in the context of the character relationships as they evolve," he was saying. "I can give you my card if you're interested, Ms Hannigan."

"Right ... sorry, Travis, did you say it was some sort of arthouse cinema project?" Mum asked.

"Oh Christ," I muttered to Ross. "Your turn-of-the-century pervert mate's trying to get my mum into his erotica."

Ross snorted. "Never stops, does he? Reckon she'd be up for it?"

I glared at him. "No I don't, you cheeky bugger. Come on, get him back on his lead."

He reached over me to tap Travis on the shoulder.

"Oi. Not that one, Trav."

Travis turned to smirk at him. "Aww, be a sport, Mason. I practically gutted my place to kit out your festival. Haven't I earned myself a bit of fun?"

"The sound equipment was much appreciated, mate, but not sure it quite buys you the right to recruit my girlfriend's mum for your mucky films."

Mum's eyes widened. "Bloody hell, is that what he was on about?"

I grinned. "Yeah, Mum. But don't worry, all the shagging's done to Mendelssohn. This is classy filth."

She shrugged. "In that case…"

Travis turned to her, brightening. "Really, you interested?"

"No. And watch it, sonny, I'm old enough to be your mother." She cast an unimpressed glance at his straw boater. "Although if I was, I'd probably try to hush it up."

Travis waggled his eyebrows. "And I'm not too big for you to put over your knee, right?"

"Oh God," she groaned, pinching the bridge of her nose. "I'm too old for this shit."

Next to her, Travis angled innocent eyes to the ceiling and started whistling Mrs Robinson.

Mum leaned round to talk to me and Ross. "Anyway, never mind him and his porn. Are you two going to give a speech or what?"

I shook my head. "What is it with you? You're obsessed with making me give speeches. Child abuse is what it is."

"Come on, one of you needs to. We've been working all day and we want some bloody adulation from the organisers, if it's not too much trouble."

Ross sighed. "Fine, I'll do it. It can't be as terrifying as the other ordeal your evil daughter put me through today."

He grabbed a biro off my notepad, stood and clinked it against his wine glass for attention. The buzz of chatter died down as all eyes turned to him.

"Er, right." He gave the expectant team a little wave. "Um, unaccustomed as I am to public wotsit and all that jazz, I'd like to say, on behalf of me and Bobbie ..." He looked down at me. "What would I like to say on behalf of us?"

"Thanks for your support?"

"Right. Thanks for your support." He looked at me again. "Prompt?" There was a ripple of laughter around the table.

"Ugh. You suck." I pulled him back into his seat and stood to take his place. "Sorry about him, he used up his inspiration when he was performing." I beamed round at everyone. "So on behalf of him and me, or in order of importance me and him, thanks for all your hard work. The event was a huge success and you should all raise a glass to yourselves." I waved my wine at them. "A toast to wonderful Cragport and its wonderful people, always there when you need them."

There was a chorus of cheers and glasses chinking.

Ross turned to his dad, seated next to our Jess bagging pound coins for the bank. "Any news on how much we've raised, treasurer?"

Keith smiled – actually smiled, a Cragport first, which meant we must've done well. "After expenses I've counted £823 on merchandise, £3362 on refreshments and £3000 on tickets. Once you've paid for everything you'll have over seven grand, lad."

"Bloody hell." Ross blinked a few times. "I mean … bloody hell."

"Is that enough to install your bar then?" Jess said.

"Yeah, and some. With the fundraising money donated by the schools and youth club it'll cover screens too. Um … wow." He smiled round at our little team. "Well, thanks, everyone. We couldn't have done it without you."

"So what's next, guys?" Jess asked.

"The biggest thing: balconies," I said. "Still waiting to hear from the lottery, but we're pretty optimistic." I beamed at Ross. "At this rate, we'll be ready to open in autumn."

"Well, I hope you're both proud of yourselves." Richie, the guy from the Clean Beaches Association who'd been at our paint party, raised his glass. "May I be the first to propose three cheers for Bobbie and Ross, saviours of the lighthouse? We all know how hard they've worked."

I blushed with embarrassment and pride as cheers

echoed around the pub. Under the table, Ross's hand gripped mine. It was hard to believe that for a mad drunken suggestion made nearly five months ago, the end was finally in sight.

Chapter 26

My summer holiday lie-in the following Thursday was cut short by the buzzing of my mobile on the bedside table. I fumbled for it, hoping it wasn't Alex – he'd been trying to call me ever since the festival, but after what happened that day he was the last person I wanted to speak to. The bruises on my arm were only just starting to fade.

But it wasn't Alex, it was Ross.

"Hi, love," I said brightly. "Listen, have you got time to read through the press release I wrote about the festival? I want to get it out asap with some of the photos."

"Ok." He sounded quiet. My brow furrowed when I heard him stifle a sob.

"Hey," I said softly. "What's up? Claire, did she—"

"Not Claire." He choked back another sob. "Charlie's gone."

"Gone? Where's he—" I broke off as my woozy morning

head wrapped itself round what he meant. "Oh ... no. I'm so sorry, sweetheart."

I paused to let it sink in. Charlie Mason ... well, he was an old man, we'd all known it had to come. But so suddenly, no warning. News like that always felt like a tree trunk to the gut.

And poor Ross. He'd been closer to Charlie than anyone. I willed myself calm, determined to help him through it.

"When did it happen?" I asked, making my voice as gentle as I could.

"In his sleep, last night. My mum found him." He made a strangled noise in his throat. "I'll miss him so much, Bobbie. Loved that old bugger."

"I know you did, lamb. Want me to come over?"

"Yes please." He paused to get his tears under control. "I mean, I knew he wouldn't be around forever, but it doesn't make it any easier knowing he's not coming back. And now there's the funeral to organise."

"You don't have to do that, do you? What about your dad?"

"That tight git? He'd stick the old man in a cardboard box and wash his hands of it. No, I won't have it done on the cheap." His trembling voice was laced with determination. "I want to give Uncle Charlie the send-off he deserves. He was like a grandad to me."

"You're a good boy, aren't you?" I said gently. "Let me know if I can help."

"I will. Thanks, Bobbie."

I sighed. If he was set on covering funeral costs himself, it was time to talk about something that'd been heavy on my mind for a while.

"Look, Ross. That 20 grand we put aside for emergencies – I want you to take your half back. You need it to live on while you're waiting for the flat sale, especially with this to pay for too."

"What? No, Bobbie. We're partners, we're doing this together."

"Please. I want you to."

"Absolutely not," he said, his tone firm. "You think Charlie would want me spending the money for Annie's lighthouse on his funeral?"

"But you need it."

"I don't, honestly," Ross said. "The cash from those big jobs I've had on'll cover it. Look, I'll see you soon for a cuddle, eh? Bye."

***

The sun blazed a joyous canary yellow and magnolia hazed the air the day we laid Charlie Mason next to his beloved Annie in Cragport Cemetery. And that seemed right, somehow.

When Ross and I arrived at church, holding hands tightly, I could see through the open doors the place was heaving. For all his oddities, the grumpy trawlerman with the pipe and smoking jacket had been well-liked around town.

Charlie's closest relatives – Ross's parents and his Aunt Lucy – were flanking the huge oak-and-iron doors, receiving cards and condolences from mourners. I was surprised to see Claire too, handing out Order of Service cards next to Molly Mason.

"What's she doing there?" I muttered to Ross.

"My mum asked her. Glad they're looking after each other, Dad'll be bugger all use."

"Shouldn't it be you though? You organised it."

"I couldn't face it. Don't think I could keep ... you know." He gulped back a sob, and I gave his hand a comforting squeeze. "Mum and Dad said they'd take condolences and I'm doing the eulogy."

When we reached the family group, Ross's dad Keith was looking the same amount of slapped-arse miserable as any other day, but his wife's eyes were red and swollen.

"So sorry, Molly love," I said when I'd given her a hug, handing over the With Sympathy card we'd brought. "We'll all miss him."

"Thanks, Bobbie." She summoned a watery smile and patted my arm. "He'll be up there roistering with your grandad like old times, I bet."

I smiled back. "Yeah, the two of them'll have drunk the ghost of Oliver Reed under the table by now. Pair of delinquents."

She managed a weak laugh. "Well, thanks for coming. Your mum and Jess are in there already." She jerked her head towards Ross, just behind me talking to his Aunt Lucy. "And look after our youngest, eh? It's hardest for him; he's never lost anyone he loved before. Not that it gets any easier, no matter how many you bury." She pinched her eyes closed for a second.

Claire, talking to an elderly lady ahead of me, heard Molly sob and stretched an arm around her. "You ok?" she asked gently. "Me and Keith can handle this if you want to take a break."

"No ... I'm fine. Thanks, Claire." Molly flashed her an affectionate smile.

I'd been avoiding giving my attention to Claire until I had to. I wasn't quite sure how to talk to her, after what happened at the festival, but I was determined to be polite. Ross was upset enough without any additional drama.

I plastered on a fixed smile as I shuffled down the line, leaving Ross and his mum to share a hug. There was an awkward pause while each of us waited for the other to open the conversation.

"Hi again, Bobbie," Claire said eventually with an embarrassed smile. Nice to know she could remember my name when it suited her. "Um ... did you know Uncle Charlie then?"

"Yes, quite well," I said, forcing myself to hold eye contact. "He was best friends with my grandad."

"Oh. Bert, was it?"

"Er, yeah." God, when it came to Ross's family she knew everything, apparently. "Did you meet him?"

"No, but Charlie talked about him all the time. Sounds like they were a right pair of hellraisers in the day. Well, I'm sorry." She shot me a significant look. "And I'm sorry. Really."

I got it. One sorry for Charlie, one for me. She was apologising for her behaviour at the festival.

I didn't quite know how to respond to that, given the feelings she obviously still had for Ross, but it wasn't really the day to be doing a Dear Deirdre about our relationship issues. I smiled weakly.

"Cheers, Claire," I said. "It's good of you to look after the family. We appreciate it, me and Ross."

She winced, but made a brave effort to repress. "You and Ross ... right. Thanks."

Had that sounded bad? No need to rub her face in it. God, was I the bitch now? This stuff was all confusing.

"Anyway, I've decided to stay another two weeks for Keith and Molly," she continued. "Thought they might need support while they get his affairs in order. Hope that's ok with you ... and Ross."

Two weeks! As if it took that long to divvy up Charlie's gnome collection.

"Oh. No, that's ... that's great. Don't you have to work though?"

"That's the good thing about being freelance. If I've got a laptop, I've got a living," she said, smiling.

God. With talk like that she'd be moving here next.

I took an Order of Service card and moved into the church to wait for Ross.

Claire's eyes were salt-swollen, just like Molly's, but she managed a bright smile for Ross as he moved down the line and enfolded her in a bear hug, her pupils sparkling like he was all she could see.

"So sorry, sweety," I heard her whisper, her lips close to his ear. "I know what he meant to you. If I can do anything just ask, ok?"

"Thanks," he murmured back. "Glad you're sticking around a bit longer, love."

So he'd known about her staying longer, had he? Known and not said a word to me. And she was offering to do anything to help him feel better: up to and including full sex, presumably.

I struggled to fight back the green-eyed thing rearing its ugly head in the pit of my stomach. No time for jealousy, not now. Not today.

Anyway, they were only doing what two people who'd

lost someone would naturally do. A hug, words of comfort ... all perfectly normal, I told myself, trying to make the voice in my head sound convincing.

And that bloody gold band glittering on Claire's finger as she rubbed it up and down Ross's back. That was perfectly normal too. For someone still in love with their not-quite-ex husband.

I almost sighed with relief when Ross let Claire go and came into the church to join me.

"You ok, lamb?" I whispered.

"I am now." He claimed my hand again. "Let's go find your mum."

St Barnabas's, known as Barney's, was 18th-century, heavy on the stained glass and brass, with that musty smell – a mixture of hymn books, melted wax and furniture polish – that old churches seem to have.

The last time Charlie Mason set foot in the place was probably when he'd come to see my grandad off four years ago. A scrappy old sinner with a patched-up soul, he'd once described himself to me – made me see where Ross got his poetic side from. Nevertheless, Charlie kept his faith in his own quiet way.

I scanned the old oak pews and spotted Mum, Jess and Gareth near the middle. We made our way over.

Ross slid in first, next to Gareth, who slapped him on the back.

"All right, mate?" Gareth said. "Sorry about your uncle. Let me know if I can do anything."

Ross slapped his back in return. "Thanks, mate."

"No worries, mate."

I was fast working out that a back-slap and a hundred "mates" a minute was some sort of lad code for expressing sympathy. Jess caught my eye and shook her head with a resigned smile.

She leaned over Gareth to squeeze Ross's hand. "Sorry, Ross. We all loved Charlie, he was a soppy old sod under those scary eyebrows."

Mum didn't say anything. She was staring ahead, clutching a hymn book she seemed to have forgotten about.

"Mum? You ok?" I asked.

My mum had been at least as close to Charlie as Keith and Lucy Mason growing up – probably a fair bit more – and I knew it was a bit like losing an uncle for her too.

I remembered what she'd told us at the painting party, how Charlie and Annie had looked after her when she was just a broke teenager with two demanding babies, and felt a stab of sympathy. She looked so lost, somehow, and child-like. There'd been a similar expression on her face the day we buried Grandad. One by one, the parent figures who'd helped her through the most difficult patch of her life had disappeared – Nana while we were still just babes in arms, then Annie, Grandad, and Charlie last of all.

"Hmm?" she said vaguely, lost in memories of her own.

Jess slipped an arm around her. "Ross is here, Mum. Don't you want to say something?"

She shook her head to bring herself back to where she was. "Oh. Yes." She turned to Ross with an expression of camaraderie in loss that was different than all our condolences. "Hi, Ross. You ok, my love?"

"Yeah, I'll be all right in the end," he said. "You?"

"Same. Bearing up, best as I can." She flashed him a sad, warm smile. "Me and you can have a chat in the pub after, ok? Do our remembering over a drink, that's what he'd want."

"That sounds perfect. Thanks, Janine."

I couldn't help smiling at the way we all were together. It was a sad time, but it was sort of nice too, the five of us saying goodbye to old Charlie. It really felt like we were a family now, each pair with their own special understanding. If it wasn't for the nagging presence of Claire, I might've felt that deity of choice was in his or her heaven and all was right with the world.

Chapter 27

A hum of conversation ripped through the mourners as the music started up and the pallbearers carried Charlie's coffin in. Eyebrows raised like a Mexican wave. There were even a few muffled titters, drawing stern looks from Wendy, the vicar, behind the pulpit.

"Erm, Ross ... did you choose this music?" I whispered.

His sober expression cracked into a grin. "Nope. Charlie did."

"Sorry, what?"

"He left instructions he wanted this playing when they brought his coffin in. My dad tried to veto it and have Abide with Me instead, but I dug my heels in and said if I was paying I'd have what Uncle Charlie wanted. Soon shut Dad up when there was a risk he'd have to pick up the bill."

"Good for you." I struggled bravely with the giggle I could feel rising. "The daft old sod. Why did he want this then?"

"It was the tune playing when he first saw Annie. Sweet, don't you think?"

"Yeah, but ... *In the Mood?*" I shook my head. "Never thought I'd go to a funeral where the pallbearers were soft-shoeing to Glenn Miller."

"I think it suits the occasion. Charlie'd want there to be laughter and not tears."

I squinted one eye. "Really? You think Charlie would want everyone to have a laugh at his funeral?"

"All right, no. He'd want everyone to be uncomfortable as hell so he could have a laugh at their expense." Ross scanned the embarrassed mourners, all struggling to decide whether they should laugh, cry or get up and have a boogie while the jaunty dance tune accompanied Charlie's coffin to the front. A few feet had started to tap unconsciously. "So I'd say that worked out pretty well. The old devil'd be pissing himself." He made a choking sound in his throat. "God, Bobbie. I'll miss him so much."

Suddenly his head drooped to his chest, his body convulsing as he gave in to grief. But he was laughing too, between the sobs, as if he couldn't help himself. Laughing, and crying, while the empty shell of old Charlie Mason made its way slowly to the front against the merry sound of a tenor sax.

I stretched an arm around him and shushed softly, glaring at an old lady in front who'd turned to give him a dirty look. What did she know about Ross's relationship with Charlie, or how it was appropriate for him to grieve? Judgemental cow.

After a minute, Ross recovered himself. He wiped his eyes and sighed.

"Daft to cry, isn't it?" he said, patting my hand resting on his shoulder. "I mean, he was no spring chicken. And for him to stay independent right to the end, just go quietly in his sleep ... not a bad way of seeing the sun set on the old bugger."

"Doesn't stop you missing him though, does it?" I said gently. "You cry all you want, my lamb."

He managed a watery smile. "Thanks, Bobbie."

"Anyway, he's with your aunty now," I whispered. "If you believe in all that."

"He believed it, that's what matters. And it's a nice idea, isn't it? The two of them back together, watching us work on the lighthouse."

"Yeah. We'll do them proud." I ran a gentle finger down his tear-stained cheek. "Been a weird few months, hasn't it?"

"I know. It's funny to think if it hadn't been for Charlie, we'd never have met again." He let out a wet snort. "And if we hadn't, I'd feel a right pillock when his will was read out and I discovered I'd inherited a bloody lighthouse."

I shot another glare at the old woman, who obviously

thought "bloody" wasn't appropriate language for a place of worship and had turned to give Ross evil eyes again.

"It does feel strange, the way it all turned out," I said. "Like fate or something."

"I know." He shuffled a little closer to me against the hard wood back of the pew. "Best thing I ever did, telling that bloke you had chlamydia."

Lady bloody Muck in front of us didn't have a problem with STD references in church, I noticed. She hadn't bothered looking round this time. I almost giggled as I imagined her pondering what a lovely name Chlamydia would be for her little shih tzu or something.

"So you want to come round mine after?" I asked Ross. "I'll make you my famous phone call to Domino's, we can get into our PJs and have a cuddle?"

"God, sounds great." He sighed. "But I should probably spend the evening with the family, do my duty as son and nephew. Not fair to leave the parents to Will and Joe while I'm getting snuggles really, is it?" He nodded at his older brothers, seated near the front with their wives and kids.

I felt a stab of worry. Was he bailing out again? It felt like this had been happening more and more lately: the evasive-sounding fob-offs, the excuses.

No ... I was being paranoid, wasn't I? Of course he wanted to grieve with his family. I mustered a reassuring smile.

"I guess not. Come round after if you get the chance, eh?"

"I will." He gave my shoulders a squeeze. "Best girlfriend ever."

Mum leaned round with a finger on her lips. She jerked her head towards the vicar, who was standing expectantly behind Charlie's coffin waiting for hush.

It's traditional after a funeral to say it was a lovely service, but this one really was something special – perhaps because Charlie had planned it himself. The hymns had an appropriately nautical flavour, beginning with the men of the Cragport Fishermen's Choir singing Those in Peril on the Sea. Charlie had been a member himself for years, before his Dublin pipe finally cost him his smooth baritone.

After Mum had recited Do Not Stand at my Grave and Weep, Ross gripped my hand. He looked flushed and twitchy, the way he did before he sang.

I gave his hand a reassuring squeeze. "Sure you're ok to do this eulogy, Ross? You're upset."

"I have to. Needs to be me."

"Guess it does." I kissed his cheek. "Good luck."

Wendy introduced Ross and he made his way hesitantly to the pulpit.

He cleared his throat and gave everyone a shy wave. Judging by the old woman in front's tut that was some sort of etiquette breach, but it seemed to help him feel less nervous.

"I met Uncle Charlie the day I was born," he began. "But I didn't know him till I was seven years old. The day he taught me to play cricket."

He skimmed his notes then pushed them away, looking over the crowd of mourners. Seeing how many friends had come to say goodbye seemed to give him confidence.

"We'd been through the basics, down on the beach," he went on. "How to hold the bat, the leg before wicket rule. It was while we were taking a break that he told me the story of how he met his wife Annie. And that's when I knew Uncle Charlie. Because you couldn't know him, not really, without knowing how he felt about the love of his life."

He paused to look over at me. I blinked back a couple of tears and smiled encouragingly.

"They met the year of the coronation, 1953, at a dance hall in town. The Cragport Palais – the building that's now Tuxedo's cabaret club. Uncle Charlie was at the bar with his old national service buddy Bert Hannigan when he first saw Annie. Those of you who remember this pair of likely lads will probably have seen them propping up a few bars in their day."

There was a ripple of laughter, and a few knowing nods from the older folk.

"That night a beautiful brunette on the dancefloor caught Charlie's eye. Red silk dress, pouting cherry lips, tiny waist just the right size to curl an arm around: a proper little darling, he told me, the spit of Jane Russell. So he winked at her, hoping she might come over." Ross laughed. "Well, that wasn't Annie. But she was dancing nearby to that old tune you just heard. She thought the wink was for her, gave her partner the slip and went to join Charlie at the bar."

There was another chorus of laughter. I was laughing too, listening attentively. I'd never heard the story of how Charlie and Annie met.

"Ever the gentleman, Uncle Charlie didn't let on he'd been winking at someone else. Instead he did the chivalrous thing and bought Annie a port and lemon. The two of them talked for hours, and by the end of the night they were engaged. Never one to waste time when he was onto a good thing, my uncle."

More laughter from the amused mourners. As eulogies went, this one was going down a storm.

"And that was it," Ross continued. "From that moment until she died 18 years ago, I don't think Charlie and Annie spent more than a day apart. He told her the night they fell in love he'd never let her go, and he never did." He made a choking noise, but struggled bravely to the end. "That was the love story that helped me know my

Uncle Charlie. Warm, impulsive, mischievous, fierce, eccentric, kind, quarrelsome Charlie Mason, who selfishly I'll miss every day, even though I know he's back in the only place he ever wanted to be. With his Annie. Thank you."

He descended hurriedly, and I could see from his twitching features that his tears wouldn't be held back any more. Instead of coming over to us, he strode up the aisle towards the door.

In her pew near the front, Claire turned to watch. I thought for a moment she was going to go after him, but after a second she turned back to comfort a tearful Molly.

Gareth nudged me. "Is he all right?"

"Think he just needs a time out," I whispered. "Wait till the next hymn, then I'll go check on him."

When the congregation stood to sing Guide us, Pilot, to the Harbour, I slid quietly from my seat and slipped out of the side door to find Ross.

I had an idea where I'd find him, and when I wandered out into the cemetery I saw I was right. He was standing by a headstone in blue-grey marble – Annie Mason's grave. Next to it, a man-sized hole waited to receive his Uncle Charlie.

I walked over and slipped my hand into his.

"That was a lovely story, sweetheart," I said gently.

"Felt like the right one to tell." He laughed through his

tears. "And to be honest, there's not many of Charlie's anec-dotes fit for church."

I laughed too. "Bit blue, were they?"

"Yep. You should've heard the one about the cabin boy, the can-can girl and the avocado."

"Sure I can use my imagination," I said, smiling. "So what happened to the other lass? The fit one Charlie was really winking at?" My eyes widened. "Oh God, it's not that old woman who keeps giving you evils, is it?"

"No, the Jane Russell lookalike's not around any more. You'll know the name though," he said, turning to flash me a tearful grin. "She married another navy buddy of Charlie and Bert's. Harry Hasselbach."

"You're kidding! Not—"

"Yep. Gracie Hasselbach née Holt, of bench fame. Bit of a raver apparently. In the fifties she was known as Hot Lips Holt round here."

"Bloody hell. She really did seize every day."

"Yeah. Along with a few other things, from what Uncle Charlie said."

"Ha! Naughty Charlie." I gave his hand a squeeze. "Come on, Ross, we'd better go back in. It's nearly over now, then we can do our remembering at the Crown."

"Yeah. Spose we should."

I turned away from Annie's gravestone to look at Ross. He was smiling at his memories of Charlie, but his lip was trembling and his cheeks were soaked. I remembered it: the emotional rollercoaster of loss.

"Hug first?" I said gently.

He blinked hard to push back his tears. "Yes please."

I wrapped my arms around his middle, thinking about Charlie, and Annie, and me, and Ross ... and the lighthouse. Always the lighthouse. Ross was right: all those things were twined together, like ivy. Their love story, and ours. Their lighthouse, and ours.

"Thanks for today, Bobbie," said a muffled voice from my hair. "Couldn't have got through it without you."

"Anything for my Ross," I said, pressing my lips to the nearest bit of him, the skin of his neck just under his ear. I sighed. "Love..."

"What?"

"There isn't anything you need to tell me, is there? If there's something wrong ... I'd rather know."

He sighed too. "Can't hide anything from you, can I? Yes, there is something."

Oh God ... was he finally going to tell me what had been happening? The lack of free time, the excuses? My stomach lurched unpleasantly.

"Charlie's death – that's not the only bad news I got that day," he said. "I didn't want to tell you right away, let you deal with the other thing first ..." He blinked down at the grass, resting his crown on my forehead.

"God, Ross, tell me quick. What is it?"

"The lottery bid. It's a no-go. I'm so sorry, Bobbie."

"What?" I sagged in his strong arms and he gripped me tighter.

"You know it was never a done deal. That's the most competitive source of funding."

"But – but what can we do? We've tapped everyone else. It'll take forever to raise what we need if we're relying on community fundraising alone."

"There's one other source though, isn't there?"

I shook my head. "Not the emergency fund. It's your own money, Ross. You need it."

"I don't, I told you. Anyway, I'm not spending our lighthouse money."

"Are you sure though? You don't know how long it'll be until the flat's sold."

"Hey." He planted a kiss on my cheek. "If you're willing to do it, so am I. Partners, aren't we?"

"Yeah." I smiled at him. "Yeah, we are, aren't we? Thanks Ross, I—"

I bit my lip before the word, that scary word beginning with L, slipped out.

"Come on, we'd better go back in. We can talk in the pub." Ross released me from his embrace and we headed into the church to say one final goodbye to Charlie Mason before he joined his Annie at last.

Chapter 28

"Hope your sister didn't hear that," Ross said as we lay panting in bed one Saturday evening.

"We honed our selective deafness skills pretty well when we were teenagers. She'll have the telly on full blast downstairs."

"Good." He grinned. "Because I've never heard you make that noise before."

"I make a lot of noises I've never made before when I'm with you." I leaned forward to kiss him. "Thanks, Ross."

"You're welcome. Er, for what?"

"For being sweet and gorgeous and great in bed."

"Oh. Well, right back at you." He returned the kiss with interest.

"So you fancy getting dressed and going down the pub?" I said, stretching. "Feel like I need a drink after that."

"That bad, was it?"

I laughed. "Let's just say my knees are still wobbling."

"Sounds good, but I shouldn't," he said with a sigh. "I need to go home and get some lyrics down, it's been ages since I've done any writing."

"Oh." I tried to keep my voice light. "Well, I could come too. Maybe I'd inspire you."

"Yeah, I know what you'd inspire me to do," he said, nuzzling into my neck. "I'd never write a word."

I giggled as he kissed along my shoulder. "Is that so bad?"

"No." He detached himself from me and threw off the covers. "But I really should go. You and Jess have a girls' night instead. I'll see you soon, eh?"

When he'd left I pushed open the door to the living room. Jess was reading with Monty on her lap.

I threw myself down opposite and sighed heavily. She didn't look up.

I sighed again, louder this time.

"All right, all right," she said, slapping her book down. "What this time, drama queen?"

"Him."

"What's he done then? Popping his cork too quickly?"

"He's off again. Won't tell me where, won't tell me why..."

"So?" she said. "Don't need to live in each other's pockets, do you? You already spend most of your free time in bed together or working on that bloody lighthouse."

"It's not that he isn't with me, it's that I don't know where else he is. He's so cagey."

"Did he not tell you where he was going?"

"Well, he said he was going home to write lyrics, but..."

"Then that's where he'll be," Jess said, picking up her book as if that ended the conversation.

"It's not just today though, is it? It's been going on for ages. Did I tell you what happened after Charlie's funeral?"

She gave a resigned sigh and put the book down again. "No, what?"

"I asked if he wanted to come back here for a cuddle." My face twisted in sympathy as I remembered his tear-stained face. "Thought he'd need one. But he said he wanted to be with the family."

"That's understandable, isn't it?"

"That's what I told myself. But when I rang he wasn't there. Molly said he'd left ages ago. And he wasn't answering his mobile."

Jess shrugged. "Well there's only so much of Keith the lad can probably stand in one sitting. Went home for an early night, I bet."

"Just seems odd he wouldn't come round here, that's all."

"Everyone grieves differently. You remember what Mum was like when we lost Grandad: she didn't leave her room for two days."

"Yeah." I blinked at the memory. "Poor Mum."

"Anyway, you're reading too much into it. Trust me, sis, he loves you to bits."

I sighed. "That's another thing. How soon would you expect someone to say they loved you, Jess? I mean, if things were going well?"

"What, has he not said it yet?"

"No. He tells me he likes me, tells me I'm special, tells me I'm beautiful, but he never tells me that. He's sweet as hell but it's like he goes out of his way to avoid it."

I made a clucking noise to call Monty to me. He jerked awake and bounded off Jess and into my lap. I petted the little guy absently, glad of the company.

"Oi. Dog thief," Jess said, frowning. "Anyway, Ross does love you, take my word for it. Thinks the sun shines out of your backside."

"Wish I could be sure of that. It'd be nice to hear it anyway."

"Then you tell him first. Not sure if it's made its way to the rock you hide yourself under, but there was this little thing called feminism a few million decades ago."

"Dunno. What if he doesn't say it back?"

"Look. Is this about that prick Alex Partington cheating on you again?"

I twirled Monty's white curls around my fingers. "No."

"Right. So you're not paranoid that Alice in Wonderbra's back down the rabbit hole with nipples set to stun then."

"Who, Claire? No."

She raised a single eyebrow. Jess could say more with one eyebrow than Roger Moore with a bloody facial tick.

"Ok, yes," I admitted. "Come on, what am I supposed to think? She's his wife, Jess. She as good as told me she's only here to get him back, and he's busy all the time, won't tell me where he's going..."

"You can't believe he'd cheat on you though?"

"No. But at the same time I can't help remembering I would've said exactly the same about Alex."

"Well, Ross isn't Alex."

"I know." I sighed. "Just wish I knew what was going on, that's all. If he's getting sick of me or whatever."

"He isn't getting sick of you," Jess said, waving an impatient hand. "Ross Mason's just about your ideal man, love, so stop being a knob and relax. If there's something up he'll tell you, soon as he feels ready."

"Or we could settle this now." I looked at her, eyes glinting with determination. "Hey, you had a drink?"

"No, got a shift at nine. Why?"

"Good, you can drive. Let's find out what he's really up to tonight."

"What? I'm not doing that!"

"Come on, just to set my mind at rest. I have to know, Jess. I just ... I have to know."

"Absolutely not." She folded her arms. "I'm having no part in your weird boyfriend stalking. Find yourself another stooge, darling."

***

Half an hour later we were parked outside Ross's flat, watching the light in the bedroom window.

"Happy now?" Jess said. "Look. He's working on lyrics, just like he said."

"Give it half an hour."

"All right, but then that's it. Told you, I'm working at nine."

"Aha!" I said, grabbing Jess's gearstick arm with both hands as Ross emerged ten minutes later carrying a large holdall. He chucked it in the boot of his Mini and got in.

"Aha nothing," she whispered back. "He's probably going down the gym. Pretty obvious you don't get a physique like that without working out." She dug teasing fingers into my hip. "Unless he's gone all *Rear Window* on us. Reckon there's bits of Claire in there?"

"Er, no. I might be willing to entertain the idea a man's been thinking with what's in his pants, not that he's a psycho killer. Come on, he's pulling out."

At a little distance, we followed the Mini through the garish lights glistering in multi-colour from the drizzle-drenched streets.

"Aha!" I said as we passed the turn-off to Cragport's only gym.

"All right, all right. Sure there's a reasonable explanation."

Eventually Ross pulled into a car park down by the pier. Lurking up a side street, we saw him take his holdall from the boot and head towards Tuxedo's, Cragport's down-market cabaret club.

I frowned. "What the hell's he doing at this dive?"

"Exactly. Not a place you'd bring a date, is it?" Jess said, looking smug.

"Unless you wanted to take them somewhere you wouldn't be spotted. Only tourists are dumb enough to come to Tuxedo's."

"He probably knows the barman or something. Look, I'm going to be late. Can we go home now?"

"No ..." I let my gaze dwell on the flashing bow tie in glaring yellow neon above the club. "No, I'm going in. You go back."

She pressed my shoulder. "You sure, Bobs? Don't like leaving you here on your own. Not again."

"I'll be fine. Ross is in there somewhere. He'll see me home ... if it's all ok."

"It will be."

"I think so too." I narrowed my eyes. "But I have to know. See you later, Jess. I'll text you."

***

When I'd finally followed the snaking queue to the door of the club, a burly skinhead in black tie and neck tattoos stepped out to confront me.

"Any ID, love?"

"Nope. What you going to do about it, you fat bastard?"

The man glared at me. Then he broke into a broad grin and flung himself forward to envelop me in a muscly hug, to the surprised mutterings of the mob queued up behind. Probably wondering if this was the kind of place where it was obligatory to let the bouncer cop a feel before you could get in.

"Hiya, Gary," I said through a mouthful of dinner jacket. "Missed you too."

"Nice to have you back, Bobbie. Been a while since you came to see me."

"Sorry, been busy. Got a lighthouse."

"So you said, you mental cow."

"That's me." I untangled myself from the hug. "Look, Gary – do you know a lad called Ross Mason?"

"What, the musician guy? Yeah. Good bloke, always shakes my hand on the way in. What's it to you?"

Always shook his hand?

I tried to sound nonchalant. "Just wondered if he was in tonight, that's all."

"Yeah, he's in." Gary lowered his voice. "Hey, if you want to see him I can sort you a VIP token, get you in free."

I smiled gratefully. "Cheers, Gary."

"All right, here," he said, surreptitiously pressing a gold

disc like a poker chip into my hand. "And if anyone asks where you got it you never heard of me, ok?"

"I won't grass, no worries. You're a good mate, Gaz." I turned to head into the club.

"Er, Gary ..." I said over my shoulder. "Did you see Ross with anyone tonight? Ginger lass, big boobs, sort of pretty?"

His brow furrowed into a puzzled frown. "Well, no."

"Ta, love. See you later." I nodded goodbye and strode into the club.

Tuxedo's was the same hive of mirrorballs, peacock feathers and sweat, full of tourists looking for the traditional cheesy seaside night out.

An illuminated semi-circular bar studded with diamante curved around the back of the room. In front of it, about 30 round tables were laid out for groups of six. A stage was backed by a black curtain dotted with little white lights, another huge neon bow tie, in blue this time, over the top.

Tonight there seemed to be some sort of Elvis tribute on, which meant a big crowd of middle-aged women in. The bloke was currently belting out his version of Love Me Tender while he wiggled his hips: typical end-of-the-pier stuff. Still, he wasn't as dire as a lot of the variety acts that passed for entertainment in Tuxedo's. Chuck in a few dirty jokes for his between-song patter and he could probably even make it to the dizzy heights of Southport.

I scanned the club, and felt my stomach lurch horribly when I spotted Claire. She was tarted up to the nines in a little black dress with cleavage practically touching her chin, sitting on her own at a corner table. Well, not on her own, or at least only temporarily. A man's grey jacket was draped over the chair opposite, and there were two glasses of wine on the table. Red wine. Ross's drink.

"Right, like that is it?" I muttered. "Ok, Mrs Mason, let's do this." I marched over to the table to confront her, face blazing with anger and humiliation.

But as I got closer, the only thing stronger than pure stomach-churning rage started to take over – good old-fashioned British awkwardness. By the time I'd weaved my way through the crowded tables, my march had turned into an embarrassed shuffle.

"Er, hi," I said to Claire, not making eye contact.

"Oh. Hello, Bobbie," she said, looking up from her wine in surprise.

"Look, I just came to – is Ross here?" I blurted out, my cheeks the colour of her drink.

She frowned. "Well yes, you know he is."

Oh God, humiliation overload. Could he really have done an Alex on me? Had I been duped by the kind of love rat who'd lure his ex to a club on the pretence his girlfriend knew all about it?

No, he couldn't, surely. Not Ross.

"Bobbie," a man's voice behind me said. "Didn't expect to run into you."

I spun to face him, shock written all over my face. It wasn't Ross. It was bloody Alex.

"Alex, why're you ... you're here too?"

"Clearly." He flushed to the roots of his blonde mop. "I've been trying to call you for weeks, you know."

"I know you have. I didn't want to talk to you."

"Look, about the festival. I'd had too much to drink or I never would've ... I mean I never meant—"

But I'd already turned away from him to Claire. "So would you like to tell me what the hell's going on?"

"We're on a date," she said. "Nothing wrong with that, is there?"

I blinked in surprise. "What, you two? Why?"

She shrugged. "Why does anyone? He asked, I said yes."

"We met at your music festival," Alex said, sinking back into his seat. "I meant to tell you. You wouldn't take my calls."

I curled my lip. "You've got to be kidding me. You turned up at the festival, told me you loved me then asked out my boyfriend's wife?"

He flushed. "No. Other way round."

"My ex-boyfriend and my boyfriend's ex." I shook my head. "There is something seriously wrong with you."

Claire's eyes had widened in shock. "You're her *ex*?" she said to Alex.

"What, you didn't tell her?" I said.

He fumbled nervously with his wine glass. "I thought she might change her mind."

"Well you were right," Claire snapped. "Jesus, Alex!"

"And you brought her to Tuxedo's," I said. "Classy, mate, proper fucking classy. Look, have either of you seen Ross? I know he's here, I saw him come in."

Alex let out a shocked laugh. "You're joking."

"What?"

"Honestly, Bobs, you must be joking. You don't know where he is?"

"Well, no, or I wouldn't ask, would I?"

"God, do you really not know?" Claire said.

I was starting to feel dizzy now. I leaned against the back of an empty chair for support.

"Don't you start. Come on, where is he?"

"Up there."

She pointed towards the stage. I gasped, actually staggering backwards as I looked more closely at the Elvis impersonator gyrating his pelvis for the appreciative crowd.

It was Ross.

Chapter 29

I mean, Ross Mason, my boyfriend Ross, playing his guitar right there on stage dressed as fucking Elvis Presley. Rhinestone suit, quiffed wig, medallion: the works.

Quickly I lowered my gaze, but it was too late. His eyes flickered over the crowd to me, looking uber-conspicuous in my scruffiest clothes, and he flinched with recognition. His face flushed scarlet as he struggled manfully on with Let Me Be Your Teddy Bear.

"You honestly didn't know?" Claire said.

"No, I ... he never told me." I shook my head, trying to free it of the mist filling it. The whole thing felt like a dream.

"You!" I said, spinning round to Alex. "God, that's pathetic."

He blinked. "What?"

I lowered my voice to an angry hiss. "That's why you brought her here, isn't it? To humiliate him. You petty, sad little bastard."

Claire stared at him. "Is that true?"

Alex flushed and looked down into his drink.

"Oh God," Claire whispered. "Did you even really like me? Or was this always about Ross?"

For a moment there was silence.

"Look, he deserved it, ok?" Alex burst out at last. "He's not good enough for her. And he's been lying to her too, see?"

"That's hardly something for you to get on your high horse about, is it?" I said.

"No," he mumbled. "But I told you, Bobbie, I've changed."

"And I told you I think that's bollocks."

"You can't deny he's a liar though, can you?" He nodded to Ross on stage. "Did he tell you about this?"

I hesitated. "No," I said finally. "But that doesn't mean—"

"And God knows what else he's been hiding from you. Ok, so I brought his ex here on a date to wind him up after she told me where he worked. I'm human, and I was jealous. But I'm still right." He brought his gaze to mine. "Think about it."

"He's never cheated on me. He'd never hurt me," I said, glaring back defiantly.

"You really believe that?"

"I really do."

He scanned my far from club-ready hoodie and jeans. "Then why are you here checking up on him?"

I flushed. I didn't have any answer to that.

"You know, there're still bruises on my arm," I said.

Claire stared at him. "Why would there be bruises on her arm?"

Alex looked down into his wine. "It was an accident," he muttered.

"It bloody wasn't." I turned to Claire. "At the festival, after you'd gone. He grabbed me and wouldn't let go."

"I was drunk, ok?" Alex said. "You know that's not really me, Bobs."

I shook my head. "I don't think I know anything about you any more. Not sure I ever did, not really."

"You did that to her?" Claire regarded him with undisguised disgust. "God, you're a piece of work, aren't you? Tell you what, Alex." She picked up her wine and threw it in his face. "Drink up, love. You've pulled."

He jumped to his feet, spluttering.

"Son of a *bitch!*"

Claire laughed. "Suits you." She stood and came over to take my arm. "Come on, Bobbie, let's get out of here. This date's over."

She led me to the exit, leaving Alex dripping and seething at their table.

***

Outside, Claire nodded to one of the wrought-iron benches that dotted the pier.

"Want to sit for a bit? I think we could do with a chat."

"Yeah, I'll join you in a minute. Just need a word with the bouncer."

Claire left me and I approached Gary, who was by the door doing his no trainers routine.

"Thanks for that, Gaz," I said, handing back the token he'd given me.

"No problem." He squinted into my face. "Everything all right? You kind of look like crap, no offence."

"Ta very much, mate." I managed a smile. "I'll be ok, just got a bit upset. Hey, fancy doing me a favour if I promise you'll enjoy it?"

"What?"

"Can you throw someone out for me?"

He frowned. "Well not without a good reason. Won't make me very popular with the management if I start chucking customers out all over the place."

"He's dripping red wine all over your starched tablecloths, if that's a good reason. It's Alex."

His scowl deepened. "What, that dickhead who was knobbing around on you?"

"That's him."

"Right." He rolled his sleeves up. "That's a plenty good enough reason. Back in a minute."

"Cheers, Gaz," I said, giving his tree-trunk arm a squeeze. "I'll just be on the bench over there. Have fun."

Smirking, I walked away to join Claire.

"You'll enjoy this," I said as I sat down. "Watch the door."

Two minutes later, Gary's huge frame emerged holding an obviously protesting Alex by his wine-stained collar. "Now bugger off, mate: you're barred," I heard him say. "And we'll be sending you a bill for that tablecloth as well, you little prick." He shoved Alex roughly out onto the pier.

"Ha!" Claire said. "You're right, I did enjoy that."

I turned to face her. "So. I guess we need to talk."

She sighed. "I owe you an apology first. I'm sorry, Bobbie, I've been a right bitch. It wasn't fair."

"Then why do it?"

"I think you know."

I glanced down at the ring glittering on her third finger. She followed my gaze and smiled sadly.

"Well, you're right. High time I took this old thing off." She twisted it from her finger and tucked it safely into her handbag.

"So did you come to get him back?" I asked.

"Sort of," she said, wincing. "I told myself I just wanted to see him, but the truth was our separation period was nearly up and I'd started feeling panicky about it being finally over."

"And you thought he might change his mind?"

"I thought he might want to give it one last shot before we closed the door on us for good," she admitted. "And then when I saw the two of you so close, everything I'd lost – God, it hurt."

"Bet it did." I reached over to press her hand. "I'm sorry too, I've been a selfish cow. I knew it was wrong, getting involved with him before the two of you were divorced. But he was so certain it was ok, that there was no one to get hurt ... it was only when I saw you together I realised you still loved him." I smiled. "We're neither of us perfect, eh? Trust a lad to get us acting like a pair of hormonal teenagers."

"I was worse though." She sighed. "And I don't know if I am, really. In love with him. I thought I was, when I came. Then there was Uncle Charlie's funeral, and when we hugged, it sort of felt like – something else. I hated to see him upset, but ..." She gave her head an angsty shake. "God, it's confusing. I don't know what I'm feeling these days."

"Did you love him when you separated? He told me it was a mutual decision."

"No ... well, yes. But it was a more friendly sort of love, we both knew it."

"So what changed?"

"I did, I suppose. All on my own suddenly in the city where it'd always been me and him. Oh, it felt great at first, all this new-found freedom and independence. The novelty of having my own place, dating again." She laughed. "I felt like Sheffield's answer to Carrie Bradshaw for a while. When me and Ross bumped into each other occasionally on nights out, it just felt nice to catch up. But then he moved back here."

"Why should that make a difference?"

"I'm not sure really. I suppose I always knew he was close by in Sheffield, even though we weren't seeing much of each other – there if I needed him, you know? As soon as he was gone for good, I just couldn't stop missing him. Then I noticed when he rang me about the flat my stomach flipped, like it was the highlight of my bloody life just to hear his voice."

I gave her hand a sympathetic pat. Poor lass. Maybe she had more in common with Corinne than I'd realised.

"When I was down a few months ago, we got laughing and chatting like old times, and I started thinking maybe we'd made a big mistake." She swallowed. "Then I came back, saw how he only had eyes for you, and that made it worse than ever, knowing it was too late. Except after the funeral, I wondered..."

"What did you wonder?"

"If I really was in love with him or if I just, you know, loved him. If I was missing those early days when we were two young people with all the future ahead of us, rather than Ross himself. Know what I mean?"

"Yeah, I get it. What did you decide?"

"I still haven't. But it doesn't matter." She turned to me with an odd expression of mingled wistfulness, resignation and a gladness of sorts. "He's yours now, Bobbie. And I'm happy he's happy, even if it hurts to let go."

I fixed my gaze on a discarded chip wrapper, flapping about from its prison under one leg of the bench. "If I haven't gone and ruined it."

"Trust me, he doesn't give up that easily." Claire's hand reached for mine and gave it a squeeze. "You thought he was here with me tonight. Didn't you?"

"Yes," I admitted. "Or I was afraid of it. He's been so evasive recently, I didn't know what to think." I nodded to the club. "How did you find out about this, the night job?"

"He told me last time I was in town. Thought it'd give me a laugh."

I shook my head. "Can't believe he's been lying to me. Why would he do that?"

Claire shrugged. "Embarrassed, probably. Bit of a weird one, with the costume and everything. Do you mind?"

"It is weird. But ... no. I don't care what he does so long as he's him. I just wish he'd been honest."

"You must know he'd never cheat on you though. Ross isn't like that."

"That's what my family kept telling me. God, I've been so stupid. There was something that happened, when I was with Alex ..." I pinched the bridge of my nose. "Well, you might as well have the story, while we're doing the bonding thing."

"What story?"

I pointed to the right of Tuxedo's, down the narrow ginnel between the nightclub and the novelty rock shop. "See that passage?"

"Yes, why?"

"About a year ago, some bloke tried to drag me down there and rape me."

Her eyes widened in horror. "Fuck! Were you ok?"

"Physically. Took me a while to recover from the shock though."

"God, Bobbie ... and you were still with Alex then?"

"Living together. But apparently his libido wasn't able to cope with a girlfriend struggling to get her head together after an attempted sex attack. That's when he started putting it about behind my back."

"He never! What, while you were ... shit, what a bastard." She curled a comforting arm round my shoulder. "I'm so sorry, love."

I looked at her when I felt the friendly arm go round me. Her eyes were wide with a sympathy that told me she understood, and I felt a wave of warmth towards the woman.

"You know, Ross was right. You are nice."

She laughed. "Not always, but I have my moments. So you want to share a taxi home now we're besties?"

"I can't go without seeing him."

Her eyes flickered over to the alley I'd pointed out. "You sure? I don't like to leave you."

"I'll be fine. My mate Gary'll look out for me."

"Well, if you're positive. Take care of yourself, Bobbie."

"You too," I said. "Thanks for ... well, whatever this was tonight. It's been nice. Or cleansing, anyway."

"Has, hasn't it? See you soon, I hope."

Squeezing my shoulder, she grabbed her handbag and headed off to the taxi rank.

Chapter 30

Over an hour later, I was still waiting. I'd been staring at the club's door since Claire left, not daring to look away even to text Jess.

I had no idea what I was going to say to Ross. When I thought about what I'd suspected, that stupid, corrosive jealousy, my belly clenched with shame. But I felt elated too, my pulse racing like I'd somehow be seeing him for the first time. Now I knew he was just Ross, the deep, dark secret he'd been hiding not another woman or a cupboard full of body parts but a daft second job, all I wanted was to get him into my arms and make things right.

If I could. The words burrowed lead-like into my brain. He'd forgive me ... wouldn't he? I mean, he had lied, neither of us could really claim the moral high ground.

And in and amongst the worry, occasionally, randomly, I'd burst out laughing. Because my boyfriend wasn't cheating on me. He was a bloody Elvis impersonator, and the whole thing was so completely absurd.

Oh God ... I felt my brain and stomach do a synchronised double-flip when Ross came striding out of the club, still in his ridiculous costume, looking around as if he expected me to be there. I ran to him before he could disappear.

When I got close I saw that under his wig he looked a combination of puzzled, angry and hurt. I winced when I registered the last emotion. I'd hurt him. I could put it on Alex all I wanted but in the end it was me, me and my stupid suspicions.

"Bobbie." His tone was confused; accusing. "Did you follow me?"

"Yes. Ross, I'm sorry." It was with an effort I managed to keep from launching into his arms uninvited. "I'm really sorry, I – it was a mistake, that's all."

"Let's not do this here. Come round the side." He took my elbow to guide me away from the front of the club, where Gary and a gaggle of interested smokers were watching us. Well, it wasn't every day you saw Elvis having a barney with his girlfriend in the street. One of them was already holding up his iPhone to get a video.

"No." I jerked back as Ross tried to direct me down the little alley. "Not down there."

"Oh. Right." His tone softened slightly. "Let's go over to the seafront then."

He guided me across the pier to the railing overlooking the beach.

"So how mad are you at me, on a scale of one to ten?" I asked quietly.

"You've seen *Spinal Tap*, right?"

"If you're doing jokes you can't be too angry." I tried to put my arms around him, but he held me back.

"You're wrong, Bobbie, I am angry," he said, his voice trembling. "But what I mainly am is confused. I want to make it right again, but—" He broke off, flinching with emotion. "God, do you know the torment it's been, making it through this last hour? Wondering why you were here, what you were feeling, and still having to do –" he gestured down at his white rhinestone suit "– well, this. It's not easy getting through all eight verses of In the Ghetto when you know your girlfriend doesn't trust you."

I narrowed one eye. "Was that another joke?"

"I'd call it gallows humour myself. Come on, tell me the truth. What did you expect to find when you came here tonight?"

"I ... don't know. I thought – well, no, I was worried you were here with ..." My voice faltered. "With Claire."

He shook his head, that ridiculous quiff wobbling in a way that would be comical if right then it wasn't so bloody depressing.

"We made a promise, Bobbie, to always talk things

through. You said you trusted me." He pressed his eyes closed. "And I believed you. What an idiot."

"I did trust you – I mean, I wanted to. I just needed my peace of mind back, that's all. You were being so evasive." I glared at him, my gaze lingering on the wide lapels of his disco suit. "And you're not so innocent, are you? How long have you been lying to me, Ross?"

He directed an ashamed gaze to the bare boards of the pier. "Since the beginning. It's just such a daft thing, I didn't know how to tell you."

"You told Claire."

"Yeah, but I'm not sleeping with her, am I?" He blinked, and when he spoke again his voice was choked. "In spite of what you thought."

"I didn't, not really. It was just, after Alex – it was so similar. The excuses, the caginess about where you'd been." I frowned at him. "Look, why didn't you just come clean instead of letting me fret?"

"I was embarrassed, wasn't I?" he said, going bright red. "New girlfriend and everything. It's not beyond the realms of possibility to think that sticking on a sparkly suit and thrusting my crotch like a twat at a room full of horny old women might damage my sex appeal to some extent."

I couldn't help smiling. "Nothing can do that, you good-looking bugger. Anyway, Elvis was pretty sexy. Well, he was for a bit."

"But Elvis didn't look like an Elvis impersonator, did he? He looked like bloody Elvis."

"Listen, you could be a drag act for all it bothers me. I don't care about that stuff, Ross, I care about ..." I trailed off into an exasperated sigh. "Look. Mate. Can you take that daft wig off if we have to have a blazing row in public? Feel like I'm about to get papped by the *National Enquirer*."

He folded his arms and turned to face the railing. "No."

"Ah, go on, grumpy Elvis. For me." I grasped his elbow and guided him round to look at me, my lip starting to quiver upwards. In a second it had caught him too, and before we knew it we were in fits of helpless laughter, stumbling instinctively forward into each other's arms.

"Can't believe ... I thought ... you might be having an affair with your own wife," I gasped, tears stinging my eyes.

"Can't believe I'm a fucking Elvis impersonator," he snorted. "Oh Christ, Bobbie..."

When the laughter subsided, he reached up to take the wig off and threw it down next to him. "There. Gone." His voice was soft as he hugged me to him. "So now I'm me again, how about a make-up kiss?"

"You were always you. Elvis wishes he was you." I tilted my lips up to meet his, running my fingers through his own gorgeous rusty hair as we kissed.

"I'm sorry, Ross," I murmured when he drew away. "You're

right, I should have trusted you. You're not Alex, I know that."

"No, it was my fault. It wasn't fair, sneaking about like that when I knew what you'd been through. God, what were you supposed to think, really?" He sighed. "The whole thing just felt so bloody ridiculous, I didn't dare 'fess up. Thought it might put you off me."

"Nothing could put me off you. Ever. You should know that, Ross." I stood on tiptoes to plant a kiss of forgiveness on his nose. "Tell me how it happened then. I'm guessing the Elvis tribute scene isn't something you just fall into."

"It kind of was actually. Answered an audition call in the *Free Ads*, about a month before we met again." He snorted. "'Wanted: talented baritone with own guitar for Elvis act, costumes and wig supplied.' Something like that. It was good money and the extra cash came in handy while I was waiting for the flat to sell. And then we needed investment for the lighthouse, Charlie's funeral ..." He breathed a heavy sigh. "Once the summer season started they told me I could have as much work as I wanted and I took the lot. More gigs, more sneaking around ... God, what a pillock. Should've known it wouldn't bother someone like you."

I squeezed him tighter, pressing my cheek against his heavily sequinned chest.

"Can I tell you something, Ross?" I whispered.

"Me first."

"Why you first?"

"Because I can guess what you're about to tell me, and I want to be first. Wanted to say it for ages, just ..." He nodded at the wig on the ground next to him. "Worried about that daft thing, I suppose."

I sighed as I felt him nestle his face into my hair. "Go on then."

"I love you, Bobbie. Have done for so long. I hope you know that."

I found myself choking on a sob as the words wreathed around me.

"God, Ross ... I love you too. So much."

He pressed a kiss into my hair. "Come on. Let's me and you have a romantic walk down the seafront holding hands like the old folk do, eh? I'll buy you a candy floss from the kebab van. And then if you're good I'll let you take me home and ravish me."

"Oh, right. One candy floss and you think I'll put out for anyone."

"And?"

"Yeah, go on. I love candy floss."

"Thought as much," he said with a smile. He ducked down to plant a kiss on my forehead. "I'll just go change out of this God-awful suit first."

"And what if I prefer you to leave it on while I ravish you?" I said, grinning suggestively.

"Seriously?"

"Ha, no. Just wanted to see the look on your face. Go on, lover, take it off; you look a right tit."

"Oh right, ta very much. You know, just for that I think I will leave it on."

"Don't you bloody dare, Disco Stu."

"Hey," he said, bringing his mouth close to my ear. "I've got late '50s Elvis at home."

I glanced up to meet his eyes. "The army uniform?"

"Yep. Goes down well with hen parties."

"God, bet you'd look well hot in that."

"Ta. I do actually. So, you want to dress me up like GI Joe?"

"No wig?"

"No wig."

"Well … twist my arm," I said, smiling. "You'll have to keep the hat on, mind."

"Course. Hey, did you mean that about not caring if I'm a drag act?"

"Yeah, why?"

"It's just Sunday's burlesque night, and, well, there was this Rocky Horror costume I had my eye on, with the fishnets and everything…"

My eyes went wide. "You are kidding me."

"Heh, yeah. Just wanted to see the look on your face." He leaned down for another kiss. "Back in a minute. Love you."

"Love you too, Ross." I hugged myself as his rhinestones twinkled back into the club, feeling the sudden freedom that comes with a last barrier to happiness disappearing.

Chapter 31

I shot off a quick text to Jess before we went to bed, letting her know what had happened and that I'd fill in the details next day at The Cellar. Ross was booked to play there in the evening, and he'd also talked Trav into letting The Karma Llama, a young band who went to my mum's youth club, play a set. They were just after him on the bill and since they'd never played to an audience before, Mum had asked us to go along and lend moral support.

We picked up Jess in the Mini and parked up outside Travis's mirror-panelled monstrosity around ten to seven. Ross, who was running late for his set, dashed off ahead to get ready, leaving us to make our own way.

Inside, we found a surprise waiting for us.

"Jesus, they're everywhere!" I muttered to Jess.

It was obvious this was some sort of theme night Ross had forgotten to mention. Goggles, brass and velvet top hats abounded. And cogs – oh God, so many cogs. I staggered backwards to let a well-bearded man in a leather kilt and colonial soldier's helmet barge past me to the toilets.

"Is this steampunk?" Jess whispered. "It's a bit ... rivety, isn't it?"

"Yeah, that does seem to be a theme." I giggled. "Hey, you ever wonder who Steampunk Zero was? Like some goth just woke up one morning, looked at himself in the mirror and thought 'hmm ... needs more pistons'?"

Jess laughed. "Or a Newton discovering gravity thing. One day your goth was sitting in the pub when an antique blunderbuss fell on his head, and eureka! Steampunk."

We pushed past a man in red leather armour and a Hannibal Lecter-type face mask to get to the bar. Red leather bloke was chatting to a heavily tattooed woman in a Victorian wedding dress and Doc Martens, her face painted down one side to look like a Day of the Dead skull. The most surreal touch to the whole thing was when I overheard a snatch of their conversation, conducted in broad Yorkshire accents and apparently about the difficulties the woman was having finding a decent handyman to lag her pipes.

"Ladies," Travis said smoothly when we'd fought our way through. "Bit underdressed, aren't you?"

I glanced down at my black pencil skirt and skin-tight green top. I'd actually made a bit of an effort, but when the person behind you in the drinks queue is in a polished brass basque with an ear trumpet and part of a hairdryer sticking out of the breastplate it's hard to compete.

"Yeah, if Ross had told us you were having a theme night I might at least have stuck on a topper." I grinned. "So you must feel right at home tonight."

"Actually it's rubbish. There's people who look even weirder than me, I'm getting bugger all attention," he said. "This gear doesn't come cheap, you know. Still, thought it'd be good to try something new, drum up a bit of business."

"Seems to be working." I scanned the throng of customers, reluctantly impressed. "You know, for a confirmed perv you're not a bad little businessman, are you?"

"Thanks. So what can I get you?"

"Couple of white wines please," Jess said.

"Coming up." He turned to pour the drinks.

"You're very well-behaved today. Not got any lines for us?" I asked while he busied himself with the wine bottle. "I've probably got a ladder in my tights you could exploit for chat-up purposes."

"Sorry, Hannigans, I'm afraid The Orgasm Machine's off the market." He handed over our wines with a broad grin. "Met her at your festival. Tell your mum not to be too disappointed."

"Bloody hell." Jess shook her head in disbelief. "What's wrong with her then?"

He pulled himself up with an affronted air. "Nothing,

she's a lovely girl. Chantelle." He nodded to one of the tables. "That's her."

I looked round, wondering if Chantelle came with either a labrador or a strait jacket. It was neither, but she did come with a distinctly Travisy vibe, steampunk with a flapper spin. She was all long pearls, fringed dress and purple hair, with the random addition of a golf club leaning against her chair. She also looked at least 45.

"She's a bit older than you, isn't she?" I said to Travis.

He shrugged. "Well I'm not going to start being picky now, am I? Mind you, if the pair of you want to reconsider that film offer…"

"We're good, thanks."

We paid and headed to a table before Travis could crank his lechery up a notch and his new girlfriend came over to sort us out with her vicious-looking nine-iron.

"Right," Jess said when we were seated. "You want to run that text you sent past me again? I'm still confused."

"Why're you confused?"

"Because last night at work I opened a text from my sister that basically read 'All fine. Just an Elvis impersonator. Off to bed.' Which even by her standards is pretty crazy. What does it all mean, Bobs?"

"What it says. He's an Elvis impersonator, that was the big secret."

"Not an axe murderer?"

"Nope. Just a little old Elvis impersonator."

Jess frowned. "What, like a closet one? Did you catch him parading round the bedroom in motorcycle leathers going 'uh huh huh' or something?"

"No, duh. He's been working down at Tuxedo's."

"So this isn't a sex thing?"

"Thankfully, no." I grinned when I thought back to the shenanigans of the night before. "Well, maybe when he's in the army uniform."

"All right, never tell me." Her eyes went glassy again. "Sorry, sis, you'll have to go over whatever you just said again. I drifted off into the weirdest daydream where you said Ross Mason likes to dress up in a sequinned disco suit and pretend to be Elvis Presley."

"Yep." I giggled. "That's my boyfriend, all-round hottie and Elvis to the stars."

"I see." She blinked a few times. "Ok, I'm not really down with what the kids are into these days, so maybe this is a stupid question. Still, humour your baby sister while she's on a learning curve." She paused to take a deep breath. "Why the fuck is he an Elvis impersonator?"

"For the money, obviously," I said with a shrug. "Apparently it pays quite well, the old impersonatoring. The club offered him all the work he wanted over the summer."

"Oh." She paused, then gave a final shrug of acceptance. "Ok, makes sense. Better than standing down the docks selling favours to lonely sailors, I suppose. Although with his pretty face he could rake it in."

"You are not pimping out my boyfriend, young Jessica. Ask Gareth to do it if you're so keen to get into the sex industry."

"Heh, he would as well. Fiver a scrum and 20 quid for a nice, hard tackle."

I snorted into my wine. "Stop it. You know I get giggly when you say tackle."

Her eyes glazed again, like she was still struggling to get her head around the whole thing. "God, does he have to wear the wig and everything?"

"And worse. There was a medallion."

She looked over at him on his stool up front and shook her head. "The poor lad. So how do you feel about it?"

I followed her gaze to Ross making love to his microphone, his eyes tight closed. It was a romantic song, low and sad, and his features were twitching with emotion. I felt a twinge of compassion for whatever he was feeling; a sudden desire to put my arms round him. His songs could get you like that.

"Well, it's surreal," I said at last. "But once I'd got over the shock I just felt relieved really. Considering what I was worried about, Elvis impersonating's no big deal." I glanced at Ross again, noting how tired he looked. Ok, that was partly because we'd stayed up late for some sexy fun, but

I was still concerned about the long hours he'd been working. "I suppose my biggest worry is he'll burn out, working at the club on top of the day job and the light-house."

"He does look shattered. You'd better look after him, Bobs."

"I will." I blushed, fiddling with my wine glass. "Guess what he told me last night after we'd kissed and made up?"

"No!"

"Yep. Said he'd wanted to say it for ages, but he was worried about the Elvis thing."

"Aww. Told you, didn't I?" She stretched an arm round my shoulders. "Happy for you, sis."

"Cheers, Jessie." I smiled. "You know, I actually had a great night, weird as it was. Found out my boyfriend isn't either a cheat or a serial killer, heard him say he loves me, watched my knobhead ex get a wine in the face and made my peace with the femme fatale I thought was after my bloke. And then there was candy floss, cuddles, sex and more cuddles with a fit man in uniform. Result."

"All right, Priscilla, now you're just making me feel like a low achiever."

"Why, what delights did your stint on A&E hold?"

"Well I made up a new game. Want to play? I call it Sick or Thick."

I sighed. "Go on then."

"Ok, I'll tell you the symptoms, you tell me if the person's genuinely ill or just dim. Easy one to start you off. Stomach cramps and flatulence."

"Sick?"

"Nope, thick," Jess said. "Daft cow had been doing that cabbage soup diet. Sent her home with a prescription for a bag of pasta. Right, next: bleeding from the ear."

"Thick. Cleaning their ear out with a safety pin or something."

"Correct. Except it wasn't a safety pin."

"Well, what was it?"

She shook her head. "A bloody Black and Decker drill. Switched on. Pillock said it was itchy in there."

"Ouch. And what did you prescribe for that one?"

"Well I wanted to prescribe withdrawal from the human race on the basis of Darwinism, but apparently I'm not allowed. So I just sent him home with some cream."

Ten minutes later, Ross had done with his set and was helping the youth club band with their equipment. As much to escape Jess's manky A&E stories as anything – they were definitely getting worse – I suggested we wander over and watch.

"Can you keep a secret?" I whispered as we grabbed our drinks and headed towards the stage area.

"You're a closet Madonna impersonator?" Jess said. "That's no secret, love. I found the pointy bra in your knicker drawer yonks ago."

"Not that one." I nodded to the band. "Something them lot don't know. This isn't really a gig, it's an audition."

"Audition? For what?"

"The lighthouse opening. We need a talented young band to open and Mum reckons they've got what it takes."

"She's always biased about her youth club kids though."

"I know. That's why Ross organised the gig, so we'd have a chance to judge them in the wild. Don't say anything, will you? They'll be bricking it as it is."

Ross was helping the lead singer, suitably steampunked for the night, assemble the drum kit. The lad looked terrified, and as we crept into earshot it sounded like Ross was doing his best to pep him up.

"Don't worry, son," he was saying. "Everyone feels like that. Means you're going to be good. It's over-confidence that'll kill your voice, not nerves."

"Or it means I'm going to piss myself live on stage," the boy said, looking seven shades of scared shitless. It was young Josh, the scruffy artist who'd been the talent behind our wall mural months ago. In his top hat and velvet blazer, he looked like a young, fair-haired Laurence Llewelyn-Bowen.

Ross finished tightening a screw and stood to slap Josh on the back. "No you're not. Just do that thing if you're nervous."

"What thing?"

"That thing they always say to do. Imagine the crowd naked."

"Are you kidding? I'm 16, I spend most of my time doing that." Josh's eyes widened in sudden horror. "Fuck! I just thought of the only thing more embarrassing than pissing myself."

Ross laughed. "You're not going to piss yourself and the last thing you'll be thinking about when you get going is sex. Trust me, I've been playing 12 years. Had all the anxiety dreams – public nudity, losing my voice – but they've never come true. The worst thing that happened was when our drummer exploded."

Josh blinked. "What, seriously?"

"No." Ross narrowed one eye. "You've seen *Spinal Tap*, right?"

"Spinal what?"

Ross shook his head. "Kids," he muttered. "No appreciation of the classics."

"Good with them, isn't he?" Jess whispered to me.

"Yeah," I whispered back. "He'll be great once we get the workshops up and running."

"Do I really have to imagine everyone naked?" Josh asked

Ross. He lifted his red top hat to wipe his brow. "My mum's here."

Ross grinned. "Best not then. Just get up there, shut your eyes and sing. Ask yourself, what would Kurt do?"

"Yeah ..." Josh's eyes clouded with Cobain worship. "He'd just get on with it, wouldn't he? Let the music take over."

"Yep, and so will you. Janine told me how good you guys are. Bound to be better than the band I was in at your age, and we managed a few years without being booed off stage."

Josh looked at him in surprise. "You were in a band? What were they called?"

"Er ... can't remember."

Ross looked over when he heard me snort and shot me a grin.

"That's my girlfriend. Think you've got this if I leave you to it?" he said to Josh.

"Yeah, no worries." Josh followed his gaze to us and frowned. "Sorry, which one's your girlfriend?"

"Both of them, if I play my cards right."

Josh's eyes turned saucer-like, and for a moment it looked as though Ross might topple Kurt from his pedestal as hero of choice, until he grinned and explained he was joking.

"Oh. Right." Josh looked disappointed that he wasn't about to pick up any tips. "Hey, thanks for sorting this, man. No one ever let us play before."

"No problem," Ross said, slapping his arm. "Good luck, lad."

"You should've told him," I said when Ross joined us. "Stalin's Budgie Smugglers is no worse than The Llama Drama."

Ross shook his head. "Karma Llama. And Nietzsche's Jockstrap, as you well know, funny girl. What is it with you and band names?"

"Maybe I just like my versions better," I said with a shrug.

After we'd been to the bar for a top-up, we reclaimed our table and waited for Josh and the band to start.

"Think they know why they're really here?" I muttered to Ross.

"Not a clue. Good thing too, they're nervous enough as it is."

"Reckon they'll be ok?"

"Dunno," he said, shooting a look at Josh's perspiration-soaked brow. "But if they manage this, I think they'll do a good job for us."

"They better," Jess said. "People are going to have some pretty high expectations for the opening."

I glared at her. "Thanks, sis. No pressure, eh?"

"Don't start giving me evils. It's Ross we're not talking to, remember?"

Ross lifted his eyebrows. "Why, what've I done?"

"Why didn't you tell us the place'd be full of Victorians in fetish gear?" Jess demanded. "We look well weird."

"*We* look weird?" he said with a laugh. "There's a bloke over there dressed as a steam-powered Ghostbuster."

I squinted at the man Ross had pointed out. He had a home-made ghost-sucking thing on his back that'd make Jules Verne's eyes water: all wood, cogs and wires. You couldn't fault someone who'd gone to that level of effort, I decided. His commitment to battling the legions of Victorian ghosts was just too inspiring.

"Yeah, but in this lot he looks normal," Jess said. "It's us who stand out. Even the bloody band kids are dressed up."

"What would you have done if I'd told you then? Gone the full steampunk?"

Jess shrugged. "Might've. Quite fancy myself in one of the basques."

"You'd better watch yourself saying stuff like that around Trav, he'll be dashing upstairs for his video camera," Ross said with a grin. "So what've you two been talking about?"

"You." I drew my finger across a dark circle under his eye. "We're worried about you."

"Me? Why?"

"Are you sure you can manage all this, Ross? Two jobs plus the lighthouse?"

"Oh, I'll cope somehow. It won't be for long, I hope. The flat's bound to go sooner or later."

"And if it's later rather than sooner?" Jess said.

"I'll find a solution. Move in with my parents maybe."

I curled my lip. "Yeesh. Not sure I could stand going back to living with Mum now, she'd drive me insane." Jess nodded her vigorous agreement.

"Yeah, I know what you mean," Ross said. "Me and Dad might well end up killing each other. Still, it'd only be temporary."

"Just take care of yourself, ok, Mason?" Jess said. "No offence but you look shagged out."

Ross cleared his throat, lifting innocent eyes to the ceiling.

Jess shook her head at him. "All right, sex maniac: I did actually mean in the metaphorical sense. Go careful, that's all. I don't want to end up seeing you in a professional capacity."

"I will. Thanks, girls." He smiled at us. "Nice to have you both looking after me."

"Don't go saying stuff like that around Josh," I said with a laugh. "I thought his eyes were going to pop out when you did that threesome joke earlier, poor lad."

"Shush now," Jess said. "They're starting."

We all turned as The Karma Llama's drummer finally mumbled his "one two three four" and the band launched into their first song.

Josh was sweating heavily under his topper. The poor

lad looked like he was about to dive head-first into a horde of teenage girls baying for his flesh, and he didn't know whether his dreams or his nightmares were coming true.

But there was something about these musicians, the ones who really believed in it. Josh touched his fingers to his Fender guitar – and he was gone. Within a minute he was leaping around the stage, eyes closed, belting out a cover of Smells Like Teen Spirit for all he was worth.

"Bloody hell," Jess said, looking taken aback. "Mum was right, they are good. And bloody energetic."

"So, Bobbie? What do you think?" Ross said.

"I think we've got ourselves a band."

Chapter 32

September furnished an Indian summer, but the educational elite showed no mercy. Come the 19th I had to go back to work at Cragport Community College, and the long summer of the lighthouse came to an end.

I was back to squeezing everything lighthouse, and everything Ross too, into my suddenly very limited free time. With the November launch event creeping closer and Ross working every spare hour down at the club, it wasn't long before things started to take their toll.

Things came to a head one Friday about three weeks into the new term, when I arrived at the lighthouse straight from work to find a throng of men in high-vis bustling around the place.

Fear gripped me instantly. We hadn't booked in any workmen. My brain jumped from one terrifying possibility to the next. Had the council plotted something? Had Alex got his revenge by teaming up with Langford to scupper us right at the last?

"Oi! What's going on?" I demanded of a burly bloke having a fag by the door. "Who authorised you to be here?"

"What's it to you?"

I glared at him. "This is my property, mate. So you'd better tell me what you're doing to it without my consent pretty sharp, before I call the police."

He looked me suspiciously up and down. "You aren't the owner. We've got paperwork signed by the owner." He dug into his pocket and pulled out a dirty receipt. "Mr Mason, says here."

"Mason?" I blinked in shock.

I pushed past the man and shouldered open the door. The inside was a flurry of sawdust that got up my nose, making me sneeze. There was a loud buzz of machinery, and huge planks of wood stacked up against the wall.

"I'm the owner!" I shouted to a man operating a circular saw over a workbench. "What're you doing?"

"What?"

"WHAT WORK ARE YOU DOING?"

The man gestured to the wood. "Balconies, love."

"What? I never authorised that!"

He shrugged. "I just do as I'm told. Better take it up with the gaffer outside if you've got a problem."

"Right. I'll do that." And I stumbled blindly back out of the door.

The balconies were the biggest, most important, most expensive part of the whole renovation. They needed careful thought and planning. And now it looked like Ross had booked some cowboy company to fit them without saying a word. Without even consulting me! What could he have been *thinking*?

"Hey, you really the owner, love?" the burly foreman said as I stood by the door, my eyes caked with sawdust and angry tears.

"Joint owner."

"So are we to carry on then?" He looked a little nervous now he'd had the chance to think about it.

I hesitated. "Yes," I said at last. "You might as well now you've started. I need to have a word with my business partner though. Expect a phone call."

Seething, I jumped into my car and drove straight round to Ross's flat.

"What the *hell* did you go and do?" I demanded when he answered my knock.

"Oh. Hi, Bobbie. Er, what?"

I pushed past him into the living room. He closed the door and turned to face me, looking bemused.

"Have I done something wrong?"

"I'll bloody say you have, mate. I've just been up to the lighthouse."

"Ah, right, good. Have they started the balconies?"

"Yes, they've started the balconies. I got the shock of my life when I found the place overrun with workmen. What the fuck did you think you were playing at?"

He looked puzzled. "I thought you'd be pleased. I know you think I haven't been pulling my weight recently, and you were tired after going back to work ... I wanted to make it up to you."

"Make it up to me?" I exploded. "By booking in some dodgy company without telling me? Jesus Christ, Ross!"

"They're not dodgy, honestly. Travis recommended them."

"How much?"

Ross looked guilty. He shuffled his feet with a schoolboyish air.

I frowned. "How much, Ross?"

"Twenty-five grand."

"*What*? But that's the entire emergency fund! All the remaining fundraising money too!"

"I did manage to negotiate it down from 30. Trav said that was the best price we were likely to get so I just went with it."

"What, you didn't even get any other quotes?"

"No. I didn't think there was any point. Travis knows what he's talking about." He rubbed at one eye with his knuckles. "God, I'm tired."

"I can't ... Christ! I just can't believe you'd do something so reckless. Make a massive, expensive decision like that without even telling me." Angry tears prickled my eyes. "I thought we were partners."

"We are partners." He reached out to embrace me but I held him back, staring in stunned disbelief.

He sighed. "I'm sorry, Bobbie. I wasn't thinking. It won't happen again."

"Well it can't now, can it? We're skint." I shook my head. "This has got to stop, Ross. You can't go on like this."

"Like what?"

"You know. The long hours, leaving me to pick up the pieces on the lighthouse. This isn't the first poor judgement call you've made recently, is it?"

First there'd been the LCD screens. I'd let Ross source them from some seller on eBay, and when they'd turned up we discovered they were wired for a US power output and wouldn't work in the UK. We'd had to return the lot, at our own expense.

And then there'd been the safety documentation for the launch event. We'd almost missed the deadline to get it in to the council when Ross remembered at the last minute he'd forgotten to post it. But this ... nothing had shaken my confidence in him as much as this.

"I'm sorry, Bobbie, I really am. I guess I just wasn't seeing it from the right angle. I don't function well when I'm not getting enough sleep." He took a deep breath. "Look, I'm glad you came over. Me and you need to talk."

Oh God. Those words. They never heralded anything good.

"Here, come sit down." He guided me to the sofa and took a seat next to me. He looked nervous, his eyes glittering as if he was coming down with a fever.

"What is it, Ross?" I asked in a low voice.

"You're right, I can't go on like this. I'm exhausted." He rubbed at his eye again. "And the summer season's nearly up, then they'll cut my hours at the club to weekends. There's a difficult decision I've had to make."

"Are you moving in with your parents?"

He shook his head. "I spoke to them about it, but there isn't room. They've already got Joe, Sal and the kids with them while they wait to move into their new place. No." He looked down at the carpet. "I'm going back to Sheffield, Bobbie."

"*What?*" I exploded. "But ... you can't! No, Ross!"

"Not forever, just until me and Claire get shut of the flat. I'm going to live in it while we wait for our buyer to get out of their chain. It's the only way."

"But what about the lighthouse?" I felt a tear escape and trickle down one cheek. "What about us?"

"I'll come back at weekends. Lots of people do long-distance. And it's not so very far away, really."

"But ..." I tried to fight down a wave of nausea. "... but *she'll* be there!"

Ross frowned. "Who will?"

"Don't give me who. Claire! She'll be right there, round the corner, while I'm nearly two hours' drive away. How's that supposed to make me feel?"

"You trust me, don't you?"

"I trust you not to cheat on me. I don't trust you not to fall for the gorgeous not-quite-ex-wife who's still in love with you when I'm out of sight and she's on the doorstep." I could hear my voice getting shrill. I knew I sounded unreasonable but I didn't care.

"That wouldn't happen, Bobbie. I love you."

"Oh really? Have you filed that divorce petition yet then? You're over the required separation period now."

He flushed. "I've been busy, that's all. It's on my to-do list."

I gave a grim laugh. "I see. You love me enough to leave me, to let me sort the lighthouse out while you're living it up in the big city with the missus. Why don't you tell the truth, Ross? You're running away, aren't you?"

"What? No! That's not it at all. Come on, Bobbie, you're being daft." He reached for me again but I jerked away, sobbing uncontrollably now.

"Right. I'm just a daft little girl who should count herself lucky her boyfriend wants to move miles away while she fixes up the lighthouse he talked her into buying in the first place." That wasn't true and I knew it, but all I could feel were sharp, sickening pangs of resentment and hurt. He wanted to run away, to leave me – me and the lighthouse. "I knew this would happen. I've always known," I sobbed, batting away the hand that had reached for mine. I jumped to my feet. "Well, if you don't want to be with me any more then let me make it easy for you. Goodbye, Ross. Enjoy your new life."

"Bobbie, wait!" he called after me. I ignored him and marched out of the flat, slamming the door behind me.

***

Back at the cottage, I slumped on the sofa and cuddled Monty to me, the only comforter within reach. Jess was at work and I knew Mum would be running the youth club for at least the next few hours.

So that was it. He was leaving me. Leaving me to go back to Claire in Sheffield, Claire who'd told me she still loved him. How long before the old feelings rekindled for him too?

And the lighthouse. Our lighthouse. I'd told Jess once that the lighthouse went with me and him. That bond severed, I could understand exactly how Charlie Mason must've felt about the place. Without Ross, I didn't know if I could even bear to look at it.

Jesus, and the 20 grand. All our investment, gone in the snap of his fingers – without so much as asking me!

But as I sat twisting Monty's white curls around my fingers, letting his little warm body across my legs relax and comfort me, I started to feel calmer. The sobs subsided and I tried to think more clearly.

Had I been too hard on Ross? Yes, the balconies had been a big, expensive error of judgement, but he had genuinely been trying to help. And his situation, the money worries and long hours: that wasn't his fault. He couldn't force the flat to sell any faster than it was doing. I pictured his handsome face and crinkling eyes, recalling all the sweet things he'd ever done for me: how he'd remembered my birthday after ten years, the toy boat he'd given me, the song he'd written for me. How he'd told me he loved me in that ridiculous Elvis costume. Our first kiss, back when we were kids. I couldn't help smiling as the memories washed over me.

Monty gave my hand an encouraging lick.

"Oh right, so you're on his side now, are you?" I muttered. The little dog just blinked at me.

Ross. My Ross. God, I loved him. I couldn't lose him, not over this. I yanked out my phone and stared at it for a second, wondering whether to ring him.

Still. Leaving me, going back to Sheffield while I sorted out the lighthouse problems his negligence had caused.

Spending the emergency fund without consulting me! If he wanted to talk I'd talk, but I wasn't going to be the first to apologise: no way. I set my phone on the arm of the sofa and glared at it resentfully.

I must've wallowed until well into the evening, Monty now fast asleep in my lap, and I was sitting in near-darkness when the phone finally buzzed with an incoming call.

Ross. So he was ready to talk things through. Thank God.

But I frowned when I looked at the screen. It wasn't Ross, it was Jess.

"Jessie? I thought you were working."

"I'm on my break." She sounded hushed, worried. "Look, you have to get to the hospital, right away. It's Ross."

Chapter 33

I sagged back in shock. "Shit, Jess, what's happened? Is he there?"

"Yes. They brought him in a few hours ago, I just found out."

"Tell me quick, please! Is he ok?"

"I can't tell you anything over the phone. I shouldn't really be ringing at all. Just get here, can you?"

"But is he ok? Please, you have to tell me."

"He's ... stable. That's all I can say. Please, Bobs, hurry up."

"God, yes ... I'm on my way. Tell him I'm on my way."

I don't know what thoughts went through my head as I drove like a demon to the infirmary. I don't even remember the drive, or arriving: I think I must've gone into autopilot. The next thing I knew, I was hurtling along a sterile white corridor to Ross's ward.

When I'd been shown into the waiting room by one of

the polite, starched nurses, I discovered Ross's parents Keith and Molly already there, along with both his brothers and ... someone else.

"Claire?"

She looked pale and worried, but she managed a smile for me. "Hi, Bobbie. Don't worry, he's going to be ok. They said he should be able to see us in about half an hour. He's conscious now, he just needs rest."

"Thank God. Oh, thank God." I sagged against the wall. "What the hell happened?"

"He was attacked, up at the lighthouse," Molly said.

"He's got some head trauma and a broken rib," Ross's brother Will told me. "Nothing care and rest shouldn't fix, the doctor told us."

"Hang on ..." I looked around at Ross's family. "How long have you lot been here?"

"We came straight away," Molly said. "I think it was three hours ago the hospital called. Where've you been?"

"Well, at home, since none of you bothered to ring me!" I exploded. "For God's sake, Molly!"

She frowned. "Didn't the hospital call you?"

"No, why would they? I'm not next of kin. Our Jess did." I turned to Claire. "Who called you?"

She blushed. "Molly. Sorry, Bobbie. I didn't know you hadn't been told."

I spun to face Molly. "You called her and not me?"

She looked guilty. "I thought he'd want to see her."

"And it didn't occur to you he might want to see me?" I almost yelled, my voice strangled with rage.

"All right, calm down. Try to remember this is a hospital," Will said, coming over to lay a restraining hand on my shoulder. "We're sorry, Bobbie, ok? It's a stressful time, I don't think any of us were thinking too clearly. No one's questioning your right to be here, if that's what you think."

I glared at him. "And you're no better, Will Mason. All my life you've known me, we were in nursery school together. You couldn't tap out a quick text to let me know your brother was in hospital?"

"I should have. I said sorry. We were just worried about him: that was all we could focus on."

"Well so am I worried about him. And I'm sick of being treated like an afterthought by the lot of you. I'm his partner, not Claire. He loves me." Suddenly, I burst into tears. "He loves me," I whispered.

Ross's family were staring at me in surprise. No one seemed to know quite what to say. With an impatient gesture, I turned and stumbled out of the room.

The hospital was a labyrinth of identical corridors and wards, and it didn't help that I was half blind with tears. By the time I finally made it to an exit, I must've passed the same sign for Acute Admissions three times.

Outside I managed to locate a sad-looking smokers' shrubbery, overrun with brambles and the flowerbeds full of dog-ends. There was an old bench and I sank onto it, giving in to sobs.

I had to see Ross, had to make sure he was ok – we were ok. The fact we'd had a blazing row right before he'd been hurt was tearing me up.

I felt sick wondering if he was really going to be all right. The others said he would, but head trauma – that was serious, wasn't it?

"Oh God, please just let him be ok," I muttered to no one in particular. "I don't care if he moves to Sheffield or London or Timbuctoo, if he'll just be ok."

I looked up as someone sank onto the bench next to me and a comforting arm wrapped around my shoulders.

"Took me a while to find you," Claire said.

"Not surprised. This place is a maze." I ran the back of my sleeve over my eyes. "Can I see him yet?"

"Not yet. Another 15 minutes or so, they said." She sighed. "I'm so sorry, Bobbie. I had no idea Molly called me and not you. I didn't even think ... I was just so worried about him. Jumped straight in the car and drove over, never even stopped to consider the family politics."

"No, I'm sorry. I overreacted." I paused. "Actually, no I didn't. But I don't blame you." I burst into a fresh round of tears and turned to bury my face in her shoulder. "Oh God,

Claire, what if he isn't ok? What if it's worse than they think?"

She shushed me softly. "Don't worry yourself. This is a hospital, they deal with cases like this every day. They'd know if there was serious damage."

But the tears wouldn't stop. They just kept coming and coming, until I felt like I was on the verge of hysterics.

"Hey. Calm down," Claire said gently. "He'll be fine, I promise."

"It's ... not just that," I gasped. "He's going ... away. We had a big row this afternoon, and I said ... I said..."

"What did you say?"

"I said if he wanted to go I'd make it easy for him and stormed out. It's ... my fault. I bet if I hadn't upset him this wouldn't have happened."

"Come on, you know that's not true." She frowned. "Wait, did you say he was going away?"

"Yes. Didn't he tell you? He's going to live in your old flat. Work'll dry up at the club when all the tourists go home in a few weeks and he won't have enough money coming in for the two places."

"But what about the lighthouse?"

I gave a wet laugh. "That's what I said."

She was silent for a minute, and I tried to fight back my tears. I didn't want to have swollen eyes when they let me go in to Ross.

"I might be able to help," she said at last.

I sniffed. "You?"

"If he's really struggling that much for design work. I've got plenty on at the moment, more than I can handle. I got offered a big job last week doing page layouts for a women's magazine. I was about to turn it down, but ... well, I could hire Ross to do it as a subcontractor. And anything else I get in too, if he's got the time."

"You'd really do that?"

"Of course. He's done it enough times for me when I've been short."

"But he could go back to Sheffield. You could—"

I broke off. She could win him back, were the words I'd choked over.

"... you could see more of him," I finished lamely. "I thought you'd like that."

"Not as much as I'd like seeing him happy," she said quietly. "He loves you, Bobbie. There's no point kidding myself about it. No matter where he is, he loves you."

"He told you that?"

"He didn't need to. I knew it that first day I came to your house ... the way he looked at you." She sighed. "He never looked at me like that."

"Course he did," I said with feeling. "You were his wife. And I know he loved you, he told me."

"Yes, he loved me. Very much, once. But he never looked at me the way I've seen him look at you."

367

"How does he look at me?"

Claire smiled, a little sadly. "Like there's no one else there." She let go of my shoulders and stood up. "Come on. I think he can probably see us now."

***

It was Will who spotted us first when we'd snuck back into the waiting room. I saw him lean over to his mum and whisper something. Molly looked up and smiled warmly at Claire.

No. Not at Claire. At me. To my surprise, she got out of her seat and came over to give me a hug.

"Bobbie, our Will thinks I owe you an apology and I quite agree with him," she said. "I've been a selfish old thing, haven't I? Of course I should've called you first."

I blinked as I gave her back a vague pat.

"I should've made more of an effort generally," she went on. "We all should. I never wanted you to feel we preferred Claire to you, I just never thought. After all the years I've known your family ... look, can we start again? How about when Ross is better you both come over for dinner?"

I glanced at Keith, who was having a muttered conversation with his oldest son Joe – something about all his taxes going to the NHS and it still not managing to provide a decent cup of tea. An entire dinner date in his company didn't exactly sound like a laugh a minute, but I appreciated the invitation all the same.

"Thanks, Molly," I said, giving her a squeeze. "I'd like that."

She smiled at me. "Friends again?"

"Friends again. And I'm sorry too. I should've talked to you instead of bottling it up. A hospital's no place for a family bust-up, is it?"

"Oh, don't apologise. We're all on edge tonight."

The crisp ward nurse poked her head around the door. "Mason party?"

"Yes, that's us," Will said.

"He's ready for you now. Who'd like to go in first?"

Molly stepped back and nodded at me. "Go on."

"I can take two of you," the nurse said, glancing around the others. Joe made a move to stand up, but Molly shook her head at him.

"Let Bobbie go on her own. We'll get our turn."

I smiled gratefully. "Thank you."

"Well. One of the family now, aren't you, dear?"

I followed the nurse out of the waiting room and past the rows of ugly metal beds. Finally we reached one with the curtains drawn all the way round. The nurse nodded to it.

"Here's your friend. Try not to tire him out too much, won't you? He's still a bit woozy."

When I'd fought my way through the curtains, I found Ross sitting up, looking pale and drawn. There was a bandage round his head, and the shape of the hospital gown he was wearing told me there must be another where the poor broken rib was.

He smiled weakly when he saw me. "What, no grapes?"

"You daft sod." I threw myself at him for a hug, bursting into tears. "Don't you ever, ever do something like that to me again."

"Mind the rib, eh?" he said as he embraced me. "Don't cry, love. I'm ok."

"Who did this to you?"

I felt him shaking and looked up into his face, concerned it was some side effect of his concussion. I needn't have worried. He was laughing.

"What's funny?"

He shook his head. "Just my wounded pride. Also I think they gave me morphine. Tell you what, it's good shit."

"Who did this, Ross? Tell me."

"I don't know if I can without losing all my macho points forever." He sighed. "It was the bloody graffiti kids. I mean, they were literally kids: the oldest looked about 14. I'm telling you, if the head injury doesn't kill me I might just die of shame."

I shuddered. "Don't joke about that."

"Sorry," he said gently. "I really am ok, promise. It's like a bad headache, that's all."

"How many kids?"

"Six or seven. I felt really bad about the balconies after you walked out so I thought I'd go check on the work."

"I knew it! Oh God, I knew it was my fault. I'm so sorry, Ross, I never should've—"

"No, I deserved it." He winced slightly, and shuffled a bit to get comfortable. "Anyway, I caught them in the act. They'd obviously tried Zaheer's door with no luck and decided they'd go to town on the outside instead." He rubbed at his head. "Little buggers just set on me. One of them had a bloody cricket bat."

"Jesus Christ!"

"The police said I'm lucky it wasn't a lot worse. Apparently someone scared them off and called me an ambulance. I don't remember, I was unconscious by then."

I held him tight, as tightly as I could without hurting him. "I'm so glad you're safe. Don't ever scare me like that again."

"Hey. Look at me."

I lifted my head from his chest to gaze into his face. His pupils were dilated with the morphine, but I could still see that keen expression in his eyes, the one that seemed to go with me and the lighthouse.

"Bobbie, this afternoon..."

"Oh God, I'm so sorry. I didn't mean it, about making it easy for you. I just didn't want you to go."

"It'll only be for a little while, I promise. I'll come home just as soon as I can afford it."

"Well, maybe you can afford it now."

He blinked as I filled him in on Claire's offer to sub him some of her design work.

"Bloody hell," he said. "I had no idea she was doing so well."

"So can you stay?"

"Well yeah, if it's a big enough job. Did she really offer to do that for me?"

"Yes. She says she wants you to stay here and be happy." I blushed. "Says you love me."

He smiled. "I don't think anyone can have missed that." He patted the mattress. "Here, come sit with me."

"Am I allowed?"

"If I say no, will that stop you?"

"Ok, good point."

He shuffled to one side and I swung myself up onto the narrow single bed next to him.

"Typical," I said, smiling at him. "Up to your eyeballs in morphine and you've still managed to get me into bed."

"Well I've got a reputation to maintain." He gave my neck a kiss, wincing as he changed his position. "Ow. Still, it might be a few weeks before I'm back to full sex god status."

I sighed. "Ross ... you do really want to stay, don't you? There's not a bit of you that's secretly disappointed?"

He put one finger under my chin and twisted my face to his. "Not still jealous, lass?" he asked softly.

"A little," I confessed. "I do trust you. Claire too, she's a lovely girl. But I can't help being a bit jealous when I see the way you still care about her."

"Hey." He leaned forward to plant a feather-soft kiss on my lips. "Claire means a lot to me: she always will. But I'm in love with you, Bobbie. My feelings for her ... well, I want her to be happy. But that's all, I promise."

"Really?"

"Really. You're the only one for me. Not sure I didn't know that the night you forced me to drink a tequila slammer and sold me half a lighthouse. Not sure I didn't know back at school, in a strange sort of way."

"Maybe I did too." I reached up to draw one finger down his perfect face, around the contour of his cheekbone, my eyes flickering over his features. Maybe it was love talking, but he even looked good in the bandage. "You're a pretty thing, my boy in the band."

He smiled. "There's just me now, love. I'm not in a band any more."

"No. But I always remember you like that."

"You want to know why I love you, Bobbie?"

"Because my incredible body drives you mad with lust?"

He shrugged. "All right, yes. But not just that."

He took my cheek in his hand and stroked it tenderly with the tip of his thumb.

"Ok, no joking, I'm being serious." He pointed to his lips, pressed into a firm line. "See? Serious face. This is now a banter-free zone."

I couldn't help smiling, but quickly settled my face into a deadpan expression. "Sorry, go on. Serious faces."

"All right, here goes then." He took a deep breath. "I love you because you make me laugh. Because you're sweet and beautiful and clever, and sometimes crazy, and always bossy. Because you bring out the best side of me and make me do mad, fun things." He reached up to twist a strand of my hair around his fingers. "But mostly, I love you because life's always been better those times it's had a Bobbie in it. You make everything in my world new and glossy. Like our lighthouse." He blinked, and I noticed a little droplet at the corner of one eye. "Thank you," he said, so gently it was almost a whisper.

"God, Ross …" I didn't even bother to blink back the briny pearls that had started to fill my eyes, letting them trickle freely down my cheeks. "I love you so much. I can't even…"

"I love you too, Bobbie. More than anything."

"Well you better kiss me now, that's all."

"Well then I will. Bossy." He claimed my lips for a long

kiss, his rough, tender fingers caressing my cheek and brushing away the tears.

"It's funny," Ross said when he eventually drew away. "But when I was lying on the cliff wondering if that was it for me, the first thing I thought about was Charlie."

I stroked his hand, following each vein and contour with my fingertips. "Why?"

"I don't know. The cricket bat maybe, reminding me how he'd taught me to play." He gulped down a little sob. "And I felt peaceful then, because I knew I'd be ok. I knew I couldn't die with the lighthouse not finished and leave you to work on it alone. The universe wouldn't let me."

I smiled. "That morphine really is strong, isn't it?"

"Yep. I'm high as a kite. Jealous?"

"Maybe." I leaned over to kiss his ear. "Thanks for not leaving me, Ross," I whispered. "Don't ever."

"They'll never take me off you without a fight."

We were interrupted by the sound of the curtain drawing back. I drew away from Ross's ear to find Jess standing there in her blue scrubs, arms folded.

"And what do you think this is, *Carry On Matron*? Get your dirty mits off the patient, Roberta Hannigan. And get your feet off the bed while you're at it."

I shot her an apologetic smile. "Sorry, Jessie. Still, my boyfriend did nearly die. He's allowed a cuddle, isn't he?"

"Not the kind you like to give him, that could finish him off. Come on now, his family's waiting."

"She's scary when she's at work," I whispered to Ross.

"She scares me all the time," he whispered back. I giggled and clambered off the bed.

"Will you come back later?" he said as I turned to go.

"Yes, love, I'll be right outside."

He smiled. "Thanks, my Bobbie. Love you."

"Love you too, Ross," I said, ignoring Jess making gagging noises in the background. "Get better soon, eh? Me and you have got a lighthouse to finish."

Chapter 34

Lying in bed one morning, I felt the ribbon of muscle that ran from my thighs to my neck tighten with an overpowering feeling of elation.

The sensation came partly from knowing I was in love and that the person I loved loved me back. And it came partly from excitement, because today, finally, the lighthouse was opening and all those dreams we'd nursed for the past seven months would be real, solid – ours.

But mainly it came from Ross Mason thrusting into me, making love to me with that mixture of tenderness and unrestrained animal energy I'd come to love in him. It came from the trembling tension in my nerves, taut as a guitar string, while my beautiful man pressed me closer and closer to orgasm.

"Oh God, Bobbie," he gasped into my ear when he heard me moan. "I'll never get enough of you, of this ... never."

I couldn't answer; my talking breath was gone. He'd had

it all, claimed it with his hot kisses and shivering touch, and now there was only the occasional brush of my lips and the throaty noises of imminent climax left for him. But he seemed happy enough with those. I pushed my hands up into his hair, coiling them through the rust-brown strands to press his scalp with my fingertips.

"Luh ..." I managed.

He laughed at my lack of speech, that sexy panting laugh he had, his thrusts speeding up as he sensed us getting closer to the end.

"Love you too, sweetheart," he panted, guessing my meaning with the telepathy of lovemaking. "Jesus, you feel good, so ... warm ..." He let out a guttural groan, and I knew we were nearly done.

"Kiss ..." I gasped. I wanted his mouth on me, to feel his lips, his tongue, when any second the tremors from his body echoed into mine.

"God, yes ..." He gave me his lips and I let out a muffled moan into his mouth as I stopped holding back and let the orgasm take me, one of many but each somehow sacred because it came from him. I felt him harden in me as my shuddering flesh helped him join me at the peak, but he didn't take his lips off mine, pushing into me with his tongue and his body until I couldn't bear it. God, he was addictive, that boy of mine...

And just when it felt like I might explode with the sweet,

pure pain of it and I had to pull away from his lips to cry out, the sensation ebbed into that gentle ripple of throbs that comes after and we sank into the mattress, cuddling tightly and panting into each other's necks.

"How did you get so good at that?" I gasped when we'd got our breath back.

"Maybe you inspire me."

I cocked one eyebrow at him. "Really? Best you've got?"

"Well I could say practice, but it seems in poor taste."

"Oh. Ok, slutty, I'll take the first answer."

He shuffled his head along the pillow to nuzzle my nose with his. "Good," he said softly. "Because it's true. Never felt this way about anyone, Bobbie."

"Me neither," I said, blinking back a happy tear. "I take it your rib's feeling better."

"Noticed that, did you?"

I pressed my lips against the tender area over his poor broken rib, the skin a brownish-purple now as the bruises faded. "So have you decided whether you're going to play later?"

He shook his head. "Don't think I should. The young people are the focus, it's not a vanity project. Let Josh and the lads have their time in the spotlight."

"You should do Dark Sentinel though. That one goes with the lighthouse." I tapped the tip of his nose. "And maybe I can't help showing off my talented boyfriend as well."

He laughed. "Well he better hope he doesn't run into me then, eh?"

"Stop being modest, you know how good you are."

"Only because you're always telling me." He looked down at me. "You know, one day you'll have to let me return the favour."

"Sorry?"

"Your novel. You told me ages ago you'd think about letting me read it."

"Oh. That. No ... not yet, Ross. Let's finish the lighthouse first."

"You know as well as I do we'll never finish it. That's who we are to this town now, the bloody lighthouse people," he said. "Come on, I thought you didn't need to hold anything back from me."

"Don't push," I said, frowning. "I'm not ready, ok?"

He leaned up on his elbow. "You realise you've never told me what it's about?"

"Change the subject, Ross."

"Or start something new. Might remind you what you used to get out of it."

"I've asked you to leave it twice," I said, my scowl deepening.

He looked puzzled. "What, are you mad at me now?"

"No ... look, let's get up. Lots to do today."

"Ok." He still looked concerned. "You promise you're not

mad though? You're always telling me to have more confidence in my stuff, I just want to do the same for you."

"It's not the same." I smoothed my frown with an effort. "I'm not mad, promise. I've just got too much on to think about it now."

"Right. If you're sure." He swung himself out of bed to find his clothes, still looking puzzled at my sudden shift in mood.

The truth was, the more I thought about the manuscript sitting in my drawer, the more I was afraid of it. I could almost hear the little bastard, shuffling its leaves at me like the bloody tell-tale heart, origami edition.

I couldn't bear to look at it, still less let anyone else see it. This thing had come straight out of my actual brain, the one I kept in my head for use in emergencies. What if Ross didn't like what he found out about me? What if he thought it was terrible? What if...

God, I wished he'd just drop the subject so I could forget about the damn novel for the next year, or ten years, or the rest of my life.

***

I was making the bed when I found it, tucked under my pillow. A flat, square envelope with "LISTEN" scrawled in biro on the front.

"What's that?" Jess asked when I went to seek her and Monty out in the living room.

"CD. Ross left it for me. Him or the tooth fairy, anyway."

"What's on it?"

"Dunno yet."

She dislodged the dog and reached under the sofa for our old laptop. "Well, let's find out."

"Looks like audio tracks," I said when she'd popped the CD in the drive.

I double-clicked the first file and Ivy Only Grows for the Wicked started. I hadn't heard it since the night Ross and I became a couple.

But this version was different. Polished, professional: Ross at his very best, not some Saturday night job with dodgy pub acoustics.

"This is brilliant," Jess said, looking impressed. "Not heard it before."

"This is the one he wrote for me."

We sat in silence, listening to the lyrics. The lighthouse, and us, and the feelings we had for each other. Firm, grounded, indestructible. That's what I heard in it now.

There were ten songs on the disk and we listened to them all. They were in Ross's familiar, haunting style, but there was something ... an emotion, a sound that was new to him. Something completely original, the essence of Ross Mason.

By the end, Jess was staring at me with round, tear-filled eyes.

"Did he really write you all those songs?" she asked quietly.

"I think so. Me and the lighthouse."

"You lucky cow." She nodded at the screen. "There's one more, look."

"So there is." I double-clicked the file.

"Hi Bobbie," said a shy Ross voice through the tinny speakers. "It's me. But you probably know that, because ... it's me. Er..."

I smiled at Jess. "Yep, that's him."

"So, um, I call these The Lighthouse Tapes," the pre-recorded Ross voice said. "I wrote them while we were working on the lighthouse, and because I had you for inspiration, I honestly think they're the best things I've ever written." He paused. "I know you're there, Jessie. Hope you're getting all this, your mum'll want a report."

She grinned and gave the screen a little wave.

"So anyway. Bobbie. I wrote these for you, and when I got out of hospital I had them all recorded to sell at gigs, maybe even send out to a few people in the industry if they're really good enough. I never thought I could do it before, but ... then I met you. And once I'd drunk a tequila slammer, renovated a lighthouse and played a set in front of hundreds of people, I started to think maybe I wasn't just a pub singer or a corny seaside tribute act. Maybe I really did have something, like you'd always tried to tell me. And I'm proud I know you, and I'm proud you love me, and I'm proud you're my Bobbie and I belong to you. And that together we seize every day, just like Gracie. Er, sorry for waffling."

"Pause it," I whispered.

"You all right?" Jess asked, stretching an arm around my shoulders.

"Yes, just … God, Jess, he's the one. Isn't he?"

"Well, yeah." She smiled. "Always the last to figure it out, eh? Me and Mum had this conversation months ago."

I laughed. "I bet you did, psychic busybodies. Play the last bit then."

She hit the play button.

"It was because of you I had the courage to do this." Ross's voice was earnest now, nerves lost in sincerity. "So don't sell yourself short. You've got a talent too, and I believed in it long before we grew up and fell in love. I'm proud of you, and I believe in you. Never forget, lass, and never give up. I'll see you later."

The mic crackled to sleep as he switched it off.

***

When Jess and I arrived at the lighthouse that afternoon to prepare for the grand opening, Ross was outside with a paint bucket, examining the helter-skelter stripes for cracks.

"Hi girls," he said brightly, putting down his brush.

God, look at him, carrying on as if nothing had happened. As if he hadn't made me feel almost sick with emotion. You'd think he recorded albums for women every bloody day.

"Jess, turn around," I commanded.

"Right. Er, why?"

"Because there's about to be some snogging and I want to spare your delicate maidenly sensibilities. Stick your fingers in your ears too."

"Ugh. This is worse than when we shared a room." She turned to face back down the clifftop path, blocking her ears and humming softly.

I ran to Ross and threw myself into his arms, carefully avoiding the sore side.

"Oof. Missed you too," he gasped, winded by the impact. "What's brought this on?"

"As if you don't know," I whispered, squeezing a tear into his jacket.

"You liked it then?"

"You kidding? It was beautiful, sweetheart. So proud of you." I looked up to flash him a loving smile. "Tell you what, in a year or so Peter Frampton'll be boasting about how he once stood next to Ross Mason at a urinal."

"Heh. Let's not get ahead of ourselves, eh?"

"So how about a snog for your number one groupie?"

He shook his head. "Groupies might be alright for the hoi polloi, Mick Jagger and those lads. I call my girls Rossettes."

"Yeah? How many have you got?"

"Well, just you so far. But I'm thinking if the album sells well, I could have as many as two, even three." He softened his voice. "I love you, you know. Wanted to show you."

"Me too, Ross." I lifted my lips to his for a long, tender kiss, pressing myself as deep into his arms as I could burrow.

"You know, I can still hear you," Jess said loudly. "I can hear the sucking."

Ross pulled away to grin at her. "Alright, twinnie. You want to take over painting duty so we can go have a proper snog in our lighthouse?"

"Alright, if you must," she said, dropping her fingers from her ears and turning around. "But make sure it's just a snog. People are coming to see a band, they don't want to be greeted by your bare bumcheeks bobbing about on stage instead."

Ross shrugged. "We might get more donations that way though."

"Not off me you wouldn't." She slapped his arm as she came over to claim the paintbrush. "Nice songs, by the way. Think you've really got something there."

"Thanks, Jessie," he said, smiling. "Good to get some feedback from the non-biased twin."

He took my hand and led me into the lighthouse.

Every time I went inside and compared it to how it'd looked all those months ago, coated in that sickly layer of dust and droppings, it took my breath a little.

The semi-circular wooden stage where Josh and the band had already set up their equipment now filled half the floor space, with the other half reserved as a little mosh pit for anyone who fancied a dance. A camera above the Project Phoenix mural was hooked up to three screens, wall-mounted to give those on the balconies the best view of the acts, with a speaker either side. We'd decorated the place with second-hand vinyl sleeves, mounted in curved frames to suit the shape of the walls.

There were three crescent balconies with staircases between them, finally reaching the loft opening to The Lantern Bar. Strings of red and white bunting were currently hanging from the brass balcony rails, giving the place a party atmosphere. A banner behind the stage announced *Project Phoenix – Grand Opening!*

"So do I get that snog now then?" I asked Ross.

"In a minute," he said. "Something I need to tell you first."

I frowned. "Nothing bad, is it?"

"No, the opposite. Got some good news this morning."

I looked up into his face. His eyes were shining, and a little smile twitched the corner of his mouth.

I clapped a hand to my mouth. "You sold the flat!"

"Yep. Claire texted to say the new owners have signed on the dotted line."

"Oh my God, that's brilliant!" I said, hugging him tight. "So glad you don't need to worry about it any more."

"There's one thing I still need to worry about." He held me back to look into my face. "Your half of the emergency fund."

"Oh, never mind that," I said, flushing. "It all worked out in the end."

"That was just luck. You were right, Bobbie, I let you down." He fished in his pocket and pressed something into my hand. "Take this."

I blinked at it. It was a cheque for £10,000.

"No, Ross."

"Please. I won't feel right unless you do."

"And I won't feel right if I do," I said, tearing the cheque down the middle and stuffing it back in his pocket. "I told you, it's James's money. I never wanted anything off him and I don't want it now. Let him pay his debt to Mum and Corinne with the lighthouse."

"Are you sure?"

"I'm sure," I said firmly. "Not that you weren't a right pillock to spend it without asking me. But I forgive you."

He smiled. "You know you're some girl, right?"

"No arguments here."

"Well, if you won't take the money then I hope you'll take this," he said, pulling out a little gift-wrapped package. "Wanted to give you it before, but it didn't feel right until the flat sold."

He handed it to me, and I noticed he looked nervous: his twitchy, flushed stage fright face.

"Another present? You really need to stop giving me things."

"This isn't something new, it's something I gave you once before. Open it."

I frowned as I started to unwrap it. It was Ross's 50p, his lighthouse money.

"But it's your lucky keyring," I said. "Why're you giving it back?"

"If you take it back I won't need it, I'll be the luckiest bloke in the world. Unwrap the rest."

I did, and discovered a key, shiny and freshly cut, dangling on the other end.

"For my flat," Ross said softly. He tilted my face up so I was looking into his pretty silver-flecked eyes. "I'm asking you to move in with me, Bobbie. I don't want to be anywhere else but with you, and I think we're ready for the next step. Come share a life with me, lighthouse girl."

I gasped and swallowed at the same time, making a

strange choking noise in my throat. For a minute, all I could do was glug at him.

"Bobbie?"

"Yes," I finally managed to gasp out. "I mean, no."

"Right." He blinked. "Er, wow. That was a pretty quick turnaround."

"I mean, I'll move in with you. But not your flat. It's too small."

"Oh. Why, have you got an Imelda Marcos-sized shoe collection or something?"

"No, but I've got Monty. And Jess." I brought my eyes to his. "Can't you come to me?"

He frowned. "What, with your sister and the dog?"

"Would that be a problem?"

He looked thoughtful. "No, I'm up for a houseshare if that's what you want," he said after a minute. "But ... you don't think Jess'll mind?"

"Well, let's check."

I went to the lighthouse door and flung it open.

"Oi!" I called to Jess.

"What?"

"Can Ross move in with us?"

"Yeah, if you like. The pair of you'll have to go halves on a louder telly though."

"Cheers," I said, shooting her a thumbs-up.

"Sorted," I said, going back to Ross and snuggling into

his arms again. "I'll come round next week and help you pack."

He laughed. "Bloody hell, why do I feel like whenever I'm with you I've just been for a spin in a revolving door? Not so fast, crazy girl. Need to give notice on my letting agreement first."

"Oh. Well, you can start moving some bits in."

"Suppose I should be flattered you're so keen." He buried his lips in my hair. "Can't wait to wake up with you in my arms every morning, bonny lass."

"God, yeah." I blinked a few times. "That sounds … wonderful."

"Give us that mouth then."

I pressed my lips to his for a long kiss.

"Can you believe we made it this far on the back of two tequila slammers and a drunken snog?" he said when we separated. "Moving in, opening up…"

"I know, it's unreal. You excited about today?"

"Well I feel like I might be sick, so that's either excitement or terror. You?"

"Yeah, got a few butterflies. But it's fine, we've been planning this for ages. I won't say 'what can possibly go wrong?', that's just asking for trouble, but I think we're on pretty safe ground."

"If I was feeling pedantic, I might point out the ground we're on is at the top of a massive fuckoff cliff."

"All right, smart-arse. You're the metaphor king, work it out."

"Do the volunteers all know what they're doing?" Ross asked.

"Yep. You're downstairs with the band, I'm doing my meet and greet up on the second storey balcony, Mum on the third, Trav on merch, Gareth on bar and Jess offered to mind Anthony." After pulling us in plenty of press for the music festival, we'd been badgering Anthony to do the official lighthouse opening for months now and Jess had finally managed to twist the old luvvie's arm.

Ross shook his head. "So weird how those two hit it off."

"Isn't it? Shared love of winding people up, I think. Come on, let's unload the car."

As we left, the rows of merry bunting fluttered us good luck.

Chapter 35

2 pm. The time came, the bell tolled and it tolled for thee. I mean, me. We. Me and Ross. Well, it didn't because we didn't have a bell. But if we did it would've tolled good and ominously, with an extra big couple of dongs.

"What're you giggling at?" Ross asked when he heard me snort.

"Nothing. Not dongs."

"Er, right. Strange girl."

As the faces of Project Phoenix we'd both changed into our best for the launch, and there was a distinct embassy ball vibe that left me feeling we should be handing round pyramids of Ferrero Rocher. I was in a pale blue organza dress that'd cost me a small fortune, and Ross had gone for his favourite Man in Black look of dark shirt and matching skinny tie. He looked fresh-minted somehow: sexy as sin.

You'd think the formalwear would help us feel more

confident, but all I mainly felt as we stood at the back of the excited crowd gathered in front of the lighthouse was equal parts terrified and conspicuous.

"Hey, seen who's here?" Ross pointed into the crowd, and I noticed Claire looking at us. She waved when she saw she'd got our attention.

"Oh good, she made it," I said, waving back. "Who's the lad?" Claire was leaning against a tall, ash-blonde, placid-looking man with one arm curled lazily around her waist.

"That'll be the new boyfriend, Derek."

My eyebrow flicked up. "Derek?"

"Yeah, poor sod. Still, he sounds nice."

The lighthouse door opened and Jess made her way out, Anthony leaning heavily against her shoulder. I could tell instantly from the way he was wobbling that something was wrong.

"Oh God, he's not ..." I squinted at him, tottering unsteadily as Jess bent under his weight. "He's hammered, Ross!"

"Shit, you're right! God, he was bad enough at the music festival."

"This is ten times worse. Look at him, he can hardly stand!"

I glared at Jess, who shot me a guilty smile. She left Anthony propped on the cane he was carrying, swaying and smiling vaguely at the crowd, and skirted over to us.

"Ok, how much did you let him have?" I hissed when she reached us.

"Not much, I swear! He had a couple of whiskies at the bar, that's all. Said he needed it to help with the stage fright."

"Yeah? Then how come he can't seem to operate his knees?"

My eyes widened as I saw Anthony fish in his pocket for a small hip flask and take a sly gulp. There was a ripple of laughter through his audience, the journalists in the front row scribbling away on their notepads.

I slapped a palm against my forehead. "Jesus, he's got a secret stash. How the hell's he going to manage a speech?"

"Oh, he'll be all right," Jess said – but her tone lacked commitment. "He's been doing this sort of thing his whole career, hasn't he?"

"But he's not been on stage for 15 years," Ross said. "Oh fuck. Fuck fuck fuck. We're fucked."

"You kiss your mother with that mouth, Mason?"

I frowned at Jess. "No jokes, you. This is all your fault. How could you not notice him swigging?"

"Look, I'm sorry, ok? He's obviously an expert. Never even saw him take it out."

"Last time I let you babysit. Here." I reached into my handbag for a gummed red ribbon and a pair of golden scissors. "Give him these. Hopefully he won't go into a drunken rage and start stabbing hecklers to death."

With a last apologetic grimace, Jess threaded her way back to Anthony. She gave him a quick pat on the back, the old man swaying slightly under the impact, before fixing the ribbon across the door and slipping the scissors into his pocket. Then she went to join the other helpers near the throng of press.

Anthony patted the pocket with the scissors in, blinking for a moment as if he couldn't quite remember where he was. Then he pulled himself to his full height and started clearing his throat imperiously. Gradually the hubbub died down as the crowd waited expectantly for him to speak.

"My dear ladies and gentlemen," he began, his voice slurred but steady. "I am honoured and proud and ... honoured to have been invited to address you today on this historic occasion, the reopening of the Cragport lighthouse as –" he waved a dismissive hand "– well, some sort of concert hall, I believe."

"Good start," I muttered to Ross. "You told him what it was all about, didn't you?"

"Yeah, but I don't think he was listening. He cut in to tell me an anecdote about the time he played Macbeth trollied opposite Maggie Smith."

I let out a death-rattle groan. "Oh God. And now you've said Macbeth. The lighthouse'll fall down in a minute."

Ross shot Anthony a worried glance. "Still. Jess was right,

he does have a history of this sort of thing. Maybe he'll pull it off."

"He'd bloody better, or the press'll have a field day. It'd be just our luck to be responsible for a national treasure collapsing in a drunken heap at the opening."

"Will you be giving us anything from your Richard the Third today, Mr St John?" a young reporter called out.

Anthony smiled indulgently. "Dear boy. Flattered, of course, but at my age Lear is really the only great part left to me." He blinked into the ever-demonic nor'wester, his topper bobbing precariously. "And while a soupçon of 'Blow, winds, and crack your cheeks' may seem appropriate, I did not come to satisfy my own need to exhibit."

A doubtful hum suggested the crowd weren't quite buying that, but Anthony ignored them. He sent a paternal smile over the sea of heads to Ross and me, beckoning us to him.

"Bollocks!" I whispered. "Do we have to go?"

"You know we do. At least this time we've actually got a speech written."

The speech ... oh shit! Shit shit shit! I stared at Ross with wide, unblinking eyes.

He shook his head in shocked disbelief. "Oh no, Bobbie. Tell me you didn't."

"Yep. Left the bloody notes at home. Oh God, it's all going tits up, isn't it? Should've known I'd jinxed us with that safe ground line earlier." I stared horror-struck at the waiting crowd. "Fuck, Ross! What do we do?"

"We'll just have to wing it as usual, won't we?" He gripped my hand tightly. "Let's get it over with."

"Everyone's naked everyone's naked everyone's naked ..." I heard Ross muttering as we weaved our way through the crowd.

"Is that helping?"

"No. The only person I can focus on is Councillor Langford over there." He nodded to our old enemy from the town council, probably trying to pretend Project Phoenix had all been his idea for the clusters of press.

We took our places next to Anthony and grinned nervously at the crowd.

"Ah, my beautiful young people, you're here to lend some glamour to proceedings at last," Anthony slurred. "Welcome to the bearpit."

He turned back to the crowd to begin his speech. I felt a surge of relief when I caught a glimpse of his eyes. There was a sort of glint in them, a passion for performance that seemed to override the drunken fog in his brain. Say what you like about Anthony St John, the man was a pro.

He pushed his best top hat up to a jaunty angle, cleared his throat and suddenly there he was, back in the game.

"The lighthouse means something different to each of

us," he said in a thespian boom. "For me, it has always meant adventure."

He paused for dramatic effect, then went on.

"When I was small, I remember asking my dear mother the story of this wonderful building, and the old girl seating me on her knee and telling me tales of its long and glorious history in those halcyon days of Empire."

I saw Ross shoot me an amused smile but I ignored him. It was all I could do to stop my top lip wobbling.

"Of course, Mother introduced a few elements to the stories that perhaps were not entirely taken from life," Anthony went on. "Having reached man's estate, I came to question whether there may have been rather fewer pirates and rather more fishermen than in her version of events, and I believe that in reality the invasion of the Spanish Armada took place a few centuries before the lighthouse was built." His face set into a serious expression as he reached the apex of his speech. "Nevertheless, one thing I held in my heart: our lighthouse has a proud history. It has in its time saved many lives, overseen many adventures and borne witness to many great stories." He turned to us. "Including, I understand, one rather wonderful love story."

Anthony took Ross's hand and guided him round so the pair of us were flanking him. Then he held our arms up to present us to the crowd. He reeled slightly, and I shifted my weight to give him a bit of support.

"Seriously, how much have you had?" I muttered.

"All part of the game, my dear. These people came for a show, and let him whisper who dares that the old man doesn't provide value for money." He raised his voice to address the audience again. "I'll crave your indulgence a little longer, good people, and then I believe the talented youngsters inside are ready to regale your eardrums with something more pleasing than the ramblings of a washed-up old ham like Anthony St John. I should like to present –" he paused, but the brain that had spent decades learning parts was still serving him well, even under the influence "– Miss Roberta Hannigan and Mr Ross Mason, the organisers of this project. These are the two exquisite human beings who have, with vim, vigour and a rather sizeable pair of balls each, saved our lighthouse from tragic decay and granted it beauty and purpose again in its dotage." He flashed the crowd a wry smile. "A fate I think many of us would choose if we could."

There was a round of applause as Ross and I stepped forward to blush and smile and wonder what the hell we were supposed to do now.

Anthony nodded affably in my direction. "Your line, dear. Would you like a prompt?"

"Yes please," I hissed back.

"Well then, tell us the story. I believe I've fluffed them nicely for you."

"I'll do it," Ross said. Anthony's drunken showmanship seemed to be catching.

He cleared his throat. "Welcome everyone," he said. "I'll try to keep this short, I know the bar's open."

There was a ripple of laughter, which seemed to set him at ease.

"Mr St John has asked me to tell you a story I know. The story of a boy and a girl and a lighthouse. Which sounds like a kind of fairytale – and it was, even though it started with the mundane reality of a drunken kiss and a killer hangover."

There was another chorus of laughter, and I noticed some of the journalists scribbling notes. All I could do was hope Ross knew which bits of this x-rated fairytale he needed to censor before I woke up to a "Saucy shenanigans and bare bottoms in old town lighthouse" headline in tomorrow's *Cragport Chronicle*.

"I knew a girl once, at school," Ross went on. "Well, I knew a lot of girls, but one was different. One was this one, Bobbie Hannigan: the first girl I ever kissed." He jerked his head in my direction, blushing.

Anthony, the old romantic, took this as a signal to shuffle behind me and guide me next to Ross again. Ross took my hand and gripped it firmly.

"I knew then she was different from any other girl, but I didn't know ..." He paused and looked at me. "... I didn't know she was the one. I only found that out after she talked me into following my dream of opening a performance space for young musicians. And it took a lot of alcohol and at least one snog to convince me the perfect venue had been in front of me all along – my Uncle Charlie's long-neglected lighthouse."

There were a few "awws" from the crowd. I sidled closer to Ross and gave his hand a squeeze.

"Let me do the rest, sweetheart," I whispered. "I can talk now."

"You sure?" he whispered back.

"Partners, aren't we?"

"Always."

I cleared my throat, looking over the ocean of expectant faces.

"Sorry about him, he waffles when he's being adorable," I said. "I'll keep it short. Seven months ago a talented musician told me he had a dream, and I believed in it, and I believed in him. Enough to take a lot of risks, but I knew no one with that fire in their eyes was capable of letting me down. Over the summer I don't know if the two of us saved a lighthouse and accidentally fell in love, or fell in love and accidentally saved a lighthouse, but that's what happened. Through all the trials and tribulations, Ross and I managed to raise a phoenix from the ruins of the Cragport lighthouse. Today we're proud to present it back to you." I smiled. "As for the boy I got free with it, I'm keeping him for myself."

Ross pulled me into his arms for a kiss – which gave rise to more loud applause from the soppy sods watching. Between our snogging and Anthony's pissed-up hamming, they were getting quite a show.

When we separated, I turned to Anthony.

"You want to do the honours then, Beau Brummell?"

"I thought you'd never ask, my dear. I'm positively parched for want of whisky."

"Flask empty, is it?"

Anthony ignored me. He held up a hand for silence and the noise died to a respectful hush.

"Thank you all," he said. "And now it appears the time has come, as our inelegant friend the walrus once observed. So it is with great pride that I declare this lighthouse—" he broke off to glare at a premature clapper "in my own good time, sir, if you don't have a more pressing engagement. I now declare this lighthouse ... open! May God bless her and all who sail in her."

He took out his gold scissors to snip the ribbon, and as it flapped free in the wind a loud cheer echoed over the clifftop and across the bay. After seven months, or 30-odd years depending on which way you looked at it, the Cragport lighthouse lived again.

Chapter 36

Once we'd got everyone into the lighthouse, our team of volunteers took to their posts. I was on the second-storey balcony, meeting and greeting the VIPs – press, families of the band and others there by special invitation. I was just taking a breather, leaning over the brass rail drinking it all in, when someone tapped my shoulder.

"Oh. Hiya," I said to Claire, kissing her cheek by way of a hello.

"Hi, Bobbie. Ross said I'd find you here."

"Where's the new chap – Derek, was it?"

She grinned. "Upstairs with Keith and Molly. Thought I'd throw him in at the deep end."

"Ha! Poor lad." I gave her arm a squeeze. "How's it going with you two then?"

"Good," she said, flushing slightly. "I mean, early days and everything, but yeah. I think we're really ... good."

I smiled. "Glad to hear it."

The band were starting up now. I could see poor Josh on the LCD screen in front of me, looking even more terrified than the night he'd played The Cellar.

Ross got up on stage and whispered something to him. I don't know what he said, but Josh did look slightly comforted. As soon as The Karma Llama's drummer counted them in he was away, Kurting it up with the best of them. Coming through the speakers with the live sound combined, it sounded incredible.

"Not bad," Claire said with an impressed nod, raising her voice so I could hear her over the band. "So any news on Alex then? Please say no."

"He did come round a few days after the Tuxedo's thing, but when Ross answered the door he left in a hurry. I think Alex was hoping he might've split us up that night. Not heard from him since, thank God."

"Well, glad it's all worked out. Ross told me on the phone he was going to ask you to move in."

I flushed. "Actually he's coming to me. But, er, better keep your voice down, I still need to break the news to my mum. She can be a bit – intense when it comes to micro-managing my love life."

"Ah, right. I'll keep schtum then." She drew an invisible zip across her lips. "How're his ribs now?"

"Healing nicely." I stifled a smirk when I thought of our

bedroom activities that morning. "I think he's nearly back to full strength."

"Did they ever catch who did it?"

"Yep. There was an eyewitness, the chap who called the ambulance. The police picked them all up the following week. Gang of teenagers from South Bay looking to start some trouble."

"Good. Hope they get what's coming to them," she said with a satisfied nod. "Oh, by the way, I brought something for you. Call it a housewarming present."

She was grinning all over her face, and I smiled uncertainly. "What is it?"

"This." She took a piece of paper out of her pocket. "Photocopied it before I set off."

I unfolded it and stared in disbelief.

"Our decree nisi," Claire said. "Got it in the post last week. Ross was bursting to tell you but I made him promise. Really wanted this to be my surprise."

"Oh my God!" I leaned across to give her a hug. "You sneaky buggers. Thank you."

"Just a few more months and he'll be a free man," she said, giving me a squeeze. "Happy launch day, love."

***

An hour later, the band were packing up to take a break. I could see Ross waiting in the wings, and I leaned over the rail so I could send him a smile.

"Oi. You."

I turned to find a grumpy-looking Jess, a frilly apron over her little black dress and a tray of hors d'oeuvres hanging by a strap around her neck.

"Ha! You look like a French maid." I picked up a pastry thing from her tray and eyed it quizzically. "What's this supposed to be, some sort of sex toy?"

"That's a saxophone, you cheeky cow."

"I knew it was a mistake letting you make the nibbles." I popped the saxophone-dildo in my mouth and gagged.

"Bloody hell!" I grabbed one of the complimentary proseccos she was carrying and drained about half in one go. "How much chilli did you put in the bastards?"

She smirked at me. "Sorry, trade secret. But you'd better add chilli powder to the shopping list, we're all out."

"Evil twin."

"Ugly twin."

I shot a nervous glance at Josh's granny, chatting to Richie the Clean Beaches man not far away. "Look, don't be handing those things out to the old folk. With that shape and flavour combo, you could end up with a cardiac arrest on your hands."

"I won't. I'm taking a break anyway." She unburdened

herself of the tray and shoved it in my direction. "Want to hear my new housemate sing."

"Yeah, how weird is it he's moving in?" I hung the tray round my neck and slapped her arm. "Thanks for being ok with it, sis."

"Well, I don't want a man coming to break up the sister act just yet. Last time I let you out on your own you ended up getting taken for a ride by that knobhead Alex." She nodded at the miniature Ross on the LCD screen. "He's starting."

"Hi everyone," Ross said into the mic with his usual wave. "Just a quick one from me, then The Karma Llama are back for the last hour."

"Do Jailhouse Rock," shouted a young heckler.

There was a ripple of sniggers around the crowd. Ross's secret had become something of an open one over the last few months. It didn't bother him who knew now though, as long as I was ok with it.

Ross smiled. "Sorry, lad, I'm afraid Elvis has left the building. No, I'll only be doing one, then it's back to Josh and the boys."

He played the opening chord on his guitar. "Ok, so this is Dark Sentinel. Copies available from the odd-looking bloke called Travis on the third floor – trust me, you can't miss him – with 100% of profits going to Project Phoenix."

It was impressive how much more confident he seemed

now – not just singing, but his public speaking. I blushed when I wondered if I'd played a part in that too.

"Oh, sorry, quick bit of housekeeping first," he said. "Plastics only on the balconies please, guys: no bottles except at the bar. It'd help our volunteers if you could put empty cups in the waste bins provided. Don't lean right over the rails, we don't want any accidents. And, er, special announcement for Janine Hannigan, I'm moving in with your daughter. Well, both of them, technically. Thanks."

"*What?*" Mum's explosion from the balcony above mine could be heard around the lighthouse.

After the laughter and cheers had died down, Ross grinned up at her. "Thought I'd tell you while you couldn't get me. Sorry, love. Right."

He played the first chord again, and on the screen I saw his eyes close. *Watchman for the lost…*

"What did he do that for?" I muttered to Jess once everyone's attention was held by the music.

Jess shrugged. "He knew he'd have to tell her some time. By the time she gets her hands on him she'll have calmed down a bit."

"S'pose." I smiled. "Sweet, wasn't it?"

"Yeah. The man's a bloody sweetness addict." She cocked her head. "Hey, wasn't that the last verse? Why's he still singing?"

She was right, he was still going, another chorus ... and then he launched into a verse I'd never heard before.

...Partner of my soul
Best friend and keeper, anchored here
Fall with me, deeper, disappear
My pride, my ocean girl, my pioneer...

The last note lingered in the air, then faded away.

I shook my head. "He wrote me another verse for the launch," I muttered to Jess. "You're right, he is a sweetness addict."

"They're like musical love letters, his songs, aren't they?" Jess said.

"God, I love the romantic bugger." I sighed happily. "Some year, eh, sis?"

"Been a big one for both of us, hasn't it? Lighthouse, boys..."

"... Anthony," I said with a smile. "Where is he? He must be paralytic by now."

"No, he's still upright, just about. He's at the bar, drinking us out of Scotch and reciting poetry at Gareth."

"How is his poetry?"

"Let's just say if he was pinning his hopes on a laureate position to make up for the knighthood he shouldn't hold his breath." She shrugged. "He's a nice old boy though. Wants me to go visit him sometimes. I think he's a bit lonely in that big house with only the booze for company."

"Good for you." I shuddered. "Still, rather you than me. Not sure I could cope with an epic poem on hydrangeas no matter how much whisky he plied me with."

***

The people were gone, the band had packed up and disappeared, the tidy-up was finished. The lighthouse was silent again. But to me it felt like I could hear it humming, feel it vibrate under my feet, alive with fresh purpose.

Over the last seven months I'd almost started to think of the place as self-aware. I could picture it now, breathing a deep sigh as it was left alone with just me and Ross, its old friends.

It was thoughts like that which made me wonder if this whole lighthouse business hadn't turned me a bit strange...

"Good job today, my boy in the band," I said to Ross as we snuggled in the lantern room.

"Good job you, Bobbie Hannigan from school." Ross leaned over to kiss the top of my head. "Did ok in the end, didn't we?"

"Understatement of the year. At the risk of developing an Anthony-sized ego, we did bloody brilliant." I looked up at him. "Although one downside, you've been summoned to Mum's tomorrow for coffee and interrogation."

"Oh bollocks." He looked suddenly nervous. "Think it'll hurt much?"

"Nah, she loves you. Quick grilling, threat of castration if you ever hurt me, then it'll be back to happy families." I leaned across to kiss his cheek. "And that's for you, by the way. Thanks for my song, it was beautiful."

He smiled fondly, twirling a strand of my hair around one finger. "Well. Always manage to bring out the soppy bugger in me, don't you, Hannigan?"

"Wouldn't have it any other way," I said. "Oh yeah, got a present for you. In the absence of songwriting abilities." I rummaged in my handbag and pulled out a flat oval object, gift-wrapped in foil paper. "It's to go on the door. Been saving it till the end."

Ross ripped off the paper and blinked at me, touched.

It was an engraved brass plaque I'd had made, just like the one on Gracie's bench. The inscription read *Project Phoenix, opened 6th November 2016. Dedicated to the memory of Anne and Charles Mason, who loved our town and one another.*

"It's perfect, Bobbie." He planted a soft kiss on my forehead. "You're perfect. Thank you."

I flushed deeply, scuffing at the floor with one strappy shoe. "Something else for you," I mumbled.

He laughed. "And you told me off for too much present-giving. What now?"

I fished in my bag for the USB stick I'd tucked into the pocket and handed it to him.

He held it up in front of his face. "What is it?"

"It's a romantic thriller, since you ask."

"What—" He broke off. "Your book? You're letting me read it?"

"Yes. Be gentle with me, eh?"

He stashed the stick in his pocket and pulled me into his arms again. "I won't need to be, I know it'll be brilliant. What changed your mind?"

I laughed. "Well if you can write ten songs for me, this seemed the least I could manage. And ... you're right, I can't hide forever. I don't want to get to Anthony's age and realise my biggest regret was not finishing the thing."

He didn't answer. He just pressed his lips into my hair, which was better.

Through the glass we could see the town in all its night time beauty, the many-coloured lights casting wibbly, glowing spears into the ocean's midnight dark. Smaller lights clambered higgledy-piggledy up the hillside, little cottages full of little people.

"Pretty old place sometimes, isn't it?" I said quietly.

"Yeah. Like you, my lighthouse girl."

I took his hand and massaged it with my thumb. "Why did you come home, Ross?"

"Oh, I don't know," he said with a long sigh. "There's

something about the sea ... gets inside you, salt in your veins. It always calls you back in the end."

I pressed the hand I was holding. "You're a bit like that, you know. I never forgot you when you were away. You got into my veins along with the salt, Ross Mason."

He laughed. "Yeah, you remembered me so well that when I got back you didn't recognise me."

"Well, you went and got all sexy, didn't you?" I smiled up at him. "I mean it though, Ross. I never did forget you. There was still a little bit of me put aside for you when you got back ... think that's why it felt so easy to fall for you."

"You're sweet tonight, my Bobbie." He left another gentle kiss on top of my hair. "I love you very much, you know."

"Me too, Ross. I always will now."

"Aww. Give us a snog then, softie." He tilted my face up to his for a deep, tender kiss.

"So what shall we do now, sweetheart?" he asked when he drew back, his fingers playing in the nape of my neck. "Lighthouse, bed or pub?"

I laughed. "'Lighthouse, bed or pub' could be the title of our memoirs."

"It could, couldn't it? Hey, you should write it. Anthony was right, it is a good story."

"Really? You want everyone to find out we were bonking in it?"

"Good point," he said with a grin. "So come on, bonny lass, what's it to be? For once in our lives we're fancy-free. No lighthouse stuff to worry about, no Elvising to do, no big events to plan. For once, finally, it's just me and my girl."

I smiled. "Buy you a tequila slammer, handsome? Let's start the next adventure."

Acknowledgements

A lot of people helped make this book, but the biggest thanks has to go to my agent Laura Longrigg at MBA, who saw its potential while it was still in first draft infancy and with her sterling editorial advice, helped me turn it from the book it was to the book it was meant to be. Likewise my brilliant editors at HarperImpulse, Charlotte Ledger and Sam Gale, for all their support, encouragement and help, and my wonderful beta readers, without any of whom this would have been a far weaker book: Mark Anslow (who was forced to plough through no fewer than three different drafts), Kate Beeden, John Manning and Kaisha Holloway.

My nearest and dearest have been supportive and lovely as ever while I was in irritable writer mode: my partner Mark; friends Bob, Nige, Lynette and Amy; Firths, Brahams and Anslows all, and my long-suffering colleagues at Country Publications, who must be even more sick of hearing about this book than the last one!

A massive thanks too to all my encouraging writer buddies, both online and off, especially the lovely ladies of the Wordcount Warriors Facebook group and the good folk from the Airedale Writers' Circle.

I'd also like to thank Andrew Mason for kindly responding to my request for information on Spurn Lighthouse's recent renovation. And finally, last but certainly not least, a big thank you to the Marine Lake Cafe in Southport, who many years ago and without realising it, inspired a major plot point in this book!